OUR LAND!
OUR
PEOPLE!

Written by *Gary Chapman*

The Cherokee Advocate adopted as its masthead motto "Our Rights, Our Country, Our Race" for its first publication on October 25, 1843. That motto influenced the author's choice of *Our Land! Our People!* as the title for this book.

This book is in many respects a work of fiction, although historical references are as accurate as the author could make them, and documentary evidence determined the course of the narrative as noted in footnotes and works cited. Many references to historical events, real people, and real places in this book are used fictitiously. Some names, characterizations, and events, and all conversations are products of the author's imagination.

© 2014 Gary L. Chapman
All rights reserved.

ISBN-13: 978-1523630059
ISBN-10: 1523630051

CreateSpace Publishing
Charleston, South Carolina

"[I]f Cherokee blood is not destroyed it will run its courses in the veins of fair complexions who will read that their Ancestors under the Stars of adversity, and curses of their enemies, became a civilized Nation."

... John Ridge, 1826, in his essay for Albert Gallatin

Contents

Foreword

In the Cherokee Nation, 1831- 1839   4

The Day Log of Red Wolf   130

In the Western Cherokee Nation, 1839-1848   214

In Pike County, Illinois, 1850-1901   337

Afterword   431

Appendix A: Cherokee Wordlist   433

Appendix B: John and Charlotte Bell's Family   435

Appendix C: James Starr's Family   440

Appendix D: John and Willie Bell's Family   443

Bibliography   445

Acknowledgements   450

About the Author   451

Foreword

Early in our married life we met my wife's Grandpa Glen Hillmann on the wooded hill of the Gray Cemetery, two miles south of the village of New Salem in Pike County, Illinois. Memorial Day provided the occasion for the family gathering, and we paid tribute to him as a veteran of World War I, then in his sixties, and to other veterans and family members gathered there, some very much alive, and others long dead.

Grandpa was an impressive man, thin and erect in perfect posture, at five feet two inches, standing tall, or appearing to stand tall as long as no one taller stood near. His black shoes were always polished to spit-shine brilliance, and whatever he was wearing that day, likely a dark suit and tie for that occasion, he always managed to look neat. Straight black hair and dark eyes shone from his farmer sun-reddened and wrinkled skin. Strong jaw, high cheek bones, flat determined mouth that could speak in a dry tone the solemnest truth or the most rib-tickling tease.

That day was a pensive day for sharing serious thoughts and passing on the family lore to the uninitiated, with me his grandson-in-law among them. There lay his first wife, the mother of his four daughters. She was gone too soon from cancer fifteen years earlier. Beside her he would be buried, though he could not know that death would not come for him for another three decades until he reached the age of 98. There lay his father, Alfred Hillmann, the second generation German postman who served New Salem, who had raised his children after the untimely death of his wife "Lissa," Melissa Hillmann, named at birth Sarah Melissa Bell. She had swallowed a mouthful of pins while sewing, and she choked and bled to death, leaving three-year-old Glen, and his siblings—Burl and Lila Furn, who were older, and Leta Bede, who was two years younger. Alfred had raised those children alone before he married Mary Jane Seaborn several years after Lissa's death.

A hundred feet away in the center of the old cemetery, under some cedar trees, we found the graves of his grandparents, Willie Ann Gray Bell, whom he remembered living with them until she died a few years after his mother, and his grandfather, John Bell. The tombstone reported that John Bell was born July 6, 1829; he died on October 10, 1870. He grew up among the Cherokees, Grandpa Hillmann said. When he was just a child he made the trek west with twenty-one siblings. How his Grandpa Bell got such a large family, our Grandpa didn't know, but that is what his Grandma Willie Ann had taught him when he was a child, and his father had repeated as he got older. Beside them lay their first adult child to die, Allie Bell, who had died the day she was supposed to be married, because she had contracted typhoid fever a few days before, so they buried her in her wedding dress beside her father. Next to her lay a little boy, Foster Bell, dead after only a year and a half in 1866. Next to them lay a row of stones of a family with the surname of Bean. One son of John and Lissa Bell, John A. Bell, lay buried a few yards north. His was a more fortunate life, born in 1857, married to his wife Mary, buried beside him. She had died in 1928, and he died in 1939, nearly eighty years old although he had been deaf for most of his life.

That was enough story-telling for one day. Besides that there wasn't much else to tell, at least not much that was known. The stories, such as they were, were tantalizing enough, but would there ever be more to tell?

Glen Otto Hillmann, ca. 1918

Our Land! Our People!

February, 1831, Jack Bell's General Store, Coosawattee Town, Cherokee Nation

At the edge of the flagstones in front of a smoldering fire in the fireplace, Little Wolf sat on the wood floor playing with pick-up sticks, listening to the older men who sat around. They took turns talking, with the silences longer than the sentences. Uncle Jack's general store was a low-ceiling cabin with shelves covering the outside walls, filled with bolts of fabric, tools, cans of coffee, tea, and tobacco, herbs and spices, guns and ammunition.

The half-breed Jim Stone[1] spoke, drawing from his long-pipe after every few words, and letting the smoke out as he spoke, "It was not enough for them... to take the gold from the mountains. They had to take the mountains, too. Then they wanted the fields and barns... the houses and towns and rivers. They want it all, make no mistake. Until they eat it all up, eat the people, too. Like a monster alligator, crawling from the swamp." Then he accented his words with a "Hummph," the signal that he was done and another man could speak.

Jack Dougherty was next to speak, "There's no one left to stand with us. Jackson took his soldiers home to Washington. Georgia does whatever it wants. They even threaten to put the preachers in jail—Worcester, Thompson, Mayes, Trott, Butler, Clauder. It doesn't matter what church they come from, they will take them all to court, threaten to keep them in jail if they stand with us. We have to stand alone. Hummph."

---

[1] This name and the other names of Coosawattee Town citizens are borrowed from Don L. Shadburn, *Cherokee Planters of Georgia, 1842-1838* (Cumming, Georgia: Don Shadburn, 1989), 241-246. The personal characterizations are fictional.

Then Young Turkey took his turn. "We have a good crop this year. We could take the corn and buckwheat and our animals into the hills, and make our stand there. We know the land better than the Georgia boys. There we have a chance even when they outnumber us. Hunh."

"That works for us, but what about our wives and children, our old people?" Wat Sanders asked. "This has been our land for many generations. This has been our town since our grandfathers fought the Creek and won it. How can we run away from the graves of our fathers? When we leave this place we will not be able to come back, even if we make a stand in the mountains. I think we must stay as long as we can, stay in our houses, stay on our farms, until they force us out. Hummph."

David Bell had been working at a desk in the corner of the cabin with the dim light of a kerosene lamp. He stood, walked through the circle of chairs around the fireplace, and placed a couple of logs on to the fire. Little Wolf's eyes followed his father's actions, as he stirred the fire with the iron poker and teased some flame from the coals into the new dry logs. "You do not speak of the western lands and our people there. I have heard some of the missionaries say that we may have to make the best deal that we can and move there. They have not given up hope that we can hold onto what we have here, but they are thinking of our families and our people. What if Georgia continues to move into our homes, and take our towns and our farms? Would we do better to leave with something in our hands instead of nothing?" He walked through the circle back to his chair in the corner.

Wat Sanders waited some time before he spoke again. "Our people will not make another treaty. No matter what. They see the Choctaw leave, good-riddance, but they will not go so easily. They are proud. They honor our fathers' and mothers' graves. They remember when Ridge made it a law that anyone who sold our land to the white man would forfeit his life. The land is a sacred trust. Hummph."

David let the words that Wat had spoken linger in the air. Then he spoke. "No one is in a hurry to leave. Our lives are here with our people's graves. But the day may come when we must choose the lives of our children over that of our ancestors. I believe that their spirits will come with us if we have no other choice that will protect our little ones and our elders."

Little Wolf listened to his father's voice, stood up, walked over to where David sat, and put his head down in his father's lap. He did not speak. He had not spoken yet in his two years, and only rarely did he cry after his first week, when his mother had begun to think of naming him "Crying Cub." When it became clear that the name would not fit, she decided to use the simple form of her clan's name for a child, Usdi Wahya.[2] That name stuck. Since he was the firstborn for this generation in a long line of John Bells, he was also to be known with the white name, John Bell, to the satisfaction of his grandfather. David proposed the middle name of Francis, to honor his uncle, and Allie, his mother, liked it also. Francis was a favorite holy one of the white people, especially the Quakers, and her maternal uncle, Caleb Starr, who had arranged for her early education. She had also heard the Moravian missionary teachers at Spring Place speak about the saint named Francis.

Oolskuntee (whom people sometimes called by his English name "Fool") followed Little Wolf's every move with his

---

[2] The Cherokee name for "Little Wolf." All of the familiar Cherokee words used in this narrative are also found in the Cherokee Wordlist at the end of the book.

eyes. In closing, he said in a mixture of Cherokee and English, "He will be what the white folks call a 'good Indian,' since he doesn't make a sound. I couldn't even hear the drop of his sticks on the floor, so his feet will not crack a twig in the forest."

Young Turley pounced on that, "That's because you are half-deaf, old man," and some of the men laughed, some frowned.

The wooden latch of the door rattled, and into the room pushed the woman Sally Wehena, carrying some bundles under her arm. As she shut the door, for that moment, the smoke from the fireplace drew more strongly into the room.

Glancing at the men gathered in the circle of chairs, she mumbled just loud enough for them to hear, "So this is where the boys are hiding. They should be out shining in the sky, not talking to the smoke." [3] She walked over to where David was sitting at his desk, and he stood up. "I brought medicines from my lodge, and I want to trade for some buttons and cloth."

"We can do that," David said. "We need medicine."

April, 1831, Allie Bell's Farm on Coosawattee

The horses and the cows were grazing in one of the fenced lots near the small log barn, and the plow sat near the gate. David was hoeing in the field, and the sun was beginning its final descent into western horizon. At the edge of the field Little Wolf had his own small hoe and wielded it with the sporadic determination of a two-year-old. His mother, Allie, his "Uji,"[4] was

---

[3] The story of the six boys in Cherokee lore is told in James Mooney, *Myths of the Cherokees*, Cosmogonic Myths 10, "Origin of the Pleiades and the Pine," 258-259.

[4] Cherokee word for "mother."

Our Land! Our People!

within calling distance as she worked in the garden nearer the house, lifting and resetting small green sprouts.[5]

The sound of a trotting horse turned their faces to the road that ran by their house and farm. The rider was coming from the Southwest along the river road, and soon they could see the calico shirt, buckskin pants, and dark skin of Ezra, a trusted slave belonging to Uncle Jack. He turned his horse in David's direction as soon as he saw him standing in the field.

"Your brother been arrested," he said breathlessly to David as he slipped off the horse. "Happen this morning near New Echota, when Jack out to buy some salt pork for his store. Not know what happen to him when he not come back when he said."[6]

"Who arrested him?" David interrupted.

"Georgia Guard. I find out when I go find Jack. Wife of old man Sawney see it happen and tell me. The soldiers come up the road with white man who claim old man's place belong to him. Jack not happy and get mad. Tell white men to go back and leave

---

[5] There is no convincing record of the name of the mother of John Francis Bell. Both Emmett Starr and George Morrison Bell, Sr., list their relative John Francis Bell as the first son of David Bell, but they do not agree on his mother's identity. This author has adopted Allie Phillips, as the name of his mother. She died as a young woman, and she was a sister of the Elizabeth Phillips whom George Morrison Bell identifies as John Francis' mother. Elizabeth was married successively to Edmond Bean, William Thornton, and David Bell. She was already residing in Arkansas during most of the early years of this narrative, if the Georgia land sales record from 1831-1832 is accurate, and Edmond Bean and Elizabeth Phillips Bean moved west at that time. (Don L. Shadburn, *Cherokee Planters in Georgia*, 320, 334-335)

[6] The account of John Adair Bell's arrest comes from *The Cherokee Adairs*, prepared by the Adair Family Reunion Book Committee, published by the Cherokee Nation 2003, page 26, and it includes a quote from *The Cherokee Phoenix*, April 16, 1831, used later in this chapter.

old man alone. Soldiers arrest both and take 'em away. Say they will sell 'em for slaves."

"Do you know where they took them?"

"No. I go back to New Echota and tell Mr. Boudinot what I find out. He gets his man Caleb and they go to look for him."

"Thank you, Ezra. Come with me and we'll get something for you to eat. I've got to think about this. The Georgia Guard no longer has to have a reason to do what they do." David took the reins of the horse and led it back to the stable.

Allie and Little Wolf had come up behind them and heard their words. Allie escorted Ezra to their house and offered him the basin, water pitcher, and towels sitting on the porch for washing hands and faces, and they each in turn used them. After she had cleaned up Little Wolf, she went inside to prepare for their meal. Spreading a fresh muslin tablecloth, she began putting brown stamped pottery bowls and metal spoons on the table, preparing for the stew that she had simmering in a black pot hanging above the coals in the fireplace. Taking the loaf of corn bread from a sideboard she cut it into thick slices on the table. She set a pitcher of goat's milk and four cups in easy reach at the center of the table. Next to it she placed a large bowl of mixed berries and a wooden spoon. Finally, she took the bowls to the pot and filled them with a steaming mixture of meat, broth, and vegetables. By that time, David also had cleaned up and come in.

David said, "Please sit down, Mr. Ezra. We are grateful to you for bringing us word of our brother."

Ezra hesitated a moment, unfamiliar with such hospitality, then sat down quickly on the bench and rubbed his hands together. The others sat down after him. David thanked the Creator Spirit for the food on their table and their guest, and asked help for his brother, and they began to eat.

"You stay here tonight, Ezra. You and your horse have travelled far enough for today," David said, after a few quiet minutes. "I will go back to New Echota and see if there is any news from Elias. If not, I will stay at Jack's store until I have been able to learn something. I just hope that Jack is able to keep his temper under control. He could make matters worse if he loses it again."

"I go back tonight," Ezra said. "My horse is strong. I don't rest here. Your brother needs me to work at store when he gone. We take road slow. Full moon tonight helps us."

"I wish you could both wait until morning," Allie said. "But if there is anything to be done, I know you want to get right to it. Perhaps John Martin could advise us. If he is here I will find out in the morning and speak with him. If he is in New Echota you must speak to him."

"Yes, I will also see if John Ridge is getting back from his trip to Washington with any news.[7] If I know my brother Jack, he will try to bribe his way out when he finds a greedy officer. Sorry to say, that is probably the best way to handle it. We don't need yet another case that stands on principles, because Georgia has none. The governor will just stand with his back to the wall and fight like a wildcat, and keep people in prison. We have to get Jack out if we can."

---

[7] The account of John Ridge's delegation to Washington D.C. in mid-1831 and his meetings with President Jackson are recorded in John Ehle, *Trail of Tears: The Rise and Fall of the Cherokee Nation* (New York, Doubleday, 1988), 240ff.

Allie added, "Please try to comfort Jennie. She and Jack are only two months married. This will be hard for her."

As soon as they finished eating, David gathered a few things for his saddlebags, embraced Allie and Little Wolf, and he and Ezra headed for the stable. In a few minutes they were on their way back toward New Echota. They rode in twilight, and then the full moon made a clear road for them as they trotted to the sound of frogs, crickets, and locusts as the road wound near the Coosawattee River toward the southwest. Near midnight they came to the settlement of New Echota, and lamps were glowing in the little white clapboard building in the center of the village, which housed the Cherokee Phoenix office and printing press. David headed for those lights.

When he knocked on the door he heard Elias Boudinot's familiar voice calling "Come in" over the racket of the printing press, where John Wheeler, the printer, and a regular helper, a black slave named Noah, were working. Boudinot reviewed the morning's events with David, and showed him the article he had written for the Phoenix, which included the line, "We understand on Wednesday morning Mr. John A. Bell of Coosawaytee was arrested by a detachment of the Georgia Guard. Mr. Bell is a native and what the charge was we are unable to say, and in fact it is impossible to know, for these law officers go to work without a written precept."

"That says it right," David commented. "What do you think we can do now? I'm guessing that Jack has already made an offer as a bribe, though they'll call it bail."

"That's what John and I thought. They would not let us see him. I don't know what shape John or Sawney's in, or whether they've been beaten or not. I wouldn't be surprised."

"How much do you think the Georgia officials will want for Jack and Sawney's release?"

"My guess would be around hundred dollars, but you don't want to start there. It's barter like Jack's good at. See if he can make a deal first, then protest that it's too much, that it'll be more than you can afford," Elias answered.

"I'll talk to Jack's partner, Joseph Lynch, and John Martin. We'll come up with it, one way or another" David responded. "I just hate to pay what old Sawney could have used to buy his own place two times over. There's no fairness in it."

"It's not about fairness. It's about survival, isn't it?" Elias said.

Red Wolf's Map of the Cherokee Nation 1831-1838

July, 1832, Allie Bell's House on Coosawattee

Little Wolf's mother Allie loaded the brick oven at the side of the fireplace with loaves of risen bread on a narrow wooden paddle. Her long black hair was tied with a leather band and fell in one plait down her back. Her floor-length dress showed vertical bands of ivy and flowers separated by lines—all in silver and red—against a solid brown background. She stood thin and still, with her hands on her hips, while she considered the tasks she could accomplish while the bread baked. Little Wolf knelt on the bench at the table so that he could reach the table top, looking at a copy of the Cherokee Phoenix laid out on the creamy oilcloth. She decided that everything else could wait while she could read the paper with her three-year old. She would take advantage of his interest in the squiggly marks while his curiosity was aroused. Other work could wait.

He hadn't spoken aloud yet, although she knew he understood some language, both Cherokee and English. He would answer with a nod or shake of his head any simple yes or no question. He would do his simple chores whenever asked. His hands signaled any request a child might have, and she had learned to interpret his increasingly complex hand signals. She felt confident that he could speak whenever and whatever he wanted, but he just did not. Was he possessed by some kind of spirit? Was he going to be a shaman or diviner of some kind?

She missed her mother, Ruth Harlan, and her father Joseph Phillips, since they had left with the rest of the family for the Arkansas frontier in the spring. She regretted that her brothers were not close enough to consult for their fatherly guidance of Little Wolf. Ellis Fox and John were so many miles away, and Joseph had died of consumption the winter past. Ellis was the oldest at 22, but he was not as responsible as her own husband, and brother John was barely 16.[8] Even her sister Elizabeth had married Edward Bean, and they had sold their property and moved west in February.[9]

Her husband David frequently took Little Wolf with him as he worked in the fields or kept the general store for his brother Jack, while Jack was spending more time away on trading trips, or tending the store with his partner at New Echota, or enjoying his new home there with his bride Jennie Martin. David did more than most Cherokee fathers with their young sons. He enjoyed working in the fields when other men kept the traditional attitude that the fields and crops belonged to the women. He hunted and fished as well as any Cherokee man and was eager to teach his son about all of it.

Little Wolf smiled as Allie took her seat beside him at the table and began to point her finger at a line on the newspaper. She read aloud about the Cherokee National Council meeting at New Echota. They had decided that their present crisis made political campaigns for their national elections unwise, so they had voted to keep their present leaders in office indefinitely, with John Ross as Principal Chief. Major Ridge had spoken against the action, arguing that their Constitution not only required elections, the debates were necessary to help the people understand the hard choices that they faced. The Council adjourned with no plan to deal with the impasse caused by the State of Georgia's opposition to the Cherokee Nation, and the refusal of U.S. President Jackson to interfere with the Georgia's

---

[8] Phillips and Harlan family information comes from David Keith Hampton, *The Descendants of Nancy Ward* (Cane Hill AR: ARC Press, 1997).

[9] The record of property sale from February 18,1832, for Edward and Elizabeth Phillips Bean is found in *Cherokee Planters in Georgia 1832-1838*, page 320.

Our Land! Our People!

"States' Rights." They rejected the concerns of Major Ridge, his son John, Elias Boudinot, and anyone associated with them.[10]

"I don't know how you can understand this, Little Wolf, because I can't. We are both white and Cherokee. The blood is mixed in us in equal parts, like milk and water mixed for bread, yet the leaders of the white peoples cannot see us as we are, people like them. They even put in jail and mistreat their own people who befriend us. It has been so since the days of Grandmother Nancy Ward. She wanted peace and honor between Cherokee and white. She found that she could trust some whites but not all. She tamed her warrior blood for the sake of peace, but she never put away her warrior courage."

She stopped abruptly with her reading and exclaimed, "English is so hard to read. It makes no sense. They spell 'nation' with a 'ti' which should be an 'sh,' but sometimes it's a 'ch,' and all these can be spoken differently also. We are so lucky to have the syllabary that Sequoia devised and Dr. Worcester put into print for us.[11] When words are printed in Cherokee we know how they are supposed to sound. We don't have to memorize so many different possibilities. You can grow up reading our language in a sensible way and don't have to learn English, which is just too confusing."

"Here it says, 'On July 19, 1832, Chief John Ross proclaimed a fast to be observed throughout the Cherokee Nation.' A fast is when people decide not to eat for a little while. Their hunger reminds them of something they must remember.

---

[10] Ehle, ibid., 259.

[11] Dr. Samuel Worcester designed the printing fonts for Sequoia's syllabary, and organized the 77 syllables into a memorizable format. See *Beginning Cherokee* by Ruth Bradley Holmes and Betty Sharp Smith, 2nd Edition (Norman, OK, University Of Oklahoma Press, 1976),12-14.

'Whereas the crisis in the affairs of the Nation exhibits the day of tribulation and sorrow, and the time appears to be fast hastening when the destiny of this people must be sealed; whether it has been directed by the wonted depravity and wickedness of man, or by the unsearchable and mysterious will of an all-wise Being, it equally becomes us, as a rational and Christian community, humbly to bow in humiliation.'"[12] She looked down and saw that Little Wolf had bowed his head as they did when they sat down to eat at the table, ready to pray. Then he looked up and smiled at her again. What would she do with this little mystery boy? She wished that she could walk over to Springplace and talk to her teacher, at the place where she had spent her girlhood, where she had learned to read and write in Sequoia's Cherokee syllabary, and where she had learned more about being a Christian. The Moravians were a peaceful people and loyal to the Cherokee people, too, but they had escaped across the border into Tennessee to avoid being arrested and put in prison by Georgia's laws against white people working with the Cherokee Nation.

A strong gust blew through the west cabin windows, prompting Allie to stand up and hurry to the door. "Let's see what the wind is bringing." Little Wolf slid off the bench and scrambled toward her as she walked through the open door onto the shaded porch. She looked toward the northwest and saw the dark front of rolling clouds reaching high into the sky above them, blocking the form of Fort Mountain to the north. The leaves of the corn were rustling, and the bean and squash leaves bowing and bobbing. "We will have Sky Woman's tears to freshen the crops. She does try to take care of us."

---

[12] James Mooney, *Myths of the Cherokee* (New York, Dover, 1995), 119-120.

Our Land! Our People!

August, 1832, on Coosa River

Two men paddled a hand-hewn log canoe up to the river landing. David paddled in front, tanned but light-skinned. Steering at the back sat a much larger man, Elijah, coal black in color. Between them in the canoe sat David's little curly, black-haired boy, John. They all wore trousers in coarse-woven dark colors, plain bleached cloth shirts soaked dark with perspiration, and brimmed misshapen hats. In the background loomed the steamy blue outlines of the Sleeping Bear Mountain above the plains of the river valley. David pushed himself up from the canoe, and still hunching his back stepped out into the shallow water, yelling out, "Siyo! Osiyo! Udoda.[13] Your son, David, come to see you!" He pulled the canoe onto the beach, and lifted the boy out of the canoe onto the dry sand of the landing, while Elijah climbed out and finished beaching the canoe and stowing the paddles.

They walked up the wide path that led up a gradual slope to a wood clapboard, two-story house that stood clearly visible on a rise above the river. Several people working on the roofed porch that surrounded the house had turned their attention to the riverfront.

"David! Elijah! Little John! Good to see y'all! What a bonnie surprise y' bring us this hot day!" yelled an older man as he jumped off the porch and came running down the path. As they met he put his hands lightly on the sides of both shoulders and then reached down and picked up the boy and hugged him to his chest as they both laughed. "And have ye started to talk yet, me wee one?"

---

[13] Osiyo or simply Siyo means hello. Udoda is a word for father.

The boy just shook his head and continued to smile broadly.

"Don't blame ye a bit," Grandfather John Bell said. "Wait till ye have somethin' right good to say. Now y' all come to the porch, and let's have somethin' cool to drink and a bit to eat. Then ye can tell me what has brought y' here this day, me son."[14] He put the little boy back on the ground on his own two feet, turned around, and led the group through the other people who had come down from the porch, who now stretched up the path in different spots to greet the arrivals. Their procession halted every few yards to repeat the clasping of arms and embraces. David's cousin, Asa Bell and his wife, Barbary,[15] stood toward the end of the line, and waiting on the porch, stood Grandmother Charlotte Adair Bell, her arms outstretched and beckoning. Soon most of them brought chairs from the farther sides of the porch, as it wrapped around the house, and they seated themselves in a broad circle, while Charlotte sent servants into the house to get drinks and food.

Grandfather Bell began their talk, "I suppose y' saw some surveyors out along the river as y' came down, doin' their dirty work."

---

[14] John Bell, Jr. is recorded as a blacksmith living in Will's Valley, Alabama, in *Cherokee Adairs*, page 7. As the son of a Scot immigrant and Cherokee mother, he is assumed to have a transitional speech affected by Scottish, English, and Cherokee speakers.

[15] Asa and Barbary Bell were recorded in the U.S. Census of 1850 as living in Madison County, Alabama, having been married there on August 5, 1846. Asa was born in 1802; Barbary in 1808. They lived beside Francis Bell, born in 1780 in Greenville, South Carolina. [John Bell, presumably Francis' brother, had been born in 1778 in Greenville, South Carolina.] In the 1860 Census Asa and Barbary were living in Cherokee County, Texas. Their three oldest children were recorded in both places, including Victoria (age 7 in 1850), Uriah (age 11), and Osborne (age 15).

"The signs of them anyway," David replied. "Marks and blazes along the river, every so often, settin' up 160 acre parcels for the land lotteries Georgia says will start this fall. Then we'll see even more white Georgia citizens movin' into the Cherokee Nation, grabbin' everything they want from the improvements we've made and pushin' us out."

"It won't be long until Alabama'll follow suit," Asa chimed in.

"Do you expect it soon? Have Alabama officials started to do it, too?" David asked.

Grandfather said, "They've naw passed a law yet, but from what I hear, the Statehouse has a mind to draft a law like Georgia's, and forcin' Cherokees out o' Alabama, too. Then Tennessee'll follow, sooner or later. We won't have a spit or a hair to our name. Did y' bring us other news, son? What else is on y' mind?"

"I don't know what all you've heard, but when all of this comes to pass, we must leave our place at Coosawattee, we'll have to have a plan for where to go. I don't see the Georgia Guard rustlin' everyone out at once, but little by little pushin' people out, until we're all disorganized and desperate. We have to make some plans and be ready when the time comes to make arrangements for one another, and make common cause as much as we can. I don't expect that Alabama or Tennessee will provide a secure haven for long, but if they delay their efforts to expel us long enough, maybe we can use your lands here as a staging area to move west." David finished his thoughts and looked hopefully at his father.

Grandfather Bell picked up the conversation. "We feared for many years it would come to this. Even before I set up my blacksmithy here, when I left my Pa's travelin' trader life behind, I wondered how long it'd be 'fore greed for Indian land would poison the hearts o' people, and cancel all the fine treaties the government made. We could pretend we were all white and Scot. Some o' us might blend in and make our peace, if we were naw found out, but what good would come o' that? We could play Rob Roy for a while, but have naw to show for it in the end. Sure, y' can come here for a time, if we're still here. I wonder though, with Chief John Ross bein' at Head of Coosa just upriver. I reckon we won't be safe here long. Georgia will pick on him for bein' so stubborn, push him out among the first. Alabama will want to clear us out as an example to all our kin everywhere else. Yae, I been thinkin' about it. I remember what I saw out west when I was travellin' with me old Pa."

Two black serving women came out of the door with a couple of pitchers and a tray of cups, and they began to pour a dark-colored tea for everyone around the circle. When John and his son David were speaking, everyone was attentive to their words. Even little John seemed to be paying attention.

"Thank you, Udoda. If we came here, we would bring what we could, knowin' that we would just be movin' on as soon as we could, but goin' together, if it be your mind to do. What are our choices where to stay?"

"We do have some choices. Cheap land can be had for straight up purchase. Brother James stays in Kentucky,[16] well-settled. But if too many o' us try to join him when the Cherokee are bein' pitched out, he'll lose his cover, and be known as the mixed blood he is. Some o' us could pass for white and buy back

---

[16] James Bell, in Kentucky at this time and in subsequent years, was recorded as having been born in the same South Carolina County (Greenville) as John and Francis, and near to the same ages.

land here after the lotteries have done their damage, but waitin' for that, we'd have to settle somewhere else or hide out in the mountains for a time. I'd just as soon travel to the Western Cherokee lands and settle there, in Missouri or Arkansas or the territory to the west. There's good land in Illinois, too, available for little to nothin' to us 1812 War soldiers.[17] Most o' the tribes are movin' out o' Illinois, and they'll all be gone soon. It'll be easy enough to buy land cheap there."

Asa interrupted, "I like the idea of Texas myself. John Bowle settled there. Sam Houston's just gone there.[18] Word is that they may try to make it an independent republic, and I like the idea, if it happens soon enough to matter to us. There aren't many people there yet. We might be able to make a settlement for ourselves there. David's younger brother Devereaux was standing beside Asa, and nodding his head in agreement. Asa continued, "David, yuh spent more just gainin' your brother Jack's release from jail, than yuh'd need to buy a sizable farm there."

With the mention of Jack, Charlotte was eager to pursue another question. "How is Jack? How's he been after his release from jail?"

"As near as I can tell, he made it through with no lastin' injury. It took longer than any of us expected, but in the end it turned out much as we thought. One hundred twenty dollars

---

[17] The Military Tract constituted Pike County in Illinois, and was available to Revolutionary and 1812 War Veterans according to *The Pike County History* (Pittsfield, Pike County Press, 1964).

[18] The relationship of Chief John Bowle and Sam Houston and the record of the early Cherokee settlement in Texas is summarized in Chapter 14, "Expulsion from Texas," in Stanley W. Hoig, *The Cherokees and Their Chiefs* (Fayetteville, University of Arkansas, 1998).

paid his way out, and they dropped charges against him. I know it shook him up though. He doesn't talk much about it, and you can tell he's given up on stayin' here much longer. Now that Elias has resigned the Phoenix...."[19]

His father, surprised, asked, "When did that happen?"

"Just a few days ago. Ross insisted that the Phoenix not print anything about making a deal with the Federal Government for removal to the West. Elias thinks that the Nation needs to know that their cause in Georgia is hopeless, and soon we'll have to leave whether we want to or not."

"Ross will naw consider that. He thinks he must oppose any deal that makes us leave our land. He thinks his standin' with the Nation is at stake; his position as Principal Chief depends on opposin' any deal," his father said.

"That is so," David continued. "Elias wants the people to know the truth. Otherwise they will continue to have false hope that they can stay. They won't have time to adjust to the idea that they must be ready to move or they will lose everything. Elias thinks we can still make an agreement with the government that will be to our advantage as a Nation. There are enough people in government willin to pay us to leave and to resettle in the west."

"Do y' think it's possible still? They already have the upper hand. Why would they pay us even a fraction o' what our land is worth?"

"I doubt any agreement will be to our advantage. I doubt that Ross and the Council will accept one. I doubt that anything

---

[19] Elias Boudinot resigned from *The Cherokee Phoenix* on August 1, 1832. See Ehle, ibid., page 260, along with references to the Georgia land survey in the Cherokee Nation.

we sign will be honored by the government anyway. You know me, Father. I don't expect much good to happen."

"It's still a terrible disappointment. Ross forced Elias to leave the newspaper he worked so hard to create. It's been a mouthpiece for truth. Without him, who'll run it?"

David answered, "One way or another John Ross will run it. Elias has steadily lost ground on all sides. He helped me with Jack's case, but he wouldn't show his face at the jail or the court. He knew they wouldn't deal with him. They've already had too many run-ins as it is."

The serving women had been busy setting up a table with fruits and vegetables, breads, cheeses, and meats. "Let's have somethin' to eat, then think about this some more." With that John Bell stood up and motioned for the others to join him at the table. Elijah, who had been seated and listening on the outside of the circle of chairs, started to walk toward the back of the house where the servants met, but David caught him and asked him quietly to stay with him and eat here. His father saw him and said nothing.

September, 1832, along Coosawattee

The first rays of the rising sun fringed the high dark clouds with red and orange hues. Allie and Little Wolf made their way along the narrow path above the sandy landing in front of her farmhouse to the rock-lined bathing basin for their morning immersion. David had already left before sunrise to go into town to open the store. She knelt and untied the leather apron from Little Wolf's waist, and she pushed the straps off her shoulders and dropped her own cloth shift onto the ground. Taking her son's hand, she walked with him into the river waters, and lowered herself into the water until they both were covered, dunking their heads, and opening their eyes again to the sunrise.

They listened for a few minutes to the birds' morning songs. Then she added her voice, "Thank you, Spirit of All, for this new day, made for all your children, plants and trees, birds and creatures who walk, and crawl, and simply sit and wait. You are the Maker and to you all the things you make shall return. You are Udoda to Jesus, your firstborn Uweji achuga,[20] and you let your Spirit bride come into all the things you have made to bring us back to you and tie us to each other."

She remembered how her teacher, Brother John Gambold, had argued with her about her ways of mixing Cherokee stories about God and creation with the Moravian teachings. He was kind and gentle with her, but he grew frustrated with her stubborn adherence to the stories her mother had told her. She had promised her mother that she would not let go of the old stories, even while she worked in the gardens, wove on the looms, and cooked the foods at Springplace. She was just a child and Brother Gambold an old and dying man, so she agreed with him to his face, but she continued to pray in the way she knew was right. The Great Spirit of God must be woman as well as man, and in charge of both. The baptism she received at Springplace when she came of age was renewed every morning as she bathed in the traditional Cherokee way of going to the water.[21] Then came David, only three years older, who said he had admired her from the first time he saw her at Springplace,

---

[20] Uweji achuga is the Cherokee title for a son.

[21] The Cherokee traditional ceremony of "going to the water" is described by James Mooney in *Sacred Formulas of the Cherokees*, 1891. The Baptist and Methodist emphasis on baptism found ready acceptance, according to John Ehle, ibid., pp. 192-193.

when he came to deliver an order from his older brother Jack's store. Then God had granted her the precious life of Little Wolf.

"Whatever comes in this day, Loving Spirit, give the strength to face it and hold on to your peaceful ways." Brother and Sister Gambold said they did not believe in slavery, or the superiority or inferiority of any race of people. They did hold slaves in the name of the church, so they could protect them, they said, and teach them like the rest of the students at Springplace. I wondered sometimes if their actions matched their words. They did not believe in war, or the murder of people who were different. They did believe in the Cherokee Nation.[22] She agreed with them in these things, even though they were not here any longer to support these beliefs, and it was harder now to stand for them.

Allie moved toward the river bank, allowing Little Wolf to stay and play in the water while she began to dry off. He crawled out dripping as she began to put on her shift again. She beckoned him follow up the path. He would dry before they reached the house, soon enough to dress for the day. They went through their routine of breakfast and reading lessons and were ready by mid-morning to enter the gardens for tending and harvesting vegetables when she heard the sound of men calling nearby.

Followed by Little Wolf, Allie walked out to the lane in front of the house and peered in the direction of the men's yells. She saw a man standing beside a tripod with a strange device on

---

[22] On the work of John Gambold and other Moravian missionaries at Spring Place and other mission schools in the Cherokee Nation, see *The New Georgia [online] Encyclopedia* on "Cherokee Missions." On the paradoxical relationships with the institution of slavery see Tiya Miles, *African American History at the Chief Vann House* (University of Michigan, 2006).

top. Dressed in dark clothes, jacket, breeches, and boots, white blouse and knee socks, he was obviously not in Cherokee working clothes. He was yelling directions to someone unseen in the distance. These were representatives of the State of Georgia, surveying land as David and the Phoenix had warned her to expect.

She was not standing where the man would see her, but she decided that she was not going to hide either. She had not met a white man whom she could not meet as a physical equal. She had grown up in a large family of boys and girls. Even at Springplace, where the boys outnumbered girls three to one, and the teachers held the strange idea of feminine weakness, roughhousing and wrestling were common among the boys and girls. How else could she learn to defend herself, since she was a legitimate heir to Nancy Ward?

She moved out into plain view in the middle of the lane, and she could see the man turn and notice her and Little Wolf at her side. She told Little Wolf to stay where he was, then she walked casually toward the man. When she was about fifteen feet away she stopped, and he turned toward her.

"You are the surveyors we were told to expect," she said, without the polite greeting of welcome.

"Yes, we are marking the land for its new owners. Do you live here?"

"We do."

"Who should we record as the previous owner of this ground?"

Our Land! Our People!

"We belong to the land. The land does not belong to us. But as your people think differently about ownership, I would say that the people of the Cherokee Nation own this ground."

"Not any more. I want to know who is the man whose name should be listed as previous owner?"

"If you had been on this land very long, you would know that women have the stake in land. Men do not own it. This land, these fields and gardens, and the buildings you see belong to me as long as I need it and take care of it. My husband is David Bell, but he is free to come and go. This land is my responsibility."[23]

"You speak like an educated woman, but you sure have strange ideas. I'll make a note that this farm has belonged to David Bell. I'm leaving markers, but even if you remove them, we know where they belong, and you won't be able to prevent the new owners from making their claim to this property. You might as well pack up and leave as soon as you can."

"Then our conversation is finished." With that she turned and walked back to the house with as much confidence and dignity as she could display. Little Wolf watched her as she returned to him, seeing her eyes become teary as she walked and her shoulders sag just a tiny bit, but perceptible to him. She took his hand when she reached him, and they returned to their house.

---

[23] The role of women as farmers and land holders is described by Theda Perdue in *Cherokee Women, Gender and Culture Change, 1700-1835*. (Lincoln, University of Nebraska, 1998). On page 116ff. she summarizes the transition from women as farmers involved in animal "husbandry" and the holding of land in common to the later practice of men farming and holding land in the Nineteenth Century.

Inside she sat down on their woven cane chair and pulled Little Wolf onto her lap, letting the tears flow from her eyes even while she continued to look at him.

"The day is coming soon when we will have to leave this home, and find another place to live."

"Where will we go, Uji?" Little Wolf said. Though her eyes opened a little wider at these first spoken words, she answered without pausing.

"I don't know yet, and I don't know when, but the Spirit who led us to this place will lead us to another place to live. And this land will not forget us."

Little Wolf pulled himself closer to his mother, and she wrapped her arms around him. When David returned from the store that evening, after Allie had put Little Wolf to bed, she told David that Little Wolf had spoken his first words and what had happened beforehand with the surveyors.

David said, "We knew he would speak when he was ready. It troubles me that his first words are about leaving this land. A child is lost when his tie to the land is cut."

"He will not be lost. We must make sure of that," Allie replied.

Little Wolf was not yet asleep. He listened to his parents talking, and pulled the quilt closer.

January, 1833, Bell-Lynch Store, New Echota

"Little John, you and Sarah stay here in the trading post while Jack and I join the men over in the Council House. We are meeting with Reverend Worcester. I told you about him before. He just got out of Milledgeville prison after spending sixteen months there. It's a good day. Sarah, send Little John to us if you need any help. I don't expect anyone to come in, but you never know." David pulled his heavy wool coat off the row of pegs by the front door, buttoned it, and went out.

Little Wolf looked at his aunt, thirteen years old, nine years older than he. She was a few inches taller than he was, thin, and dark-haired, and he hadn't seen her for many months.

"We ought to get to know each other better," Sarah said. "I used to be in the same school with your mother at Springplace. That was before she met my brother and they decided to get married. She was eight years older than me, and I always thought they would be the most perfect couple in all the world. Then you came along. After that I came here to the Oothcaloga Mission School, and our father moved to a new place on the Coosa River down in Alabama. You went there a few months ago, I heard."

"I saw Ududu and Ulisi[24] Bell in the summer, when it was warm. It took a long time to get there by canoe. We slept one night outside on the way down, and we stopped and stayed at a big white house coming back. That was Major Ridge's house. I got to meet him."

"How exciting!" Sarah replied. "I have seen him a few times coming here, and his son John also. They are very friendly with Mr. Boudinot and his younger brother, Stand Watie. I admire all of them, and I get to stay with the Boudinot children sometimes. Mrs. Boudinot is not very strong. She needs my help.

---

[24] Ududu is Grandfather; Ulisi is Grandmother.

Mr. Franz, my teacher, lets me help take care of them when she needs me."

Little Wolf looked up into his aunt's eyes and thought how much she talked and acted like his mother. Just a little bit younger.

"I hope you get to go to school when you are ready. There is a lot of talk about having to close the schools and the missionaries having to go away."

"Uji teaches me at home," Little Wolf said.

"She'll teach you well, I know, because she was a good student. Do you read already?"

"Some. Mostly we read together. She lets me read easy words, and she helps me with harder ones."

"Show me. Here. I'll get the newspaper." Sarah went to a chair near the fireplace where the latest edition of the Phoenix lay on the seat, for anyone who came in to pick it up and read. She gestured to Little Wolf to come and sit on the chair beside her, and unfolded the paper onto their laps. "Here is the article about Reverend Worcester, the man my brothers and other men are meeting today." They took turns reading the words, and Sarah spoke aloud all the long ones.

> Samuel Worcester, a minister of the American Board of Commissioners for Foreign Missions, and a friend of the Cherokee Nation, has been released from the Georgia State Penitentiary, by order of the governor. Worcester's release comes a year after the Supreme Court of the United States ordered the State of Georgia to release him because he had been unlawfully detained by the state. Worcester had refused to take an oath of allegiance to the state because

American Citizenship should be valid in any state, and his presence among the Cherokee Nation was authorized by lawful actions of the Cherokee Nation, and the treaties of that Nation with the United States, and the direct permission of the President of the United States. Georgia, however, had defied the federal authorities and asserted state sovereignty, with an implied threat that even the annihilation of the Union itself would not change its decisions to require the submission of white residents of the Cherokee Nation.[25]

"There are a lot of big words," Little Wolf said. "I don't understand much of it."

"Nobody else seems to be able to either," she said. "As near as I can figure, the Georgia people put the Reverend Worcester in jail, but they shouldn't have, but no one could do anything about it, so he stayed there, until something changed their minds, but I don't know what that was."

"I think there are a lot of mean people in Georgia."

"I think so, too. It's too bad, because it is a pretty place to live, with all the pine trees, and good soil to grow things, and mountains, and rivers. Nobody wants to leave it. We work hard to plant gardens and fields, fruit trees, and build buildings, but Georgia is giving it all away to other people."

Sarah got up to stoke the fire and put some wood on it. The chilly breeze outside made its way through some of the cracks, and they needed the wool garments as well as the linen ones that Sarah had learned to weave at the school.

---

[25] Newspaper account summarized from John Ehle, *Trail of Tears*, pp. 262-264.

"You know what I'd like to do?" she said suddenly. "I want to write to you, and you write back. Would you write back to me, if I wrote to you?"

"I've not learned to write."

"But you could. I know your mother will teach you how to use the syllabary. You won't have to write much. We could just tell each other how we are doing, since we don't live close to each other, and we don't know where we are going to be, but we could write to each other and tell each other where we are and what we are doing.

"My Uduji[26] Jim Foster used to come to visit every other month, and stay at the Vann House at Springplace where I stayed. He checked on my brothers and me and made sure that we were making progress in our work. When he couldn't come to visit, I started to write to him, but he has to have help writing back to me, too."

"I don't know Uduji Jim Foster."

"Oh, I didn't think of that. Your mother's brothers either live far away, or they've died, haven't they? You don't have someone who is supposed to help teach you, so other people have to fill in. You would like our Uduji Jim. He is a lot of fun. He used to organize big contests for the stick ball game. The people came from all over to play. That's how they first got to know him at Springplace. Brother Gambold told me that my uncle planned a big game near Springplace, and he was afraid they would run over their planted fields and ruin their crops while they were

---

[26] Uduji is an uncle. In traditional Cherokee families the maternal uncle bore major responsibility for raising and teaching his sister's children. See Marcelina Reed, *Seven Clans of the Cherokee Society* (Cherokee, North Carolina, 1993), 8.

playing. My uncle came and talked to him and promised him they would protect the crops and fields, and he kept his promise. That was many years ago, before I was even born. They stayed friends after that."[27]

"I'd like to get letters from you," Little Wolf announced, "and I will try to write back."

The latch rattled and Elijah pushed the door open. His big body filled the doorway, and he quickly pushed it shut to keep the warm air inside. "I've come to relieve you from your busy work behind the counter."

Sarah laughed. "It hasn't been so busy. We haven't had one customer since we've been here. We've just been trying to keep warm."

"Your Uncle Jack sent me over to put you to work, then, but my son Will would like to have your company, Little John. He's practicing target shooting with the blow gun, and he's got a blowgun and darts for you to use. Would you like to join him?"

"I sure would. I was just telling Sarah about our trip down the river last summer."

"David and I would never have made it without you, Little John."

"You're funny, Mister Elijah." With that comment Little Wolf put on his leather coat and rabbit hair cap and headed out the door.

---

[27] Manuscript of *The Missionary Journal of the Moravian Missionaries at Springplace*, p. 100849, copied from the manuscript photocopy at New Echota State Park library.

May, 1833, Jack Bell's Store, Coosawattee Town

David stood behind the counter with his hands in his pockets, looking uncomfortable, and wishing he was working in the field instead of listening to several angry and raucous men.

"What does your brother think he's doing, joining the protest against Chief Ross at Council?" Young Turkey said, louder than necessary in the small store cabin.

"Well, what do you expect him to do?" Jack Daugherty yelled. "Ross is a dreamer, but he doesn't see the plain truth staring back at him. We don't stand a chance of keeping our nation together here. They're picking us off four and five at a time, people seizing the house and land as soon as one of us leaves to go hunting, or to visit a friend. We could go home right now, and find our wives and children kicked out and crying."

George Arnold spoke more evenly, trying to calm the waters. "Even Ross' brother Andrew, and his nephew Cooley disagree with his position. Major Ridge spelled out the whole story at the Council. He went into great detail and made the case. So I don't blame Jack for signing the petition asking Ross to explain himself and stop delaying. We've got to get the best deal we can, before we can't make a deal at all."

"Wasn't Chief Ross trying to do that when he went to Washington? I heard he tried to get twenty million at least, since there's that much gold in the mountains, let alone the value of the land," said John Otterlifter as he tipped the chair he was sitting in, balancing on the back two legs.

Quickly Jim Stone slipped in, "Then why won't he admit it and get it out in the open?"

"He's afraid of losing the support of most of the fullbloods, I say."

"He's not going to make us leave without a fight. He's not going to settle for a pittance like his brother, either."

"We're not going to fight. Ross is no fighter. Can't you see that? Ask Black Hawk and the Sauk tribe how much good it did them to fight out in Illinois. I just don't see why Ross doesn't knuckle down and negotiate a good price. He knows how to make a bargain. If he can't, get his brother Lewis to do it. He could dicker the shell off a turtle. "

"You're much too quick to give up."

"Why did Jack and the others agree to let Ross wait until the October meeting to explain himself?

"They don't know what to do either."

Little Wolf looked from man to man as they responded so fast to each other. He hadn't heard men talk so quickly to each other before, even interrupting each other, and not allowing one man to finish before another spoke. It was confusing. Why were they so angry with each other?

They finally stopped talking and several of the men were looking at David. "I don't know what to tell you. I've tried to stay out of it, and I haven't had a chance to talk to my brother. I think everyone is just trying to do the best job they can, and time is running out. Now, I'm going to go home to Allie, and try to explain to her what's going on, when I don't know myself."

He started blowing out the oil lamps, and putting away the record book, and making it clear that it was time to close the store. "You can stay and talk as long as you want, but I don't know what good it's going to do us. I know it won't help if we come to blows. Fighting each other is the last thing we need at a time like this." The men were headed toward the door, and David had Little John's hand in his own. Soon they were walking toward home.[28]

"Why is everyone so mad all the time?" Little Wolf asked his father.

"I think it's because no one knows exactly what to do. When people are afraid and don't know where to turn, they get angry and upset. Instead we should keep alert and watchful, like the owl and the hawk, to see what's happening and when to take to wing. We have to see the whole view like the eagle, and every little thing that happens like the hawk. If we fuss with each other and don't use our brains, we'll act more like frightened mice or rabbits, and fall prey to people who would hurt us."

"The white people of Georgia?"

"Some of them. Enough to make our lives miserable if we are not ready. I think we have to be ready to move, and ready to use the strength we still have. We must make an agreement that will help us move to a place where we can live the way we want to. At the same time we have to keep learning how to live with people who don't understand each other. We can be our own enemies, if we don't figure out how to live together. But we also have many enemies outside our people. We have to figure out how to live with them too."

Their cabin came into view as they walked along the path that ran midway along the bluff above the Coosawattee River.

---

[28] John Ehle, *Trail of Tears*, p. 265 provides a summary of the Council meeting controversy between John Ross and Major Ridge.

The last glimmers of twilight reflected patches of color onto the rippling water, and the lamplight glowed an evening welcome through the window glass. "Siyo, Allie, we're home," David called out, as they stamped their feet on the porch to alert her of their arrival. David opened the door and saw Allie sitting at the table under the yellow glow of the hanging kerosene lamp, with a leather bag open on the table, and the familiar white turtle bones spread out before her amid a scattering of dried sage. "You have the medicine bag out. What are you learning?"

"Don't you laugh at me," she answered.

"I don't laugh at what I don't understand. I leave that to others."

For a moment she looked hard at him, and then a little smile began to appear. "I was seeking some help. I want to know whether to plant a crop this year or not. I pray about it, then I decide to ask turtle to help me decide. Will it be a waste of effort and seed? If we have to move before harvest, then we will want that seed later."

"Did you hear about the arguments at Council? Is that why you are puzzled?"

"I saw Susannah and Sally Wahena today. They were telling me the news. They both thought it would be foolish to plant a crop. I didn't agree, but they at least planted the seeds of doubt again. I remember how John and Anna Gambold drew lots to decide whether to baptize any of us. It took a long time before they finally baptized Margaret Vann, and she was their first convert. They drew lots whenever they made other big decisions.[29] So why not seek turtle's help, I say?"

---

[29] John Ehle, *Trail of Tears*, p. 92

"What does turtle tell you?"

"She says, plant, this year. And next year. Then she says, no more. It's hard to believe after all the talk and worrying, but there it is. Ulisi taught me how to read the bones when she gave me the bag. I think it's what God wants me to do."

"Then that is what we will do. We won't worry about tomorrow or next year. We'll just take care of today. We'll be like the flowers in the field and the birds of the air. Isn't that what the Reverend Gambold taught you also?"

"Yes, it is. You and I will continue to plant seeds. I will wait to decide when we will leave this place, and where I will go."

July, 1834, Coosawattee Trail

Followed by Little Wolf, David herded two large oxen down the path past the last cabins of Coosawattee Town as they headed toward home. "Now I have this problem," he said half to himself. Little Wolf looked up at his father, but didn't say anything.

"How do I tell your Uji that I spent most of a year's income on these oxen?" They walked on for a while in silence, only the swishing of the oxen tails and the clop of their hooves making any sound to compete with the midsummer locusts. "Do you suppose it will help to tell her that I bought them from Samuel Lattamore? That's her clan udo,[30] who's married to your Uhlogi[31] Rachel, even if we don't see much of them." Little Wolf just kicked a little dust in reply.

---

[30] Udo is a brother or sister.

[31] Uhlogi means "aunt."

"I suppose we'll know soon enough if she minds my buying them. I could take them back if I can't persuade her that we'll need them, but I hope that I can."

A small outcropping of limestone, typical of the region along the lower river, gave way to the clearing where their first field showed the corn in full tassel, and the squash and bean vines growing abundantly between the stalks.

"Just a little bit farther and I'll have my answer."

Not far from their house David saw Allie standing in the small cotton patch, inspecting the blossoms. He called to her. "I think you'll have a good crop of cotton," he called as soon as he thought she would see him.

"Where'd you get those?" she answered. "I don't remember talking about buying a team of oxen.

"You're right. We didn't yet. I saw Sam Lattamore in town. He delivered a new wagon to John Martin. He drove it all the way from the Hiwassee River in McMinn County, and I was admiring this pair of oxen. He said he'd sell them, too, since he'd raised them, and didn't need them himself, and Judge Martin already had ten good teams. So I offered him thirty dollars, and we settled at forty. But if you don't think we should buy them, I'll take them back."

Allie pursed her lips and began to examine them, as she thought about it. She rubbed her hands over their flanks and examined their mouths and teeth. "No, I think you did all right. I'd been wondering how we would move our stuff when the time came, and a good working team will help us in the field wherever we are. So you are safe this time. But I don't want you to get used to spending our money without talking to me. This time I agree that you did well in buying them when you did."

David breathed a visible sigh of relief and gave Little Wolf an open-eyed look and a wink. "Little John helped me make the decision. He's going to be a bargainer like his Ududu, I think."

"I suppose so," was all that she said. "Did you hear any news?"

"Sam says your clan relatives are all as well as can be expected. They heard from Arkansas. Your mother Ruth is strong as ever. She is herding more cattle. They heard from your aunt-mother Nancy Starr. They are prospering with their mill and holdings there at Evansville. They said they are ready for more of their family to join them and hoping it will be soon."

Allie answered, "It's already been ten summers since Nancy and Caleb moved out there. I didn't dream we would even consider going there. It's been hard to have the family so far apart."

David continued, "The people are getting ready for the Green Corn Festival. There are special preparations at New Echota, the largest festival ever, they say, a full week of stomp dancing, fasting and fresh corn feasting, stick ball, scratching ceremonies, everything. I suppose we should plan to go."

"Hmmph. I don't think I want to leave Old Coosawattee Town this year. We should prepare a gayugi[32] to take care of old Deaf Nancy's fields, and it seems strange to me to leave Old Coosawattee when it may be the last time we get to celebrate here. There has been a green corn festival here for as long as

---

[32] A gayugi was a communal show of support.

anyone can remember. The old people would surely miss it if everyone went to New Echota instead."

David stepped close to her and wrapped his arms around her. "I'm glad you feel that way. I'd rather be here myself, and, you're right, Deaf Nancy could use our help. That should come first. We can get a dozen or so to form a gayugi for her, and then we can celebrate in the old style, even if most of the town goes away. Besides, even with the ban on liquor, someone will sneak it in when the crowd gathers at New Echota. Someone is always spoiling the old ways." Then he and Allie shared a strong kiss, even while Little Wolf stood silently looking at them.

"One other piece of interesting news, though I don't know what it means. Sam said that his brother-in-law James Starr, and another of your clan brothers, John Walker, Jr., are in Washington with Andrew Ross, trying to negotiate a plan with Andrew Jackson."[33]

"They can't do that!" Allie protested. "They don't have any authority. They can only get into trouble with the people!"

"My feelings exactly. But that is what he said, and that is what I heard from the four winds as well, though less politely."

"It's already being talked about, then. This will be awful for them. "Allie paused for a moment before she continued. "We should name them Cain and Abel."

"What?" David asked, confused.

---

[33] John Ehle, *Trail of Tears*, p.266

"The oxen. We should call them Cain and Abel, because of the division growing among the Ani Yun'wiya.[34]" She then sat down with Little Wolf and explained to him the bible story that gave the oxen their names.

September, 1834, Springplace

Tall, blond-haired John Martin stood nearly a foot above and looked nearly twice as old as the slight, dark-haired David Bell. They waited in the square courtyard between the brown-stained clapboard-sided buildings that were formerly the Moravian School and Mission at Springplace. Not far away James McDaniel and William Dowling also awaited their turns to testify at the murder trial of fellow half-breed James Graves.[35]

Judge Martin spoke to David, "This town has certainly deteriorated in the two years since Georgia took possession of it and forced Reverend Henry Clauder out. The buildings and orchards and fields, everything looks abandoned. The Moravians and James and Joseph Vann had made this into a showplace that we could be proud of. Now it's falling apart."

"The white people who are coming into the area have neither the skills, nor the education, nor the love of the land to do much with it. They are obviously in charge here. This is a nasty business we are a part of," answered David.

"We all heard James Graves, loud and drunk, boasting about killing that white man."

---

[34] The Ani Yun'wiya are the Principal People, the traditional self-designation of the Cherokee Nation. The name "Tsa' lagi (brought into English as Cherokee) is of uncertain origin and meaning.

[35] The account of this trial comes from *Murray County Heritage*, Chapter 2, "Murray County's Early Years," the online publication of the Murray County Historical Society, Georgia.

"If we hadn't tried to find out who it was, or where it happened, or what James did with the body, we wouldn't even be having a trial. We never found any evidence that he was doing anything more than wanting to kill someone, but we did not hide what we had heard. We wanted to find out if it was true. So how can they take a drunken man's bragging for evidence?" David asked.

"We must cooperate with the Georgians who are in charge. We're trying to salvage some trust and goodwill, until we no longer need to be here. God willing, we can leave before they turn everything into a shambles. They have us in a vice, David, you know that, and they'll squeeze us every way they can. Any excuse, and we'll lose the little we have left here, and have nothing to show for a lifetime of work."

"So, if we don't testify to what we heard, we will put our families in even more jeopardy. I see how it works. Graves will pay the price, whether he actually did what he said he did or not."

John responded, "Elias will put the best face on the testimony as he translates the Cherokee into English. He'll make sure the jury understands it's all hearsay, but I doubt the jury will care much about the life of one half-breed."

There was a commotion in the area outside the square, as a man rode up on his horse and slid off the saddle. He announced loudly enough for all four of the men in the square to hear, "Jim Walker's dead."

"The hell," McDowell said loudly.

David took a couple of steps backward as if trying to avoid a blow. "I knew he was in bad shape. He didn't have much of a chance to survive being shot in the back. He lost too much blood."

"Allie will take this badly, won't she? She's known him all her life. And, like me, he leaves two wives to take care of. He did not deserve that."

"Nobody deserves that. As I heard it, three men snuck up on him at Muskrat Springs and, like cowards, shot him in the back. For what? Because he talked with Jackson about coming to terms with the Principal People and moving west? If everyone who had thought about that would be put to death there would be no chiefs left, nobody who could read or write, nobody who knew anything!"

"They suspect he has already made a secret deal."

David answered quickly, "How could he? The President would not make a deal with one or two men, expecting all the rest of us would go along. It takes a lot more people than that to make an agreement. We saw that when Andrew Ross tried it. The Senate has to have more of an excuse than that to make a new treaty with our people. We still have some political support on our side, but even the missionary societies want us to come to terms."

"The hotheads do not listen to that. Ross does not seem to understand it either. He keeps playing both sides, but he won't admit to the full-bloods that we have to get ready to leave."

"John, we all saw the violence in the crowd at the Red Clay Council. Tom Foreman called the advocates of a treaty "enemies of the Cherokee Nation." Elijah Hicks manipulated the crowd into impeaching Ridge and his son John, and David Vann, the very people who should be the leaders we follow. I would not be at all surprised if Tom and his brothers, James Foreman and Anderson Springston, were the ones who shot Walker."

"Mark my words, David, they will not be brought to justice, and Walker will be only the first of many to die for his people."

"I hate to tell Allie. She will be even more certain that we have no good choices left."

The next day toward evening David was completing his ride from Springplace to Coosawattee Town on the Federal Road, and the familiar landmarks of Bell Mountain and Horn Mountain came into view. His house at the foot of Bell Mountain, and the village and river running between, had been his home all of his life. He stopped his horse for a few minutes and looked at the two mountains on the near horizon. The caves, the springs, the rich fields along the river, the fish weirs, and the ancient town had been his playground and his livelihood. He felt sorry for Little John who would not know its motherly embrace for much longer. He wished that he did not have to report the news to Allie. Her prediction of the killing of Abel had come true.

He had taken her as his bride when she was barely nineteen years old. Now that she was twenty-four, fully a woman, rightfully confident in her own abilities and independence, now that the killing had begun, would she be able to stay so far away from her mothers and sisters?

November, 1834, Running Waters

Neat tents and shelters spread across a recently cut hay field that lay to the north of John Ridge's fine new two story white frame house. The house sat among several farm buildings and slave quarters, the young orchard, and the bountiful Running Waters spring that supplied the hundred men and women gathered there. Several fancy carriages parked nearby, and horses were grazing in a part of the pasture that had been fenced off and not mown. None of the usual festival arrangements for stick ball or stomp dancing were visible. The serious character of the gathering showed to any observers, and there were observers representing men who refused to take part in this council. Occasionally people around the tents and buildings caught sight of silent sentries in the woodlands out of earshot.[36]

David, Little John, and Allie shared a canvas tent at the edge of the orchard. They were standing outside their tent, sharing late morning cups of coffee, talking with his brother, John Adair Bell, "Jack" to all who knew him, who looked much like David—short, slim, and dark-haired, with little obvious evidence of his half-Cherokee ancestry. Soon they were joined by two older men who shared their stature and features.

"Osiyo, Ududa," said Jack and David almost in unison, "Siyo, Asa," likewise. "You got in late last night, I hear," Jack continued.

"Right," the elder John began, "we've plans to continue traveling, regardless o' how this meetin' turns out, y' must know. Devereaux, Asa, and I'll head west after. We'll stop at brother James' place in Kentucky to see his family. We'll travel on to St. Louis, through Missouri, into the Western Cherokee lands. There's the land I heard about in Illinois, too, newly opened in Pike County. The Sauk and Fox have had to cede their land in that area, after Black Hawk's ill-fated stand. Just because his tribe canna' live in it doesn't mean that no Indian people can. I know some settlers in Missouri and we'll talk with them. O' course we have many people in Arkansas and farther west and

---

[36] John Ehle, *Trail of Tears*, p. 272.

Bowle and his people in Texas. We'd some work to finish before we came here. Be gone for about a month at least. We'll ride light, and, if the weather holds, we might even get back afore the worst o' winter."

"Do you plan to move west, then? What about the prospects in Texas?"

"Devereaux and Asa think they want to go and stay there, join with John Bowle. There's a lot o' open land, and Sam Houston wants the Cherokee in it, but we've got some enemies there, too.[37] Still too unsettled, to my way o' thinkin'. Later on maybe, but movin' when and where is still a question. I do aim to stay with the Old Settlers in Arkansas, if we can, but we all must hedge our bets. They tell me Pike looks much like McMinn County, rolling hills and forests, deep ravines and plenteous water. Soil there is rich and dark like Coosawattee bottomlands, not red and clay. It'll be good for growing crops, good for livestock, too. Might be a good investment, I think, whether we wind up there or naw. First, we must see what we can do here. Later, if Texas becomes secure, and they settle who's in charge there, whether or naw they'll respect claims we might stake, then we can look in that direction again. Who knows?" Asa nodded his head quietly as his Uncle John was making his comments.

---

[37] Chief Bowle, also called Duwali, had led a group of Cherokees into northeast Texas in 1820. In November of 1835 he and Sam Houston agreed to a treaty granting a large amount of land to the Cherokees. The Republic of Texas did not confirm the treaty, as some Cherokees had sided with the Mexican government in their fight for independence and other Texas leaders opposed native autonomy. Carol A. Lipscomb, "Cherokee Indians," *Handbook of Texas Online* (www.tshaonline.org/handbook/online/articles/bmc51), accessed April 07, 2015. Uploaded on June 12, 2010. Published by the Texas State Historical Association.

David knew that this was the first time that Allie had heard talk of either Illinois or Texas, and he felt her stiffen at the thought of being so far away from her roots, and her grandmother. He wondered again whether he should have discouraged her from coming to this meeting, but she was determined to be a part of any decision they might make. He knew that any effort to discourage her participation would only make her more suspicious and difficult to persuade later. He would have to suggest a walk toward the Oostanaula River, so they could talk and clear the air.

Little John got brave enough to ask his question when the older men paused in their conversation. "Ududu, did Sarah come with you?"

"Naw, Grandson, she's stayin' home these days, doin' her work there. She do like to get your letters, though, and she likes to write to ye. So if y' can, write a little letter to her. I'll take it to her. It tickles m' ears to hear y' talk."

"Thank you Ududu," Little John said.

They were soon engaged in speculation about what decisions they would make while they were here. Soon they would eat together, and they already smelled the roasting carcasses of beef and lamb that the servants of John Ridge had put on spits and begun to turn regularly since early in the morning. Major Ridge and Susannah were comfortably accommodated in their own house six miles west. With them also, were Stand Waite and Elias Boudinot. Boudinot had recently returned from a lengthy stay in New England with the family of his wife, who had died in the spring, and with friends from his years at Cornwall School. John Martin and old Chief John Walker, father of the murdered man, John, Jr., had guest rooms in John Ridge's house. Jack and David had already greeted

John and Ezekiel West, Archilla Smith, James Starr, John and David Vann, and Alexander McCoy, whose tents were set up nearby, or who had taken shelter in one of the barns. They had seen Jack and David's brother, Samuel, at breakfast, but he had left after that to talk with someone else. There were scores of other familiar people, and Allie had some catching up to do with all of the Phillips, Hildebrand, Starr, Candy, West, and Bean clan relatives who had arrived from McMinn County.

Little John had clan brothers and sisters to see, and other children his age and older. Enough youngsters had come to divide into teams for a stick ball game. Little John carried the racket he and his father had made, as a clear sign that he was ready to play, whenever anyone else was. Not much time passed after lunch before he and several other boys and girls were batting and running across the open field south of the spring that gave Running Waters its name.

Allie was consoling and commiserating with her sisters, aunts, and cousins over the death of John Walker, Jr. They talked about where they would go when some Georgia lottery winner would come and claim their property and send them away. When they retold the story of John Ross coming home to his plantation at Head of Coosa, just seven miles to the southwest of where they were talking, and finding it occupied by a stranger named Stephen Carter, they laughed a little. Ross had to move just over the state line into Tennessee, but he still didn't understand that what was happening could not be stopped. The same threat was too close to all of them for them to laugh a lot.

At the afternoon assembly they quickly reached a general agreement. They would have to form a party of Cherokees that would favor making a treaty with the United States. It would have to compensate well for the loss of their ancestral lands. It would have to make it possible for them to reestablish themselves as a nation in the Arkansas region alongside the Old Settlers there. They knew that they had a lot of work to do. They must develop a strategy that would win as much support as possible among the rest of the people, and to arrange the best terms for a treaty that would benefit all of the people.

David found Allie, and he asked her to take a walk with him toward the Costanaula River, where Major Ridge had his home and ferry. The path between Running Waters and the river was well-worn from frequent traffic between the two Ridge family plantations. David described the discussions and the consensus that was developing about their course of action.

"The full-bloods will never accept another treaty," Allie predicted. "They will turn against those who make it, and our people will fight each other instead of our common enemy."

"What choice do we have? We lose everything if we try to stay. At least we can gain enough to reestablish ourselves if we trade for land in the west and make them pay us for what we are giving up."

"We don't have a choice. I'm just saying what I know to be true. The people will fight it. The fight will be Cherokee against Cherokee, not against the white people who take our land away. I don't want to be in the middle of the fight."

"We already are, aren't we? I thought we could keep building our people up, adopting the good that we found in our father's ways, and rejecting the bad, honoring the ways of our mothers and staying together as a people, but I don't see how we can do it. We have too many divisions."

"The white people know only division. They brought us their religion, but it comes in different forms. Even though the missionaries can work together on some things, they still argue about many. They brought us tools that help live off the land, but they cut the land up into little pieces and want us to fight each other for it. They brought us many slaves, but the slaves no longer become part of our families. We are supposed to treat them more like cattle or pigs. I think the white people like to make us fight. At the same time their religion teaches us to make peace. I cannot understand them. I don't want to try to get along with them anymore."

"Then we have to move to a place where we can set up our own way of life as much as possible. We don't have a chance to do that here."

"So you and your father have been planning to go to Illinois or to Texas? Our people will never go there. It's like the rumor about John Ross and others wanting to resettle in Mexico. It's not going to happen. If we go anywhere it must be to join our own family in Arkansas, not to divide into yet more small pieces."

"That's my father's plan, not mine. You know him by now. He's a trader by nature, always buying and selling. He thinks about possibilities, and he's willing to go and invest in a little bit here and a little bit there. Later he'll make up his mind what to keep. He'll not want to settle in Illinois if he can't keep his slaves, and people in Illinois haven't made up their mind on that.[38] You heard him talk about the unpredictability of Texas, so he's not ready to do anything there yet. Anyway, that's him, not me. I

---

[38] The complex story of the slavery issue in Illinois is told in *The Pike County History* (Pittsfield, Illinois, 1964).

heard him talk about it before, but I have made no plans to join him in it."

"I understand. You must know by now that I will not agree to have slaves, and I will not live off the work of slaves. I will do my own work, and I will treat slaves as my own family. I won't follow your father or your brothers or anyone else who mistreats other people like the white people do. Why imitate the white people when they treat us so badly? We can live without slaves. The people who are slaves can surely live better free than they live now."

"I see the way you see, and we have lived this way for six years. I have not taken a slave, and I have not made anyone work for me, if he did not want to. Ezra and Elijah are my friends, not my slaves, and I have paid them or traded work for anything they have done for me. You and I see alike. This will not be an issue between us."

"I am grateful, husband, because it cannot be. As to making a treaty, I cannot bless you in it, because I know it will not bring our people together, even if we have no choice. We will surely suffer for it, and our people may suffer for it forever." Allie and David had been walking side by side, and she was stunned to see unfamiliar tears in David's eyes when she looked at him face to face. She stopped and turned fully toward him, and they embraced for a few quiet moments in the middle of the path, before they turned around and walked in silence between the pine trees back to their camp.

February, 1835, Coosawattee Town

Allie recognized the backs of two women, the tall form of Wehena and the shorter, more rounded form of Susannah, a hundred hands ahead of her on the path, as they approached the small log cabin of Deaf Nancy at the east edge of Coosawattee Town, near the mouth of Talking Rock Creek. Smoke was curling out of the crooked stacked rock chimney at the opposite end of the cabin from the front door. Both women were carrying bundles, as was Allie. She had a large pack of newly cut cane, tied with leather straps, slung over her shoulder. She knew that Wehena was bringing food to Nancy, and Susannah had agreed to bring cloth to work on a new dress. They disappeared inside the door, without stopping to knock, since Nancy was expecting them and wouldn't hear their knock. Soon Allie opened the door herself and entered into the dim tallow-lit room. Deaf Nancy was hunched over her fireplace, appearing always shorter and more bent than the last time Allie had seen her, her head held sideways from her body. She was lifting the black kettle from the iron brace, and she carried it over to the table to pour a black tea into cups. As Allie's eyes adjusted to the light, she saw that Katharine Dougherty and both Betsy and Dorcas Kahena were there kneeling on mats on the dirt-packed floor. They greeted one another, and Nancy spoke in syllables that were barely understandable, but which Allie took to mean that she was happy to have company and their help for the day's projects. She would keep talking through much of the day, and sometimes Allie could understand enough to piece an old story together that she had heard Nancy tell before.

"Soon Ganugogv'l[39] will arrive, and we'll go up on the mountains to gather ramps[40]," Katharine said. "We'll need to find some for Nancy, since she prepares the best stews." They talked for some time about the ways that they used ramps to flavor various foods, and sipping the strong tea.

---

[39] Gaanugigv'l and gilagoge are Cherokee words for the season of spring.

[40] A wild onion.

Gradually Allie unpacked and sorted the cane that she had brought. "I found these along Talking Rock Creek, just as you told me, Dorcas," she nodded to the gray-haired woman across from her. "There are not many cane brakes left in the area."

"The people are using more oak and hickory strips lately, but they do not make good water baskets," Dorcas replied. "Anyway, Nancy loves to make the old baskets, and she is good at it."

Soon Nancy had joined Allie, kneeling on a shared mat, and Nancy caught up with and passed Allie in forming a round base, weaving the cane firmly and deftly into a familiar pattern. Soon the sloping sides of her basket were taking shape.

The women managed for a long time to avoid the topic that they all dreaded, but eventually had to discuss. First they talked of recipes and skills that people were losing in their eagerness to buy cloth, metal utensils, glass and pottery dinnerware. Then they were talking about the removal to the west. Allie could almost hear a collective sigh when Katharine asked them whether they had heard about the group that had signed up to go west to Arkansas.

Wehena said, "What I heard was that they got as far as Springplace. Some of them used the money they were given for travel to buy whiskey, so they were so drunk that they couldn't go any farther."

Betsy added at that point, "And some of the women were so disgusted that they took what they could carry, and their children, and ran into the woods. They had already been on the road for many days and they had gotten no farther than Springplace."

"I don't know exactly what happened, but a couple of hundred people had taken the offer to go, received part of their payment, and at Springplace the group disbanded. They had already given up their homes and fields, so they didn't have anything to go back to. Most had to go to relatives in different places. I don't know anyone from our town who was part of that, and I'm glad of that. We have enough lazybones and drunkards as it is," Katharine concluded.

"Is this an example of what 'removal to the west' means to our people?" asked Allie. "Giving up what we have made, packing up what we have left, getting drunk on the way, and finally disappearing into the woods before we have gone forty miles? If that's what it means, our cause is hopeless."

Betsy stated firmly that she's not budging. "They'll have to carry me out."

Katharine continued, "Many of our people have made the trip west over the years, without being bribed to do so, except for the promise of land in the west. You have family in Arkansas already, don't you, Allie?" Allie nodded. "Your brother-in-law and his father have been back and forth several times already. It must be possible, if we have to do it, to make the trip. I don't want to, but if we have to, to live life the way we choose to live it, and not the way the white people of Georgia do, I think we can do it."

"We will have to do it," Sally Wehena said. "Just look at what happened to Joe Vann at Springplace three weeks ago. Colonel William Bishop and his soldiers took over his house, and kicked him out, from the nicest, prettiest house in the nation. Joe had to move his family over to their little farm at Ooltewah. They were fortunate to have a place to go. Most of us don't, but that won't keep the whites from taking over our places. If they don't respect a man like Rich Joe Vann, they'll steal from us without a buzzard's look around."

An awkward silence followed Katharine's remarks, which no one seemed to want to break, until Deaf Nancy asked, "Would anyone like more tea?"

March, 1835, Fish Weir in Coosawattee

Little Wolf, Will, Runner, and Richard Martin had stripped off their clothing in the warm sun, and were wading into the cold flowing water of the Coosawattee inside the rows of heavy rocks that formed a series of V-shapes pointing downriver. Each of the boys carried a spear and coil of woven twine in their hands, as they formed a line moving steadily toward the far point where a series of heavy stakes allowed the water to flow through, but the larger fish could not pass.[41] The boys passed the place where one V of rocks channeled the water into the short last V, and put the woven frame in place that prevented fish from returning upstream. They could now see the larger fish assembled in the lower pool, among the boulders placed to isolate them into separate pools. They were laughing and pointing excitedly, ready to try to spear the fish or to try to catch them bare-handed.

Little Wolf had watched as the older boys and men had worked the fish weir last year, but this was his first time to try to catch the fish himself. He was surprised at how fast they moved to avoid his hands, and how slippery their skin. The other boys had more experience, and were soon stringing their fish on the line they had brought. At last he cornered a trout in a small pocket and had his hands firmly around it, slipping his twine

---

[41] Allen Lutens documented the Coosawattee and other fishweirs in the region in his Masters' thesis, *Prehistoric Fishweirs in Eastern North America* (Binghamton, State University of New York, 1992, updated by the author in 2004).

through its mouth and gill the start his line. He was all smiles. Finally, tired of the effort and resorting to the spear, his line was as full as he dared carry, and they all headed toward the bank where they had left their clothing. Their feet and legs were so cold that they could barely feel them, but the sun was warm, and they were soon dry enough to put their clothes back on.

"How long has this weir been here?" Little Wolf asked his friends.

Richard answered, "My father says that it was already here before the Creeks lived in Old Town, long before our people came. He thinks it was made at the time the ancient ones built the mounds at Etowah long ago. That was when they built Old Town also."

"The rocks are so heavy. Giants must have built it," Little Wolf said.

Will added, "It took a lot of men a lot of work. But I'm glad they did it. It's so much fun to catch fish in it."

The boys all agreed to that. They would prepare a fire to roast some fish for lunch, with the bread they had brought from home. They had enough to take home for their families to eat later. Richard and Runner busied themselves with the fire, while Will wanted to show Little Wolf something from his pack. He unlaced the leather ties and lifted the cover to pull out the loaf of bread he had brought, and, after it, he removed a bundle and unwrapped it to reveal a brown leather-bound book.

"You and your mother are always reading from the bible or the newspaper," Will said. "I wanted to show you the bible that my father got from the preacher at Springplace ten years ago. This is what I used to learn to read. Dad said I could show you, if I was careful and brought it back."

Little Wolf took the book carefully in his hands and fingered through the well-worn pages. "It is beautiful," he said. "It looks just like ours."

Will and Little Wolf looked for some of the stories they liked to read. Little Wolf found the fish-catching story at the end of John. He decided their experience at the fish weir was more fun. Their mouths were already watering at the smell of the fish that Richard and Runner were roasting. Will wrapped the bible again and put it back in his pack, and they took the loaf over to the fire to be ready to eat. Richard used his hunting knife to remove a fillet from one side of the fish and lay it on a chunk of bread, and then did the same with the other side. Then he picked the rest of the flesh from the bones with his fingers and ate it directly, while the other boys divided the bread and fish.

After eating, they doused and covered the fire with soil, picked up their lines of fish, and headed upriver along the path toward town. They stopped to check a rabbit trap they had set on a run in the pine woods on the way earlier. There was no catch yet so they continued up the path. They came to Richard's home, a large two-story frame house set high on the bluff among many small cabins and stables overlooking the river. There they found an outside table, and they cleaned their fish and lay them in the sun to dry.

With the work done, Richard slowly revealed what he had been thinking about. "My father told us something he wanted to keep a secret, but I'm going to tell you anyway. Will you keep it a secret?" The boys nodded eagerly. "He says that once a treaty is finished to give up our claims to this land, our family will move west. We will leave everything behind. We won't wait any longer.

Our Land! Our People!

We will pack what we need, and my family and our slaves, and we will move on our own to join the Old Settlers in the Arkansas land."

Runner frowned, "You'll leave all of your houses and stables and everything? How can you do that?"

"Father says we can't keep any of it. He already knows a buyer, a man named Carter. We have no choice."

"When will this happen?"

"Father expects the treaty to be done in the fall. We will finish the harvest and leave soon after."

"I wonder what will happen to the rest of us?" Runner spoke sadly.

"You will come later in large groups."

Little Wolf listened to the two older boys and looked at his friend Will. He had listened to talk about moving all of his life. The talk of moving west reminded him of the nightmare that he often had about a great mountain higher than any he had ever seen or climbed, a great monster of a mountain that would awaken and eat any creature that tried to climb it. He wondered whether he had the strength to try.

April, 1835, John Bell's Farm, Coosa River

David sat on the familiar benches on the porch of his father's house along the Coosa. The elder John Bell and cousin Asa sat beside him. They watched his younger sisters Sarah and Charlotte as they came from the stable west of the house, after leaving their horses with a servant who had travelled with them.

Sarah pressed a few books against her breasts with her folded arms.

"We went to the school at Creek Path. We study with the teacher there, Miss Charlotte Brown," she said to her brother David's unasked question.[42]

"I didn't realize the Mission School there was still open. They were forced to abandon all the schools around Coosawattee."

"Oh yes," Sarah replied. "Daniel Butrick, the preacher here, says he will stay with us wherever we are. He will stay here as long as the people are here, and he will go west when the people go west. He looks very stern when he says it, and I think he will. And Miss Brown says she'll be here as long as she's needed."

"I'm glad to hear it. Reverend Sam Worcester lost his house in New Echota. I understand he plans to go west to get ready for the rest of us, to be there when we get there." David reached into his vest pocket and pulled out a crumpled envelope. "Before I forget, here's a letter from Little John for you. He's always eager to send a letter. I know he loves to get one back from you."

Sarah quickly took the letter from David's hand, and went into the house, with Charlotte following. Their little brother, James Madison, heard them at the door, and came to meet them, looking much like his nephew, whose letter she carried, but nearly a year older at age eight. They went up the stairway from

---

[42] The school and teacher at the Creek Path Mission until it closed in 1837 are recorded in *The Brainerd Journal*, Edited by Joyce B. Phillips and Paul Gary Phillips (Lincoln, Nebraska; University of Nebraska Press, 1998), 400.

Our Land! Our People!

the entry hall to a sitting area at the window at the top of the stairs. There Sarah took a seat on the window bench, with James and Charlotte on either side. She opened the envelope and began to read the Cherokee symbols.

> Dear Sarah Caroline,
> Udoda is coming to see Ududu and asked if I want to send a letter. Yes, I do. I was surprised to learn that Ududu and Udo Asa[43] had been gone so long on their trip west. They got stuck in snow. I've never seen much snow except on the mountain. I heard they saw his Udo James in Kentucky. They met Richard Bean, Uduji of Edmond Bean who married my Uji Udo. I never met these people. I wonder how people get spread out so far and live in so many places. Someday I will learn this, since everyone always talks about leaving Coosawattee. Will we travel together? Udoda says he plans to. I hope so. I would like to be with you more. I hope you are well. Uji always helps me with the letter. We have a printed book that helps us choose the right syllables. We will soon plant crops. Uji says it is our last crop here. Say Osiyo for me to Charlotte, James and little Martha.　　　　Yours truly, Usdi Wahya

On the porch the men were talking about another letter, one sent from President Andrew Jackson to the people of the Cherokee Nation.[44] "Not many people will read it, or understand it, and those who do are already persuaded we must come to terms," David said as he handed a printed copy of the letter to his father.

---

[43] Udo is a loosely applied word for sibling, brother or sister. It is also appropriate for a clan cousin, but here it is used for a cousin who was probably of a different clan.

[44] John Ehle, *Trail of Tears*, pp. 275-278

"There's nothin' new here," the elder John said as he read through the letter. "The details are much like the ones last reported to us by John Ridge and Elias. This line will not win any friends—'You will ultimately disappear, as so many tribes have done before you.' He listed all the stipulations we asked for—money for schools, agricultural instruments, domestic animals, and missionary establishments—but I do naw think they're enough to satisfy Ross or anybody with him.

"I suppose y' want to hear about our trip west."

David simply nodded.

"I did naw expect to see so much winter, but it turned out all right. We'd a good stay with brother James in Kentucky. When Asa and I got to St. Louis, the river was still open, but trails were blocked with ice and snow. So we didn't go to Pike County. We invested in provisions to take to our Arkansas friends. We had enough money, and James Starr had asked us to do that if we could. His father Caleb had complained of the lack of provisions and trade goods in the new territory.

"While we were trading in the area just west of St. Louis we met a man I'd heard about, named John Bell, whose wife has the same name as Asa's wife, Barbary. Like me, he's a veteran o' the War in 1812. What an oddity, to have so much in common! He's settled next to Daniel Boone, Junior's, homestead in Franklin County. I was visiting with Daniel and Nathan Boone. They introduced us to me namesake. Both Bell and the Boone family already have land in Pike County, Illinois.

"Bell doesn't know what he'll do with the land there. If he doesn't move there himself, he'll sell it to his nephews, who seem to be interested in it. Says the soil in the area is mostly dark and rich. The politics seem to be settlin' down some. It won't be a

Our Land! Our People!

slave state, but you'll see Negro workers there. There's a settlement o' mixed bloods and Negroes near his property, led by a freedman named Frank.[45] He thinks it's a good sign we could get along there, if we decided to settle there. There's enough open land for many families to homestead at very low cost.[46]

"We were tempted to go north to 'vestigate, but the weather wouldn' break. So we booked passage on a flatboat and floated down to Memphis, found the Military Road west to Little Rock was dry and passable in the bottomlands. Bought two teams and wagons, loaded 'em, and headed southwest to Little Rock. The road was much better than last time. It still could go to ruin fast if weather was wet, and travelers rutted it, but for us it was in bonnie shape. The Arkansas River was low, so we continued on the post road till we got to Van Buren. Then up the mountain we went to travel a ridge road to Evansville and Caleb's mill and lands. In dry weather, this will be the route to take next time we go. Otherwise, the southern river route will be easier on passengers."

"You know best, Father. No one's made more trips back and forth," David said, as his father stopped talking, tamped some tobacco into his pipe, and lighted it.

---

[45] The community of New Philadelphia was established in Pike County by Free Frank McWhorter in 1836. The John K. Bell properties were a mile to the west. The John Francis Bell properties in the 1850's were a mile east of New Philadelphia-related homesteads.

[46] John K. Bell is recorded in Pike County, Illinois, real estate records as acquiring land on November 20, 1831, and, with his wife Barbary, selling it to his step-sons, John and Moses Decker, on March 8, 1836. The latter transaction occurred at the Franklin County, Missouri, courthouse. Details of the John K. Bell family were found through the Franklin County Historical Society.

Asa resumed the story. "We traveled around a bit and checked out some locations. The area around Caleb's settlement will remind everyone of home. You come down off the steep mountainside as you come to the Vineyard Post Office, and a broad plain opens before you, with the river providin' good flow, just a little less than the Coosawattee. Plenty of timber, good grasslands and fields, too. Not as dry as farther west. John and Ruth Bean are well-settled there. Noon and Ellis have stakes a few miles west, and Ellis and Deliah have just put up a cabin. The Starrs and Beans all say there's plenty of room for more of us to settle. Even if we had a bad first winter, I think the area would provide enough shelter and game."

Comfortably sucking on his pipe, John continued to speak, "We went north into Delaware country. Found good lands there as well. The Old Settlers are mostly settled on the lower Illinois and Grand Rivers and along the Arkansas. I'd rather leave that area to them, though I 'spect newcomers'll crowd in where Old Settlers've already got a good start. We found a welcome everywhere. No one seems anxious about several thousand more o' their people comin' to live with them. They don't know yet what they're goin' to face.

"We sold the teams and wagons along with the provisions, and bought four horses for ourselves. When the weather settled down, Devereaux and Asa wanted to go south o' the Red River and find Bowle's settlement in Texas. We made our way south and found 'em about two weeks later. Bowle's group's grown to about eight hundred and they have impressive farms and herds. They still don't have legal papers, and the future of Texas is murky, to say the least. Devereaux wanted to stay. I tried to talk him out o' it, but he's an adult an' he's got a mind o' his own. We divided our earnin's, so he had a bonnie stake. I left him with Bowle, a man I can trust. Asa has his father and a woman to look after, so he came back with me. We came back by way o' Memphis, and took the usual route 'cross south Tennessee, goin' from County Seat to County Seat, always findin' 'commodations and supplies to suit us."

Asa hurried to add, "It's not goin' to be easy for a large group, no matter which way you go. We have few worries when we travel light, but a wagon train with hundreds of people and animals is somethin' else."

"That's what I've been thinkin' about, too," said David. "So much depends on the weather. It could go hard but well, or it could be a disaster. I'm glad you're both givin' it your full attention. The next part of our journey leads to the next Council meeting at Running Waters. John Ridge is tryin' again to host a full Council meeting in May, but it's goin' to be the middle of plantin' season. I doubt he'll have enough people attendin'. Still he's workin' hard to bring a crowd and provide a full Cherokee welcome, as he puts it." [47]

"We found that welcome in the West and in Texas," said Asa, "but I think it's disappeared hereabouts. Everywhere we go we find silent watchers, ready to report to John Ross. He posts sentries at every gatherin' and watchin' the homes of other leaders. I fear what he may be willin' to do. He's like a cougar stalkin' prey."

August, 1835, Allie Bell's House on Coosawattee

"I'd like to go to Running Waters for the green corn dance. Not because of the money John Ridge is spending on it. It'll be elaborate, I know. But this may be the last chance to persuade

---

[47] John Ehle, p. 280

anyone else that we should agree to a treaty for removal," David pleaded with Allie, though she mutely stood her ground.

"This is a poor time to go south," Allie stated emphatically. "We have dozens of the Creek people pouring into our neighborhood trying to escape from the military roundup of the Creeks in Georgia and Alabama. They couldn't have been more poorly treated. They are desperate and need our help. You know as well as I do, no matter how many people come for the corn dance, and I have no doubt many will come, nobody is going to change their minds about a treaty.

"Besides, David, there is something else we need to talk about. I've been waiting to tell you until I was sure. I've missed the flow that comes with the moon, for two moons. I have the dawn sickness."

"Oh, Allie, that is good. You will give birth in the spring then."

"Yes, we've wanted another child for years. But I've decided that I must go to be with my sisters while the baby grows inside me. I need to be with them when the child comes. I know that will disappoint you."

David was silent for a few minutes. "In ordinary times I would want to keep you with me. These are not ordinary times, and we both want this baby too much to pretend that it would be safe to stay here. You have foreseen that we will not plant here next year. I have nothing to keep you here. I know that everyone will leave this place sometime in the months to come. I would take you to my father's, but you would not be comfortable there, with the slaves doing much of the work. I know you need to be with your sisters in McMinn."[48]

"I knew you would understand."

"It's a lot to take in. I'd go and stay with you, but I still have so much to finish here. The harvest. The settlement of our land claims. The work with Jack. I have two fears. You have to travel many miles when you shouldn't. I'll go with you now, of course. I don't need to go to a green corn dance. But I'll have to come back here. Another thing troubles me. You may not want to stay with me when you've had the pleasant company of your sisters."

Allie looked at him and nodded her head, "I don't want to travel, but I must. I must do it while I still can. I'm glad you'll take me. To that other silly worry, I make you a promise. I will be with you and we will make a home together. I don't know where it will be, but you come to me, and we'll figure it out. There is one more matter, and I want you to consider my thoughts. Little Wolf must have a safe home, too. I want to take him with me, and he would have the care of my clan, but you are the best Udoda to him. He does not have an uncle near enough to teach him. Maybe he could stay with you for the winter, if you think he will be safe. I would like for him to join me in the spring. Maybe you can join us, too, by then. He could go to school at Candy's Creek, while we stay near there. If you can't come then, maybe even if you can, my cousins James and George Starr will surely be willing to provide a home for us; they are next in clan kinship. Cousins George Starr and George Washington Candy are married to your

---

[48] McMinn County, Tennessee, was home to many of the Phillips, Starr, Candy, West, and other relatives, as well as the Indian Agency for the Cherokee Nation at Charleston, and the temporary national center at Red Clay after Georgia's confiscation of New Echota.

sisters; they will have a double obligation to provide for Little John."

"You have thought about this more than I have. I thought we'd be together through this whole mess. Now that doesn't make sense. I need a little time to think. You are my beloved, Allie. You are my warrior udali'i.[49] Let me think about this for a few days. I will wear these ideas like a belt, and see how they fit. I'll see if I have anything to add to them, if I can make them feel right." David took Allie in his arms, and gave her a long kiss, and whispered in her ear, "I love you, Allie, till death; I never want to be apart from you. I never want you to send me away. You bring me the happiest news, and the saddest, both at the same time."

November, 1835, John Martin's House

Jack Bell sat next to his wife Jennie in her father's well-furnished parlor, David sat in a chair by himself, and John Martin sat with his second wife Nellie. Little John was looking through the shelves of books John Martin kept at the end of the room. One of Martin's slaves entered the room carrying a flask of wine, and poured glasses for each of them.

"How is the new man-without-a-wife?" John Martin directed his question to David.

David grimaced. "Not too well. It's been three weeks since I left her in the care of James and George Harlan Starr on Conasauga Creek. Little John and I both miss her. Right now she is staying with her Aunt Sarah.[50] Her husband died just a year ago. It already seems to me like a year since Allie left. I don't think she'll be happy there, but it's relatively safe for now."

---

[49] Udali'i means wife.

[50] Sarah Harlan West, widow of Jacob West who had died in Tennessee in 1834.

"We can't say that for our position here, can we?" John Martin said. "I'm sorry for your separation. I hope it's only for a few months. Lucy and Nellie have kept my beds warm for many years." He sat straighter in his chair and stretched his hand toward David, "The best news we've had in a long time came with the formation of the joint committee, five from the Ross Party and five from the Treaty Party to negotiate with the government about a treaty for removal.[51] We may finally have a united front to deal with the government."

"John Ridge is very enthusiastic. He thinks we've made a breakthrough," Jack Bell added. "I'll believe it when I see it, but John seems confident."

David said, "In view of that agreement, John Ross' arrest couldn't come at a worse time. When Colonel Bishop took the Georgia guard across the line into Tennessee to arrest him and John Howard Payne, what was he thinking?"[52]

John Martin responded, "He probably thought he could force him into cooperation. He doesn't know John Ross very well, does he?"

Jack said, "Payne is a well-known writer. That could swing back and hit Bishop, too. Payne already felt sympathy with the plight of the Cherokee. He's sending letters and articles all over the country complaining about the bad treatment. I understand, also, that Payne and Rev. John Schermerhorn have been rivals since college days. With Schermerhorn as the government negotiator, the controversy becomes even more complicated. I don't know how this could work to our advantage.

---

[51] John Ehle, p.289

[52] John Ehle, p. 290-292.

It may just stiffen Ross' resolve against Schermerhorn. He already calls him the 'devil's horn.'"

David added, "Absolom Bishop is holding Ross and Payne in a shed at Springplace. Is there something we could do to help Ross? He might appreciate an effort from us on his behalf. We could try to build some goodwill with him."

"John Ridge is already on his way to Springplace to try to see Ross and persuade Bishop to let him go. We could join in the effort," Jack said.

"I like that," John Martin said. "Let's pay him and Colonel Bishop a visit. The worst Bishop could do to us would be to arrest us, too. Then our united front would mean even more to Ross."

December, 1835, Council House, New Echota

David and his brother Jack Bell stood outside the Council House at New Echota. Little John was at David's side. All wore their leather coats and gloves against the chill, but the day was calm and clear, and the mid-afternoon sun was shining.

"No sign of anyone from the Ross Party except the blanketed sentries in the woods," David said in a low tired voice. "I don't know if we helped to secure Ross's release so soon, but the whole episode seemed to strengthen his resolve to oppose the removal treaty."

Jack answered, "What I think happened was due to all the publicity Payne created with his writing. Sometimes the pen is mightier than the sword, in wreaking havoc anyway. The backlash against the mistreatment of one white man made half the country feel a little guilty for what they'd done to all the civilized tribes. Ross sensed that the political winds were blowing in his direction for a while. He might glide in them to more advantage, but whether it's his own advantage or the advantage of the whole people, who knows?"

"Do you think the public sentiment has truly changed? If so, what are we doing here?"

"No, Georgia has not budged one inch. Nor has Jackson or anyone else in his administration. The southern and western members of Congress will hold steady with them. The Northeast and the Old Whigs will mostly oppose the Treaty, but with no other plan of their own to aid our people. It could be a close vote when it gets to the Senate, but if they vote it down, there will be no advantage to our people, just more wasted time and more arguing among everyone concerned. The public attention won't last. So, I think, what we're doing here, is playing our part, to see if we can settle things, so our people come out with something instead of nothing. If we can make a treaty, we can get on with our lives."

"Everything is in it that we discussed—equal land and more land in the west than what we yield in the east, settlement money for the properties that we leave behind, money for the people to move west, and an annuity for every person and for the whole nation to rebuild. Money for schools. And full support for the first year, when people won't have food and shelter and clothing without help. The only question I have—will the government keep its promises this time?"

"Probably not. They will make an effort, but it won't be enough. The people will be disappointed."

"Udoda, will you sign the treaty?" Little John asked.

"No, son. I will support the ones who do sign. The Ridges and Boudinot will sign. Your Uncle Samuel and Uncle Jack will sign. Many other friends and relatives, and most of the educated leaders of the nation will sign, but I promised your mother that I would not, so I will not."

"Little John, no one has an easy decision. Your father made a promise to your mother, but everyone knows by now that he supports the treaty, whether he signs or not. Those of us who do sign will have enemies who will make life hard for us. They will call us traitors, even though we are trying to do what is best for all the people. They may try to kill us, but we will be brave. We will do everything we can, but we will not go to war. It would be a war that no one would win. We will try to be a peaceful people."

"That's what my mother wants, isn't it, Uduji Jack?"

"That is what your mother wants most of all. I think she came to the conclusion that no one would gain anything by signing or not signing, by planning or not planning, so we might as well just live day to day the best way we can. She may be right in the end."

David wanted to say something to his son, but he could not figure out what to say, so he put his hands on the boy's slight shoulders, and held on in silence.

May 1836, Mouth of Talking Rock Creek

Reverend Evan Jones and Jesse Bushyhead stood on the bank of the Coosawattee River where Talking Rock Creek joins, surrounded by a crowd of Old Town residents. Jones' voice boomed out over the crowd, echoed by the banks and hills along the river.

"If God's providence does not favor a people, they cannot prosper," Jones was saying, needing no interpreter in the Cherokee language. He listed the sins of the people that were a burden to them. "All men are sinners. Not one is righteous, no, not one. We look around and see the signs of God's wrath, people leading lives of destruction, in drunkenness, profanity, and profligacy. These sins are among us as much as they afflict the white man, and they are a burden to everyone. The Cherokee people have adopted the white man's ways, and if these sins were not bad enough, some among you have accepted the sin of black slavery. God in his patience and longsuffering might have overlooked the common sins that plague mankind, but how can God forego the very sin that afflicted the ancient Israelites in slavery in Egypt? He heard their cries and he led them out. God will hear the cries of the people who are enslaved today, and those who do not free their slaves will become slaves themselves."

The words stung Little Wolf and Will standing side by side in the crowd, as they looked around and saw a few other black slaves standing here and there. These were brave words for Jones or Bushyhead to speak, when the homes of the leading Cherokee men in the community were only a mile or two away, surrounded by the cabins of their slaves.

Soon they were speaking of the remedy for sin that Jesus Christ provided and inviting people to join them in the river to renounce the evil in their midst and accept the salvation that came from Jesus with the washing of baptism. Dozens of men and women who had already become part of the Baptist community in Coosawattee Town joined them in the river, forming lines of support for any converts that might venture into the river after them, leading right up to Evan Jones and Jesse Bushyhead in the middle of the river.

Will and Little Wolf talked quietly with each other. "They baptized my daddy here last year," Will said. "He told me it would be my decision when the time came."

"Mama was baptized at Springplace when she was a girl," Little Wolf responded, "but they don't do it there anymore. I want to be baptized here."

"Let's do it together, then," said Will. They wove their way through the crowd as they descended toward the river's edge, and joined about twenty other people entering the water, taking the offered hands of those standing in the river to steady them, as they walked in the water among the rocks. They were the youngest of those who were pressing forward. One by one Jones talked with the converts who presented themselves to him. Some were quickly accepted and grasped by the shoulders and lowered completely under the water of the river and lifted out in one smooth motion. With others the conversation continued for minutes, and some left without being baptized.[53]

---

[53] As early as 1823, the Baptists opened a mission and school at Coosawattee.... When the mission became a preaching station as well, the Coosawattee residents often gathered for services at the home of... Judge John Martin. Martin also sent one of his children to the Baptist mission school. The Baptist missionary from the Valley Towns, Evan Jones, visited Coosawattee on numerous occasions and usually stayed at Martin's home. . . . Martin offered to pay the [American Board of Commissioners for Foreign Missions] for another teacher. In spite of the Baptist initiatives, however, missionary Butrick referred to Coosawattee as "that dark place," a reliable indication of the community's continuing cultural conservatism. Coosawattee remained on the Baptist preaching circuit even after the school and mission closed ..., and in the summer of 1836, Evan Jones found a great increase of interest in conversion. More than 20 Cherokees were baptized, some in Talking Rock Creek, in 1836-37

Our Land! Our People!

Will stood in front of Jones and told him about his father's baptism and his words of permission when Will was ready, and about his own desire to be a Christian and be baptized. Then Jones asked him what name he would be called, and Will answered simply "Will is my name," so Jones baptized him and embraced him before he let him go. Will stood back a few steps and watched as Little Wolf came forward.

Jones said that he knew Little Wolf's father and mother, and all of his family, and asked why he wanted to be baptized.

Little Wolf said, "Because I believe in Jesus as my Savior, as my Uji taught me."

Jones studied him for a moment, and then he asked if Will was his friend.

"My best friend in all the world, along with Jesus and my parents," he answered.

Jones smiled, "Do you understand that a man cannot enslave another human being if he is going to be a Christian?"

In 1838, the pace accelerated. Convert and missionary Jesse Bushyhead baptized 47 fellow Cherokees in May, 10 days before removal began. While Martin, with 69 slaves and 315 acres of improved land, was unquestionably the wealthiest Cherokee at Coosawattee, his neighbor John Adair Bell was also affluent and influential. . . . Bell owned a two-story house, store house, smoke house, shuck house, corn cribs, stables, a dairy, slaves, and more than 100 acres of improved land. In 1836, Bell became the disbursing or issuing agent for "poor and destitute Cherokees" in Coosawattee. He traveled to Calhoun, Tennessee to pick up rations made available by the federal government and was ordered to use the distribution as an opportunity to impress upon the recipients the necessity of complying with the treaty. Agent Albert Lenoir at New Echota told him which Cherokees were allowed to receive rations. An estimated 600 Cherokees lived at Coosawattee at the time of removal." From *Cherokee Removal: Forts Along the Georgia Trail of Tears*. Draft Report by Sarah H. Hill under a joint partnership between The National Park Service and the Georgia Department of Natural Resources/Historic Preservation Division).

"That is what Uji taught me, and that is how my Udoda lives, too. I want to live as a Christian, too, even though some of my family do not."

"Do you still think of them as your family?" Jones asked.

"They are, but I will not live like they do."

"They are my family, too," Jones said as he smiled, "even though I want them to change and become Christian, too. You have answered well." Then he said, loud enough for many to hear, "The Lord Jesus told us we must enter the Kingdom of God like children, and we have two here that will enter ahead of the rest of us." Then he spoke quietly to Little Wolf again, and asked him what name he should call him, and Little Wolf answered, "Tsan[54] is enough." So Jones grasped him by the shoulders and lowered him swiftly into the river, and John thought of his mother in her daily trip to the river and vowed to remember this day, every day, as he continued to come to the river.[55]

May, 1836, Federal Road to Conasauga River

A blue haze wrapped the ridge of mountains north of Fort Mountain, east of the Federal Road as it angled toward Tennessee. David and Little John rode horses side by side on the road. David's shoulders sagged, his eyes out of focus, his tone soft and flat as he spoke, "We'll be leaving the main road soon, and head north toward the Starr settlement. We'll follow the trail

---

[54] In Cherokee the name 'John' is pronounced 'Tsan.' Little John is 'Tsan Usdi.'

[55] Jesse Bushyhead and Evan Jones preached against slavery and baptized 29, including seven at Coosawattee, according to John Ehle, *Trail of Tears*, pp. 300-301, and Bushyhead baptized 47 fellow Cherokees in May, 1837, just 10 Days before the removal began.

along the Conasauga River. I thought we'd be taking this trip before the birth of your little sister."

"I don't understand what happened, Father," Little John said.

"I don't understand it either. It just happens sometimes. The baby started to come earlier than we expected. She wasn't born the right way. When she tried to come out, she couldn't, and your mother started to bleed too much. She wanted this child very much."

"We did, too, didn't we, Udoda?"

"Yes, we did," and he fell silent, with his mind lost in the afternoon haze on the mountains.

They continued their course along the river into the late afternoon. Little John asked at some point, "Where will I stay when you go back to the Old Town?"

"Your mother wanted you to stay with her, and the rest of your near relatives. She had made that plan with her sister, aunt and cousins. She told me she wanted you ready to go to school at Candy's Creek. They have a mission school there that's connected to the Brainerd Mission. It's near where your maternal uncle George Washington Candy lives. He's my brother-in-law also, though we haven't seen him for a while. I think it will be good for you to have more schooling. It's one of the few places you can go right now. I will miss you, though."

"I will miss you a lot. I miss my Uji; I can't believe I won't see her again." Little John was silent for a time, and neither spoke, until he said, "I want to go to school, but I don't want to be so far away from you."

"It's must be for a little while. We don't have a home now to go back to. I didn't sign the treaty, so we can't stay at the farm. A white man from Georgia has already claimed it. Jack can stay at his place for a while, because he did sign. Jack now has a government job. He'll be the disbursing agent for the Old Town people, so he will be traveling back and forth to the government agency at Charleston, Tennessee, to pick up supplies. That's just a few miles north of where you will be staying. I will help him with the store and with the food rations and supply shipments. I can travel with him when he comes, and at least I'll be able to spend a little time with you. I'll see if I can bring Will when I come."

"I'd like that, Udoda."

Just before dusk they came to the settlement along both sides of the Conasauga River, where the Starr houses stood. David headed toward a small cabin that hid behind a larger one on the south side of the river. The little cabin sat at the edge of a field of newly sprouting corn and in front of an orchard of apple and peach trees. At a corral and small shed they dropped from their horses and let the horses drink from a trough, before removing the saddles, blankets, and gear from their backs. Before they finished, Aunt Sarah came walking slowly from the cabin. She was a short, stout woman with a weathered and wrinkled face, and a crooked wry smile. "Osiyo" they said to each other. She grabbed Little John under his arms and lifted him up, exclaiming how much he had grown in the six months since she had seen him. Then she put him down, turned toward David. Little John could see that they both were shedding quiet tears. Taking Little John's hand Sarah led the way back to the cabin.

After their supper together, they sat near the fireplace in the cool of the evening, and David reported all of the changes he could think of. "Young Turkey and a few others have headed north into the mountains, where they intend to live in hiding as long as they have to. John Martin has sold all of his holdings to a man named Carter, and he and his wives and family, and their slaves, have headed west to Arkansas. Most of the people of Coosawattee will stay through this season, although much of the land is being confiscated. They can't plant crops. People expect to begin receiving their payments in the fall. Most of the Creeks who took refuge near Coosawattee are still there."

"How are the people going to have food to eat, if they can't plant a crop? Sarah asked.

"The government has promised to supply what the people need. That is part of the preparations for removal that the treaty arranged. Jack's been hired to haul supplies from Charleston. We'll distribute the rations from the store. The largest share of those rations will be dried and salted. There will be no fresh fruit and vegetables. We will have to find as much fresh food as we can on our own, or our people will suffer. Next year the military will begin a roundup of the Cherokees just as they did to the Creeks. The people of Coosawattee will have to leave as a group, all six hundred or more of them." David paused for a long while, and with tears in his eyes he said, "I need you and the family to keep Little John while I am going back and forth, at least until he can start in school at Candy Creek."

"I will be pleased to have him as long as he can stay. Maybe we can help to mend each other's hearts where they are torn. Soon enough he will go to school, and soon enough we must travel the long journey west to join our family there."

"I am in your debt, Uloghi Sarah."

August 1836, Rattlesnake Springs

Little John walked along the road with his cousins, those who were his own age and older, while the smaller children and the older women sat with Uncle James and Uncle George in the wagons pulled by teams of horses. Warm, clear weather had favored their journey toward Rattlesnake Springs for the New Corn Festival. Other Wolf Clan members and their spouses and children would join them there within the next day. They were coming into the Dry Valley, a broad valley between low hills, where fields and pastures occupied more of the landscape than the remaining stands of trees. They would soon enter the depression formed around the abundantly flowing springs that had been a traditional gathering place for many uncounted years. Two long days of walking made Little John tired, but playing games, dancing and feasting would soon replenish his and his kin's energies. Here he would finally meet his Uncle George Washington Candy, who would soon provide a home where he would stay with his cousins. His uncle would try to arrange for his enrollment when school resumed in the coming weeks, either at Candy's Creek, Brainerd, or Red Clay.[56] Whether he would be able to enroll was increasingly uncertain. Many schools were closing or reducing enrollment in anticipation of the move west.

---

[56] The roster of students at Candy's Creek School does not record either the children of George Washington Candy nor any of the Bell family. Brainerd Mission records do include some members of both families, although no evidence of John Francis Bell's enrollment. *Candy's Creek Mission Station 1824-1837*, by William R. Snell (Cleveland, Tennessee, Two Penny Press, 1999); and *The Brainerd Journal*. This author assumes that most, if not all, of John Francis' education occurred in family surroundings by those who themselves had received mission-sponsored education.

Our Land! Our People!

Uncle Ezekiel Starr's family had returned to visit from the Cherokee Nation in the West, where they had emigrated several years earlier, and they had borrowed the use of a cabin in the valley near the springs, so they welcomed James' and George's families as they arrived, and pointed out the corrals and sheds that would provide grazing and shelter for the horses, while the families set up tents and fire pits in the field south of the springs and the creek that flowed east full of the water that rushed from the side of the small hill. Plenty of water filled the creek for a crowd to drink and bathe.

Pork and beef carcasses roasted in the spits above the fire pit near the house that sat next to the spring. A wide veranda surrounded the sides of the house, so the women found ready shade from the late afternoon sun to begin their sharing of news of recent events. In spite of tired feet the cleared pasture area beckoned to the youngsters to play stickball as soon as the tents were up.

Uncle Ezekiel and Aunt Mary had eight children so far, but only Caleb and Leroy joined them in the field. Ruth was helping with the food preparations, and Sarah, Elizabeth, Ellis, Ezekiel Junior, and Mary Jane were too young to join in the running games. Of James' seventeen children, Samuel was Little John's size, and Field, Washington and Mary—all children of Aunt Nellie Maugh, James' first wife—joined in the game, except Joseph, who was taking care of the horses, and Leroy, Rachel, Janie, and Caleb were too little to play. James' second wife, Aunt Sukie, sister to Nellie, had given birth to eight children—Ellis, James Junior, William, and Bean, who came out to play, too, and Thomas was working with Uncle James setting up camp. John and Ezekiel were toddlers, and little Jennie just wanted to watch.

Little John surveyed the players, most of whom were older than he. Between two families there were enough players to get started. By the time the Wests, Phillips, Walkers, Vanns, and Hildebrands[57] arrived, there would be a crowd. With the younger children growing up, and the newly-marrieds with more children to be born—Uncle George and Aunt Nancy Bell Starr, Uncle George Washington Candy and his wife, Aunt Elizabeth Bell Candy, Uncle John and Aunt Lucy Too-Yah Bean, and there were more aunts and uncles to count—there were plenty of ball players for all of the foreseeable future, past the years when he would be playing with the young adult men. He felt the security of numbers for the first time in his life. If only Will were here.

There were some black "servants" among the people yet to come. Not everyone agreed or held to the standard, but the shadow of their Quaker grandfather Caleb Starr cast long upon this gathering, for he had employed many slaves, but insisted that they have considerable personal freedom and eventually freedman status. All of his relatives held his standing invitation to come and join him in Arkansas, whether they held slaves, or "servants," as some of them preferred to say, or not.

As the sun was nearing the western horizon and coloring the sky, the play sagged to an end. Everyone gathered at the rows of tables and benches near the house, while men and women began to lift the roasting meats from the charcoal pits and serve the food. Little John filled his plate, found Aunt Sarah, and sat down next to her. Soon after he had begun to eat he pushed his plate aside and laid his head down on his folded arms

---

[57] The interrelationships among these families are documented in *The History of Adair County*, (Cane Hill, AR: ARC Press, 1991) and *The Descendants of Nancy Ward* by David Keith Hampton (Cane Hill AR: ARC Press, 1997).

on the table, no longer able to stay awake enough to eat. Eventually he leaned toward his aunt and slumped into her lap, his head and shoulders resting on her legs, his body stretching out on the bench, while her left hand kept him from falling off.

"Poor little fellow," Sarah said to her sisters and nieces. "He's too tired to eat." Conversation soon turned from the travel of the last two days to the long journey that would be coming.

"How long do you think the trip will be?" Lucinda asked.

Sarah answered, "David says that we should plan for at least three months if we travel together in a caravan. When his father took them on a trading trip, they could make it easily in a month, but they were a small group, riding horses and pulling only two or three wagons."

"Why should it take so long then?" Lucinda interrupted. "I heard the plans called for most of the people to go by riverboat."

"David thinks the rivers aren't dependable. If we're lucky we'll be able to travel on the rivers, but more likely we'll have to go overland most of the way. Not many of our people trust river travel anyway. We'll want to stay together to make sure everyone gets through the river bottoms and crosses the rivers safely. With children and older folks, and cattle to drive, we won't be able to travel far in one day. We'll have to buy provisions along the way. The weather will probably cause delays. We'll surely travel in spring or fall, not in the winter cold nor the summer heat. I don't know whether we'll be making the journey next year or the year after."

"My husband, Looney, hasn't decided yet what we're doing. He thinks we may stay here, and take the offer to become citizens of Tennessee. I don't like the idea of giving up my own nation," Lucinda said, "but the Prices are not all Cherokee. Looney says we have to choose who we will be. Either way we'll leave part of the family behind."

"Allie and I went to talk to Great-Grandmother about this," Sarah confided.

The sisters seemed surprised. "You did?" they asked.

"You went to Grandma Nancy's grave, didn't you?" stated Nancy. "I think about going to talk to her, but I live so far away. I haven't made the trip."

"It wasn't so far for us, though I didn't want Allie to go. She insisted. I probably shouldn't have let her go," Sarah responded. "Sometimes I take a day and ride over to Womankiller Ford on the Ocoee River.[58] I remember when we were children visiting her there at her inn, taking care of her herd of cattle. She would take us in and provide for us, along with anyone else who happened by. She was a great chief for our people, honored by all who came, Indian, white, or mixed blood like us."

"We had good times there. I miss those days," said Ruth.

"Anyway, we went there to her grave about five moons ago. I told her how we have come again to a great parting of the ways. Her children are divided and don't know what to do. I asked her why she accepted slaves."

"You didn't!" Lucinda said, sounding horrified.

---

[58] On this book's cover is a recent photo of the gravesite of Nancy Ward, surrounded by tokens of the prayers and respect of her descendants.

"She reminded me that she was the Beloved Woman, and she was honor-bound to accept the gift of slaves after war. She felt that she should provide for them as part of her family—food, work, and house—and they should be free to come and go as they chose. So she did not keep slaves as people do now. She didn't think that she owned them. They were like the land, to be respected and trusted, allowed to give and receive their full share, and returned to themselves.

"I told her that things were different now. We have become more like the whites, treating our people as superior, and black slaves as inferior. Yet the whites treat us both as inferior and take the land for themselves. They pretend to own both people and land. I told her that her dreams of living together peacefully have been broken.

"She was silent for a long while. We waited for her to answer. She finally said that she wanted us to move west together as a nation. Not everyone will, but most of us should. Someday we would come back and live side by side again, red, and white, and black, and mixed blood, as she had hoped. Allie and I talked afterward, and she heard the same thing."

Ruth said, "I want to live long enough to see that."

Sarah answered, "I have the feeling we won't get to. Maybe our great-grandchildren will, or their grandchildren. Ghigau[59] is very patient now. She has learned how to wait and not rush anything."

Little John opened his eyes briefly. He had been listening while his aunt spoke, but he was too tired to make a move. He mumbled his question, "When will we see her?"

---

[59] Ghigau is the Cherokee name of Nancy Ward, the Beloved Woman.

Sarah answered, "She's dead, Little John. Like your mother but many years longer. I haven't seen her for a long time, but I talk with her anyway, and I listen for what she has to say. We'll only see her again when we die."

March 1, 1837, New Echota

John Adair "Jack" Bell and David Bell stood at a table in the building that had served as the Cherokee Supreme Court. All of the former Cherokee buildings served as the Federal Military Headquarters for Georgia. Jack's slaves, Demaris and Ezekiel, stood alongside. An Army officer sat at the table, pouring over the books that recorded the property assessments for Coosawattee Town. At his side sat a government agent certifying the script that could later be exchanged for dollars or gold by the people who were still owed payments for their property.

"You will see that each of these Indians receives his payment?" the officer said. "By my count only twenty-two remain to be paid. Everyone else has already collected what he was owed. You and Samuel can stay in your houses until the people are all assembled at the Agency at Charleston. You'll be among the last that have to leave, since you signed the Treaty. Boudinot is still here. John Ridge and the Major plan to leave in a couple of days, unless the Major is not feeling well enough. I hear he is having a round of breathing problems or something. He was going to leave in January, but his daughter Sally announced she was going to get married, and he postponed his plans, and got ready for a big wedding instead.[60] Otherwise the soldiers will have everyone within an outpost stockade within the next two months, and we should be sending groups west by mid-April."

---

[60] The dates of these two early migrations come from Stanley W. Hoig, *The Cherokees and Their Chiefs* (University of Arkansas 1998), 164.

"That sounds too optimistic to me. It's going to take longer," said Jack, but the officer said nothing in reply. "We will prepare the wagons and corral the livestock, so we can make the trip to Charleston. My wife and children are already near there, in the house her parents had near Ooltewah. We can use the ridge just east of the agency, where there are cabins, room for many tents, and good water available. There we'll assemble the Coosawattee townspeople and our family members who will make the trip together. I need to keep our group separate from the others, but most of the nation will gather there, only a few miles apart. There are enough hard feelings. I don't want more fights to break out."

"That's your problem," the officer said.

John, David, and the others went outside into the sunlight, and looked at the remaining carriages, the covered wagons and teams of oxen, the horses, and the cattle that jostled one another inside the pens. In a few days the last of these would be gone, along with all of the living people of Cherokee heritage who had centered their lives and their hopes in this capital city. Only the graves would remain.

May 1837, Candy's Farm, Mouse Creek

All of the people in the valleys of Mouse Creek and Candy's Creek were out working in the fields on the warm spring days, preparing the ground and seeding it. A month earlier Charleston Agency officials sent word to the surrounding neighborhoods that they should spend the year preparing for the move to the far west. Meanwhile, the Federal Agents would build and provision outposts within the former Cherokee boundaries, complete the removal of the other tribes this year, and prepare for the final Cherokee removal next year.

George and Elizabeth Candy applied themselves to raising as much food as possible in the coming season, since there would be no planting next year. They recognized and discussed how different this was from the traditional Cherokee way, which depended on the Great Spirit to provide in every year what was needed for that year, not saving food for another year ahead. Instead they read about Joseph in the book of Genesis, who encouraged the saving of food from good years for years of famine. They were aware that many people of the nation were sticking to the old ways and still resisting any suggestion of leaving their lands. Even at the last Green Corn Festivals across the nation people had argued about whether they should burn the last of their food from the previous year, or save it and add to it for the coming year. Every decision that the people made seemed to be part of the same argument about staying or leaving.

The Candy children were young. John Candy was eleven, just three years older than Little John; Maria was seven; Samuel Worcester, five; Charlotte, three; and Martha, one year. Yet they were all out in the gardens and orchards whenever they could be.

Little John was hoeing in the gardens when he saw his father at a distance, riding his horse, with a boy riding another horse alongside—Will! At last he would get to be with his friend! He dropped his hoe and ran toward them.

When they came together David slid off his horse and picked Little John up in a strong embrace. Will dismounted quickly also and stood at David's feet, reaching out to pat Little John on the back.

"It's been too long," David said. "I'm sorry I could not come sooner. We've had our hands full. "

"I've been working hard, too," Little John answered. "We've had orchards to prune, fields to plant, animals to feed and water. Every day is full."

"So it is. You've grown, my son. Are you doing well?"

"I am. But I miss you."

"It isn't easy being alone," David said, losing his smile. He gently lowered Little John to the ground. "I've brought a companion for you. Will needs to work on his studies, too, and he no longer has field work at Coosawattee, since we no longer have any fields. He might as well pursue his studies here alongside you at the mission school.

"Your Uncle Jack has the contract with the government to relay supplies between here and Fort Gilmer, which the Federal Army is building upstream from Coosawattee. I'm helping him. We have to continue to supply the town as well. Jack has let Will's mother, Demaris, serve as an interpreter for the Army as they round up the Creeks. She knows the Creek language well. She can find her way anywhere through the hollows and crevices of the area, so she's a good guide for the soldiers. There must be a couple hundred Creek runaways who've been hiding out for the past year.

"Let's go see my sister and George. Maybe they'll put me up for the night."

David boosted Will back onto his horse and lifted Little John up to ride behind him. He climbed back onto the back of his horse, and they headed toward the mission buildings.

"Does Butrick still come to preach?" David asked as they rode along. "I hear lots of rumors. I don't know when the missionaries from Brainerd will close the last of the schools and head west. I saw Joe Vann at Charleston. He said he's moving his household this year. He's been living just west of here at Ooltewah since he lost his home at Springplace."

Little John asked, "May I come back to Coosawattee when you're helping people pack up for moving?"

"I don't think it's wise, Little John. Some of our village people are still very angry about moving. I don't know how they will act when the Army is knocking at their door. Uncle Jack is trying to get people ready to leave before it comes to that, but I don't know if we'll be able to. The white settlers are unpredictable, too. I'd prefer to keep you here closer to the Charleston Agency where most of our people will gather."

"Will you be safe, Father?"

"I don't want you to worry. I can't say that I'll be safe, but I'll protect myself. I'll come back for both of you, wherever you are."

August 1837, George Candy's Farm

The afternoon sun was shining on Will and Little John as they were reaching into the loaded branches of a peach tree, gathering fruits and passing them down to two smaller children below them who placed them in baskets. Peach trees extended out in every direction, filling a ridge top clearing with scores of small peach trees that had been planted by George Candy. In a shelter at the edge of the orchard the sweet luscious fruit would be prepared to be eaten raw, dried, cooked into jams, squeezed into liquid and fermented, or pounded into leather-like strips. In a smaller adjacent field old and new apple trees would soon be bearing their fruit and ready for picking. Across a ravine a path

Our Land! Our People!

led to another apple orchard which Reverend Bushyhead owned and, like Candy, provided to the school for their use.

Little John was surprised to see his maternal uncle, James Starr, walking up, accompanied by his sons, Joseph, who was the same age as Little John, and Samuel, who was just a little older. "Osiyo, Little John. Osiyo, Will," Uncle James said.

The boys climbed down from the tree and clasped hands and arms all around.

"I suppose you weren't expecting to see us today," Uncle James said.

"No, I wasn't. It makes me wonder what's happening. Has something bad happened?"

"Nothing bad, but I wanted you to know that we're planning to leave soon for the West.

If you wanted to come with us, I'd be glad to have you. I would talk to your father of course, but I don't want to leave my clan sister's son without some understanding between us."

Little John looked at Uncle James while a rush of thoughts and feelings filled his head. "I don't know what to say. Thank you for asking, but if my father isn't going yet, I don't feel ready yet to come. I think I want to stay and come with him."

"You are the same as my own son, and my sons know you as a brother. So I want you to know you can come with us, or you can wait and come with your father. Either way, when you get to the western lands, you have a home with us whenever you want. That is what I came to tell you. That is what my family wants you to know. There is always a place for you. You are not an orphan. You belong to a family."

"Wado, Uduji. You too, Joseph, and Samuel, wado. I will keep your words in my heart."

"A detachment of people who accepted the Treaty will leave the Agency in about a month. We're gathering what we need now. An Army Lieutenant, named B. B. Cannon, has accepted the job of conducting us. I expect about four or five hundred people in all. I will settle near my father's mill near the western border of Arkansas. Many members of our family are already settled there. I will see your father soon and talk with him. If you decide to come, send word to me at the Agency, or just come."

"I hope you can stay here for a while today?" Little John inquired.

"Yes, I saw cousin George to find out where you might be. He was a good host as always, and I wouldn't miss the chance to enjoy the pleasure of his table. You think about what I said."

"I will. We'll finish our work here and we'll find you." Little John and Will watched Uncle James and his boys walk back toward Uncle George's farmstead, then Little John turned to Will. "He didn't say anything about you, Will, I'm not leaving here if you can't go too."

"He knows I'm not going anywhere without Uncle Jack's permission, and I know you're not going west without your father's permission, so my guess is—we're going to wait here until we're told to go."

"I don't think my Udoda is ready yet. He and Uduji Jack are working with the people of Coosawattee Town, trying to prepare them for the trip. I expect to stay here until we all can go together. It's good to know my Uduji James is willing to make a place for me, with as many children as he already takes care of, but I will wait with you."[61]

---

[61] This early detachment had as many problems as the later ones. In the fall of 1837, General Nathaniel Smith, who replaced the deceased Currey as superintendent for Cherokee removal, started west with a party of 365 Cherokees, mostly treaty supporters. Lieutenant B.B. Cannon kept a journal of the arduous trip, and he conducted the party, which traveled by way of the northern overland route. The group set out from the Cherokee agency on the Hiwassee River on October 14, 1837. The crossing of the Cumberland Mountains took four days and "severely taxed the endurance" of the people, many of whom started the journey suffering from dysentery and diarrhea contracted while waiting at the emigration depot. On October 25, around Murfreesborough, one of the children in the party died.

On October 28, the group reached Nashville, where several Cherokees [including James Starr] visited Andrew Jackson. Cannon led the party into Kentucky where, on November 3 near Hopkinsville, another child died. The consumption of stagnant water and wild grapes in Illinois caused violent illness among many of the travelers, and several Indians and a few of the wagon drivers dropped out of the party to recuperate before continuing the journey. The party reached the Mississippi River November 12 and another child died before Cannon completed the crossing into Missouri of the entire party, which took two days because of high winds. Although Cannon reported "sickness prevailing" among the emigrants, the detachment made 13 to 17 miles a day across southern Missouri.

The party rested on November 23 to allow stragglers to catch up and on November 25, Dr. G. S. Townsend, the detachment's physician, advised Cannon to suspend the march because at least 60 people were too ill to travel. Four days later Cannon moved the sick two miles to a schoolhouse, where they would be out of the cold weather while they recovered. Four members of the party, including one of the black wagon drivers, died before Cannon restarted the group on December 4, although there were not enough wagons to carry all the sick. On December 8, another child died and Cannon reported another problem with drunkenness. After the party passed Springfield, Missouri, on December 16, Cannon halted the group for two days because of extreme sickness and the snowy weather, and three more people died. Two more died by December 24, when the party reached "X Hollows," probably the site of the present-day town of Cross Hollow, Arkansas, in south-central Benton County, northeast of present-day Lowell.

On December 26, Cannon wrote, "halted at James Coulter's on Cane Hill, Ark," where the group buried "Alsey Timberlake" the next day. By the evening of December 27, the party was in Cherokee country. Cannon completed his duties on December 30 and surrendered responsibility to another Army officer. Fifteen people, including 11 children, died during the march. From Charles Russell Logan, *The Promised Land: The Cherokees, Arkansas, and Removal, 1794-1839*. (Little Rock, AR. Arkansas Historic Preservation Program, 1997), 38-39.

Little John's father and Uncle Jack had their hands full bringing food to the residents of Coosawattee Town and urging them to prepare for the move to the Indian Agency at Charleston. Near Coosawattee Town the soldiers had built a stockade, and they were forcefully gathering people from the countryside and holding them there before taking them on to the Charleston area. The residents of the Old Town could see the soldiers at work and knew that Uncle Jack was making it possible for them to remain in their own homes for as long as possible. They resented having to leave, but they were mostly grateful for Uncle Jack's efforts on their behalf. When the soldiers had moved all of the people out of the stockade they told Jack that they couldn't wait any longer. Jack and David spread the news and helped the six hundred residents load their belongings and make the move to Charleston. The whole process took most of the winter and spring of 1837 and 1838. Little John wondered whether he would ever get to see his father again.

July 28, 1838, Charleston, Tennessee

Jack Bell's wood framed, bark-covered hut sat about twenty feet inside the stockade that circled the top of the ridge a mile east of the Indian Agency buildings at Charleston. As the federal soldiers herded hundreds of people into the area, Fort Cass had taken shape as several stockades, from the closest on that ridge to the farthest twenty miles to the south. The Agency buildings also served as the headquarters of the Fort.

Jack's hut looked nothing like the big white clapboard house that Little John remembered at Coosawattee. His father, Will, and he shared a tent just south of Jack's hut. Rows of tents and several other ramshackle huts crowded the inside of the stockade. Filling the available spaces, fire pits provided families cramped quarters to squat and prepare their rations into the meager meals that salt pork, bacon, beans, corn meal, and buckwheat could provide.

Federal soldiers guarded the stockade entrance, and checked people in and out, allowing only those with passes, like Uncle Jack and David, the freedom to come and go. Little John and Will sometimes got permission to leave the fort with Little John's father and Uncle Jack as they continued to gather the supplies and equipment they would need for the long journey that was coming.

On several trips out of the "holding pen," as the soldiers called the stockade, the boys visited the soldier barracks east of the small harbor that brought boats out of the Hiwassee River, or the Agency offices on the opposite side of the bay. They met General Nathaniel Smith, who was in charge of arrangements for the removal, and Lieutenants Edward Deas and R. H. K. Whiteley, who were preparing to lead the first groups from the recent roundup west to Arkansas.[62]

On a longer trip on June 5th and 6th, the boys rode in a supply wagon down to Ross's Landing on the Tennessee River at Moccasin Bend. They looked around in wonder at the large river, snaking through the wide valley, under the hulking form of Sleeping Bear Mountain, and they saw the fleet of flatboats, anchored along the Tennessee River above Ross's Landing. Each flatboat was one hundred thirty feet long with a two story house built on it nearly to each end, and outdoor stone-lined hearths at each end for cooking. They watched as several hundred Cherokee people came in army wagons, Lieutenant Deas and other soldiers with them, and climbed aboard six flatboats. As soon as they felt the shifting of the keelboat decks several people

---

[62] John Ehle, *Trail of Tears*, pp. 338ff.

left the boat and refused to go, but most of the people settled in. The flatboats were lashed to a steamer, and then they moved slowly out into the river and downstream until they were out of sight. The boys returned to the stockade late that night, exhausted but excited.

Another group left the Agency area a few days later to board the boats at Ross's Landing, but shortly afterward rumors started to circulate through the camps. Some people said that the flatboats ran aground and had to be abandoned before they got very far. Others said the boats were sinking because they were poorly built. Some claimed many lives had been lost just like the Creek Indians had lost many lives in a boat mishap on the Mississippi a year earlier. Stories of cholera and other diseases killing many of the travelers made other people fear the trip. Already crowded conditions in the several camps within a few miles of the agency were allowing cholera and other diseases to spread like the rumors. Old-timers remembered the traditional Cherokee stories about river monsters and evil river spirits and concluded that trying to go west on the rivers would only bring more grief.

The truth came out when the lieutenants' reports reached General Smith. The first group did have trouble navigating rapids in the river, and found water levels too low to navigate. They had to shift to railroad passage at Tuscumbia, then back to another keelboat and steamer. Later they ran into low water again on the Arkansas River. Lieutenant Deas thought that over three hundred Cherokees, almost half of his boarding number, had turned back in the process of shifting from boats to trains and back again. But no one had died. The second group, led by Lieutenant Whiteley was less fortunate, with even more low water problems and hotter weather. In one incident hot weather and a supply of green peaches and fresh corn, consumed in haste by people long deprived of fresh food, led to much sickness. By the time they finally reached Fort Smith, Arkansas, marching many of the last miles, close to 275 of the original 875 had died.[63] The truth did nothing to comfort the people whom the rumors had agitated.

The third group sent out by General Winfield Scott on June 17 numbered over a thousand.[64] To avoid the problems in the rapids of the upper Tennessee River they began their journey by foot and wagon for the first 250 miles to Waterloo, Alabama, but five people died on the way. The flatboats were waiting there. Assistant Chief George Lowery and other leaders petitioned General Scott to let them stop and wait in Alabama until rain raised the water level and cooler weather arrived. Scott went to see for himself and accompanied the group all the way to Little Rock, but over 300 desertions reduced the number who arrived.

A hundred Cherokee leaders petitioned General Scott to wait for cooler weather before sending out the fourth group, and Scott set the target date of September 1. Meanwhile conditions worsened in the stockade camps. Nobody had made plans for sanitation for a long-term encampment, so refuse and excrement began to pile up. People complained about the poor quality of the food available, and alcohol began to show up in sufficient quantities to make drunkenness a problem. On the whole the camps remained quiet, but diarrhea and dysentery spread, followed by other contagious diseases—measles, whooping cough, pleurisy, and bilious fever. By the end of July scores of

---

[63] John Ehle, *Trail of Tears*, p. 339

[64] Ibid.

people had died in the several camps that surrounded the agency.

Jack and David ran water wagons back and forth from the Coosawattee people's stockade down the valley to Rattlesnake Springs for the clean water supply available there, and they continued to take care of the oxen, cattle and horses and to procure wagons and supplies for the trip.

One evening at the end of July Uncle Jack came back to his shack furious, stomping and pacing like Little John had never seen him do before. David followed him quietly and held Little John on his knee while his brother fumed. The firm grip in which his father held him told Little John that he was upset also.

Uncle Jack cleared his throat several times before he began to speak. "I knew this would happen when the Council got permission from General Scott to take over the removal effort. When they put John Ross in charge of the arrangements, he and his brother Lewis managed to negotiate for nearly $66 dollars per person for the trip. At that rate they must plan to be on the road for a year! They're going to use up so much money there's not going to be enough left for rebuilding when the people get there. Half of it will wind up lining their own pockets."

"We thought that forty dollars per person would be plenty for food and support arrangements, didn't we?" David said.

"It is enough. It doesn't waste money that will be needed later. It doesn't make the people rich who are in charge either."

"Is General Scott providing $40 per person to us and $66 to Ross?" David asked.

Our Land! Our People!

"No, he says he wants to be fair, so we'll get the same per person amount that Ross gets, but he will be in charge of ten thousand or more. We'll have no more than seven hundred in our group. The worst part is that Scott thinks I'm a trouble maker for criticizing the arrangements they've made. He's going to send Lieutenant Deas with us, while Ross's groups will have no military escort."

"Deas has made the trip back and forth as many times as we have. He may be a help to us," David suggested.

"I know he will be. He's a decent man, and he knows how easily things can go wrong. But Ross's group leaders have no experience traveling west at all. They're the ones who will need the help. Even with leaders like Bushyhead and George Candy, they'll have a tough time."

"I see your point, but I don't know what we can do about it. Ross is in charge here, and it will be hard to keep him from taking over when we join our people in the west. The newcomers will outnumber the Old Settlers."

"That's what I'm afraid of," Jack said.[65]

---

[65] Vicki Rozema, *Voices from the Trail of Tears* (Winston-Salem, NC, John F. Blair, 2003), 117-118. On July 23, the members of the Cherokee Council sent a letter to General Scott formally asking permission to be allowed to remove themselves. Scott agreed to the proposal on the condition that their emigration start by September 1. A few days later, the Cherokees held a council meeting at the Aquohee camp, south of the Hiwassee River near Charleston, Tennessee. At that meeting, they formally elected John Ross and six others as their official committee to oversee arrangements for self-removal.

"I wish Father were here," David said. "He always seems to know how to handle these things. We haven't been in touch with him in weeks. I suppose he's ready and still waiting for us to let him know when we are leaving."

"That's the way we left it. He said he would be ready to leave with two days' notice, and it will take him six days to get to Brown's Landing to join us there. Until then we have our hands full here, trying to keep people from getting sick."

"More people are getting sick by the day. We've been penned up here far too long. But it's not going to get easier on the route. And it's not going to be easier when we get there in the middle of winter and have no houses to stay in."

"That's where we have an advantage that many of our people do not have," David added. "Caleb and his family have been preparing for us."

The contract Ross negotiated with the government set a cost of $65.88 per person for the entire journey. It allowed $.16 a day per person for rations and $.40 a day per horse or ox. Ross included costs for wagons, horses, drivers, physicians, interpreters, conductors, and other support personnel. On August 2, Ross and the Emigration Management Committee—Elijah Hicks, James Brown, Richard Taylor, Whitepath, Situwakee, and Edward Gunter—requested that soap be added to the list of emigration costs covered by the government. Scott agreed, although the army considered soap, coffee, and sugar to be unnecessary. Later, Ross transferred the contract to his brother Lewis, who was considered a better businessman.

John Adair Bell, one of the Treaty Party leaders who had not yet emigrated, was furious when he learned of the arrangements the government had made with Ross. The Treaty Party feared that the funds being appropriated to Ross would deplete the money that would be made available for distribution. It also felt that the per capita removal allowance was lavish—forty dollars per person was more reasonable. It presented to Scott who replied that the pro-treaty faction would be treated equally. Bell and the Treaty Party resented the power bestowed on Ross by the government in allowing them to control removal. They correctly feared that the power would carry over upon arrival in the West. General Scott and officials in Washington became suspicious of Bell and blamed him for stirring up problems in the Ross contingents. Scott ordered Lieutenant Deas to accompany the Treaty Party to the West, while the Ross-managed detachments went unaccompanied by military officers.

"Yes, and there are others, too, who have been building shelters and putting food aside for their relatives and for whoever comes, but there will be too many coming and too few ready."

Little John stayed alert to all of these words, troubled by the tone of anger and fear that they revealed from the two people who were the strongest ones in his life. That night, when he and Will were alone together in their tent, and ready to fall asleep, they talked about what was coming.

"I don't want to stay here, where people are getting sicker, and Father wants Grandpa to know what's going on. I think we should go to Grandpa," Little John said.

"Your father won't let you go alone," Will said.

"I won't be alone, if you go with me."

"You know what I mean. He'll be worried."

"He's worried already, but we can leave him a note, and he'll know where we are. I know I can find the way. We've been to Moccasin Bend, and we just have to follow the west side of the Sleeping Bear till we come to the tail of it, and the river where Grandpa lives."

"Let's sleep on it. I'm tired," Will said.

August 2, 1838, East of Fort Cass Headquarters

A few days later, when Uncle Jack's girl, Andromache, had contracted the measles, after a visit to the stockade with her father, and a boy from Coosawattee Town whom they had known all their lives had died of cholera, Will was ready to go with Little John. Jack and David were away for a couple of days, so Little John penned a letter to his father:

> Will and I are going to Ududu. Too many people here are getting sick. I want to see if Ududu and Ulisi are packed and ready to go. We'll meet you when they join you on the trail west. Don't worry. I know the way.   Little John

He said aloud, as much to himself as to Will, that they needed to get used to walking if they were going to walk all the way to Arkansas.

They packed two canvas sacks with a blanket apiece and some dried meat and hard bread they had saved, and threw them over the back stockade fence. Little John forged a note on Uncle Jack's stationary that said they were supposed to meet Uncle Jack ten miles southwest at Candy's Creek where he was maintaining a corral of oxen and wagons. The guards at the gate could barely read but accepted the note anyway, since it was prepared in neat printing, and they let the boys through. The boys collected their bags behind the stockade and started down the road they had travelled earlier to Candy's Creek.

All the way they had to listen carefully for riders and wagons, and keep watch for other hikers. The note they had used to exit the stockade might not fool everyone who looked at it, especially those not inclined to like Jack or David Bell. Cherokee people of any age were not supposed to be walking freely down a road in those days. They were supposed to be waiting patiently for removal west. So they watched and listened, and sought out boulders and bushes and the large trunks of trees, upright or fallen, where they could hurriedly hide themselves if someone was coming. Fortunately, not many people were on the road.

After several miles, when they finally left the low rolling hills and sparse trees, the wide and well-worn trail ran along the creek and into a narrower wooded valley between taller hills. The creek itself was abnormally dry, with pools of stagnant water in many places, reminders of the unusually dry season that had postponed most river travel this summer. Occasionally they found a fresher pool, fed by a spring, so they could quench their thirst.

When they found black raspberries, ripe currants, and mulberries, they grabbed a handful and kept walking. They reminded each other that they hadn't had much sugar lately, so they would have to be careful with the fresh fruit that tasted so good. They took a bite of some bread and meat with the berries. No nuts were ready to gather, but they recognized a few edible plants that they could chew on. When they neared Uncle George Candy's place toward evening, they found a small field of standing corn, and took a couple of ears. The kernels were past the tender stage, tough to eat, but still good enough.

Little John remembered a rock shelter near the creek where he had sometimes rested in the heat of the day, where they could spend the night without being seen. If Uncle George or Aunt Elizabeth had seen him, they would put an end to their journey, and make them go back to the stockade, but they were busy with their own preparations. Little John had learned earlier that Uncle George had made a promise to Reverend Bushyhead to go with his contingent and to provide several teams of wagons and oxen. They kept their stock in the corrals that stood just a short distance away from the creek downstream. They would have to sneak past in the morning without alarming the dogs that his uncle kept.

They laid out their blankets, but didn't need to wrap up in them because of the warm summer night. If they travelled far enough, the next evening they would lie in the rocks near the head of the Sleeping Bear, the Lookout, above Moccasin Bend and Ross Ferry across the Tennessee River. Choruses of crickets, katydids, and locusts filled the air around them, and down the valley the distant call of a whippoorwill lulled them to sleep.

When the birds were fully singing their morning greetings to the sun, Will whispered, "Are you awake, Little John?"

"Doyu,[66] who could sleep? I'm listening. There weren't so many different songs at the stockade. More crows, blackbirds and turkey vultures there. I like these songbirds better, but they sure are noisy."

"I had a dream that an old woman came up out of the river. She said I looked sick, so she took my hand and led me to the river's edge, then we stepped into the water, and she led me under the water to a trail that led to the world below. People lived in a town there just like where we used to live."

"Was she a witch?"

"I don't know. I's scared of her. They had a big table set up in the middle of the village, and I's afraid that I's the one they was goin' to eat. Then I woke up."

"You must of heard about the cannibal people who live under the river waters."

"Maybe I did, but I don't remember hearin' about 'em. Do they really do that?"

Little John thought for a while before he answered, "No. My Dad said people made up stories to explain why people

---

[66] Doyu means an emphatic "yes" or "really."

disappeared under water when they drowned, and sometimes they couldn't be found afterward, 'cause their bodies got caught in snags underwater or they floated too far downstream. That story's one reason why some people are afraid of rivers."[67]

"I'm just glad we won't be going to Arkansas on a boat, especially after that dream," Will said.

"We better get up and get going, if we're going to rest tonight at Moccasin Bend."

Little John and Will rolled up their blankets, and used a branch to erase some of the evidence that they had lain on the floor of the rock shelter.

August 3, 1838, on Lookout Mountain

Will and Little John picked their way up the vertical climb through the rocks, brambles, and vines, and between the trees that managed to keep a foothold. The sun was setting in the west and cast long shadows across the mountainside. When they came to a flat rock sheltered by an angular boulder at its side, they decided they had gone far enough for the day, sat down and looked behind them. The wide Tennessee River snaked down from the north, flowing toward the base of the mountain, and abruptly turned west to flow between the mountains to their left. They could see all the way down to the landing in the distance, where men were trying to herd some balky, mixed breed cattle onto the ferry for the trip across the river, but they could only imagine the herding calls and the words they were using. Still farther upriver one of the great barges sat tied to moorings at the riverside, and it looked like some of the housing

---

[67] Mooney, *Myths of the Cherokee*, 349.

structures built so recently atop it were already being dismantled after the decision not to depart by boat.

"Those cows don't want to cross the river any more than our people do," Will said.

"Can't blame 'em. They aren't used to feeling the world rock underneath their feet either. But it sure is a pretty view from up here."

They sat quietly for a while, then pulled out some of the hard bread and dried meat they had packed to chew on, and rolled out their bedding as the darkness continued to descend. Only a few strands of high cirrus clouds reflected the changing red hues of the sunset before the sky itself began to darken into deeper blue and finally black.

The evening was still hot, and the rocks radiated stored heat from the summer sun, but soon Little John was complaining of the chill and wrapped himself tighter into his blanket.

"It's not a bit cold, Lil' John," Will said, but when he held his hand to Little John's forehead, he could feel the fever that was bringing on the chills. "You caught somethin'. We didn't get away soon enough, I'm fraid." The shivering continued, until finally Will lay down beside Little John and held his own blanket around him, until his shaking subsided, and they had both fallen asleep, exhausted from the long day's travel. A few times in the night Little John's rasping and coughing brought them both awake again, but not for long, and sometime in the night Little John's fever broke and he was drenched in sweat as if he had been running in the midday sun.

"I had my own dream about the river last night," Little John said after the sun's warming rays awakened them. He finished emptying his bladder at the edge of the rock platform, and waited for Will before continuing. "I was a wolf standing at the river's edge, and a great serpent rose out of the water, with a panther's head, and before I knew what was happening, it swallowed me whole and took me back into the river."

"I like my dream better," Will said, "not that it was much fun. Your fever's probably talkin' to you, and the river here below lookin' so much like a snake with its twists and turns. What d'you think the medicine people would make out of 'em?"

"A lot, I spose. It's just fear of the trip we have to make, all the rivers we have to cross. We're not used to it. I'm afraid somethin' terrible's goin' to happen. But we have to keep goin' anyway."

"Should we go back to Fort Cass? I's worried about you last night, when you was getting sick."

"Nah, we'll keep goin' forward. We're almost half-way to Grandpa's anyway. We'll be better off there than in the stockade."

"We'll be better off if we don't get caught on the way there, and if you don't get sicker."

Although Little John was a little shaky and slower in moving, they soon found a trail around the west side of the mountain heading toward the south along the edge of the Great Bear's giant torso.

As the day wore on, more and more clouds began to show up over the peaks of the ridge of hills to the west. They came first in small clumps, then in larger and higher masses, and later they merged into a solid darker bank. The boys began to look for shelter amid the overhanging rock ledges of the mountain's flank. Will became aware of Little's John's flagging energy, and knew they would need to stop sooner rather than later anyway, so when they saw an overhang that would provide good shelter from the rain they stopped. Will collected as much firewood as he could find nearby and stored it under the sheltering rock, and they waited for the rain. It had been weeks since they had seen a good rain. Even on this day it took its time coming, but when it began, it kept coming. Gusts of wind brought spray into the space where they sat, which ordinarily would have felt refreshing on a hot day, but clearly Little John was again feeling chilled, so Will built a fire and kept it going next to Little John propped against the rock, in and out of sleep with bouts of coughing.

Will was aware of their need for drinking water, with rain pouring into the woods around them, so he placed their one tin cup under one of the rivulets that streamed off of the rock that sheltered them. That would not be enough to keep them through the rest of the day and night. He decided to go out to see how he could secure more water and maybe some fresh food, but he didn't want to get his clothes wet for the cool of the night. He stripped off his clothes and walked out into the warm rain. The shower felt good, washing off the sweat and grime of several days' walking. A catalpa tree grew nearby, and he gathered several large leaves, rigging them with sticks into bowls in a line below the drip edge of the rock.

Toward the base of the mountain, where the land flattened out, a stream was flowing, and along it grew a stand of willows. He broke and cut several thin branches that he would later strip for bark and offer Little John as medicine for his fever. He gathered several blossoms from purple coneflowers. Finding a thicket of black raspberry canes, he gathered as many as he could carry in a burdock leaf. With his hands full he returned to the shelter.

Little John roused as Will was building up the fire and preparing a tea with the tin cup and pieces of the burdock leaf and coneflowers.[68] "I'm sorry, Will. I didn't want to get sick."

"Don't you worry, Lil' John. We'll rest here as long as we need to, and you'll get better."

"What if you catch what I've got?"

"Then we'll help each other, but I've already been sick with lots of things. Maybe I'll stay well. Anyway, I'd rather be sick here than back in the stockade. We've got what we need, and we've got each other."

"Thanks, Will. You're the best." After a while he drank some of the tea that Will had prepared, and chewed on some of the willow bark. He wasn't hungry for anything else and returned to sleep.

Near dark the far off solitary howl of a red wolf brought him awake again. "Is he calling me?"

"If he is, he's calling you to go south. The rain's let up."

"That's where we're going. I feel weak as a baby. Can you help me get up, so I can empty my bladder?"

Will helped him stand up and walk to the edge of the rock to relieve himself. Then they returned to the fireside and

---

[68] The use of these plants for medicine is recorded in J.T. and Michael Garrett, *Medicine of the Cherokee; The Way of Right Relationship*, (Santa Fe NM, Bear and Co., 1996), 54, 76.

stretched out beside each other, between their blankets for the night.

August 5, 1838, Western Flank of Sleeping Bear

The sun rose August 5th on a partly cloudy sky. After a fitful night's sleep with Little John weak and coughing a large share of the time, Will decided to spend the day where they were, hoping that he could get Little John to eat something before the day was done. He found a box turtle mid-morning and made a stew with some wild onions and other edible greens. By mid-afternoon he was successful in getting Little John to eat as well as drink some more of his tea.

At the next sunrise Little John insisted that he wanted to walk the trail south, so they moved slowly, resting often, until afternoon, when he had reached the limits of his endurance and could go no farther. Will caught a fish, and they cooked and ate it with some of the hard bread they still carried. The fever returned, but not as high, and he seemed to rest easier through the night.

They didn't walk as far the next day, but still made progress. Every other day seemed to be better, but the illness didn't leave. It just allowed Little John to keep going, and to remember not to press too hard. "This isn't like any of the sickness we heard about at the fort, is it, Will? It's not gettin' worse, but it's not gettin' much better, either."

"It is different. You din't break out in red spots, an' you din't have a whoopin' cough. You din't get sick to your stomach or have a bloody stool like some people has. They all got sick in a hurry an' either got over it slow or died in a hurry, too. So, I don' know what 'tis, but I think we're goin' to get to your Grandpa's place an' let you rest for a while."

Our Land! Our People!

The hot days continued, with no more rain on the horizon, though some dark clouds and rumbles of thunder came and went, making them stay on the lookout for shelter both along the way and in the afternoon when they needed to stop for the rest of the day.

They stayed away from the main trails, knowing that they had to avoid being caught, especially as they neared Fort Payne, where the people of the area were confined in yet another stockade. In spite of the increased danger of being seen, they knew they had only two or three more days of walking before reaching Grandpa Bell's Coosa River plantation.

August 6, 1838, East of Fort Cass Headquarters

"I keep thinking about Little John and Will. Where are they now? Are they all right? Will they make it to our father's place?" David paced in front of the cabin that he was sharing with his brother Jack. "If I had signed the treaty as you did, Jack, I could have kept my son out of this confinement. If Allie's brothers were around, instead of out west, he would have someone else to watch over him. If, if, too many ifs."

"You can't do that to yourself, David. I think they'll be all right. They've made trips before, even if not so far. They know mostly where they're going. They'll find their way."

"What if they're caught? Sure, Will is in the most danger. He doesn't carry any papers to show who he belongs to, not that anyone who's not a Cherokee would care."

"We've gone over this. You wouldn't have much chance of finding them if you went hunting. You've just got to wait it out."

"We've got too many other things to do, I know. And I don't blame the boy for wanting to leave this place. We can't wait to leave. Everyone wants to get out of here. I just wish I'd seen the signs of what he was planning."

"Do you really think you could have stopped him?"

"I would've tried. Just to let him know how much it would trouble me, how worried I am, not to know where he is, how they're doing, whether they'll get there safely?"

"When we get the wagon train ready to go, one of us will have to let Father know we're ready, and bring him and the rest of our folks back to join us. That's when we'll get to see Little John and Will. Not before. Father will keep them with him until he hears from us. I have no doubt about that."

"I know. I keep reminding myself of that. The boys are just always on my mind. The other question you just mentioned—which of us goes to get Father? You're the one in charge of the whole detachment, but you also have the travel permit, in case someone tries to arrest you on the road. The officers only let me accompany you in this immediate area."

"We'll either have to get a permit for you—if they'll do that for someone who didn't sign the treaty—or I'll have to go. You're better handling the livestock than I am, and—I don't like to admit it—you're stronger for the heavy jobs. While you're assembling the train and moving it down to Ross's Landing, I could make a quick trip down to get father, maybe take Ezekiel[69] with me, and meet you at the Brainerd Mission. You could hold up there for a few days, if I were delayed. We'd get Father's wagons in position to meet us, say, at Brown's Ferry."

---

[69] Ezekiel is Will's father in this account. The author found no record of most of the names of the Bell family slaves.

"That would work. The people who are left at Brainerd could put us up for a few days. It would keep us in as safe a position as we could find, away from any of the other detachments, while we're waiting. Away from the hot bloods that want to cause us trouble. Most of the other conductors plan to cross the river here at Blythe's Ferry where the Hiwassee flows into the Tennessee."

Jack thumbed through the recording journal he carried with him. "There's still so much to get before we leave. If we could count on trading fairly wherever we went, and getting good deals instead of second-rate goods, it'd be different. But we have to carry a good share of the heavy material. We need more oiled canvass, tents and tarps, for protection of our supplies and for shelter. We could use another fifty wool blankets, but they must be clean, or people will refuse to use them, with the rumors about diseased blankets."

"We'll be carrying enough disease from the stockades already. People are understandably afraid of diseased blankets and poisoned food," David interjected.

Jack continued, "That's right, whether there's truth to the rumors or not. We've scoured the area for more teams of oxen, but we need at least ten more pairs, if we can find them, if we have to go all the way to Cincinnati."

"We've got at least twenty barrels of corn that's only usable to feed animals, so we've got to replace that," David said. "So far about half of the grain and dried meat that the agency supplied is worth taking. The rest is waste."

"I think we'll have better results with foodstuffs when we get to western Tennessee. The people there haven't seen a caravan like ours before. They'll be willing to sell their excess produce, meat, and soap, for the cash that we carry, unless they've been so hurt by the drought that they don't have anything to sell."

"It'll be even worse for the several detachments that are heading northwest into Illinois. After the first groups go through, there won't be much left."

"That's another good reason for going the direct route west. We're familiar with it, we won't have to interact with the anti-treaty people, more trade will be available locally, as well as the extra dry conditions make some of the river bottoms much easier to cross, unless we have more rain, which, of course, is always possible. It's a chance worth taking, I think, but we could pay for it if the mudflats of the Mississippi get a lot of rain. We don't want to get stuck in the mud on the other side of Memphis for weeks like the Chickasaw did last winter."[70]

David added, "The other issue no one wants to talk about is the coming winter. The later we wait to get started, the more chance we have of getting stuck in snow and ice. If we could start before the end of this month, I think we'd be safe, but if we have to wait until October, we won't finish the trip without some cold weather. I wouldn't want to be in Illinois, trying to cross the Mississippi, in December or January."

Jack closed the record book abruptly, and made a loud 'humph.' "Me neither. Who thought this was a good idea, anyway?" Then he smiled and shook his head.

---

[70] The story of Captain John Millard's party of Chickasaw stuck in the swamp of the Military Road west of the Mississippi is recounted in the Arkansas Historic Preservation Program research paper on *"Memphis to Little Rock Road—Village Creek State Park, Newcastle Vicinity, Cross Country,"* undated. Also in Grant Foreman, *Indian Removal: the Emigration of the Five Civilized Tribes of Indians* (Norman, University of Oklahoma Press, 1932).

August 13, 1838, Coosa River Valley

Little John and Will stood on the edge of the Coosa River Valley, looking down the sweep of land, and the sparsely forested bottomland toward the river. They had begun to notice mosquitoes for the first time again after the rain a week ago, as the late afternoon heat brought them into this steamy lowland.

"We know we're on the west side of Will's Creek where we're standing—did you remember this area used to be called Will's Valley—named after you!"

"Yeah, sure."

"Well, Grandpa's farm and homestead lies near to where the creek joins the Coosa River, so we can angle east and expect to find it."

"If you say so. I never be here before. I'm glad you know where we's going."

"I'd never made it this far without you, Will. That old snake would've swallowed me up somewhere along the way."

The boys headed down the slope toward the river, finding the deer paths and clear spaces that were still off the regular trails. Out of the corner of his eye Little John saw the blur of mottled red fur and tail, and said, "Will, did you see that?"

"What?"

"About twenty paces to our right, and just ahead. I saw a red wolf."

"No, I din't see it this time, but sometimes on the way, I thought I saw one. Never saw it clear 'nough to be sure of it."

Still scanning the brush as he picked his way, Little John saw the open sky through the trees that revealed a clearing, and they angled toward it, finding the rounded edge of a field of uneven corn, all standing over their heads. They proceeded along the edge of the field until they found the farmer's lane, which led through the woods about a hundred paces to a fenced pasture with about two dozen cows grazing. Across the pasture they could see several log cabins and board-sided buildings and, rising behind them, a white clapboard plantation house surrounded by a roofed porch.

"Galieliga![7] At last we're here," said Little John softly. "We must make sure Ududu is here, that nothing has happened to him. But this is the place! See that low shed about thirty paces to the right of the house, with the big brick chimney. That's Ududu's forge and blacksmith shop. There are some horses in the corral beyond."

"I sees rows of wagons lined up 'tween the cabins, and oxen eatin' at a trough this side of the wagons," Will said. "Two men walking on the other side of those cabins, dark-skinned like me."

"I can't tell who they are from here. We have to get closer, but we don't want to be seen until we're sure Ududu's here."

The two boys crept slowly along the edge of the woods around the pasture, just inside the trees, until they were about two hundred paces from the nearest shed. They could see several people standing and working on the porch.

"You see the young woman gathering clothes from the clothesline?" Little John asked. "I think that's... I'm sure...that's

---

[71] "I am very happy!" in Cherokee.

my Uhlogi Sarah." He jumped up, broke through the trees into the clearing next to the fence, and began running toward the buildings, Will right behind him. They saw people turn to look at them, point toward them, shading their eyes from the sun.

Little John yelled out, "Osiyo! It's Little John, and Will! We found you!"

The young woman at the clothesline dropped the clothing she was holding and, staring at them, she began to run across the yard circling a fence. She was in front of several men coming toward them from different directions.

She was the first to call out, "It is you! How in the world did you get here?" As she came near she paused for a moment about ten paces away and looked at Little John and Will. She was about a foot taller than Little John remembered, and she looked at him questioningly, too, before she came up and threw her arms around him, then she turned and hugged Will too. "What a surprise! We weren't expecting to see you come out of the woods. You look like a couple of scraggly dogs that haven't seen a meal bowl in months." Meanwhile the other men arrived.

Little John recognized Cousin Asa, although he wore a beard that Little John hadn't seen before, and the slaves, Kodjo and Jeremiah, and the youth, Caesar, who had grown so much since Little John had seen him that he towered over everyone else. Then at a distance little John saw his still clean-shaven Ududu coming also, and Ulisi Charlotte a few steps behind.

"We're amazed to see y'here, "Grandfather Bell said as he grabbed Little John, lifted him up and gave him a bear hug. "Ye're light as a feather. It's a wonder ye did naw blow away. And Will, my friend, ye're naw much meatier. What happened to ye on your way down here?" Not waiting for a reply, still carrying

Little John, John Bell started for the house with long strides, and everyone else followed.

On the porch John Bell lowered his grandson into a wicker chair, asked Will to sit next to him, and took a seat facing them, "Whate'er possessed y' to come all this way?"

Little John described the conditions in the stockades at Fort Cass, the spreading diseases and the lack of good food and water while the people waited in confinement. He reported that he had listened to conversations between his father and uncle. They were working hard to relieve the shortages and to prepare for the trip west, but wondering aloud whether their father was ready and "how they were going to bring you, Ududu, into the wagon train when the time came. So we decided to come see you. We figured it was better to try out our walking legs getting here than waiting there and getting sick, but I got sick anyway, and Will is the one who got us here."

Grandfather Bell sat back in his chair, quiet for a moment, then said, "Try out your walking legs, huh? Well, y' sure did that. As to being ready to go, just a few days ago I sent my sons Sam and James and my servant Elijah to meet with your Pa and Uncle Jack to let 'em know we're right randy and bristlin' to go. My blacksmith shop is now aboard a wagon, with whate'er I need to keep us rollin'. But I do naw reprimand y' for your efforts."

Grandmother Charlotte meanwhile had secured bowls of soup for both boys and stood over them until they had drunk it down. She strongly advised them that there would be a lot more to eat until she had "put some meat on those bones."

Will reported the events on the trip down, and Grandfather took some interest in the dreams that they had told one another. "Ye are but nine and ten winters old and already ye're dreamers. Aye, my grandson here is still small, but I think he must have a new name, no more "Little John" or "Little Wolf." "Red Wolf" ye shall be. "Gigage Wahya."[72] Do y'all hear now? This my grandson shall now be called Red Wolf for his dream spirit and his journey."

Little John began to think of himself as Red Wolf during the next days, as his family began to call him that. He mostly slept and lay around during the evenings and mornings, and walked along the river and around the farm with Will and Sarah Caroline in the afternoons. Grandmother provided an ample board for her people, though Red Wolf reported that he was not hungry much of the time. The coughing that Red Wolf had begun during the travel, the fever through the evening, the night sweats, the pain in his chest, and the lack of appetite gradually subsided, although the Grandparents noted the symptoms. They had seen them before in the illness that their people usually called the "white man's cough."[73]

Red Wolf and Will noticed that Grandfather and his nephew Asa seemed to be spending time apart, wrestling with something. They could not overhear what their elders were saying to one another, but they could tell that it was an animated discussion. They asked Sarah if she knew anything.

"Cousin Asa has decided that he and Barbary will buy more land in western Alabama, where his father Francis already has a little land, instead of going west with the rest of the family."

---

[72] "Red Wolf" in the Cherokee language.

[73] It was more generally called "consumption" or, later, tuberculosis, although there was no confirmation of this disease in Red Wolf, and children who manifested such symptoms early did not usually survive it to adulthood.

Red Wolf was surprised. "But Asa's talked about going west for years. What changed his mind?"

"Mostly his father, I think. Uncle Francis doesn't think he can make the move. He's not as strong and adventurous as my father. But he has other reasons too. He thinks the people will fight with each other. We'll have many enemies since we support the treaty. Asa thinks he and Barbary can pass for a white couple and live here in peace. That's why he's grown a beard, even though it's not especially full. He thinks people won't recognize him as Tsalagi.[74]"

Red Wolf said, "I was hoping we all would be living together as one people, not spread out over so many miles as we are now. My Uji's people have been many miles apart my whole life. I don't even know some of my clan parents and cousins yet. I'm looking forward to living with them and getting to know them."

"Me, too. Cousin Asa and Barbary have always been a part of my family living near us. I don't like to think about us being so far apart. Father has been trying to persuade Uncle Francis and Cousin Asa, but they're stubborn."

"They're not alone in that," said Red Wolf.

One evening after supper Sarah brought out a book-sized package wrapped in brown paper and gave it to Red Wolf. "Open it."

"I don't have anything to give you."

---

[74] The common Cherokee word for "Cherokee.".

"You will, when you open this. It isn't a present, or maybe I should say, it isn't just a present. It's a job."

Red Wolf unwrapped the book, opened it, and he found it full of blank lined pages. "What's this for?"

"It's for your writings. We'll do lessons as we travel; your job will be to write in the journal every day about what is happening, what we are seeing, and what we are learning. I will write, too, and we will read each other's work. Just like you have written letters, and you learned by doing that. We will continue to learn to make the syllabary and the English letters, as much as we can of both. Later, maybe we can work on cursive writing, but not right away."

"I don't have a pen or ink."

"I do. You won't get out of your lessons with that excuse," Sarah laughed.

August 23, 1838, John Bell's Farm, Coosa River

Sam, James, and Ezekiel rode into the area, dismounted, and left the horses with Ezekiel to unsaddle and wipe down after the long, hot ride of the day. Ezekiel stood tall and broad next to the younger men. They decided to head for the house to see whether their father was there. They found Red Wolf, Will and Sarah sitting and reading aloud in the shade of a live oak in the yard.

"Sarah, who are these young men you're entertaining?" Sam asked.

"You don't recognize your nephew, John Francis, and Elijah's son, Will?" Sarah asked in turn.

"I wondered. This is the young fellow our brother David's been worrying about, and he's living the life of leisure here at his grandfather's. You look like you've grown a foot since I saw you last."

Red Wolf looked at Sam soberly and said, "No, Uduji, I always had just two, never had any more nor less than that."

"Hmm. Must've grown a sense of humor at least, in the three years since saw you last. Not any meatier though. From what I saw at Fort Cass, you made a good decision to come here. This place is a lot healthier than those cattle pens on the Hiwassee. Do you know where Father is?"

Sarah directed him toward the house, and all of them followed. They found him sitting by himself on the porch on the opposite side of the house, facing the river. John Bell stood as he saw them approach, and hurried to meet them. "Glad to have ye back! Come, sit a spell, and tell me the news."

Sam answered, "It was a good trip. Dry all the way, except for some showers along the west side of the mountain on the trip north. The drought continues throughout Tennessee, we hear, so no one has moved yet. There was a council meeting at Rattlesnake Springs, that they now are calling Aquohee Camp, on August 1. Ross' people made up the majority of the people there, but Bushyhead and George Candy were there, too, and we were able to talk to them afterward. Ross led the assembly to condemn the Treaty again, even while they are doing all they can to benefit from it. They also decided they would keep the same constitution and the same leaders when they move west, and not accept the government that our people in the west already have in place."

"I suppose I should'a seen that coming," their father interjected.

Sam continued, "They have over six hundred fifty wagons ready for the removal, and hundreds of livestock. They're all planning to take the northern route through Kentucky, Illinois, and Missouri, so it looks like our group and Benge's group from Fort Payne will have the southern route to ourselves. Bushyhead and some of the other captains are trying to set up forage depots along the route, so they won't have to carry so much food for the livestock along with the people. It's a huge mess. I've never seen anything like it."

"A good luck to 'em! They'll need it. With winter a'comin on, for a certainty," their father answered. "I canna' see that forage depots will help us much. That's one of the advantages of goin' a separate way. With smaller numbers we won't be depletin' the supplies of people who stay along the route. We can expect people to help without being overburdened. I canna' envy anyone tryin' to find supplies enough for twelve thousand people on the way. It's hard enough to plan for seven hundred. All it'll take is one big gully-washin' rainstorm, and we can find ourselves stuck in the mud, especially in one o' the big river valleys we have to cross."

James said, "Surely we won't have to worry about that, as dry as the summer's been."

"Y' canna' know, son," John Bell responded. "We're due for a change in weather. We can hope the weather holds dry for us to make the trip all the way, but we must be ready to change our plans in the middle if we need to, and that's easier to do with smaller groups, than one multitudinous caravan. I'd have more fears for the way they're tryin' to go, than for the way we are, which'll be fearsome enough for any mortal."

Sam continued his report, "Ross expected to start the first detachment around the first of September, and spread them out a few days at a time. That way they won't run into each other, unless there's a major snag somewhere, but stragglers from one group can be picked up by the next."

"As sick as many people are, there are bound to be stragglers, and more sickness along the way," James added.

"Aye, there will be; it's good they look to that and plan for it," John Bell added as he tamped and lit his pipe. "Now tell me how Jack and David are doin' with our plans. I've heard enough about those we can't do a thing about. Are they ready to go? Should we start movin' our stuff north to meet them at Brown's Tavern, or further downriver?"

"Jack told us, as soon as Lieutenant Deas returns and is satisfied with their preparations, they'll start. He'll leave David and Deas and the other assistant conductors in charge, and he'll high tail it down here to let us know when they're getting underway from the Agency and to help us get moving. They'll wait for him to rejoin them at Brainerd Mission, then they'll start the river crossings. Jack figures we'll have plenty of time to push north to meet them at whichever ferry crossing we choose, Brown's or Kelly's." Sam watched his father's expression to see whether this plan was acceptable.

"I would'a started yesterday if I could'a. This waitin's naw easy. Jack needs to collect his wife and young'ins, too, I canna' doubt, so we can all travel together and help each other out. We'll be ready and eager as hungry bears in early spring."

September 30, 1838, at Fort Cass

Standing in General Winfield Scott's temporary office in the Charleston Agency, Lieutenant Edward Deas saluted and turned back to Jack and David, "We have our field orders, gentlemen, and our first measurable rain since May. Let's get our detachment together and go." They nodded in response, turned with him and headed out the door.

The Agency Post door opened onto a porch overlooking a broad bay that held flatboats and other vessels tied to docks around the edge. Across the bay the makeshift wood frame barracks held many of the soldiers. They took turns overseeing the remaining stockades that stretched for miles to the south. Beyond the rise to the east, fifty-six wagons parked in front of the stockade that held most of the former residents of Old Coosawattee Town. Several corrals held over three hundred head of horses and four dozen teams of oxen. Barrels and crates of supplies and stacks of heavy canvas tents waited to be loaded.

"We will pass the word that we have permission to go," Jack said to Deas. "We take comfort in knowing you've gone west five times before, with groups as large and larger. You've learned from bad times as well as good, and people commend you for each time you've gone. I have reliable assistants and translators, and Doctor Eddington will go with us.[75]

"I know you, Jack. You're not the villain Ross makes you out to be. You could handle this endeavor on your own if you had to, but we'll do our best together and make an easier job of it

---

[75] Wayne Dell Gibson concludes that Lieutenant Edward Deas was disbursing agent and John Bell was conductor. Serving Bell as assistant conductors were D. S. Walker, D. M. Foreman, Ellis Harlin, and Luther Rankin. Watt Foster, W. M. Boling, and John Sanders served as interpreters, and Dr. J. W. Edington served as physician. Wayne Dell Gibson, "Cherokee Treaty Party Moves West: The Bell-Deas Overland Journey, 1838-1839," *Chronicles of Oklahoma* 79 (Fall 2001), 328.

than it would be otherwise. God knows it will be hard enough if the weather's with us. They say it's a more treacherous route, heading straight west, but we both know it well; it has advantages and disadvantages, but we'll make a go of it."

The men stopped on the ridge and looked south where a plume of smoke was filling the air. Deas commented, "It looks like the soldiers have put the torch to the Gunstocker Spring camp. The last of its occupants is probably just out of the gate."

David said, "I don't think anyone would want to turn around at this point. There was too much sickness there. They're probably saying 'good riddance.'"

Jack spoke, "As soon as everyone in our detachment has the word and knows what they're doing, I'll take my leave. I'll tell Jennie and the children to meet you at Brainerd, and Elijah and I will get my father started from his place on the Coosa. We'll come back together and meet you at Brainerd. Probably a week to ten days."

David put his hand on Jack's shoulder and said, "I think we're well-organized to do this. We've gone over the plans several times, so no one should wonder what their duties are. You should be able to go without looking back. Say 'Osiyo' to little Andro, Maria Charlotte, and Hooley for me. I know they're missing their Daddy. I'm eager to see Little John. Meanwhile I know our first challenge will be to keep our distance from the Ross detachments until we're clear of this area. I'll do all I can to keep any hotheads from making trouble."

As they approached the stockade several men came out to meet them, eager to hear whether they had the 'go ahead' to do the final loading of the wagons and be on their way. Excited voices responded to the news.

Activity started before sunrise the next morning. They still had several days for loading and checking their supplies before heading toward Brainerd Mission. Immediately after breakfast Jack and Elijah saddled up and headed for the Martin farmstead near Ooltewah, where Jennie and the children were staying in the company of several servants. Her parents and siblings had already been gone for several months.

Lieutenant Deas wanted to make sure they didn't cross paths with any other group on the road, so they waited until several of the groups had cleared the area. The other groups were headed west or northwest, while the Bell detachment was headed south. They were certain to run into each other if they didn't coordinate arrangements with the other groups. Hair Conrad and Daniel Colston had made the earliest start, leading a group out on August 28. Other conductors who followed with their detachments during the next month were Elijah Hicks, Sittuakee and Rev. Evan Jones, Captain Old Field and Rev. Stephen Foreman, Rev. Jesse Bushyhead, Choolooka, Moses Daniel, James Brown, George Hicks, and Richard Taylor. Jesse Bushyhead's group included Aunt Elizabeth, who was Jack and David's sister, and her husband George Washington Candy. Cousin Peter Hildebrand would conduct the last detachment to leave, the first week in November.[76]

The Bell detachment left their stockade on October 10 and 11. Lieutenant Edward Deas and the assistant conductors moved their caravan of wagons, livestock, and 650 people south of the Agency along Mouse Creek, then along Candy Creek toward Ooltewah, and directly south toward the Chickamauga

---

[76] The list of detachment leaders is found in Stanley W. Hoig, *The Cherokees and Their Chiefs: In the Wake of Empire* (Fayetteville, University of Arkansas Press, 1998), 173-174.

Creek crossing at Brainerd Mill and Mission. They did not encounter any other group of Cherokees along their two day journey, and the weather was warm and pleasant. Jennie Bell and her children were the first to greet them at the Brainerd Mission. She reported that she expected her husband Jack to arrive at any time.

October 7, 1838, Red Wolf's Day Log

All of my life has led to this day. My family and I join our people's march west to the new home of the Cherokee Nation. Today my Ududu John Bell starts traveling north with his family, his wagons, the tools of his blacksmith shop, and a few cattle. Everything else will be left behind for someone else to take over. I am excited and I am afraid. I will see my Udoda and the people from my village, Coosawattee Town, in a few days. Udoda was upset when Will and I left the Agency stockade to go to Ududu. We nearly didn't make it, because I became so sick. My best friend Will helped me and the call of the red wolf kept me going. It's a long way to Arkansas, with many problems to face along the way. I don't know if I can make the trip. We are going to a place I've never seen. We are leaving behind everything I've known, including my mother's grave. My Udoda and Ududu and Uduji Jack have gone west before when they were trading, so I know we won't get lost. My Uloghi Sarah Caroline will help me write, so I can correct the spelling and grammar and learn while I write. This will be my school. Most of our teachers have already gone. There won't be a school to go to yet when we get there. We have to build homes and schools and everything from scratch.

October 8, 1838, Will's Town, Fort Payne

We slept on blankets under the wagons last night. The oxen were unhitched so they could rest too. The sky was clear and the evening was warm. Ududu said we travelled about twelve miles yesterday, and that was good for the first day. We should go farther today. We will pass Will's Town, which is now called Fort Payne, tomorrow. There are many people there preparing to make the trip. Uduji Jack will report to the fort commander that we have left the Coosa River plantation. The new owner can claim it. I know Ududu hates to do that. He says he is glad that he could stay there until time to go, because he signed the treaty. No one who refused to sign could stay at their own place. They were all rounded up by soldiers and kept in stockades like the one where we stayed at the Agency. We had to stay longer than we should have. Conditions were terrible. Many were sick and the food was bad. There was not enough water to get clean or to drink. That was why Will and I decided to leave. I think my Udoda understands that. I hope so.

We don't have much to do while we are on the trail. We walk alongside the wagons. When the wagons stop, we stop. We make camp at night. We help feed and water the animals and gather wood for the campfires. We feel very tired at the end of the day. I will mostly write in the log in the morning or when we take a break midday.

Sarah reads what I have written and corrects it. She shows me how I can write better with the syllabary. I write on the left page of my journal. She marks mistakes and makes suggestions on the left page. Then I make a good copy of our work on the right page. The journal will fill up fast that way. Only the right page will be good to read.

October 7, 1838, Red Wolf's Day Log

We are not far south of Fort Payne. We can see the smoke of campfires and chimneys, not as many as we expected. The Cherokee people have already left the camp, led by a conductor named John Benge. Samuel and Jack rode ahead to the Fort to report our presence to them. They already learned of our plans a few days ago.

Just a few weeks ago Will and I were hiding in the forest near the base of that mountain. We made our way along it, always trying to stay out of sight. I feel much better not having to hide. We travel openly on the roads. When we meet someone, soldiers or others, we don't have to hide. The most Ududu or Uduji Jack has to do is explain what we are doing and show some documents. Some people ride around us at a distance. They are afraid they might catch something from us.

Uduji Jack and Ezekiel will ride on ahead of us soon to meet the main wagon train at Brainerd Mission. He's waiting until we are well past Fort Payne, in case someone there tries to make trouble for us or detain us, he says. We have to stop there today and make a final report. Will and I want to ride with them when they go, so we can see our fathers. Uduji Jack has not decided. We might slow them down. He wants to get there as soon as possible.

Asa and Barbary have two children—Osman is five summers, and Sarrah is one. They are going with us in our train. I talked to Asa yesterday evening. I asked him why they won't travel with us all the way west. They plan to leave the train when we reach the plateau and travel south along the Tennessee River. They will live with his Udoda Francis. I am named after Francis. I have never met him. I don't remember meeting him. They will settle on land he has bought in Alabama. He said he wants to live like white people. No one will know he is half-blood. He wants to go to Texas which is a new country now, not part of Mexico. Now he is waiting for things to settle down there. He thinks our Chief Bowl may have trouble after Sam Houston is no longer president of Texas. Houston could not get a new treaty ratified between the Cherokees and Texas.

Asa doesn't believe that Cherokee people will be able to stay long in the new lands along the Arkansas. They have already had to move farther west outside the new state of Arkansas. He thinks the United States will keep moving Indian people west until there is no more land for us.

I asked Asa why he did not decide to go to Illinois where he and Grandfather could get land. He said he wanted to have servants. Illinois does not allow servants. He meant slaves. He prefers to use the word servants. He wants to have a large plantation like they had here and have slaves work on it. In Texas that is legal. In Illinois it isn't. I must think about that. I didn't know that we would have slaves in our new home. I don't think that is right. One person should not own another person. That is what my Uji taught me.

October 11, 1838, Red Wolf's Day Log

We stopped at Fort Payne yesterday. It took many hours to stop there and get some new papers with permissions to travel. We did not get to travel very far. After they talked with the officers at Fort Payne Uduji Jack and Elijah decided to stay with the train until we get to the river landings. We will all go together to meet the whole detachment, they said. I don't know why they changed their minds about riding ahead. They seem to be worried about something, but Sarah does not know what it might be.

Every evening we have been lucky to find a spot near a river or creek for a camping place. I like to bathe and wash off trail dust and grime. We use running water for a morning dip before anything else is done. Our life on the trail will be strange. If we can take a morning dip, it will be like home.

Yesterday I told Will the story of the Great Sleeping Bear that my Uji told me. We were walking along and admiring the smooth sides and flat top of the mountain. It is not like the pointed shapes of most of other mountains. Uji said this mountain is one of the giants, a great bear. The bear fell asleep after the time of creation. She said the age of man was like a long winter's sleep for the Great Yonu. Every hundred years the bear wakes herself up and looks out at the land. If the Ani Yun'wiya are still living here in peace, she will fall asleep again. Uji said some people call the mountain "Lookout Mountain" because the bear looks out to see the Cherokee people. When she was little the bear woke up and the earth shook. Everyone was afraid. The shaking lasted only a short time, and then the earth was quiet again. The bear went back to sleep. That was a time when the people had many old men preaching about the need to return to their old ways and reject the white man's ways. Ghost dances and gathers were held around the country. The earth's shaking tore up some of people's villages in the West along the Father-Water. People saw it as a sign that they should stay in their own lands in the East. Uji said that her Ulisi Nancy Ward told her there was no reason to be afraid as long as they stayed in their land. The bear would be happy. If she woke up and saw only white faces, she would be angry. Then everyone should be afraid.

Will had never heard the story. Sarah told me she had never heard it either. Her Uji, my Ulisi Charlotte, told her some animal stories, but none like that. I was sad for a while after I remembered my Uji telling me that story. Will and I did not talk for a while after that.

October 12, 1838, Red Wolf's Day Log

The road has been good. Uduji Sam said the army cleared the road a few years ago, the whole length of Will's Valley. It makes easy walking. The wagon wheels and horse's hooves stir up a lot of dust. I suppose I should get used to that. We will follow main roads like this one across the counties of Tennessee and Arkansas all the way to Ududu Caleb Starr's home. I have never met him. I am looking forward to meeting him. Everyone says he is a nice man and they miss him. He moved to Arkansas before I was born, when it was all Western Cherokee land. Now he and Ulisi Nancy Starr live at a place called Vineyard Post Office. It is at the east border of the Western Cherokee Nation. Many of their grown children already live with them there—that is where Uduji James Starr lives now—but a few are still here. They are part of the last big groups to travel west. I will be glad to see many clan brothers and sisters and cousins. We have not played together for many months since Rattlesnake Springs.

October 13, 1838, Red Wolf's Day Log

I feel really tired tonight. Some of the coughing has come back. I think it is the dust from the road that makes me cough now. I've listened and looked for the red wolf. I haven't seen or heard any sign of him. He will stay clear of so many people and wagons. Ududu says I can ride in the carriage with Ulisi, Barbary, and the girls if I want to, or on a wagon seat. I will walk as much as I can. I can't get stronger if I don't walk.

October 14, 1838, Red Wolf's Day Log

I rode on the wagon-seat today with Ududu. I was ashamed of not being strong enough to walk on my own. He was nice about it and funny too. He said he could not walk all the way himself. He had to ride as much as he could, and he hadn't been as sick as I had been. Then he made fun of my shoes with cracked soles and my toes peeking out. Most of the time I go barefoot. The nights and mornings are getting colder now. I like to wear shoes when I'm working with the horses or oxen. They don't mind stepping on my feet. They leave their poop all over for me to step in. Ududu said he'd get out some leather and start making some new shoes tonight when the rest of his work is done. I told him I'd like to learn how to make shoes. He said I could help him make them. I told him about walking over the rocks and wearing my shoes out. He said rocks do wear your shoes out. If you walk on the earth in the summertime, you don't need shoes at all. We'd best get shoes for when we need them and enjoy the times we don't. Riding on the wagon is bumpy, but I've never had Ududu all to myself to talk and see things as he sees them. He pointed out the birds getting ready for winter, some flying south and some coming from the north. They travel more miles than we are traveling, and they do it every year. We should be able to manage it, unless we're not as smart and brave as birds.

October 15, 1838, Red Wolf's Day Log

Sarah helps me a lot with this writing, using Sequoia's syllabary. She is more than a teacher, and more than a Uloghi to me. I would say she is more than a Udo or sister, but I never had a sister to know what having a sister is like. She smiled when she read that and said she did have a little brother, James, but he would not sit still to learn from her. Her older brothers just liked to tease her. Her younger sisters Charlotte and Martha Jane got into her things and made nuisances of themselves. Of course she liked them and took care of them anyway. I think she is lucky to grow up with several brothers and sisters. She is high in my affection and respect, and she could not be higher. We talked about these words and decided they are fine to use. Sarah has an interest in a man. She doesn't tell me his name. She said he is quiet and soft-spoken like me. I don't need to know any more than that. She will wait to see what the future holds. Will he have an interest in her when people settle in the West? I've never thought before about having a family, becoming a father, or taking care of children. I would like to have someone as a wife who is like my Uloghi Sarah Caroline. Tomorrow we will reach the Tennessee River.

October 16, 1838, Brown's Landing

We reached Brown's Inn and Brown's Landing today. The inn stands on a low rise about a mile above the Tennessee River. The whole property is just a short way west of where Will and I climbed the Sleeping Bear to look down on Ross's Landing. Dozens of our people are already here with Ellis Harlan and Luther Rankin, two of the Assistant Conductors. We learned that the some of the detachment are just across the river, and some are waiting on the east side of the river at the Brainerd Mission. No one wanted to cross until Uduji Jack had gotten there, but Deas insisted they get started anyway.[77] Maybe they will all be happy to see Jack tomorrow. I wanted to cross the ferry and go to meet Udoda. I was too tired after a long day. We are waiting on the south side of Brown's Ferry until the whole detachment joins us. Where I am sitting I can see the two story inn that Brown built. It will take two days to cross the river two times. Maybe tomorrow Will and I can cross over and see my Udoda and Elijah.

October 17, 1838, Red Wolf's Day Log

Will and I did it! Ududu said to go ahead. We wouldn't get lost. He is so funny sometimes.

October 17, 1838, Ross's Ferry

Morning broke clear and cool on October 17, and after breakfast of cornbread and beans, Grandfather John Bell inspected Red Wolf and gave permission for him and Will to walk the half mile slope to Brown's Ferry, cross over the river, walk the three miles to Ross's Ferry, cross the river again if necessary, and try to find his father David with the caravan of wagons and horses that

---

[77] Lieutenant Edward Deas wrote to General Scott that the detachment had begun crossing at Ross's Landing on October 16, and that "many of the people [were] unwilling to proceed in consequence of the absence of the Conductor Mr. John Bell." Deas was concerned that "unless Mr. Bell on his arrival shall be able to infuse a more reasonable spirit into many of the Emigrants composing this party, I am entirely of the opinion that nothing but Force will be able to make them consult their own interest and proceed quietly upon the Route to the West." King, Duane. *The Cherokee Trail of Tears* p. 57.

should be preparing to cross the river. Red Wolf was eager to go, and Will equally game for the hike to find his father Ezekiel. Halfway there they began to meet oxen-pulled wagons and walkers from families they knew from Coosawattee Town. Jim Stone was the first, with his wife and children, Kuncheestaneeska and his family, Jack and Katharine Dougherty, Wat Sanders, Aggy Foster—the familiar faces and greetings encouraged them.

Aggy yelled "Siyo' friendly enough, but she followed with the warning, "Your fathers are looking for you, too."

Red Wolf and Will looked at each other, as if they had forgotten entirely about the discipline that might follow their long absence without their fathers' permissions.

"I have a debt to pay to you," Red Wolf said. "You can say I needed your help."

Will responded, "I don't think I can use that excuse," and remained quiet for a while.

There were long gaps between the wagons, sometimes with strings of horses between. The boys began to count the wagons and horses. When they finally reached the west side of the Ross's Ferry Landing, they saw what they expected—the long ragged line of wagons and people, horses and cattle, and a few carriages, stretching east from the opposite shore. They were still surprised by the large size of the detachment.

Lieutenant Deas and several soldiers were trying to keep some kind of order in the lineup for boarding the ferry, but it didn't take long for Red Wolf to identify his father and Uncle Samuel at the east landing, helping with the loading of the ferry. At the west ramp, two familiar men, George Arnold and John Shatteen, helped with the unloading of the ferry, which seemed to move quickly as both the animals and the people were quicker to get off than to board.

Red Wolf and Will boarded the empty ferry for the journey to the east side, felt the rocking sway of the ferry and the rushing water underneath, as the cables and ropes held the ferry in position and pulled it in an unsteady rhythm across the wide Tennessee River. Red Wolf locked eyes with his father waiting on the other side and looking very sober. When they reached the landing, David met Red Wolf at the edge of the ferry, grabbed him in his arms and lifted him in a strong embrace, saying quietly in his ear, "I missed you. I was afraid I might not see you again." Then he set him on his feet again and continued speaking to them both. "You'll need to find a safe place to watch, away from the boarding ramp. Some of our animals aren't too keen on riding the ferry. Or you can go see some of the other folks who've been wondering where you went. The crossing here and at Brown's will take all of today and most of tomorrow." Elijah released his grip on his son with a "We'll have a talk later."

The boys found a vantage point about forty paces away on the bank and watched for a while. David and Elijah talked with the teamsters and found different ways to coax the oxen onto the raft, sometimes covering the oxen eyes, sometimes speaking quietly and reassuringly, sometimes cracking a whip and giving strong pulls on their harness. Those who knew their teams had practice in crossing rivers. Others were just finding out what their teams would do as they faced obstacles.

The boys continued their tally as they watched. They decided to walk a mile to the end of the lineup along the road towards Missionary Ridge to the east. When they finished the count they added the numbers from Grandfather Bell's group.

They had a total of 56 wagons, many hitched to oxen teams, 318 horses, and 670 people headed west.

Along the way Uncle Jack showed up, riding his horse, talking with people along the way about what to expect, how they would deal with whatever unexpected events people were fearing, and keeping track of who was drinking alcohol, who was impatient and troublesome, and who was helping their neighbors cope while they waited. There would be lots of waiting times like these.

Red Wolf did not recognize his cousin Andromache when they found Uncle Jack's family near the end of the train. The measles had left her thin and weak, scarring her face, although not as badly as the more feared smallpox. At six years old, Andromache looked about a half as big as she was when Red Wolf last saw her. Also along the way he had seen a lot of other children among the families who had fared as poorly and looked as sickly because of the waves of sickness during the past four months.

Will asked Red Wolf to excuse him since he saw his mother, Demaris, working with the horses a hundred paces farther on the other side of the trail. "Of course, Will. You don't need to ask." Will ran ahead.

Aunt Jennie, Uncle Jack's wife, invited Red Wolf to join them for a lunch of bread, dried beef, and sliced apples. They sat under the shade of a maple tree, its leaves just beginning to turn yellow, with Andro and her two little sisters, Maria and Charlotte, and eight-month-old Hoolie. Months had passed since Red Wolf had played with small children; he enjoyed their play and attention to him.

"You look like you've been as sick as Andro," Aunt Jennie told him.

"Really? I suppose I do. On the way to Ududu I got sick. Will kept me alive."

"Jack told me that is when you received your new name. How did it happen?"

"I was too sick to find our way. We were lost. I heard the red wolf call. He called from the direction of Ududu's farm. Later I saw him leading us alongside the trail, and his coat was mottled with red. Ududu said I had a spirit guide, and he gave me his name."

"That is fitting. We used to call you "Little Wolf." Anyway we are Wolf clan. You're a friend of my youngest brother, Richard. He and my parents have already settled in the West, and they're waiting for us. I'm your mother's clan sister. She's waiting for us also, beyond the Western horizon. I am your mother on this journey, as long as you need me."

"Wado.[78] You are very kind."

As the day wore on, the line slowly moved closer to the landing, but when evening came, they started a fire near the side of the road. Aunt Jennie and Demaris prepared a hot supper. Uncle Jack, Ezekiel, and David returned to the campfire circle. The sky was still clear. They laid out their bedrolls and spent the night under the stars. In the early morning, before sunrise, when Red Wolf awoke, he could see the Six Brothers at their campfires overhead.

---

[78] Wado, thank you.

October 18, 1838, Finish Crossing Brown's Ferry

The sound of crackling fire and the making of a breakfast of mixed meal porridge and coffee came with the first rays of sunrise showing above Missionary Ridge. The bedrolls were damp with dew, and they left them lying in the rising sun for a hand of time until they were dry. The men downed their breakfast quickly and hurried off toward the landing. Will and Red Wolf helped water the animals and pick up the camp while Demaris harnessed the horses to the carriage and the oxen to the wagons.

By noon they were part of the tail of the long caravan, ready at the river's edge to cross the river. Uncle Jack and David had already gone ahead to Brown's Landing. Ezekiel was in charge of the last crossings. The oxen were sluggish but sure-footed as they planted their hooves on the ferry, as they had done on many previous river crossings. The horses acted eager to get across to the other side. Red Wolf and Will spent much of the morning occupying the children, so when the time for the river crossing came, Red Wolf had Andromache by the hand, Will had Maria and Charlotte at each side by hand, and Jennie was carrying Hoolie. The children looked with wonder at the wide river. They walked on the trail through the willows and the brush toward the next ferry crossing, which came in the evening. The sun was no longer in sight, but hidden beyond Raccoon Mountain. David and Uncle Jack stayed until everyone was safely across. They drove the teams halfway up the slope toward the log tavern building and set up camp for the night.

Grandfather and Grandmother Bell had directed preparations for the fire circle that night, along with Sarah Caroline, Samuel, James, Aunt Charlotte, and dozens of others. The servants were busy around a large pot of stew simmering with game and vegetables that disappeared into tin plates that almost everyone refilled, along with the breads that had fried on the hot rocks in the coals of the fire.

Sarah asked to see Red Wolf's day journal, but he had to admit that he had added nothing to it since he had left her two days before. "You've had enough to do, joining your father and my brother's family, haven't you?" she said.

"I have so much to write, I don't know where to start. I also have plenty of other things to do. I am excited to see how big this wagon train is, how much work it is, how much everyone has to do."

"This is an adventure, yes, bringing a thrill at the same time it brings sadness at leaving. My brother Jack is telling everyone they may go to the water at sunrise, if they want, while we are in the shadow of the Lookout, what you call the Great Bear. People will be looking back over their shoulder when we leave Lookout Mountain tomorrow. It'll be a sad farewell."

"Going to the water to cleanse the body will be better than drowning sorrows in whiskey," Red Wolf said.

"Many are doing that. The soldiers are watchful, afraid trouble will start as the drinking gets worse. Men lose their senses and lash out at anyone who gets in their way. I heard Deas tell the soldiers that trouble could start at the ferries. Some of our people are angry with Ross and his cousin John Brown for making money in the removal. Some are just angry at having to leave and ready to take their anger out on anyone. Deas heard rumors that rebellion was brewing."

"If people were going to rebel, wouldn't they have done it earlier? Wouldn't they have broken out of the stockades when they were so miserable? Some people hid in the mountains when the soldiers conducted the roundup. Even before that, Young Turkey disappeared. I remember him talking about hiding in the mountains years ago, when I was a little boy."

Sarah chuckled at that. "You still are little. You are nine years old. The truth is—no one ever let you be a little boy. Life made you grow up too fast. You are little, but you are also a man in many ways, Red Wolf."

Red Wolf blushed, and he remained quiet as he listened to others talk about their feelings on this last light in the moon's shadow of the Lookout.

October 19, 1838, Red Wolf's Day Log

This morning at sunrise a procession of our people moved slowly and silently to the Tennessee River. Below the head of the Great Bear we dipped in the water and cleansed ourselves. Some of the women elders shed tears, knowing they will never return to this land of our ancestors.

Father tells me that we will travel several days along the river. After we leave it far behind, it will curve around so we will cross it once again in central Tennessee. Today feels like the day we have been preparing for all my life, when we leave our land behind. We embark on a long journey to a new land to call our own. Will it be a Promised Land? Will the Great Spirit provide for us as we wander through the wilderness? Will many of us die on the way?

As I watched people the last three days, I could tell that a lot of our people are weak and sick. Measles, whooping cough, bloody bowels are among the sicknesses that are still with us. Several of us are just weak and worn out from being sick, and week. It seems like a month. We have moved only twenty miles. Seven hundred more to go. At that pace we would be on the road for thirty-five weeks, or nine months. It would seem like forty years in the wilderness.

October 22, 1838, Jasper, Tennessee River

The trek along the north side of the river is so narrow at points that wagons wheels could easily slide off. Wagons could tumble down the slope into the water. We had to move slowly and watch what we were doing, not spook the animals any more than they already were. Most of the way the road allowed no room to pass. People coming from the opposite direction had to wait until we passed. Luckily only a few wagons came toward us. They had to pull off where there was room to pass, and wait most of the day. I could see they were angry, sometimes shouting profane words at us when we passed. Most of our caravan were quiet and did not answer. Uduji Jack told us to be ready for this and avoid trouble by being quiet. I was surprised our people followed his advice. Usually we like to insult each other. We let words fly back and forth like arrows, for the fun of it. On this journey everyone seems to know we have more at stake. Old people and children and everything we own are with us.

Before camping this evening we forded the Sequatchie River. It flows through the foothills with a great mountain rising behind it. The river was only about ten paces wide at the ford, and only about a foot deep at the deepest point. We had little trouble crossing it. I am glad that we haven't had much rain because it could fill quickly and become a monster to cross.

At the end of the day we are camping at the outskirts of a settlement called Jasper. The wagons sit close to each other in a large open field. Tomorrow we will drive through Jasper, leaving the Tennessee valley, and begin to climb the Cumberland

Mountains. The horses, cows and oxen have some pasture here. They are grazing happily. Ududu says they better enjoy it while they can. They won't see pasture again for several days.

October 23, 1838, Martin Springs

We camped tonight near a cave springs in a beautiful wooded area. The cold water flows out of a cave large enough for people to enter and find shelter. The output is enough to provide a small river, very cold, pleasant to drink and to bathe downstream.[79]

I went with Udoda to see Lieutenant Deas in his tent this morning. He just received a letter from General Winfield Scott, which he read aloud to us. Then he read his reply. Scott had asked how the trip was going. Did Lieutenant Deas need more soldiers to provide security? Deas answered that "circumstances had so much changed for the better, relative to the progress of the Party under my charge, that in my opinion the presence of a guard had become unnecessary." He also wrote that "Everything at present is going on well, and all appear satisfied, and no exertions shall be spared on my part, to render their journey to the West as comfortable and expeditious as possible."

All of our leading men were there, nodding and thanking him for what he wrote. They agreed that the soldiers were a big help to us but we didn't need any more. Were we really so unruly, unpredictable and ill-tempered that we needed the soldiers to keep us in order? I don't think so. I am upset to think that General Scott may have that opinion of our people. A few men that I know are sometimes rude or rowdy. They are well outnumbered by the gentlemen who keep them in line. I think the soldiers are useful in protecting us from the fearful and

---

[79] Southeast Tennessee Tourism Association, "Cherokee Native American Guide" 2009. "Research provided by Dr. Duane King." Item 19- Martin Springs Cave.

Red Wolf's Day Log

ignorant settlers. They do not know us. They do not know how patient we have been with their mean governments.   Some men who have reputations for being rowdies bought spiritous liquors from the taverns at Jasper when we were passing through that little town. They are drinking quietly tonight. Uduji Jack and Udoda have reminded them to remain quiet so the women and children may rest. They are sitting around the campfires drinking and talking quietly They are more sad than angry at what has happened. Some talk bravely about building a new nation in the West. They will soon be asleep I think.[80]

---

[80] The full text of the letter:
Edward Deas to Major General Winfield Scott
Encampment of Indians near Jasper, E. Tenn.ᵉ
22, October 1838
To Major General Winfield Scott, Command Eastern Division
Sir,
Your letter of the 19th reached me on the 20th instant, but I am happy to be able to say, that circumstances had so much changed for the better, relative to the progress of the Party under my charge, that in my opinion the presence of a guard had become unnecessary. I have no doubt, however, that the knowledge of a detachment of troops having been ordered to attend the Party, has produced a salutary effect, & I tust that hereafter no further unnecessary delays will occur.   Every think at present is going on well, & all appear satisfied, & no exertions shall be spared on my part, to render their journey to the West as comfortable & expeditious as possible.

It having been necessary, by the route we travel, to cross the Tennessee R. three times, our progress thus far has been slow, but after crossing the Cumberland mountain our rate of travelling will be very different.   This Party being small, & taking into our consideration the number of Indians passing over the Missouri route-the dryness of the past season affecting the roads-the probability of ready supplies, all other circumstances; I have concluded that we had better pursue the route by Memphis, provided the people themselves are willing to do so. The latter must be more than 150 miles shorter, than the route thro' Missouri, & the cost thus saved would far more than pay the extra expense of running round the Mississippi swamp by water, to Rock-Row on White river, should the road thro' the swamp, be found in a bad state for wagons, upon our arrival at Memphis, which I can scarcely believe will be the case.   There is nothing further for me to communicate, I believe, at present, upon the subject of the Party of Emigrants under my charge.
I have the honor to be, sir, Very respectfully, Yo. Mo. Obt. Servt. Edw Deas, Lieut. U.S.A. Disbg Agt.

Our Land! Our People!

October 24, 1838, Cumberland Mountain

We will spend a whole day climbing the mountain before we reach a point near the top when we can begin descending. The climb is gradual so we hardly notice that we are climbing until we see the great mass of the mountain ahead through the trees. The trail runs north up a wandering little river, called Battle Creek. There is game for us to chase and practice our skills with the bow. I didn't get anything, but Will shot a squirrel to add to our supper pot.

Ulisi Charlotte said that the Great Buzzard must have been huge to flap its wings and make this mountain.[81] Ududu just laughed at her. She looks tired and more wrinkled than ever. She says she has not been sleeping well. She misses her bed. She has not slept on the earth for many years. Ududu often sleeps on the earth in his travels. He chided her for losing touch with Uji Earth, and she said, "I know. My mind is ready to rest on the earth, but my body is not." Her bones ache, she says, so she drinks willow bark tea every chance she gets. I don't want to get old.

October 25, 1838, Cumberland Mountain

This evening we arrived at the cabin of a man named Trussell who built a toll road down the west side of the mountain. Uduji Jack and Lieutenant Deas made arrangements for our train to go down the mountain tomorrow. We're enjoying the flat ground

---

Source: Lt. Edward Deas to General W. Scott, October 22, 1838, National Archives Record Group 75, Records of the Bureau of Indian Affairs, Letters Received, Cherokee Emigration, Roll 115, S1555 No. 2

[81] In a popular origin myth, the mountains and valleys of the Cherokee homeland were created by the Great Buzzard's flapping of his wings in the still-soft earth of the newly created land. See James Mooney, *Myths of the Cherokee*, p. 239.

near the top of the mountain this evening. Trussell and his hired hands cut trees, dug out rocks, and cleared a path all by themselves all the way down through the trees on the steep side of the mountain. I hear that deep ravines and cliffs are common along the route. The road itself is narrow, with barely room for single file all the way. We must be even more careful along this trail than we were along the Tennessee River before Jasper.

Uloghi Sarah is nervous about tomorrow. She is afraid of losing people and wagons if we are not extra careful. Everyone who can walk must walk. Only the best wagon drivers will be on wagon seats.

October 26, 1838, Trussell Toll Road

The day has been amazing. We started at daybreak, after a quick breakfast before the sun was even up. Everything told to us about the toll road was true. Much of the road cut steeply through the trees and large rocks down the mountain. The west side of the mountain looked entirely different than the gradual climb up a pleasant valley on the east side. The rugged and treacherous road cost us one wagon. It collapsed after an axle broke and smashed two wheels on the steep side of the trail. When he heard the crack of the axle, Otterlifter jumped off the driver's seat and landed on the oxen. The oxen were patient and calm enough to stand still while the wagon fell apart and became dead weight behind them. Oxen are such dependable workers. They never get spooked or nervous like horses. They just keep doing their jobs. Two barrels rolled out of the wagon and kept rolling down the mountainside until one crashed into pieces on a boulder a hundred paces below. Its contents of shelled corn spread out for all the small animals to enjoy. The other lodged in a clump of trees farther down. We didn't try to retrieve it.

Our Land! Our People!

I heard the sound of crashing and yelling, walking in front of Ududu's wagon with Will and Andro. We were about twenty wagons behind Tom Otterlifter's wagon. Ududu took big prybars and sledges and took charge of dismantling what was left of the wagon. He saved the two good wheels and one axle, and dumped the broken parts down the mountainside. Other men and women salvaged most of the barrels and boxes and other contents and moved them to other wagons. Otterlifter took the reins and walked the oxen the rest of the way. With everyone pitching in, the delay only took about two hands of time, and we continued our slow progress down the road.

Otherwise no accidents interrupted the journey, to everyone's relief. We just kept moving slowly, not even stopping to eat. We nibbled on whatever we had put into our pockets from breakfast and got a drink of water whenever we could, twice at springs along the way. The road often turned back on itself in sharp turns. It seemed that we made little progress, but it wound downwards almost all the way, about nine miles. We reached a level valley at the foot of the mountain after sunset, and set up camp beside a small stream.

The weather was perfect for going down the mountain. No one complained about the lack of rain. The leaves of all colors are falling steadily now, although pine woods cover much of the mountain. This evening is chilly as I write this by the campfire. I feel more tired than I can remember, but still excited by all we did and saw today. The road may be the most rugged road I have ever travelled, but the mountain was wild and beautiful. We went farther in one day and cut miles off the route we would have travelled before Trussell built his toll road.

October 27, 1838, West of Winchester

All I wanted to do this morning was sleep, but we were roused to break camp and eat at sunrise. With the mountain behind us, the roads were well-travelled through many clearings and past many farmsteads. Mid-morning we passed the town of Winchester. It had several well-built houses and many cabins. About as many people live in Winchester as we have with us in the detachment. Deas and Uduji Jack inquired at the blacksmith shops and with three wagon-makers about buying a replacement wagon. None was ready to go, and they did not want to wait for a new one to be finished.

The land rolls gently here. We look east and the mountains extend north and south into the haze. We look west and the horizon is flat. Only the trees and a few clouds show up. Udoda says we will not see another mountain until we reach deep into Arkansas, in about two months. I find it hard to believe there is that much flat land to cross. He says we will see hills and big river valleys, but no mountains until we get close to where we will be making our homes.

Andro and I both rode most of the day. Aunt Jennie put Andro on the carriage seat beside her, and, when he saw me falling behind, Ududu put me beside him on the wagon seat. I even slept part of the way. Will and the older boys kept walking.

October 28, 1838, Jesse Bean's Settlement

We made camp on Bean's Creek this evening, just across from a mill. An old friend of Ududu, Jesse Bean, settled here many years ago, when no one else was living in the area. Ududu told me that these were cousins of the Bean families that we knew in the

Cherokee Nation, related to Mrs. William Bean that Ulisi Nancy Ward had saved many years ago.[82] Jesse's brother, Richard, farms land that their father got in the Military Tract in Illinois, because he was a veteran of the Revolutionary War and the War of 1812.[83] They have relatives in Arkansas, also named Richard and Mark—Ududu knows them, too—who run a salt-works on the Illinois River in the Western Cherokee country. I wondered if their land in Illinois is close to the Illinois River. Sarah says there are two Illinois Rivers—one in Illinois and the other in Arkansas and the Cherokee Nation. They are many miles away from each other, because Ududu said that it took many days to ride a horse from one to the other.[84]

Old Jesse Bean is a blacksmith like Ududu. Mr. Bean makes fine rifles that Ududu says are some of the best. He works in a cave north of the river. Ududu bought five rifles from Mr. Bean, which he said were "worth their weight in gold." He could easily sell them again for more than he paid. Ududu's still a trader.

We crossed the creek below the mill where it was easy to ford. There was only one easy place to cross, because there are limestone bluffs on the north side of the river where they built the mill. Will and I and some other boys fished in the deeper pools near the mill, and caught some good ones.

---

[82] Carolyn Thomas Foreman summarizes some of the family history in "The Bean Family," *The Chronicles of Oklahoma*, vol. 32, pp. 308ff.

[83] Pike County, Illinois, Land records show Richard Bean living on 160 acres of land acquired by William Bean on January 1, 1818, under the authority of the Scrip Warrant Act of 1812, the northern quarter of Section 20 of Township 1 South, Range 2 West.

[84] The Illinois River in Oklahoma is several hundred miles southwest of the identically-named Illinois River in Illinois. Pike County lies between the Illinois River and the Mississippi River in Illinois.

At the mill Uduji Jack made a deal with a neighbor to buy a wagon in good condition, so Tom Otterlifter has a wagon to go with his team again. Lieutenant Deas was able to purchase additional supplies of cornmeal, corn, fodder, and tallow candles for our people and our animals.[85]

The hardest moments I witnessed today were the farewells between Ududu and Ulisi Bell and Uduji Asa[86] and Uloghi Barbary. They will take their wagons and my five-year old cousin Osmon and go south into Madison County, Alabama, where they will live with Ududu Francis. They bought a piece of ground to farm and a house already built.[87] Ududu tried again to persuade Asa to come west with us when he could. Asa will live near his Udoda for the time being, without worrying about Cherokee citizenship, like their Udo James up in Kentucky. Maybe later, when things have settled down, Asa will move west to Texas, but not to the Cherokee Nation, he says. They all

---

[85] "Part of Deas' job as disbursing agent was to procure forage for the animals and subsistence rations for the people, including such items as corn meal, flour, bacon, fresh beef and fresh pork. On October 30, 1838, he purchased 12 sacks of corn meal and 15 pounds of tallow candles from T. M. Likens, corn and fodder from R. H. C. Bagby, and 2600 pounds of flour and 30 bushels of corn meal from Sam Rosebrough. The next day on Cane Creek "near Fayetteville," he purchased corn and fodder from Thomas Hines and on November 2, "near Fayetteville" from Henry Cable. And on November 3, "near Fayetteville," he purchased corn and fodder from Logan D. Harvill." from *Treaty Party—Disbursements for Subsistence; Disbursements for Transportation*, Edward Deas Papers, Sequoyah Research Center.

[86] Here Asa and Barbary are named as uncle and aunt, even though they are cousins to David Bell and John Francis Bell. The titles of uncle and aunt are often used loosely without specific reference to generations or specific blood ties in Cherokee and English.

[87] The 1850 Federal Census lists Francis Bell, residing next to Asa and Barbary Bell in Madison County, Alabama. Asa and Barbary have sons Osborne, 17, Uriah, 11, and daughters Sarah, 13, and Victoria, 7. The 1860 Census lists Asa and Barbary (with Osman at age 25 and without Sarrah) in Cherokee County (Rusk) Texas. The marriage of Asa and Barbary was recorded in Madison County on August 5, 1846, according to a descendant, Richard DuPrees of Denton, Texas.

embraced, and the women had tears in their eyes. They have lived near each other for as long as Sarah and I can remember. Life will be different without them.

I don't know why Asa feels as he does. Ududu wants to be Cherokee, but it doesn't matter as much to Asa. My Uji planted a desire to be Cherokee in me before she died. My Udoda gets it from Ududu, too, but Asa is several years younger than Ududu. Sarah says his Uji died soon after Asa was born. Maybe he and Uduji James, who I never met, did not receive the same sense of family ties that we got. That's what Sarah and I think.

October 29, 1838, Elk River to Fayetteville

We continued on a main road through rolling country with low slopes and no creeks to ford, until we reached the Elk River. The Elk, at twelve paces, is the largest river we have forded since the Tennessee. It was easy to cross where the bank had been cut away and hewn logs had been anchored with stakes and rocks in the river.

The town of Fayetteville, County Seat of Lincoln County, lies just ahead of where we camped tonight. We can see some lights in cabins at the edge of town. Lieutenant Deas and Uncle Jack have gone into the town to let the sheriff know about our detachment. They will also secure a burial place for little Muskrat,[88] the two-year-old son of Tooka. He died today of dysentery which had made him sick for several days. He couldn't keep water or milk down. People tried all kinds of teas, to no

---

[88] Duane King, in "The Emigration Route of the John A. Bell Detachment of Treaty Party Cherokees within the State of Arkansas, November 25, 1838 - January 7, 1839," Research Paper, 2001, records the death of twenty-one people during the entire travel of the Bell detachment. No names, ages, or locations of burial are recorded.

avail. His mother Jenny Rat, is ill also, so the family is too worried about her to grieve openly for the boy. He's our first death, but there are many more who are very ill.

We stopped at Gum Springs to refill our water barrels. There the friends of Jenny Rat washed the boy's body and wrapped him in a clean blanket.

People came out and stared at us as we passed their cabins today, just as they usually do. Children pointed at us excitedly and hid behind their mothers' aprons. They have never seen so many people traveling in one group. In our detachment we have more people than live in many of the towns that we pass. I can understand why they might be fearful or suspicious. Many of our people are equally afraid of them. Andro, Will and I just smile and wave. They likely hear wild stories about Indians. Most of us are dressed as they dress, so we don't look much different than they do. The wear and tear, dirt and sweat on our clothes matches the garb of most of the settlers. I don't know whether the uniformed soldiers, who ride with us, make people feel safer or more afraid.

October 30, 1838, West of Fayetteville

The sky was overcast and the air chilly all day today. I couldn't find a place to warm up and stayed wrapped up in a blanket all day. I rode in the carriage with Uloghi Jennie, Andro, and other cousins.

Soon after breaking camp we left the main train and arrived at the burying ground at the edge of Fayetteville. Muskrat's Udoda had dug the grave in a corner where no one else was buried. Tooka laid his little boy, wrapped in a blanket, in the hole. His mother sat nearby, her head bowed, too weak and frail to stand at the grave. Uduji Jack said a few words, so did a couple of elders. Teka-Geeska[89], the oldest man among us, said he expected soon to fly across the Western sea, but Muskrat, being young and small would fly fast and high above him. The wings of his spirit soul would be young and strong. They were on the journey together, both the young and the old, so he could not get lost. This was a new idea to me. My Uji said little about the Western sea that many people seemed to be afraid of. Teka-Geeska spoke as if he looked forward to flying over it.[90] We were quiet together for a time. They shoveled the grave full. We climbed back into our wagons.

We rejoined the main train of wagons. They had nearly finished the crossing of Tim's Ford of Cane Creek in the valley at the west edge of Fayetteville. We went ahead with them through wooded hill country, wondering if the clouds would bring rain on us. The clouds colored darker blue beyond one hill, then another, and turned lighter again. I was glad to stay dry. I was already cold enough. I am still shivering as I write this.

We have one day left in October, and mornings are all frosty now. Warm days will be few and far between from now on. I wonder if I will feel warm again or have a place to lie down and rest. Muskrat does.

October 31, 1838, Boonshill Road

Stone fences lined the dirt roads in this area of neat farms and settlements. Ududu explained to me that farmers have pulled

---

[89] Teka-Geeska, recorded in Don Shadburn, *Cherokee Planters in Georgia, 1832-1838*, page 246, as a property owner in Rabbit Trap Town, downriver from Coosawattee Town, was also recorded as "probably the oldest man now on Earth."

[90] Many different stories about the land of the dead were current among the Cherokee in the early Nineteenth Century. James Mooney describes several in *Myths of the Cherokee*, pp. 253-254, 436-438.

rocks out of the land that they farm and piled them carefully along the edge of the fields to form fences. The fences both mark boundaries and keep pigs and other short animals inside. If a fence gets tall enough it will keep cows in also, but horses and deer will jump over. He said the practice is common in Scotland, according to his Ududa, who came from there. Ududu has seen it himself in New England. At home we often returned animals that wandered away from their owners. I did not know anyone who went to the trouble of building such impressive stone fences.

The roads often twisted and turned as they ran along the ridge tops, or we followed a creek until a good crossing could be made, or we zigzagged through a valley that sometimes was wide and sometimes narrow before another stream entered from its side. Ududu said that the roads often follow trails made by the first tribes who lived on this land. He remembers some of the trails from the days when no white settlers were here. Now the roads run between one settlement and another. Eventually a village will come into view with several cabins or sometimes a few frame houses. So many white people now spread out across all these lands that once belonged to native peoples—the Muskogee Creek, Choctaw, Shawnee, Chickasaw, and many other nations.

The settlers are becoming more numerous all the time. They think that no one ever knew or loved the land before them. They seem to want to live more by themselves than we do. Most of our people live in larger villages, and go out into fields and pastures that surround the towns. If a Cherokee family wants to live away from a settled town, they usually have many family members and servants that come to live with them, needing many houses and buildings. When they finish making rooms for everyone, they have a new village. I hear people making plans for how they will build when they arrive in the West. I do not think they will change much. They will not all stay in one town like Coosawattee Town. Udoda says there will never be another Coosawattee Town.

Only in larger towns do we see small church buildings or schools. We did not see any today, but we did not reach any settlement of more than ten dwellings. I do not think many white people value schooling or worship, compared to the desires of the Cherokee people. I know that some of our people do not care as much as we do about these things. Sarah says she is excited by all of the talk she has heard about building schools and churches in our new nation.

We travelled many miles today, maybe twelve or thirteen. This evening we found good water at Big Spring and refilled our drinking barrels. I wish I could walk like Will and other boys, but six-year-old Andro and I are still riding in the carriage with the children. I feel as tired as I felt when I was able to walk. Frost covered the ground this morning. Then the sun came out and shone warmly today. I almost felt warm again.

November 1, 1838, Friendship Creek

A six-year-old girl I have known since she was a baby died today. Her name was Acorn. I have seen her many times, but we did not spend any time together. I just recognized her from her family. They came to the store at Coosawattee and took part in the Green Corn or other events. She had whooping cough when we began the journey. She never gained any strength afterward, fighting to draw breath every day. I feel sorry for her because I know what that feels like. I have not had such a hard time myself. Even when I have been too weak to walk, I have been able to breathe.

Acorn's family decided not to bury her in a white town cemetery. They found a high place in the woods above Friendship Creek and buried her there. She liked to explore the woods and creeks back home, they said. She would not feel right about leaving her body spirit in a white person's town. Uji taught me that we have one spirit. In that spirit we leave the body when we die. I don't know what to think about the old way of believing, that we have more than one spirit that separate when we die. I like the way they respect Acorn's wishes about where she liked to live. They didn't mark her grave, although they covered it with stones. They didn't want anyone or any animal to bother her. Acorn's Ulisi said that her spirit needed to find her way west, but no one needed to disturb her body and make her come back to haunt them.

Uduji Jack and Udoda were there to help them bury Acorn. I wasn't. They told me what her Uji and her Ulisi said. The whole train stopped during the burial to honor her. We were soon underway again afterward. We followed a road that ran along Friendship Creek most of the day. We came to a ravine near the creek's spring source. Then we climbed the ravine that grew narrow near the end until we came out onto a broader plateau. Soon we descended into another ravine and followed Buchanan Creek until we forded it and set up camp. The County Seat of Pulaski lies ahead of us this evening.

November 2, 1838, West of Pulaski

We passed a toll gate on the way through Pulaski. The road in the wide valley near the town had been improved with a corrugated base of split logs. An iron and wood bridge sat on massive fitted stone pilings at Richland Creek, at the west edge of Pulaski. The company that built the road and the bridge charges a toll for everyone who uses it. Lieutenant Deas paid for

Our Land! Our People!

us. The river was a little wider than most of the creeks we have crossed in recent days. A mill stood at the river nearby also. We resupplied some of the ground wheat and corn we had consumed.

We learned that we are the second detachment that passed through Pulaski. John Benge led a group of 1100 Cherokees through this area two weeks ago, using the same roads that we will follow for a few miles.[91] Benge started out from Will's Valley where Ududu lived.

Udoda and Uduji Jack keep the supply wagons near the middle of the train, so anyone can get whatever kind of grain meal, jerky, bacon or salt pork, lard, salt or soda, potatoes, roots, apples or dried fruit, soap, candles, and tobacco whenever they need it, whenever they are running short. They run it just like the old store, except that it's free to everyone now. The soldiers are always standing nearby, and they help with the distribution. I guess they want to make sure no one tries to get more than they should. If people want something special they can buy it themselves when we are going through a town. Some people use their money to buy whiskey. Most of the folks I know keep their eyes out for vegetables, fruit, or fresh meat instead. The season is now so late that no one has much fresh food for sale.

Seeing my uncle and Dad looking out for what people need reminds me of home and Coosawattee Town. The farther away we get, the more I miss our home there. I think a lot about my Uji. I told this to Udoda. He wants to build a new town, like the old peace towns of the Cherokee where anyone could come and be safe, or like the Bible Salem or Siloam places. That's what

---

[91] The city of Pulaski, Tennessee, memorializes these events. http://www.nicolejordancompany.com/tot_pulaski/bridge.html

he's looking forward to, he said. We have to keep looking forward, not backward, since we cannot go back.

November 3, 1838, Farther West of Pulaski

Something terrible happened today. Last evening we let the oxen graze in a wide glade full of grasses and lots of different broad-leafed plants. Will and I were watching them to make sure they did not wander off. They were eating heartily after a heavy days' pull until Udoda and Uduji Samuel pulled them away to stake them for the night. This morning four of them were grounded and could not stand up. We couldn't make them move because they were very sick. Udoda knew Will and I felt bad about the animals. He let us stay and watch the efforts to help them during the morning. The rest of the wagons moved on down the road. Something that they ate must have poisoned the four. They died one by one in the afternoon. Four dead oxen, including my favorite, Abel.[92] Maybe we made a mistake in naming him Abel. We left their carcasses at the edge of a nearby ravine, far enough away from the nearest cabins. They will provide a lot of food for the vultures and scavengers. We didn't have time to skin them for their hides. They are too large to bury, and no one would benefit. I am sad to lose such good helpers. We will have to find out what plants poisoned them so it doesn't ever happen again. We had to ride horses to catch up with the rest, and Udoda kept his arm around me, riding on his horse. I liked having his arm around me again, like when I was a little boy. It was still hard to keep from crying for the oxen.

---

[92]The record of several dead oxen—"[the Bell detachment] arrived in Memphis on November 22 without incident except that west of Pulaski a number of oxen died from eating poisonous weeds"—comes from *The Promised Land: The Cherokees, Arkansas, and Removal, 1794-1839*, A Historic Context Written and Researched by Charles Russell Logan.

Our Land! Our People!

I wonder why they'd eat something that would poison them. I thought animals knew better than people what they should or shouldn't eat. Something about moving to a new land must make them forget. Maybe they get too tired and just eat because they know they're supposed to. In the old ways, plant spirits helped us by providing everything people needed to stay well or to get well.[93] It just seems wrong that they would turn against the best-natured animals we have.

November 4-5, 1838, North of Lawrenceburg

The frosty fall morning began as usual with David Bell and Jack Bell on their horses winding their way from the front to the back of the train, chewing on jerky and grabbing some pan bread for breakfast, making sure that everyone would be ready to move before the sun reached a full hand into the sky. They found several people dealing with fatigue and illness, including Dr. Eddington, who apologized for needing to stay wrapped in his blankets for the day.

When they reached their own family at the end of the line, they found Red Wolf still in his bedroll, though Will and Andro had packed everything else, including the tent.

"He was tossin' and turnin' and coughin' all night," Will explained. "Has a tetch of fever, too. Mostly I reckon he's still upset about the oxen's dying."

David replied, "There's not a thing we can do to help that. It looks like we'll have to keep him bundled up and haul him in the carriage and hope he feels better." He picked his son up,

---

[93] A well-known Cherokee story has the animals bring diseases to punish people for their destructiveness; the plants decide to help people by providing cures for every disease. James Mooney, *Myths of the Cherokee*, 250-252.

letting the bedroll fall away, and carried him to a place in the grass where he could relieve himself. Then he gave Red Wolf a weak tea and a biscuit and honey that Jenny had prepared, wrapped him again in his bedroll, and propped him up with blankets and cases on the floor of the carriage. The whole time Red Wolf said barely a word, seeming to be in a daze.

He was little better at noon time, taking a little broth and bread, saying he was just tired, continuing his dry cough.

When the train came near Lawrenceburg they followed a route north of the town and north of Shoal Creek as it snaked through the valley that surrounded the town. They avoided ravines and high banks, and they found clearings among the old growth oak and maple woods to set up their series of camps for the night.

Sarah Caroline came back to Jennie's camp at the end of the line to check on Red Wolf and see if he was working on his day log, but he was in his bedroll and his fever was higher in the evening. Will told her that he was "a lot like he was when we was comin' down to see you at Grandpa's place."

"Then we'll all have to take care of him like you did, Will," She answered. Jenny had prepared a warm concoction of herbs for Red Wolf to drink, and Sarah stayed with him for two hands of time until he had drunk all the tea.

"Wado," Red Wolf said weakly, when he had finished.

David went into Lawrenceburg to find a doctor who would be willing to come out and see Red Wolf and the other sick people in their encampment, including Dr. Eddington, but the two doctors he found said they had more than enough work to do already. The most that either was willing to do was prepare some medicinal syrups and salves, and David paid well for those. Red Wolf was asleep when David returned, so he did not try to wake him.

Around the campfire that evening Jack Bell asked what they should do if Dr. Eddington was not able to resume his duties.

"We've been very fortunate to have him," said Samuel. "We're not likely to find a replacement who's as competent or acceptable."

"I'd counted on the good will and compassion of doctors along the route, but I didn't expect the indifference or callousness or fear of infection that I found here. I know earlier groups have und some doctors who were really willing to make extraordinary sacrifices. Obviously we can't count on that"[94]

David replied, "Jack, don't blame yourself. We don't have the power to prepare for everything, and we'll do the best we can with what we have. We're not desperate yet. We may yet find help. Red Wolf managed to survive with just the help of young

---

[94] *Notes from Cherokee Removal*.pdf, from the 1834 contingent on the north side of the Arkansas River from Little Rock, pp.29-31: "In 1834 Harris, leader of a detachment passing through Cadron, recruited a nearby doctor, Dr. Jesse C. Roberts, and he visited the camp to tend to the growing number of sick.

On April 15, a cholera outbreak struck the camp. Dr. Roberts dutifully attended his patients. However, Harris returned April 21 from another search for transportation to find the doctor sick. He summoned a Dr. Mennifee from 15 miles away to care for him, but Dr. Roberts died the next day. Dr. Mennifee gave Harris instructions for ministering to the ill and then left "to look after his own patients." He was relieved by a Dr. Fulton from Little Rock, which allowed Harris to resume his desperate search for transport, but Fulton also fell ill and left the camp. Six teams of oxen and one five-horse team arrived at the camp that day, but word of the death of Dr. Roberts and the extreme sickness of Dr. Fulton caused other teamsters with whom Harris had contracted to return home."

Will the last time he was so sick. If we need to, we'll ask Lieutenant Deas to help secure another doctor."

John Bell reminisced about meeting Lawrenceburg's favorite son, Davy Crockett, who as a Tennessee Congressman had courageously opposed the Indian Removal Act in 1830. Crockett had taken a different path than a well-known Cherokee ally, Sam Houston, but they had both wound up in Texas, where Crockett got himself killed at the Alamo, and Houston had problems with unruly allies in spite of his own strong support for the native people's nations. John asserted that no one could foresee all the twists and turns of politics and human affairs, and his sons agreed.

November 5-8, 1838, Road to Waynesboro

The next days were little different for Red Wolf or for Dr. Eddington. The dreary, slow, bumpy progress of their carriages matched an overcast chilly day, with no sleep within a pile of blankets, just jogging and discomfort. Red Wolf was too weak to do anything except cough and open his eyes to watch the passing scenes part of the time.

The children riding with him in the carriage provided Red Wolf's only diversions. Andro brought him water and tea when they stopped to rest. Maria and Charlotte busied themselves with arranging his blankets or pillows, or holding his head in their laps, until Jennie saw that they were not really helping and told them to sit with her.

They rode along a plateau, avoiding ravines and copses of pine and hardwoods, following the edge of a prairie that showed occasional ploughed and fenced patches near homesteads. Finally they began a slow descent into a major valley through a pine forest, following the north side of a creek until they came within sight of the town of Waynesboro.

A light rain began as they were setting up camp on the 8th, adding to the chill of the evening. Under the canvass and wrapped in blankets, Red Wolf broke into a sweat sometime after midnight, and Will helped him dry off, rearrange the blankets to be dry and warm, and return to sleep.

November 9, 1838, Waynesboro to Flat Gap

I feel littl better today so I tri to rit. I lern that Sarah is sick too with sumthing. I ask Dad am I going to die. He says yes but not today. Not toomorow either. He needs my help. He makes me laff. I feel so bad some days I don't care. I wont show this page to Sarah. She wood scold me.

November 10, 1838, Indian Creek to Savannah

I sat propt up in the caraj flor today so I can see wear we ar goin. We keep crosing criks yestarday and today. See tall rok walls and cavs like at hom. Up and down hills. Bak and fourth arownd obstackls. If this is a strait way to go west I wunder wat a cruked way looks like. I feel soree four anywun who must take it.

Crossd Indian Crik abowt twelv paces wiid. Wiit pepal must nam it. We wood nam it equoni[95] sumthin. Whi nam it Indian wen no Indian can liv heer? Wen we must go far awaa. We leev lots of Indian nams heer but no Indians.

November 11-12, 1838, Tennessee River Ferry

After spending the night at the west edge of the town of Savannah the detachment roused early on November 9th to

---

[95] Equoni, Cherokee word for river.

descend to the Tennessee River ferry landing. Heavy fog delayed the ferry crossing until the sun began to burn through the fog. The river was much broader here. People were amazed to see the opposite banks so far away on the other side. Once people had crossed the river, they had to proceed through the mud flats a couple of miles to the hills on the west side of the river where they could make camp and wait for the rest to finish the crossing. While waiting many of the women and household slaves took advantage of the time to wash clothing and blankets. Those who were ill, including Red Wolf and Sarah, all well-bundled in their heaviest clothing and blankets, spent the day napping and watching the slow ferrying progress. Dr. Eddington rented a room at a Savannah inn, counting on two days and nights of rest to complete his recovery. Grandpa Bell supervised work on some of the wagons that were showing the strain of travel, replacing some wheels and axles, and putting his slaves to work in blacksmithing as he had trained them.

Deas and Jack took a group of men into Savannah to replenish their supplies, especially of corn and fodder for the animals. Most of the soldiers, David, and Samuel were busy helping the loading and unloading at the ferry. All of the people watched the dark clouds forming and dropping water to the west, fearing that heavy rains and flooding would overcome the detachment as they were trying to cross the big river, but the rains moved northward steadily even as the clouds formed and reformed during the day on the western horizon, and they did not interrupt the crossing progress.

About two thirds of the detachment finished the crossing when the ferry shut down for the night at dusk. Some of the young men, having taken advantage of the waiting time also to resupply their stocks of whisky, continued drinking around a campfire into the night, and making noise, until some of the mothers complained that they were keeping them and their children awake.

November 13, 1838, Stage Road to Purdy

The ferry crossings finished at midday, in spite of the sluggish awakening of some of the young men who had gotten drunk the previous night. Jennie's carriage and the children, Grandpa Bell's carryall and freight wagons, and a small herd of mostly dairy cows, with three others purchased by Jack at Savannah, were near the rear of the detachment. Dr. Eddington was the last to cross, saying he was feeling much better and ready to resume his duties. The entire train was again making progress on the stage road toward the McNairy county seat town of Purdy. Riding ahead of the train Deas and three soldiers reached Purdy and were able to locate and buy more corn and fodder for the supply wagons. He rode back to the encampment at Snake Creek and reported to Jack in the evening that he believed they were in pretty good shape for the next three weeks.

In spite of the last day's efforts to maintain wagons, one broke down in the late afternoon on the rocks at the Snake Creek ford. Word was passed down the train to Grandpa Bell at the rear. He and his crew hastened forward to begin work, but they had to work late into the night to finish the repair. Grandma Charlotte didn't get much rest either that night, as she was already tired from treating her children, Sarah and James, and several of the slaves for the grippe,[96] and she began to show cold symptoms herself as she watched over Grandpa at his work. Most of the young people were showing marked improvement, so she took to her own bed with that consolation.

---

[96] The grippe was used loosely to indicate influenza, a serious cold or other respiratory infection or catarrh.

November 14, 1838, Purdy and Bethel Springs

When the wagon train arrived at Purdy late morning on November 11, Lieutenant Deas and his men picked up the additional supplies. Thick woods provided shelter from a brisk wind that kept the treetops waving. Grandpa Bell made arrangements to stay at a local inn for Charlotte and himself and a few servants until she was well enough to continue the journey. Sarah persuaded him to let her stay also to help care for her mother, but James stayed with the train.

The rest of the train moved on to Twin Springs, where they stopped for a noon meal, watered the livestock and refilled water barrels. They made camp in the evening at Bethel Springs, where good water was available also.

November 15-16, 1838, Hatchie River to Bolivar

On two clear sunny cool days the line of wagons, walkers and riders, and small herds of livestock stretched out over three miles through sandy flats, pine forests, rolling hills, crossed two creeks, and entered a flat plain. Grandma and Grandpa Bell, along with Sarah and their servants, caught up with the tail of the detachment at midday on the 13th, much to the relief of Jennie, James, Red Wolf and the rest. Grandpa announced plans to seek inside accommodations again at the next town of Bolivar. Wrapped in her blankets but sitting upright on her carryall seat Grandma Charlotte was still suffering from the grippe, but she told everyone that she was much better.

As they reached a walnut grove and looked down the slope into the valley, they saw the Hatchie River, twelve paces wide. Beyond the river there stretched two miles of mud flats, recently flooded by a severe rainstorm. The river level had begun to subside, but the water had broken some of the anchors for the bridges across the river and the mud flats. We still had to pay the tolls to cross them. The corduroy road that ran from bridge to bridge through the mud flats had also washed away in places. Jack and Deas decided that they would have to double team every wagon with oxen to pull them slowly through the muck. They would have to take their time in order to do the least damage to their wagons and equipment. Up to ten oxen or twenty horses were needed for the heaviest Conestogas. To lighten the load, they dumped what was left in the water barrels as the wagons approached the river.

The lighter carriages, carryalls, and buckboards went first, with the sick among them, so they would be able to set up camp before nightfall on the far side of Bolivar. With the extra teams they passed through the mud flats with few getting stuck, climbed the short hill and found themselves passing a pretty two-story white clapboard federal-style building that served as the Hardeman County courthouse. Many people noticed that the building looked just like the buildings at New Echota.

Just forty paces beyond the courthouse, also on the north side of the street, sat a similar building with a bell atop, marked as the Presbyterian Church. Grandpa Bell stopped and knocked on the door of the house next door to the church, expecting it to be the manse, which it was. The pastor answered, and when Grandpa Bell explained his need for directions to an inn for his sick wife and some others who were even sicker among the detachment, the pastor invited them to stay in his house and the church, saying that he and his wife would be pleased to have them as guests, and they could provide better accommodations than the inns of the town. He explained that he was a supporter of the American Board missions and their missionaries among the Cherokee, and he would be honored to be able to help. By the time all of those who were in need of some shelter and care were counted, the pastor enlisted the aid of several other local families to provide space for that night and the next. Grandma Charlotte and Sarah Caroline stayed overnight in the manse. James, Red Wolf, and Will slept with several others in their bedrolls on the wooden pews and floor of the church, while the pot-bellied stove in the center of the room provided more comforting warmth overnight than they had felt in weeks.

The men struggled to begin the process of moving the heavier vehicles through the mud, and by sunset only a dozen had made it to the top of the hill and the encampment at the west edge of Bolivar. They spent all of the next day, November 14, pulling the remainder of the train through the Hatchie bottoms.

Sitting at the campfire that evening Jack said, "We've been extra lucky so far. We've had dry weather on our side and managed to get through these areas where we could have gotten trapped."

Deas agreed. "I can't help but think of the Mississippi bottoms, which could be twenty-times as hard and long to get through. We lost weeks when I let the Creek detachment travel through there two years ago, and people suffered terribly in the swamps." [97]

---

[97] "Deas party, which numbered 2,320 when it left Alabama, set out from Memphis on November 5, 1836, intending to split as had the earlier groups. A sizable group of Creeks refused to board the boats, choosing instead to follow the horse herd along the Memphis to Little Rock Road under the leadership of a conductor whom Deas appointed. The water-borne party waited at Rock Roe, but only a portion of the overland party arrived with the conductor. After waiting two weeks, Deas set back toward Strong's place on the St. Francis River to round up the stragglers. He found 300-400 starving, stranded Creeks…scattered along the route and arranged for their escort to join the rest of his band. Deas' main group arrived opposite Little Rock on November 27 and stayed there until December 9, allowing most of the stragglers to rejoin them. After moving three miles, he learned that another large group was still a few days behind him, so he again encamped until December 17. The Deas party finally arrived at Fort Gibson on January 23, 1837. His was the last

Our Land! Our People!

"Then what alternative do we have? What are you willing to do with the remaining funds that we have for transport?"

"I should have done it then, as I did earlier this summer. The best thing I can see, is to load up the heavy gear, everything we won't need on the remaining trip, everything you need when you start rebuilding, put it on flatboats at Memphis, and send it downriver to the mouth of White River, then up the Arkansas to Little Rock, maybe Cadron, or farther if we can, and meet it there, while we take our lighter wagons and livestock onto the Military Road across the river. If we find the road is impassable, we'll have to put everyone and everything on board whatever vessels we can hire."

"I doubt that will be necessary, but I'm glad to relieve ourselves of the heavier cargo. I think we'll make much better time, and be able to travel easier. Maybe we can give some of our sick people the attention and help that they need, if we're not so pressed to get everything else done."

"So we are agreed that we will spend what we need from the government allotment to hire flatboats for the extra cargo?"

"We are agreed, and I am grateful," answered Jack.

November 17, 1838, Following Ridgetops

Staying in Bolivar felt more like being at home than any place we've been so far. I've never slept in a chapel before, but we

---

major Creek removal party to travel the Memphis to Little Rock Road." From the Arkansas Historic Preservation Program research paper on "Memphis to Little Rock Road—Village Creek State Park, Newcastle Vicinity, Cross Country," citing *The Arkansas Gazette*, December 19, 1837, and Grant Foreman, *Indian Removal: The Emigration of the Five Civilized Tribes of Indians* (Norman, OK: University of Oklahoma Press, 1972), 213-214.

were inside and warm, in buildings that had a lot of room, not just shacks like we had at Fort Cass. Uloghi Jennie, Sarah, and Ulisi stayed at the preacher's house. They said they were treated like guests of the family. We all felt better in the morning. Then word came that one family lost a baby last night, and they had a hasty burial in the town cemetery. We all felt sad for them, even when we were happy to find friends and lodging here.

The preacher brought fried eggs and griddle cakes to us on the porch of his house. We ate well before we returned to the trail. We crossed one small creek mid-morning west of Bolivar, climbed to a gently rolling plateau, and followed a ridge top road most of the day. Travel was easy. We went more miles than usual, maybe eighteen. I still rode in the carriage all day. I will be glad to be able to walk with the boys again.

The best thing today was Sarah telling me that she would work with me on the journal if I felt like it. She helped me correct my spelling and grammar as usual. I am just printing. I cannot write or read writing. We have begun to work with numbers, so I will be able to add. That will be more useful to learn, Sarah says.

November 18, 1838, Clear Creek to Loosahatchie

I watched a killdeer run in front of the carriage today. The bird did its usual zigzag run as if it was trying to take us away from its nestlings, but this is not the season for that. I guess it was just practicing as our wagon train came through. It had to be tired when we all finally moved beyond its territory.

Every bird has its nest. Every fox has its den, but we have no place to lay our heads. So I heard Reverend Bushyhead say a long time ago, quoting Jesus he said. I often think about him and George Candy and his family with him, traveling far to the north of us in a land that is much colder than here. On many days a colder land seems impossible to me. None of us have a place of our own yet, but we are dreaming about it, wondering what it will look like and when we will reach it.

Ududu, Udiji Jack, and Udoda remind me that they have been to the land where we are going. We already have family there who are preparing places for us to stay during the winter ahead. If they didn't tell me this, I would be so afraid and so tired of traveling that I would just give up and curl up alongside the road, where that killdeer has its nest.

Clear Creek was easy to cross. The mud flats on the west side of it caused some problems. Tonight we made camp at the edge of the valley of the Loosahatchie River. The valley is about a mile wide, and the river about eight paces, Uduji Jack says. We are at the edge of Fayette County, and we will see the County Seat, Somerville, tomorrow.

November 19, 1838, Somerville to Bell Grove

Sarah taught me how to shape the numbers up to 100. I worked on them throughout the day as we rode the carryall with Ududu and Ulisi. I feel less like a child when I am with them instead of with Uloghi Jennie and her girls. Sarah showed me how to put the numbers in a column so that I can add them together. I remember how the older students at Candy Creek School were working with numbers like this.

A people with the name of Bell were here before us. When we arrived at an oak grove we found a road through the grove had the name of Bell. I can still dream that it belongs to us, as we camp here for the night.

November 20, 1838, Bell Grove to Wolf River

Today as we rode in the carryall Sarah helped me memorize the sums of added numbers. We crossed four creeks. Cypress Creek was the largest, only five paces wide, and we forded all of them easily without any big problems. I am tired. We did enough thinking today. 4+4 is 8. 5+5 is 10. 6+6 is 12. 7+7 is 14. 8+8 is 16. 9+9 is 18. 10+10 is 20. And so on.

We refilled our water barrels at Walker Springs. We traveled a stage road alongside a large river that shares my name and clan, Ani wahya. The Wolf River spans more than ten paces and runs deep in many places. We are nearing the town of Memphis on the Mississippi River. I am eager to see the Udoda Equoni. Many people live in this area because the river remains open all year and people are able to come up and down the river all the time.

I have never seen so many cabins and settlements. We made lists of objects that we saw along the route, counting how many of every kind—dogs, cows, carriages, wagons, horses, people, frame houses, log houses—and added numbers in our heads and also on paper. I needed all the new numbers I had learned to do the adding. When we saw a flock of passenger pigeons I didn't even try to count. There were so many that they appeared to be a large dark storm cloud that filled the sky. I would need a lot more number names if I tried to count them, but that would be impossible anyway.

November 21, 1838, Memphis on Mississippi

We crossed the Wolf River on a wooden bridge built out of large hewn logs and wide boards. The bridge felt sturdy when we crossed, hardly shaking at all, although we took one wagon across it at a time.

Then we saw it, the Father-water, Udoda Equoni. The river is huge beyond my dreams—broad, deep and dark, as if it carries blood and sap and all the juices of life squeezed from the land into its water. Even at the beginning of winter, the plants and trees along its banks are lush and full of a multitude of hues of green and brown, accented with every other color. Lieutenant Deas rode ahead and made the deal for a flatboat to carry all of our supplies and equipment not needed for overland travel. We spent much of the day sorting through our belongings, separating what was needed for the road from what we could send downriver, and repacking, then loading the freight boxes onto the flatboat.

Lieutenant Deas also bought and gave out new shoes and blankets for many of the poor families who needed them. He restocked the supply of soap that was running low. People had time to do the washing of a lot of clothes as well as bodies.

Some of our people did not want to let go of any of their belongings. They were afraid of the flatboat running aground, capsizing, or sinking, and they would lose everything they put on board. After much talking most people were able to let go of a good many things.

This will make the last miles of long haul easier. The boat will go downriver to the mouth of the Arkansas River at Rock Row, up that river, and meet us again beyond Little Rock. Lieutenant Deas has gone across the river with Uduji Jack to check out the condition of the road through the swamp on the other side. If the road is as dry and solid as they expect, we will cross the river tomorrow and continue overland toward Little Rock. Otherwise we would have to hire more boats to take us along the same route that our extra gear goes. We are waiting at campfires next to the river for them to return with their report, and the sun is down. The night is clear and the moon is shining brightly onto the river.

A few of our richer people have found lodging in the inns near the Memphis riverfront, and some of our sick are staying inside tonight also. Will says he will keep our fire going all night with the driftwood and coal we found along the riverbank this afternoon.

November 22, 1838, Memphis on Mississippi

The first wagons boarded the ferry shortly after dawn this morning. Even though the ferry is larger than the ferries we used before, the river is much broader, so barely half of our people were able to make the crossing today. The west bank of the river has little space for camping, so most of those who crossed have moved on down the road. Udoda tells us that the Military Road across the bottomlands has been built up with rock and clay and is in good condition if we do not have heavy rains while we are here. Our wagons will stretch out along the road day and night, with marshlands or lagoons on either side, until we reach the ferry at Blackfish Lake. We can't see any hills in the distance to the west. Our travel may take three days to reach higher ground.

We gathered more fuel. The night is clear but cold. Again we will stay near the fire. We'll see if we can cross the big river tomorrow. We watched a pair of eagles fishing in the river today.

November 23, 1838, Memphis

Only a few wagons remain on this side of the river, so we will finish the ferry crossings tomorrow. The steam ferry broke down today for a few hours, or we would be finished crossing. We watched the last of the cattle make the crossing today. They required even more persuasion at this crossing than they did at the Tennessee. Many local people have come down to watch. Having such a large group of Indians crossing the river near the center of the town must be a curiosity to many of the locals. I heard that the Choctaws crossed south of Memphis at the mouth of the Cypress Creek.

One fancy dressed woman approached Will, Andro, and me as we were sitting on some crates watching the loading of the ferry. She wanted to know where our parents were, so we pointed out our fathers where they were working at the ferry. She was surprised and said we didn't look like Indians. "What are we supposed to look like?" I asked her. "Different" was all she said before she hurried away. Sarah says that happened to her too.

November 24, 1838, West Bank, Mississippi

We were all across the river by noon today. If it weren't for the strong current in some parts of the river, it felt more like boating in a large lake than crossing a river. The wind across the water made steering hard. The road followed the river bank north for a little way before it branched west into the swamps. We have stopped for the night on the road in the swamps. The skies are cloudy now, and we are hoping we won't have rain, or if it does rain, we won't have much.

We are a small group now, separated by miles from those who crossed ahead of us. I am riding with Ududu and Ulisi and Sarah in their carryall at the end of the train now. Will and his parents are riding a buckboard behind us. I was sad to learn today that we have left a total of seventeen people at the side of the trail.[98] I have seen the burial of just two. I was not aware of everyone who died. Ten full bloods, three Africans, and four half-bloods, the very young and the very old and people in between, rich and poor alike have died. Every kind of person with us has made a sacrifice of at least one life to the journey that we are making. Many are still carrying sickness with them, and the worst months of winter are ahead of us. We are about half way and everyone says they wish we were there.

November 25, 1838, the Middle of the Swamps

The rain that fell last night was light, just enough to keep us in tents and to put out our fires, so the air was damp, cold and miserable for sleeping. We had to crowd together to take advantage of each others' warmth.

We pass many ponds and marshes, and the way would be impassable by wagons without the road that the military has built.[99] I have seen huge flocks of geese, ducks, gulls, and smaller birds, as well as scores of herons, pelicans, egrets, and cranes. The road remains sound, about eight paces across, with just enough room for wagon traffic in both directions, although I am

---

[98] Deas correspondence noted the purchase of 17 coffins at this point in the journey. Duane King assembled Deas's expense vouchers from the National Archives in *Report on Recent Research Regarding the Cherokee Removal*, 17 April 1996; National Park Service, Trail of Tears National Historic Trail -- Map Supplement, Maps 222-247.

[99] Lt. Frederick L. Griffth was appointed superintendent of the Memphis to Little Rock Road on January 27, 1826, with instructions to make a road "at least twenty four feet wide throughout" with all timber and brush removed and stumps cut as low as possible, marshes and swamps to be "causewayed with poles or split timber," and ditches four feet wide and three feet deep to be dug on either side of the road. "The hills on the route are to be dug down and wound round in such a manner as to make them practicable for carriages or loaded wagons," Griffith was instructed. From *The Arkansas Historic Preservation Program*, Online, "Memphis to Little Rock Road," citing Clarence E. Carter, comp. and ed., *Territorial Papers of the United States, XIX, Arkansas Territory, 1825-1829* (Washington, D.C., 1954), 187-88.

glad that we met only two wagons today. The ditches along the road are full of water. If we ever went off the road it would take a lot of work to pull a wagon out of the muck and get back on.

All the way along the road, the marshes are full of willow, cypress, and box elder, and many other scrub trees that I cannot name. Muskrats build dens that look like small domed huts except that they are in the middle of the water. Sometimes we see where beavers have been busy as well. The whole land appears to be a hunter's and trapper's paradise.

November 26, 1838, West of Memphis

By this evening I could finally see the ridge at the far west horizon if I stood on the wagon seat. Grandpa thinks we will reach Blackfish Lake by tomorrow evening, and then take another ferry across to the ruins of the ancient town, that the people called Casqui,[100] where we will reassemble with the rest of our detachment by the next evening. Then, if the weather holds, on the next day we will have yet another ferry crossing to the far side of the St Francis River.

The sky is still threatening rain, so we will spend another damp and chilly night.

November 27, 1838, Blackfish Lake

The military road ends abruptly where the swamp is deepest. This place is called Blackfish Lake. It is not a clean lake of fresh water, like we see in the mountains. Instead the water is still and dark, too deep in many places for trees to grow in it, so I would call it Black Water Lake, since we cannot see any fish to be called black fish. As the Mississippi is a solid brown with the juices of

---

[100] This ancient Mississippian center is now Parkin Archaeological State Park.

life, the water here is black with decaying leaves. Most of the people have already taken their wagons across the lake, maybe 400 paces wide, but I cannot see where they are because of the islands of trees and shrubs between us. I will be glad to have this lake behind us. I am frightened to think of what monsters could hide in its waters. We have many old stories that tell of large scaly creatures that are part serpent and part winged beast, even though Sarah tries to reassure me that such creatures do not really exist.

November 28, 1838, Casqui

A man named Ferguson ran the ferry for us to cross Blackfish Lake. I do not envy him the job of living and working there, but we made the crossing today without any troubles.[101]

We are all together again at last, all six hundred fifty of us, staying in the ruins of an ancient city that reminds us of the ruins at Etowah, just south of Coosawattee. We have travelled over four hundred miles, according to Ududu, and we find a place that reminds us of home. We all find comfort in that. He said that some of our ancestors may have lived here, or people like them. They built a two-level temple and palace mound, surrounded their village with a moat and a palisade, played stickball or chunkey in a large central plaza, and grew corn, beans and squash in the fields nearby.

Somewhere nearby are the graves of the ancient ones who lived here. We must honor them and pray while we are here. The land ahead cannot be strange to us, if our ancestors lived here before us. Their graves still make this holy ground.

---

[101] According to Duane King's research, Deas' vouchers show that the party crossed Blackfish Lake on November 28, when he paid H.N. Ferguson to ferry the Cherokees.

Few signs remain of the houses and palisade that stood here, and the fields are all overgrown now. Anyone can see this was a fine dry plateau in the middle of a land full of life and water. I wonder what kind of skin unguent they used to keep the mosquitoes away. At least the cold weather keeps them away from us now.

November 28, 1838, William Strong Visits

William Strong had become a leader in developing this section of the military road and wanted to make a living from the traffic along it. Looking out from the veranda of his four story home prominent in the bluffs eight miles to the west, he saw the smoke from many campfires at the Casqui site, He trotted his horse down the road to see what was happening. Crossing the St. Francis River on his ferry he could already see hundreds of people camped with their wagons among the ruins around the mound, gathered around their campfires, and conducting the business of a temporary encampment. To one side near the road a small group of soldiers had also set up camp and in their midst he recognized his old acquaintance Lt. Edward Deas.

Strong immediately approached Deas. "Hello, Lieutenant. I didn't expect to see you back on this road after your experience the last time, but I'm mighty glad to see you."

"William Strong, looking healthy and prosperous, I must say. We have been favored with a dry season quite unlike our earlier trials here. The road shows the benefits of much labor and a favorable season. We are glad to make use of it."

"I had heard the last trip you made was mostly by the river route, but I think you will find the road is in much better condition now and offers you many advantages," Strong replied.

"Indeed, it already has. We are hopeful that the segment from here to Little Rock will live up to the years of investment you and the government have put into it."

Strong brightened at these encouraging words, smiled broadly, and adjusted his hold on the belt that encompassed his broad girth. "I am confident that the road will live up to the potential that we have predicted for it. The land route will open up the entire southwest to settlement. Not only will Indians find it a boon. I foresee many settlers finding it useful for years and years to come, but let me take care of first things first, how can I be of use to you? I suppose that you will need the services of my ferry tomorrow or the next day. For such a large number I can certainly offer you a reasonable fee arrangement."

Deas nodded his assent.

"Perhaps I can also provide from my stores some of the necessities of travel that you will need over the next few weeks. I have an abundant supply, and until you reach Little Rock, you won't find anything comparable in quantity or quality."

"We would be interested. We resupplied before we crossed the river, but we also have some extra space since we sent our excess baggage by boat downriver. What do you have available?"

"Lots of cornmeal and beef, plenty of feed corn and fodder. A good stock of liquor and several fine rooms at my inn if your ladies would like to enjoy some comforts after their harrowing days and nights crossing the swamps."

Meanwhile Jack, his assistants, Ellis Harlin and Luther Rankin, David, and Samuel arrived to listen to the conversation between Deas and Strong. Strong recognized Jack and asked about their father, who had stopped by the inn in leaner times. Jack, hearing the last comments about liquor and staying at the inn, told Strong that he would be doing them and himself a favor if he locked up his liquor supply, but that the offer of hospitality at the inn would be appreciated, especially by the older and ill women who had been trying to recover from cold and exhaustion.

Deas and Strong then commenced to haggle over prices, and they arrived at a purchase of up to a ton of cured and salted beef at 4 ½ cents per pound, fifty bushels of cornmeal at a dollar per bushel, fifty-nine bushels of shelled corn at a dollar per bushel, and a thousand bundles of fodder at four dollars per hundred.[102] They would pay according to what was actually available at loading and what they could load and carry when they passed the storage buildings ten miles up the road on the bluff near Strong's inn and home. Deas and Strong shook hands on the agreement, and the other men joined in shaking hands before Strong took his leave. The rest of the men returned to their tasks for the evening distribution of food and fodder.

November 29, 1838, Strong's Ferry

Ududu and Ulisi, Uloghi Jennie and my little cousins were among the first to cross the ferry this morning. Ulisi and Jennie planned to spend the night at the inn tonight, along with several other women who were chosen because they needed a roof and

---

[102] Duane King discovered these vouchers in the National Archives: Four vouchers show that the party purchased supplies from William Strong. Voucher #98 shows that on November 29 & 30, Strong ferried 650 Cherokees across the St. Francis River. Voucher #34 shows that on November 30, 1838, Deas purchased 50.5 bushels of cornmeal at $1 per bushel and 1,776 pounds of beef at 4 ½ cents per pound for a total of $130.42. Voucher #99, also dated November 30, shows Strong sold Deas 59 bushels of corn at $1 per bushel and 1,016 bundles of fodder at $4 per hundred bundles for a total of $99.64. Each of these vouchers was paid off on December 2.

a stove instead of a tent and the cold for another night. Sarah and I worry about Ulis. She looks more tired and frail every day, and Jennie, too, has been suffering from the cold and trying to care for her little children. They will probably be able stay two or three nights until all the people and wagons have ferried the river and made it to high ground.

Strong's ferry is small, hard to load, taking as long to cross as some of the bigger rivers we have crossed. I was afraid the cables would snap under the load, or wagons would dump into the river. The ferry platform tipped and swayed, but no accidents happened.

I will wait to ride with Will and his parents, Ezekiel and Demaris, at the end of the line tomorrow. Maybe Will and I will walk part of the way again. I am feeling better.

November 30, 1838, St Francis River to Inn

Sarah reminded me that my middle name is Francis, so the river we crossed and I have something in common. I am glad to leave it and the little ferry behind. Today was a good day, clear and cool. Will and I enjoyed walking part of the way. We were able to watch the small animals and birds at play in the waters of the marshes along the road. We even tried to fish for a while, but we didn't catch anything worth fixing for supper, except some bullfrogs. We saw an old water line on the tree trunks of cottonwood trees that showed that floods reach up to six feet in most of the land we were crossing. That would be about three feet above the road we are travelling. I am glad we come through here in a dry season.

We are camped in the clearing surrounding Strong's four story inn. I haven't seen anything like it on the journey. Strong says it is the biggest building in the new state of Arkansas, and I believe him.[103] A porch surrounds the whole building, and it has four large rooms off a central hall on the main floor. Many more rooms are upstairs, most of which are filled with beds ready for travelers. There is a fourth floor balcony, looking out over the whole Mississippi bottomlands. I was told that people can see all the way to Memphis from there.

Dr. Eddington occupied a room in the inn himself. He visited with everyone who is ill and made arrangements for several to stay in the inn. That included many of the women, so men who were ill mostly stayed in the outbuildings or their own tents. He listened to my chest through his bell scope, but he didn't say much. He gave me a spoonful of brandy for my cough, which burned all the way down, and I didn't like the taste of it. Later I saw him deliver a whole gallon jug of brandy to Uduji Jack for those who are having cough and breathing troubles.[104] As far as I'm concerned other people can use it if they want. I don't think it helped me any.

Sarah is staying outside with her sisters, Charlotte and Martha Jane, and her brothers. Tonight she helped Will to shape the syllable signs as well as me with my journal. Some people are against Negroes learning to read, but Sarah is like my mother was. She believes everyone should be able to learn as much as

---

[103] Strong established a home at the eastern base of Crowley's Ridge in 1827, constructing a house that was "four stories high, contained twenty rooms, with a veranda extending entirely around it, supported by red cedar posts, eight inches in diameter.... It was the largest and most costly of any structure in the State at that time." The pioneer obviously planned to profit from the traffic that would traverse the only road between the territorial capital at Little Rock and Memphis. The Arkansas Historic Preservation Program, ibid.

[104] An unnumbered voucher dated December 1, 1838, reads: "Recd of Dr Eddington Four dollars for 1 gallon of French Brandy for the Cherokee Emigration." *The Promised Land: The Cherokees, Arkansas, and Removal, 1794-1839*, by Charles Russell Logan (Arkansas Historic Preservation Program, Little Rock, AR)

they can and want to learn. After we build new homes in the new Cherokee lands, we will be building many schools. Sarah will be a good teacher.

December 1, 1838, Crowley's Ridge

When we left Strong's Inn this morning we followed the Military Road up a gradual incline to Crowley's Ridge, which is the top of the bluffs along the river valley. We followed the ridge through wooded and hilly areas for several miles. The road stayed level, turning a little left and right, but not going up and down the steep ravines.

Not long after we reached the top of the bluff a doe and her fawn walked through the woods alongside the wagon train, about ten paces from the road. She kept walking alongside for at least two hands of time. Some wanted to shoot her, but my Udoda told them we had enough meat, and her sense of safety with us was a good sign. Many of our people are Deer Clan. We can take their presence as a sign that helping spirits are with us on our journey. That reminded me of seeing the red wolf on the way to Ududu's place, when I was feeling lost and weak. We feel blessed to have spirit helpers with us. It seems to be a rare and special event.

When the road turned west away from the bluff, the land became flat again. The trees changed from bare-of-leaf maples and brown-leafed oaks to pine woods bordering grass and marsh lands. In this flat area the road goes straight as an arrow. We can see all of the wagons stretched ahead of us for more than a mile. We didn't go far today, before we set up camp. Those who stayed in the inn a second night will be able to catch up with us tomorrow.

December 2, 1838, Flat Land, Straight Roads

What I noticed today was the changing colors of the soils in the land along the road. All the way from home in Georgia through Alabama and Tennessee, the soil is red. In the Mississippi bottomland and the swamps along the river, everything is black and mucky with decaying plants. After we reached the bluffs and moved west into the flatlands of Arkansas, the soil is sandy and light brown, covered with grasses and shrubs, but along the road light and silty, nearly free of rocks. No farms or settlements have shown up yet. I wonder what it would be like to try to grow anything here. The dirt along the tracks in the road is soft and powdery. It looks like it would blow away. Still we find plenty of grass for grazing here, and the oxen and horses are enjoying it. We didn't use any of the fodder in the supply wagons tonight. Rain must be enough to make everything green, unlike the dry and cold parts of Tennessee. We can find plenty of firewood in the frequent stands of trees.

After we set up camp, the women who stayed at the inn, and the men who waited with them, caught up with us. They traveled lightly and moved fast in the carriages and carryalls. Both Ulisi Charlotte and Uloghi Jennie say they feel better.

December 3, 1838, More Wetlands

The land is still flat with no hills or valleys. Even though the road is mostly straight, we ran into boggy areas today, too wet to camp in or build in. Midday the road began to turn southwest, in order to follow the river that runs just west of us here. Here in Arkansas they call a river a bayou. I don't know why.

We crossed a couple of streams today, on log bridges covered with boards to make our crossing easy. The road builders carried enough rock and clay from somewhere to build the roadbed a couple of feet above the level of the bogs. Where they've done this we will not get stuck. Gray clouds have been gathering all day. Some people said we might have snow. The air is definitely colder, so we wrapped up in blankets.

As soon as we found a clearing that was dry we made camp for the night. The bayou (river) runs about two miles west of us, but the forests are thick, blocking us from seeing it.

December 4, 1838, Camping in Cold Rain

It didn't snow. We did have a cold rain most of the day. Not knowing if we would find as good a campsite farther south, Uduji Jack and Deas decided to stay another day here. We left the tents up, but many people were cold, damp, and miserable inside. When we had a break in the rain during the day, we tried to get out and keep busy to get warm. We had to work to gather wood dry enough for fires and to keep the fires going in the rain. Uduji Samuel showed Will and me some tricks in finding wood that was dry and setting up a lean-to so that we could keep a fire going. He told us that we have to be able to take care of ourselves in order to stay alive in cold and wet weather, especially if we have a bad winter and no places to stay when we reach our land. I did not like feeling miserable today. I don't want to face a long winter that's like this or even colder.

December 5, 1838, John Cotton's Settlement

We broke camp mid-morning, after the sun had come out enough to begin to dry the tents before we rolled them up and started moving down the road. We reached John Cotton's settlement by noon. It was just a few cabins, small barns, and out-buildings. Deas bought some more grain and fodder from him,[105] not because we need it right now. He said he wanted to encourage a man who doesn't get enough business. Also we will need as much as we can get for later in the winter. All of our animals had plenty of fresh water to drink yesterday. They enjoyed dry food today as much as we did.

Cooking in the rain was not easy yesterday. We used the old method of heating rocks in whatever kinds of fires we could keep going, and dumping the hot rocks inside our cooking pots to heat our stew. You can taste the ash and rock flavor in the food.

December 6, 1838, Heading South

We travelled ten more miles today, heading south through mostly unsettled territory. We still see bogs and marshes along the road, even though the bayou is not far to the west. We don't feel like we make much progress. We just head to a place where a ferry will take us across a larger bayou. We don't have many choices of where to cross rivers in this area. We don't want to get stuck in the mud or have to build our own rafts to take us across.

We did see lots of big red-tailed hawks. They were out hunting over the marshes to find mice and rats. We went looking for muskrats or anything with fur. We caught two rabbits, and added their meat to the stewpot for supper, and scraped their hides for tanning. We hope to sew them into mittens later.

Ududu and his workers have been working hard to repair wheels and axles. They often have to stop with someone who is having trouble and then catch up with the train late in the

---

[105] The next vouchers, dated December 5 and 6, were made out to John Cotton, who lived near modern-day Brinkley south of what is now Henard Cemetery Road.

evening. He said tonight that some of our old wagons are just not going to make it all the way.

December 7, 1838, Clarendon on White River

We finally saw the Cache Bayou that has been hiding in the trees west of us. This evening we reached a settlement on the White River called Clarendon where a ferry will take us across. We camped near the river front, in view of the steamboat-ferry. The White River is more than a hundred paces across here, wider than I expected. Grandpa says the swamp on the other side is much wider, filled with channels and islands. We will take as much time crossing here as we did the Mississippi, but this is the last large river we will cross.

Nobody likes the cold, even though the skies are now clear. Everyone says, "Once we get to Little Rock, we will feel like we're going to make it." At least here we can head west again, and not go out of our way to find a ferry.

I was carrying a bundle of fodder back to our campsite when I overheard several men talking around their campfire. Wat Sanders said none of the men who signed the New Echota Treaty will be safe when they arrive in the western territory. Jack Daugherty agreed, saying they will be blamed for all the troubles people have gone through to get there, not just the loss of our eastern lands, but the suffering in the camps and the misery and hardships of travel and building anew. Sarah and I talked about this. We think our people should understand that the treaty just made the best deal we could get when the white people of Georgia forced us to move. We worry about my Uduji Jack and Ududu and people like Major Ridge, Stand Watie, and Uduji James Starr. If our people blame them, they will be in danger. I must talk to Udoda about this.

December 8-9, 1838, Crossing White River

Just as Ududu said, crossing the White River takes a long time. I counted the wagons again, fifty-six in all. We watch the steamboat carry a few wagons and animals at a time crossing the river and then disappearing into the forest on the other side. The ferry is gone for a long time. Then we hear it for a while before we see it again as it comes out of the trees and the paddlewheel pushes it across the river to load again.[106]

We have a lot of time to cook and wash clothing, feed and water the livestock, and repair wagons while we wait for our turn to cross. People have too much time to think and talk. I hear worrying about the winter ahead, where we will stay while we build new homes and stake out farms and build places to do business. Caleb and James Starr have promised shelters for some of us, but they can't provide for everyone. Some may stay in tents for the whole winter. They have to be close to the supplies the government has promised to feed the people and their animals. The closer we get the more people worry. They may have to stay someplace that is as bad as the Charleston stockades.

I talked to Udoda about what Wat Sanders and Jack Daugherty said. He does not know whether people will forgive and put the past behind them, but they should. We need everyone to work together to build our nation strong. We have to join the Old Cherokee Settlers who are already in place, the other nations who have settled nearby, and sometimes in the same lands we will occupy. We have to work with the newcomers who support Chief Ross as well as those who have supported the Treaty. It will be hard to work together, but much

---

[106] Vouchers dated December 8 and 9, paid to Richard Pyburn, the ferry operator, show the party crossed the White River at the Mouth of Cache (modern-day Clarendon) on those dates.

harder for everyone if we don't. Father says that the road we should follow is clear, but he does not know whether we will follow it. No wonder we hear worry talk every day.

December 10, 1838, Western Munroe County

We finally got everyone across the river and are underway again. The swamp or bayou was nearly six miles across, so that was why it took so long. Years ago men had to clear away cypress and other trees to open a waterway for the ferry to reach the western shore. The weather had been cold so the cypress trees are brown and dead looking. Along the trail much of the land is boggy and brush-covered. I saw little grey herons with white markings I had not seen before, as well as the large blue herons that are familiar. Midday we came to the settlement of Daniel Wilder where Deas purchased more corn and fodder that were loaded onto one of Ududu's wagons that was nearly empty.

I rode with Ududu again after the loading. He told me that when he first came west some of our people were living just on the other side of Little Rock. No one settled in this area because the land was so much different from what we were used to in the mountains and valleys. Maybe the Seminoles could adapt to this flat, swampy land, but not the Cherokees. West of Little Rock we will see land that looks like home again along the broad Arkansas River that looks something like the Tennessee. I can't wait.

December 11, 1838, on Big Prairie

We had snow during the night. Most of it melted by mid-morning. Not much else happened today. We just kept traveling and covered many miles. Because of the cold some people are very sick again. Doctor Eddington is busy checking on all of us who have had problems. He told Uduji Jack and Deas we should try to find some better shelter at Little Rock and stay there for a few days. I saw more pine and familiar bare-leaf trees like oak, walnuts, and hickories today, less swamp and wetland. Lots of big red-tail hawks were out hunting, and I was happy to see many red cardinals. They show so brightly against the patches of snow. We made camp near a log building called Mrs. Black's Public House at a north-south crossroads with the Miltary Road.[107] Some of our sick people stayed inside with her. She was a big woman with several children.

December 12, 1838, Pulaski County

We stopped for more supplies at the barns of a man named Cy Harris. He was friendly and jolly, happy to sell to so many customers. He told us that we had entered Pulaski County, where Little Rock is county seat, only about two days away. Mostly dry ground and solid road, but there was one long stretch of marsh for about a mile.

An old woman died last night. She kept saying she wasn't going to make it all the way. Did she know? Really? I think people sometimes wish the worst on themselves. I don't know whether to be encouraged or discouraged. We have less than a third of the way yet to go, about two hundred miles according to Ududu. We have to travel in the winter time, the coldest and hardest time of year. Who knows how many will make it or not?

Sarah says if we can make it through the night we can make it through the day. At night we have to lie close together wrapped in blankets to keep each other warm. During the day we can work and move to stay warm, and sometimes the sun is

---

[107] A description of Mrs. Black's Public House, taken from *Letters from the Frontier*, by Captain George A. McCall, is found in Duane King, *The Cherokee Trail of Tears* (Portland, Oregon, Graphic Arts Books, 2007), 84.

shining to warm us. If we can make it through the night we can make it through the day.

December 13, 1838, Cypress Swamp

We set up camp just a few miles east of Little Rock, almost surrounded by cypress swamp. The swollen bottoms of the tree trunks show many years of standing in this brackish water. Again the military road shows the labor of many years too, building up a road bed of timbers, rock, and clay to make a way through the swamp. We are camping on a dry clearing that rises just above the surroundings, our six hundred some people tightly squeezed into a small field of corn stubble, as the winter winds whip against our canvas tents and wagon covers. We crowd together for warmth, even when we do not all like one another well enough to be so close.

December 14, 1838, North Little Rock

The water froze hard last night. We had to chip through the ice to get to water for cooking and drinking this morning. What a relief to get under way and then in late afternoon to come into view of the cabins and clapboard buildings on the outskirts of Little Rock. It is really North Little Rock, because we are north of the river. The largest part of the town lies south of the river. Most of us will stay on this side, because we will continue to travel on the old trails north of the Arkansas River.

We are staying in the buildings and inns that line the riverfront. Will, James, and I are among the young folks and families who are in a nearly empty warehouse at the east end of a line of two story, rough-sawn board-sided warehouses. We don't have any heat inside, but piles of sacks and bales line the walls against the wind, and the barn-like building feels warmer than our tents.

Sarah and I are working in an inn parlor, where a stove warms the room comfortably. She is staying here with her mother, sisters, and the smaller children. I am glad to enjoy the home-like surroundings for a hand or two of time before returning to the warehouse, but I will be all right wrapped up in my blankets for the night with Will and James and some rocks heated in the fire.

Dr. Eddington has again made certain that the sick and frail among us have the warmest places to stay. He will be busy trying to insure they have enough comfort and hot food during the next two or three days to help them survive the last few weeks of our travel. Then, who knows? We are all glad for a few days to stay in one place, especially with the dark blue grey clouds overhead and cold winds that promise risky travel.

I doubt even the hardiest among us will go to the river for a morning dip. It looks inviting and we are long past needing baths, but it's just too cold. Maybe some of us can find favor with some of the innkeepers to share in the hot baths they brag about on their signs.

December 17, 1838, North Little Rock

Yesterday I got to share bath water after Andro, and Will after me, just like a family at home in winter. We all felt much newer and almost human again. We played along the river, skipping stones, fishing but not catching anything, and finding interesting objects that had floated to shore. We found a wagon wheel on a piece of broken axle, which Grandpa said was still usable, a wooden bucket that can be used to feed the animals, and a usable cooking pot. I had fun looking around and finding small animal tracks and burrows.

Many crows, turkey vultures, and seagulls fly around Little Rock and the riverfront. They must find plenty to eat around here.

Some of the young men made a ruckus coming in late from drinking. All of the families were upset and shamed them into silence, then made sure they woke early this morning whether they wanted to or not. While we were walking near one tavern today we had a man ask us if we wanted him to get us a bottle of something, even as young as we are. Will and I played along, even though we had no desire to get anything. Of course when I told him we had no money in our pockets, he turned away and told me to get lost.

Ulisi looks much better after two days of rest and inn food. She is still skinny and wrinkled, but that makes her Ulisi. I wish she didn't have so much work ahead of her. Ududu either, for that matter. The weather was calmer and clearer today. We expect to be on the trail again tomorrow.

December 13, 1838, Arkansas River Bluffs

We took our time packing and leaving this morning. The sky was cloudy gray blue at sunrise, but the clouds broke up by mid-morning. I heard a man say he wanted to be like the seagulls flying around the area, able to fly over the next miles and reach where we're headed with no delay. The train of wagons climbed up a ravine onto the top of a bluff above the river, then a second bluff the same way, until we are high above the river valley. I was happily surprised to see red soil and rock instead of the bottomland black and gray soils. We are about a mile north of the Arkansas River. We can see a mountain in the distance on the other side of the river. Everyone is excited to be out of the flatlands, back into the hills with soil the color it is supposed to be.

December 19, 1838, Another Cypress Slough

Though we climbed pine-covered hills to get here we are camping along another cypress grove in a slough, which is another name for a marsh. So we haven't left behind all of the flat land. This land is just like the land farther downstream the Coosa in Georgia, where Ududu set up his farm. Many small animals make their homes in these wetlands. We've seen muskrats, minks, raccoons, possums, groundhogs, and beavers, and all kinds of owls, woodpeckers, hawks, finches, and black vultures. If we were staying longer we would set some traps. I expected we would find dry ground when we climbed the hills instead of finding more marshes.

The rabbit fur-lined mittens that Ududu helped me make do keep my hands warm on the coldest days. Some of our people have fur-lined boots, hats, and jackets also. We plan to make more when we have time to settle in one place and trap. Ududu says a bearskin would be perfect for this cold weather.

December 20, 1838, Conway, Arkansas

We traveled straight north for several miles. The river is now a few miles west of us, as it circles between the hills. We came to a thriving settlement named Conway, which only a few years ago was part of the western Cherokee lands. If the western Cherokees had not made a treaty to move farther west we would already be at our new homes. I am troubled by the thought that we find lands that have been turned over to white people all the way along the long route we have traveled. People should have been able to share their lands and live together peacefully. Why not? We are not so different from each other. Are we going to have to give up the new lands when more white people come to settle beside us? Surely this moving must stop somewhere, where we can live and let live.

December 20-21, 1838, Cadron, Arkansas

The cold stays with us, and the sky is grey and overcast. We moved on today, heading west. We see tall mountains to the west on the other side of the Arkansas River.

We arrived at Cadron this evening to camp. A few old falling down and empty buildings still stand in the remains of this town. We found few usable shelters. No one lives here now. Clearly the town used to be much more than it is today. We set up our tent as a lean-to next to the one standing wall of an old cabin. We built a fire in the old stone hearth, using wood from the cabin itself. We had to clean out a nest of raccoons first. Their musty smell still lingers. This is a ghost town. I wonder what happened to the people here.

December 22, 1838, Cadron, Arkansas

This morning we were snowed in. Inside our shelters we felt warmer with the snow piled up against the walls. Little drifts formed where snow worked its way through cracks in the logs. We slept late, then built fires with the wood that we kept dry under cover through the night. We cooked stew and fried bread for the day, which we shared at two meals before nightfall.

Some of our elders and some of the sick again stayed inside the shelter of what's left of two old inns. I heard one of the stories of this town. Four years ago Lieutenant Harris stopped for many days at Cadron with a large group of Tsalagi.[108] A cholera epidemic broke out among them. They couldn't find transportation for many days. Many people died here. Because of that story we are nervous about staying here. We won't stay here any longer than the weather makes us stay, or fears will mount that we will get stranded here like Harris's party. If there are ghosts, at least some of them are our relatives. I hope they will protect us.

December 25-26, 1838, Point Remove Ferry

I awoke shivering in the night and had to go to the fireside to spend the rest of the night. James got up with me, but Will slept right through the cold, wrapped up and hibernating like a bear.

The land between Cadron and Point Remove is a broad flat plain, part of the Arkansas River floodplain. We see high hills and mountains in every direction, miles away from us. The trail is mostly straight through pine woods and brushy marshes.

---

[108] Notes from Cherokee Removal.pdf, from the 1834 contingent on the north side of the Arkansas River from Little Rock, pp.29-31: "On April 15, 1834, a cholera outbreak struck the camp of the Harris contingent at Cadron. At least six people died during the first 24 hours of the epidemic. The next day, according to Harris, three died "before breakfast and eleven in all before the sun went down." The Indians made their doctor's attempts to treat them more difficult by "scattering through the woods, building their camp fires as remote from each other as their several fears direct," until they were extended over an area of three miles. Seven more Cherokees died on April 17 and seven more on April 18. Many of those afflicted with cholera were already weak from the measles. Dr. Roberts dutifully attended his patients, treating them with doses of up to one grain of opium, and from 15 to 40 grains of calomel. Under his diligent care, the death rate dropped to one a day on April 20 and April 21. However, Harris returned April 21 from another search for transportation to find the doctor sick. Dr. Roberts died the next day, survived by a wife and several young children. On April 25, Harris recorded "several more deaths." Six teams of oxen and one five-horse team arrived at the camp that day, but word of the death of Dr. Roberts and the extreme sickness of Dr. Fulton caused other teamsters with whom Harris had contracted to return home."

We didn't get far today, reaching the ferry run by William Ellis across the creek at Point Remove. It was a flatboat about twenty paces long that almost reached from one landing to the other. I'm sure it did reach when the water was low, but with the snow melt that we had today, it had to float a small way to the other side.[109] Crossing was easy. Half of us got across today. The rest will cross tomorrow.

Sarah remembers decorating for Christmas at the Moravian missions at Springplace and New Echota. The missionaries cut evergreen bows and brought them inside. They filled their chapels and houses with candlelight on this evening and the coming day to celebrate the birth of Jesus. We are outside among the pine trees and under the stars tonight, with a blazing fire to keep us warm. She says the story of Jesus began with Joseph and Mary taking a long trip to Bethlehem, ordered to do so by a distant government, and giving birth to Jesus in a stable. We are doing something like they did. I would enjoy the warmth of a stable tonight. Otherwise our night is much like theirs. It is a good starry night to remember that the Great Spirit is with us too.

December 27, 1838, Norristown

We camped close to the river this evening, across from an imposing mountain called Nebo, and a place called Dardanelle. This was the capital of the Western Cherokee Nation until a few years ago. A thriving river port and several trading posts are set up here. People often cross the river from a trail on the south or disembark here when traveling upriver by steamboat. The

---

[109] A description of the William Ellis ferry, taken from *Arkansas Advocate* on November 14, 1832, is found in Duane King, *The Cherokee Trail of Tears* (Portland, Oregon, Graphic Arts Books, 2007), 85-86.

supplies that we shipped by boat passed this point. They are somewhere ahead of us.

We have followed the Military Road, connected to the one built from Memphis through Clarendon to Little Rock. From here on we will follow the Post Road. In some places an old Choctaw trace north of the bluffs may help us go around the marshes and stream crossings that lie close to the river.[110] Udoda says that Uduji Jack is not sure which route will be best until we get there.

I am glad to be walking instead of riding during this cold weather. It is easier to stay warm when I am moving. At the end of the day I am more tired and ready for sleep. Enough writing, Sarah and I agree.

December 28, 1838, Post Road

We had fun fighting with snowballs this afternoon. I got cold and wet. I finally thawed out and dried out, between the blankets and the roaring bonfires that we built. We pry wood loose from the frozen ground, hack wood from standing deadwood, and take some wood from the stash we carry in the wagons from the salvage of old buildings in Cadron. We set up a lean-to by the fire as a place to thaw out when we get too cold in the night. The older boys will take turns tending the fires.

---

[110] The National Park Service study shows the route staying on Highway 64 into Fort Smith, passing through Russellville in Pope County, Clarksville in Johnson County, Ozark in Franklin County and Alma in Crawford County. However, if the emigrants followed the "upper road," probably once a Caddo Indian trace, followed by Lieutenant Harris in 1834 and Lieutenant Whiteley and Captain Drane in the spring of 1838, they often would have been just north of Highway 64 traveling along the ridges so as to avoid the marshy bottomlands of the Arkansas River and of the numerous creeks that flow into it along this route. From *The Promised Land: The Cherokees, Arkansas, and Removal, 1794-1839*, by Charles Russell Logan, published by the Arkansas Historic Preservation Program.

Flocks of Canada geese made lots of noise this morning to wake us up. We followed the Post Road today into a pine forest along the Illinois Bayou. Tomorrow we will follow the river upstream until we find an easier place to cross. We are not near a town now, just out in the middle of the woods.

December 29, 1838, Cherokee Crossing to Mill

Between frozen ground and log structures there was a natural causeway for us to cross the Illinois Bayou not far above the place where we camped last night. We followed the trail up and down and around the rolling hills on this side of the big river valley. The snow is all melted now. The days are a bit warmer. The ground is still mostly solid underfoot, not muddy, because a lot of it is sand, clay, and rock.

We do not see a mill on Mill Creek. There probably is or used to be one upstream. It will be easy for us to ford it tomorrow. Some of our party already forded it. They are camping in the willow and cottonwood trees on the other side.

You can feel the excitement growing now. We are coming closer every day to Evansville. We will get to meet Ududu and Ulisi Starr who have been waiting and preparing for us. With the excitement many people are afraid also, not knowing where we will all stay. We will not have the houses, cabins, and barns that we left behind. The winter seems to be harder and colder than what we are used to. The government may be able to provide rations of beef, bacon, corn and wheat flour, and the other stuff we've been getting while on the trail, but they can't keep us warm inside tents. Dr. Eddington says he will stay with us for some time after we get there. I am glad to hear that.

December 30, 1838, Following River Curves

Throughout the day we had the Arkansas River on our left and the Big Piney River on our right. We are heading mostly north, as both rivers turned north. The valley is wide here. Now as we set up camp by a smaller stream we are turning west again. We see high bluffs in the distance to the north, when we can see through the leafless branches of the trees. People have settled in small clusters at several places along the way. We found no towns.

Another little child died last night, and she was buried this morning. The mother kept crying, "If we could have kept her alive until we got there, she would be close to us." We are still too far away, the daytime too warm, to take her body with us. She had to be buried here. The parents say that her spirit will be lonely staying here. Sarah and I don't think so. We think God will keep her company and take care of her and all the people we leave behind. I wish we could really know such things. We might be able to comfort those who worry about their beloved dead.

December 31, 1838, Spadra Creek near Clarksville

We reached Spadra Creek this evening to camp and water the animals. The men had to break ice on the river with axes to get enough water for the animals and us. Fording will be easy tomorrow, because the creek is only about seven paces wide and frozen solid. The wagons will cross the ice like a bridge.

I heard today that many of our people following the northern route are stuck on the east side of the Mississippi. The ice is too thick for the ferry to cross, not thick enough to hold up the wagons. Lieutenant Deas must have learned that back at Norristown, but the news did not spread. We have clan and family members who may be stuck in that trouble. Uncle George and Aunt Elizabeth Candy are with Reverend Bushyhead. They are probably there. Everyone is worried about them. Uduji Jack said he had disagreements with some of them, but they are still our people, and we need them.

Before sunset we could see a large mountain on the horizon far south of us, maybe twenty-five miles. We are happy to see mountains and hills that remind us of home. They will help us feel at home here.

January 1, 1839, Horsehead Creek

We all forded Slough Creek, made it through a marshy area, and forded Horsehead Creek today. Nearly all day we headed straight west, at first through gently rolling hills, then over the creeks and marshes of flatter land.

Again Udoda, Uduji, and Ududu Bell talked about where they planned to settle after we get to Evansville. Ududu and Uduji James want to go north into the old Delaware territory. Uduji Jack talks about a place called Beattie's Prairie, also north of Evansville. He plans to set up a general store. Udoda has always worked with Uduji Jack, but he surprised me by saying he hopes to find a udali'i.[111] If he can find a udali'i, then he will figure out where he will live. He hasn't talked about that before, as far as I know. I understand he needs a udali'i. We both miss my Uji, but we have to make a new home without her and we need someone to help. I know, too, that Uduji James Starr invited me to stay with him while my father decides what to do. Sarah will be with Ududu and Ulisi for a while. I don't like the idea of us living far away from each other. For the rest of the winter we may stay close together. After that, who knows?

---

[111] Udali'i, a wife.

We start a new year today on the English calendar. It's a strange time of year to call a beginning, as I think about it. Spring would be better, when we plant crops again. On the other hand, for us, it is almost time to begin again this year. In a few days we will stop traveling, and every day will be different from what we have been doing. We will make homes, and wander in the woods and along the streams. We will not be cooped up all day in stockades or wagons.

January 2, 1839, Ozark, Arkansas

Today we came up to the banks of the Arkansas River again. This will be the last time on this trip, Ududu said. Our baggage waits for us at Van Buren. Some of our men will pick it up at a riverfront warehouse. Most of us won't have to go out of our way to the river to get it. The river curves south from here. Tomorrow we will move back to the north ridge above the river valley. We will follow the Caddo trail in order to stay away from the Frog Bayou lowlands.

Five eagles were diving for fish and making a show for us, four with white head feathers, one young eagle with brown feathers. I like to see the beautiful eagles better than the many turkey vultures and black vultures that follow us and keep watch. They wait for us to leave scraps of food so they have something to eat. They would eat us, too, if we're dead. A few nights ago I even dreamed that the vultures were white people wearing vulture masks. They were making sure that we kept going west away from their lands. They were ready to eat us if we didn't keep moving. Not all white people act like vultures. The soldiers riding with us have become friends. They live like we do and share everything with us, even the agues and grippes that come. Still I can't shake the memory of the white people who stole our houses and lands, before we even got ready to leave.

Soon we will be building houses, barns, and schools again. Maybe we can forget about leaving everything behind.

The sky was light blue, and the sun sat in a gray white haze this evening. Shadows seem to spread like water ripples in all directions, instead of forming clear images extending east from the bottoms of things.

January 3, 1839, Mulberry River

The river we will ford tomorrow morning is broad and shallow, twenty paces up here where we set up camp. We can see where it cuts through rock below us and spreads out into a marshy area. We are glad to avoid the lower river as it wanders toward the Arkansas. The sky remains light gray blue. The land is quiet as if all the animals have settled down for a winter nap. We have seen deer and rabbit tracks often, so not everyone is asleep. We just want to be.

In two days we will reach the town of Van Buren and refill our wagons with the baggage we sent ahead. We will turn north for the last short leg of our trip. Some people want to change plans and go on to Fort Smith and then Fort Gibson. Uduji Jack says we will go to Evansville where we have friends and family. If some want to travel on to Fort Gibson, they can do so on their own. He does not know who will welcome us and who will not, or where other detachments will end their journeys and where people will settle. We will go first where we know we are wanted.

Our Land! Our People!

January 4, 1839, Frog Bayou & Van Buren

We have another river to ford, ten paces wide, as we begin moving tomorrow. The way we do things every day has become a habit. I feel like we have done it this way forever. Get up, get the fire going, wash quickly in cold water, fix food for the day and eat some of it, feed and water the animals, roll up blankets and take down and pack tents, hitch up, and get underway—every day the same routine, which we repeat in reverse at evening, usually with a campfire for talk and writing in my journal with Sarah before going to sleep. As Will and I are near the end of the train, we spend some time picking up what others have forgotten and left behind. We return them to their owners in the evening or leave them at the supply wagons for people to claim when they miss them. At first I was surprised that people left axes and cooking pots, which are so necessary, but now I am not surprised by anything that people forget. Today we found a bedroll again. How can anyone leave that behind? How would they sleep without warm blankets? Of course there are bottles and trash of all kinds. If it is something that will decay or food scraps, we leave it for the birds and animals. If it will serve as kindling, or can be used again, we pick it up and take it with us. Waste not, want not, Uloghi Jennie says.

Lieutenant Deas has taken wagons, his men, and some of the slaves and made the trip into Van Buren to get the baggage we shipped by river, and also to restock. Soap, coffee, ammunition, more blankets and tents, and more food are on his list. Again some of the people who want to or need to stay in inns have gone into Van Buren tonight.

Several people are still sick or have gotten sick in recent days. If someone dies here, we will wrap them up and take them with us, to bury them when we get to Evansville, or nearer to where the people will live. The days are cold enough to keep bodies for a few days before burial.

Tomorrow we will move up the hill and take the trail north. Will and I walked part way up today. We looked out over the flat lands to the south and west, seeing the Van Buren Courthouse and Fort Smith in the distance, and the Arkansas River snaking its way west. We couldn't see directly north because the mountain was in our way. We saw mountains and hills to the northwest, where the Tsalagi are settling. We saw mountains far into the horizon on the south. Under the pale blue winter sky the land looks familiar, like a pool's reflection of what we left behind, with the low flat plains to the west instead of the east and south as in Georgia.

Yesterday and today Sarah drilled me on addition and subtraction facts. I have learned how to multiply and divide with simple numbers also. This will help me keep track of money and supplies on the farm. I wish we had more time to work on writing. I can read books and print, but I can't read what people write. It looks so different from Tsalagi syllables or English letters. Not many of our people read or write English writing, but Sarah does. I don't think we will have time for her to teach me that, before she and Ududu will move north. She tells me she doesn't know what Ududu and Ulisi plan to do yet, but she will teach me as long as she can.

January 6, 1839, Ridgetops, Boston Mountains

This morning, our train climbed the long hill north of Van Buren and followed a trail along the ridge tops, up and down. It's January and the oak trees still hold many of their leaves, while the hickories, walnuts, and most of the rest are bare. On the south-facing slopes we see short-needled pine trees. We can see long distances to steeper mountains northeast of us, and hills in every direction.

Ududu says that some of the wagons are held together with wire and wishes. They will make a start for building a shack or warm fires, but not much else when we get to Evansville. Seven hundred miles of rough roads and creek crossings have taken their toll. He is tired of fixing them and trying to hold them together.

We came upon a flock of wild turkeys in one valley. Several older boys took up their bows and followed them into the woods. They came back with three. The women made a stew this evening that smells wonderful, with potatoes, carrots, onions, and turnips thrown in. I can hardly wait to eat. Not much more to write.

At midday as the hills and valleys became steeper, we came to one of the prettiest spots we have seen. A natural dam reaches across the whole width of a river about seventy paces, and a waterfall of ice and flowing water cascades down the face of the rock wall. If it weren't so cold, it would make a perfect place for bathing. When the weather warms we will have to find our way back, because Ududu says we are only a short day's ride by horse from Evansville.

We have seen only a handful of cabins since leaving Van Buren, most of those from a distance, seeing only the curls of smoke from a fireplace.

The hills here are all more than four hundred paces tall. I saw Udoda today and told him that this seems like home. He answered, yes, it does. Only one tall mountain stands between us

Red Wolf's Day Log

and the settlement where Major Lewis Evans[112] set up a store and where Caleb Starr came to build and run a mill. I will finally get to meet him. Sarah told me that Caleb Starr is a full-blooded Scot. His wife Nancy is mostly Cherokee. They usually speak English and prefer to be called Grandpa or Grandma. I didn't know these things.

---

[112] From the "Evansville" article in *The Encyclopedia of Arkansas*, online.

January 7, 1839, Evansville, Arkansas

We made it! In all we counted twenty-one deaths. Two, sadly, were in the last three days. Six hundred thirty-nine of us arrived in the train today. Other groups have come through here ahead of us at different times, but only one in the last few months. Other detachments are expected in the area in a few weeks.

I finally met Grandpa Starr. He is taller, broader and older than Ududu Bell and he has a bushy gray beard and nearly bald head. Ududu Bell has little hair on his face but a full head of black hair that he cuts short. Ududu Bell smiles often, but never laughs aloud. Grandpa Starr laughs often with a hearty loud laugh. He appeared very happy to see all of us as he made the rounds. He met all the people that he could. Grandpa Starr lifted me up, hugged me, called me "John," and said he was glad to meet Allie's son at last.

We set up a typical camp of tents and wagons along the open prairie between Evans' store, and an old walking mill that Evans built, and Evansville Creek. Grandpa Starr's mill and water wheel work on a small side branch of the creek. A rock and post dam blocks the current of the main branch. Tomorrow people will begin to move to the places where they plan to spend the winter. Many will go twelve miles west to Mrs. Webbers' depot[113] where the army will distribute supplies through the winter. The Arkansas State boundary and the beginning of the Cherokee Nation land is in the hills only a mile or so west.

Tonight we will eat from roasting hogs and common kettles that Grandma Starr has supervised with a crew of helpers all day. They learned a couple of days ago that we would be

---

[113] Eventually the Flint District Courthouse was built a few miles south of this site, and many years later the town of Stilwell, Oklahoma, developed in this area.

arriving today. Singing and stomp dancing will follow supper. Since the people missed the New Year's fire-lighting ceremony, some folks are likely to stay up all night.

I don't think I will ever forget my first view of this valley from the mountain. You can see clearly the east and west sides of the whole valley, but it extends far north into the distance. The creek flows from a narrow valley on the east, and disappears into a somewhat wider valley on the west, where many of Caleb Starr's children and several Adairs have already settled. Clearings and patches of prairie, some with corn stubble, dot the whole valley, as far as I could see. Several cabins and barns show up near the foot of the mountain and along the creek. Northeast of the river and about a mile away you can see the smoke from several cabins in a village they call Vineyard, where a man with that name has the post office concession for the area.

January 8, 1839, Caleb & Nancy Starr's House

Caleb and Nancy Starr lived in a one and a half story white frame house about a hundred paces south of the Evansville Creek. On the morning after the arrival of the Bell detachment a crowd assembled in their yard and on the long porch that fronted their house. After the completion of their morning chores Jack and David Bell arrived in the yard and walked up to the front door to knock and be admitted by James Starr, Caleb's eldest son, who had himself arrived only an hour earlier.

"Osiyo, James. You were up early. You had a long way to come, didn't you?" said Jack in greeting. David also took his turn shaking hands with James.

"Not so early. My place is just four miles west of here, along the river at the foot of Twist Mountain. You can just about see it from here. I had to come to see my people, and find out how I could help. I've been getting reacquainted with your son here, David. He's grown since I saw him last at George Candy's place." James led the way into the parlor, where Red Wolf was seated on a bench beside the fireplace, and Caleb in an armchair facing the fire.

Caleb pointed to the chairs nearby and invited Jack and James to bring them up and have a seat. "Tom will show you the cabins and barns nearby that are ready for people to use. They are scattered from here downriver into Flint and Going Snake Districts. You told me earlier that many of these folks will probably spend the rest of the winter near the Webbers' depot, but the more that we can put into good dry shelters, the better. You will have to figure out who should be where."

"That's no easy job. I'll have to rely on my associates to help with it. For our family members it's not so hard. My wife Jennie and the children will stay with her parents, Eleanor and John Martin. Brother David has some business with the Martins also. I will have to travel around until everyone is settled as well as can be expected. As soon as possible I want to start building a house and store up on Beattie's Prairie. My father wants to settle up in the Delaware District also, but my mother is ill, so she and the family will probably stay with some of their Adair relatives nearby. I understand that my friend John Ridge has gone to New York to secure more supplies for his store and his father's.[114] When he returns we will coordinate with him as we set up stores in Delaware District. After all of the rest of our Coosawatie folks have found footholds somewhere, we will load up our building materials and take the male slaves and begin to build where we can settle permanently."

---

[114] Ehle, p. 371

David added to his brother's comments, "Until I know what I'm going to do, I'd be obliged to you, James, to take care of my son. He needs to build up his strength after the long trail and many days of sickness. The slave boy, Will, is a good help to him, and will be to you also, as long as Red Wolf needs to stay with you."

"I told you before," James answered, "I'll treat him as my own son, which he is, according to the old ways of our people. There's always room in my house for another young one. You can do what you need to do, and you don't have to worry about his care."

"I'll be all right, Udoda. I'll work for Uncle James until I'm stronger, then I'll come to work for you," said Red Wolf.

In mid-afternoon, Red Wolf said an easy good-bye to his father, Grandpa and Grandma Bell, Jennie and Andro, Uncle James, and Aunt Sarah, happy in the thought that they would be staying nearby at least for the next few months. He and Will packed their clothing and personal belongings, and set off on their own horses, selected by David from the herd, down the creek-side trail four miles toward the south foot of Twist Mountain. By late afternoon they came in sight of a sprawling cabin, fronted by a long porch, and surrounded by several other log buildings and corrals, set in a clearing between hickory trees, and overlooking the valley of Evansville Creek. Smoke wafted from four chimneys that rose from the roofs of the T-shaped house, with the kitchen chimney being the largest with the most smoke at the rear.

Sam Starr was first to appear out of the door, because he had been watching at the window, rushing out to see his playmate from three summers before, at the encampment at Rattlesnake Springs. Washington, Zeke, Bean, and Field soon followed, from their work in one of the barns, to help with the horses. Sam helped carry the bags into the house with Red Wolf and Will. Once inside, in the central room, they dropped their packs and satchels and met Ellis Harlan and John, who were several years older, and Leroy, nicknamed 'Buck', who was a few years younger. Buck had to hobble over to greet him because of a crippling accident a year before.

They walked to the back wing of the house where a large trestle table sat and the women were preparing supper. Aunt Susie and Aunt Nellie, the sisters who had both chosen James for their husband, were working near the hearth, and two slave women side by side with them. Setting the table were daughters, Mary, fully grown, and Rachel, who was about Red Wolf's age. They all paused in their preparations to greet Red Wolf and Will. Janie was watching Lucinda, born in October, still in the cradle, and Caleb, a two-year old. After they made the rounds of greeting and getting bear hugs from Aunts Susie and Nellie, Red Wolf and Will followed Sam to the loft room above the east wing, where the boys all shared sleeping space. They rolled out their blankets and stashed their belongings.

When supper was announced they all assembled at the trestle table. Uncle James sat at one end of the table, with Aunt Susie and Aunt Nellie at the other end, and he appointed places for Red Wolf and Will toward the center of the table on one side next to Caleb, Buck and Sam, and across from Mary and Rachel. The youngest children sat nearest their mothers. The oldest boys—Washington, Zeke, Bean, Field, Ellis, and John—sat nearest their father. Red Wolf had asked that Will be allowed to stay at his side at the table, although the other slaves ate their own suppers in their own houses. Later Red Wolf learned that some of the slave women came to the table when one of the mothers needed help with the youngest children, or when, during menstruation, they ate in a room apart.[115]

During supper they talked about other relatives. They told him that older brothers—James Junior, Joseph, William, and Thomas—lived on their own at farmsteads in the area. Pauline was the oldest daughter and she lived with her husband nearby. Aunt Mary was married to Austin Rider and Aunt Ruth to John Bean, and they all lived closer to Evansville. Aunt Sarah had married Jesse Mayfield; they had not yet arrived with the Bushyhead and George Candy detachment. Uncle George Harlan Starr had married Nancy Bell, Red Wolf's aunt, and they were coming with George Candy also.

So began Red Wolf's experience of the busiest and fullest household he would ever know, where he went from being an only child to having twenty-one siblings.

February 15, 1839, Evansville to Webbers' Depot

The morning was cloudless and cold with an icy sheen on trees and grounds around James Starr's homestead. Joe came into the log stable where Red Wolf, Will, and Sam were feeding and brushing the horses. "Someone's coming up the trail in a carry-all, and, if I'm not mistaken, it looks like your Grandpa John and Will's father, Ezekiel." The boys went out to look and saw for themselves that Joe was right. Red Wolf and Will soon were embracing their visitors.

---

[115] In traditional Cherokee practice women separated themselves from routine work and contacts during menstruation, since they were believed to manifest extraordinary power and possible peril during their periods. These practices passed out of common experience during the Nineteenth Century, according to Theda Perdue in *Cherokee Women: Gender and Culture Change, 1700-1835* (Lincoln, University of Nebraska, 1998), 28ff.

Our Land! Our People!

"We're on our way over to Mrs. Webbers' for supplies. Thought you might like to help us and see for y'selves where a goodly number o' our people are a'stayin' the winter," Grandpa said.

"Oh yes!" came the immediate reply from both boys. They headed for the house, reported the plans, shared other news between Grandpa and Uncle James, and started west within a hand of time. On the trail that meandered along the river and between the hills, they passed the farmsteads of the Starr sons and the Adair relatives, one of which housed Grandma Bell, where they stopped briefly. Ezekiel and Will moved over to a buckboard wagon that would carry most of the supplies they were planning to get.

"How is Ulisi?" Red Wolf asked as they looked at the impressive log house of nephew John Thompson Adair. He had purchased the large two story house, built in Federal style with a central porch and entrance doorway and two wide, tall glass windows on either side of the main door, and a balcony and matching doorway above the main door. Its previous owner, Joel Bryan, was the attorney for the Old Settler Cherokees. He had built it in 1833, on the west side of Twist Mountain in an area that was now called Oak Grove.[116]

"Maybe we'll stop on the way back. Ye can see for y'self," Grandpa Bell answered. "She canna' go out much, just putters about the house tryin' to stay warm. After the long trail, she does naw think she'll ever feel warm again. She's sufferin' from an ailment the doctor calls dropsy, somethin' that comes from a worn-out heart, so I do naw feel good about how she's doin'.

---

[116] Information about the house comes from *The Cherokee Adairs*, p. 6a. It remained in the Adair family and was still standing in 2003 when that book was published.

Mostly we're hopin' to get her to warm weather so she can gain some strength." Grandpa fell silent for a few moments, then he started talking about something else.

"I wanted you to see where so many folks'll 'wait out the winter, so you can know why we're in for it. It's as hard as the trail or worse, since there's so little to do an' so little to eat. A few hardier, braver folks have slipped away to live off the land as they once did, but most are stayin' near a depot like Mrs. Webbers', so they can get at least a little o' what they need. As they wait, they get angrier, and folks keep dyin' as well."

"I want to ask you something, Ududu, something that's been bothering me."

"Ask away,' Grandpa replied.

"I keep thinking about the slaves we have—Will, who's been my best friend always, and his father and mother, and the others who've come with us. Some get even less to eat and worse shelter than the rest of our people. When will they get to be free? Will they have to stay slaves?"

"You're your mother's son, for sure," Grandpa answered. "I do naw know the answer, but I know why you ask. Can it be fair, to pass sufferin' on to others who haven' e'en a choice in the matter? Still, I ask ye, how could we build what we need without the help of these slaves? It's a quandary, it is."

"Couldn't we let them choose, Grandpa? Couldn't we treat them like we want to be treated?"

"Not if we want to build the great houses and farms, schools and gov'nent houses we used to have in Georgia. We canna' build 'em without their help."

"Couldn't we just build smaller, and everyone have one the size they need? Isn't that the way we used to live?"

"It is. It is. But we also got used to livin' the way white folks live. It's hard to go back to the way o' the Indians long ago. I canna' do it."

"I'm sorry, Ududu. It doesn't seem fair, any way you look at it."

Grandpa smiled weakly and fell silent. After a few moments he said, "You have your own mind, boy, and it's a good one."

When they finally looked down on the broad valley between the tall hills that stretched far into the distance north, south, and west, they could see the creek wandering down the center of the valley, and the trails converging to a point where the clearing of trees made the log warehouses of Mrs. Webbers' place visible on the far side of the creek. What they saw amazed Red Wolf and Will. Everywhere they looked they saw encampments, smoke from fires, tents and hastily-built shacks, and people milling around, as far as they could see in every direction.

Grandpa Bell said, "What's left o' the Coosawattee folks is on this side o' the river near to us. Some o' Elijah Hick's detachment took the center of the valley just east o' the depot. Even some o' the people who came with Whitely or Drane last summer are still here, just west o'the depot, 'cause they didna' find somewhere else to settle. Then John Benge arrived just after we did, and you see his people spread out to the south. Hair Conrad's folks to the north. Every so often someone gets a notion to head out on their own upriver here or over to the Illinois River, but they have to be ready to hunt game, 'cause they won't find much else. O' course, there's other depots scattered around. If Bushyhead ever gets in he'll be a few miles south of the Fort Wayne depot. Your Uncle George Candy and my daughter Elizabeth are still with Jesse Bushyhead. So's my Nancy and her husband, George Harlan Starr.[117]"

"How long will people stay here?" Red Wolf asked.

"The treaty says we have a year o' rations after arriving. People got here before all the supplies were ready, so I do naw rightly know if they'll get a full year or go to the treaty date, March 1, 1840. People take a while to make up their minds where they're goin' to stay, then it takes a while to build what they need. We ne'er know if the crop'll be good, once we plant it, so my guess is we'll have people needing help for quite a while."

"This looks worse than the stockades around Charleston."

"The good part here is they're free to come and go," Grandpa answered. "The problem is most people havna' place to go. They need the food and blankets they get here, as poor as those things are."

They followed the road down into the valley, crossed the creek ford, and came to the log warehouses next to Mrs. Webber's cabin. Grandpa Bell produced letters from the people he represented for obtaining their allotments of grain, meat, and blankets. John Bell closely examined the corn, still on the cob, and rejected several bushels. "More cob than grain," he said. "Mice've already eaten more than their fair share." He examined three live cows, rejecting one that he said would not live long

---

[117] Duane King wrote "Terminating Points of the Cherokee Trail of Tears," for Cherokee Heritage Center *The Columns*, June 2006. The family details come from Mack Starr's article in *The History of Adair County* (Cane Hill AR: ARC Press, 1991), 604ff.

enough to make the trip home so he could feed it to put some meat on its bones. He and the dispensing agent argued until the agent backed down, recognizing that John Bell would not.

Will and Red Wolf helped carry and load the supplies onto the wagon and cover them with an oiled canvass. When they had finished and Grandpa had some time to greet and talk with some of his acquaintances, they returned to the trail east toward Evansville.

"Ye're stronger, Red Wolf. Stayin' with your Uncle James is a'doin' you good," Grandpa said as they left the valley.

"I like it there, Ududu. I like staying in a busy house, having brothers and sisters, taking care of the animals, and Will does, too. I miss Udoda, of course."

"Well, right now, it just makes sense for ye to stay where ye are and learn what you can about farm and family life. Your father's on the road between setting up a farmstead, visitin' at John Martin's place up along the Illinois River, and helpin' Jack with provisionin' a new store. Ye've needed a chance to know what a normal life feels like. We all have. I'm glad ye're part of a family who looks out for each other."

In the Western Cherokee Nation

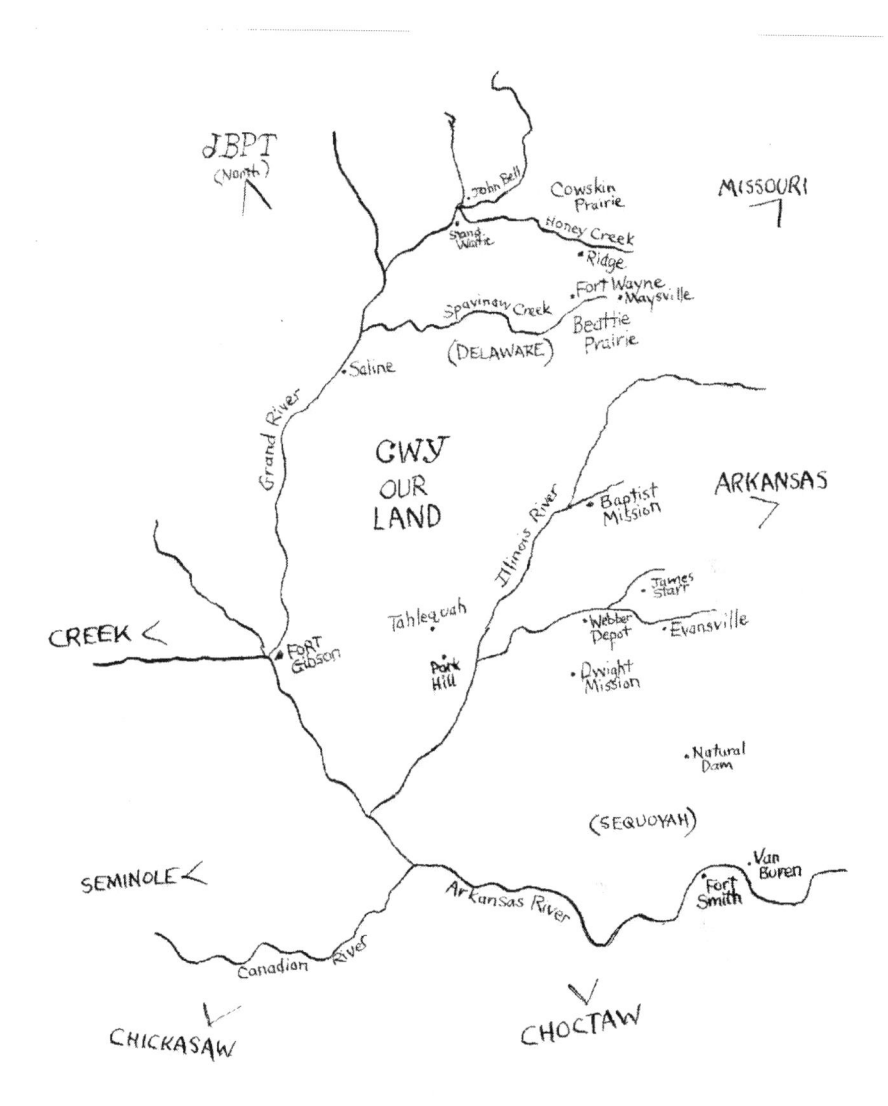

Red Wolf's Map of the Cherokee Nation 1839-1848

March 1, 1839, the Foot of Twist Mountain

David Bell came riding up the river trail from the west mid-morning of a sunny warming day after a week of cold and wet days. Everyone was eager for the new feel of spring to last. David wore a broad smile and called out "Osiyo" as he neared the house and saw Caleb and John sharpening tools on a grindstone outside the nearest shed. He dismounted near them. "Yes, I have news," he responded to their questioning looks, "some good, some not so good. First I need to see my son."

John told him that he last saw him with Sam, taking care of some new little pigs, in one of the small log buildings behind the rest, as he pointed toward it. David walked his horse back to a corral where other horses were standing, and he headed in the direction John had pointed. Soon he was lifting Red Wolf up with both arms and giving him a brief embrace. "Maybe you've gained a pound or two. You look stronger," he said as he returned Red Wolf to the ground. "And you must be Sam. I am glad to meet you. Looks like you both have your hands full from a successful farrowing season."

"We had four sows farrow," said Sam. "It's a start anyway. We've kept three of the runts alive, too, feeding them by hand, so we have thirty-five little pigs."

"I have some news for Red Wolf, that can't wait, but you can hear it too." He turned to face his son. "Jennie's sister, Nancy, has taken me to be her husband. I'll soon be going up to Delaware District where I've staked out a farm and finish building a house on it. When I have it ready I'll come back for Nancy. You can decide then where you want to be, with me or staying here with your Uncle James."

April 15, 1839, Fort Gibson

Mounted on their horses the two brothers paused at the top of the hill and turned to look back at the square stockade between them and the Illinois River landing. The grasses shown vibrant green and the trees filled with new shimmering leaves. David looked at Jack and said, "I think Deas was surprised and pleased with the sword you presented to him."[118]

"He was, wasn't he? Well, he deserved some recognition for all he did to get us here. Out of all the federals assigned to the removal, no one worked harder than Deas to make it successful. No one cared more for the people he was moving. I think we did a good thing. What's more, we need as much support and good will as we can get during these years of resettlement."

"You know the politics better than I, brother, but it was a decent thing to do. Most people feel such bitterness because so many have died. They can't give thanks even to those who eased their suffering. All are here who planned to come, many who didn't want to. What's going to happen now?"

"We've got to come to some agreement about how to govern ourselves," Jack answered. The Old Settlers already have a government in place with three chiefs—John Brown, John Rogers, and John Looney. They want to stay in place. John Ross wants to keep the eastern government and its officers in charge. The Treaty people have to side with the Old Settlers. We'll have

---

[118] *Army and Navy Chronicle* 8 (April 25, 1839): 266. CHEROKEE INDIANS.—We understand that a sword has lately been presented to Lieutenant Edward Deas, of the U. S. Army, by some of the Cherokee Indians, as a testimony of their gratitude for his kind attention to their comfort, while he was superintendent in their removal to the West of the Mississippi last winter. This circumstance is alike honorable to that officer, and to the race who have too often met with far different treatment. May they be happy and prosperous in their new homes.—*New York Gazette*.

to figure out how to come together soon. We can't have two governments. It's a dangerous time."

"Ross has a majority on his side. He's going to wind up in charge."

"We'll do what we can to prevent that. The Old Settlers and the Treaty Party will lose too much if he remains in control of everything."

"I don't know, Jack. I don't see how anyone can come out of this a winner. The best I can see is to look after my own business and hope others will put rebuilding homes, families, and work ahead of everything else."

"You have tried to stay above the fray, my brother. I will honor that. You have been such a help to me. But I can't do the same. I have to try to work things out, so everyone gets what they deserve from the treaties, and we have a fair government in place that serves all of our interests. We have a chance to set things right; when this chance passes it won't come again."

"I can't help but remember what Allie said. She was so sure there was no way out. We had no good choices. I still have to try. I have to try to build a new family and a new life for my family. That is the most important thing I can do."

June 17, 1839, James Starr's House

Their corn, squash, and beans were growing in the fields and they were ready to cut their first crop of hay. James and Tom Starr returned from the Takatoka Campground on the Illinois River where they had gone just a few days before to join the council between the Old Settlers and the new arrivals from the east. The family had already eaten supper when they arrived. Tom's tall, broad stature always impressed Red Wolf and Will, and his sense of humor entertained them. They were glad to see that he was dismounting to report on their experiences at Takatoka instead of riding on to his own place. Susie and Nellie came quickly outside to their husband and son, hustling them inside to wash up, have something to eat, and make their report about the council.

When the family had gathered, James began to address them all. "We've just seen my father and John Bell, and made our report to them. Jack and Stand Watie, Major Ridge and John Ridge, Elias Boudinot and John Martin were all present on the day we were there, June 14, and we gave support to the Old Settlers viewpoint. We formally accepted the current Western Cherokee government and agreed to wait for the election of officers in that government next July. That would keep the decisions and the treasury out of the hands of John Ross during this important first year of settlement. We were aware that Ross's Party was stirring up hatred against us, so we did not stay. Before we left we did help the Old Settler Chiefs draft a letter to Montfork Stokes, the agent at Fort Gibson, asking for the payment right away to the Western Cherokee Nation of the annuities owed to them by the federal government. Of course Ross or Lowery will never agree to that position. They have too much to gain financially by overthrowing the Western Chiefs and taking over the government themselves. I suppose they will learn about the letter and make their own appeal to Stokes, so the meeting will end with people just as divided as they were."[119]

When James paused, Ellis asked, "What do you think is going to happen next?"

---

[119] William G. McLoughlin in *After the Trail of Tears: The Cherokees' Struggle for Sovereignty, 1839-1880*, records the proceedings of the Takatoka gathering and its aftermath, 10-16.

Tom answered, "Nobody knows. We have some peacemakers who might speak up. Sequoyah and Jesse Bushyhead are the two men who might command enough respect from both sides to make some kind of deal. Will they try? I don't know. It's risky for anyone to get in the middle."

"So what you're saying is—we don't know much more than we did. We're just playing the best hand that we have," added young Caleb.

"That's right, son," James said. "We've got to wait to see how this is going to play out. The new majority has just arrived, and they support Chief Ross, for better or worse, as far as I can tell. We'll be lucky if the Old Chiefs get any say at all, and we who supported the Treaty probably won't have any."

Ellis continued, "It hardly seems fair that they all benefit from the Treaty, especially Chief Ross and his brother Lewis, yet they maintain their support politically by still opposing it. It's a done deal. They're all here."

"So they are, but they can still make money, and they can still try to control the way things go," Tom answered.

Susie then took charge. "Enough of this. You two need something to eat. If you can't accomplish anything else today, you can at least fill your stomachs and not starve."

June 22, 1839, James Starr's Hayfield

James and all the men of the household were in the hayfield, cutting and forking hay into stacks in the late Saturday afternoon, when Caleb Starr drove his horse at a fast pace up the path in his carryall. Drawing near James he waved his arms for everyone to come near, looking grave and saying nothing in greeting. The boys—family and slave—stripped to their waists and covered in dust and sweat drew close to the grandfather.

"I want everyone to hear this together," he said, waiting until the farthest workers had hurried near before continuing to speak. "Major Ridge was murdered this morning just a few miles north of here at Rocky Creek."

James staggered and slowly lowered himself to the ground. A chorus of exclamations and questions followed—Why? Who did it? Why him? Why now? What were they trying to prove? Is Ross behind this? While Caleb continued to sit on the carryall seat, the rest of them sat on the ground around James and waited for their Grandfather to tell them more. He cleared his throat and remained silent for a finger of time.

"I don't know much. The Major stayed overnight at Ambrose Harnage's cabin at Cincinnati. He was heading south to Van Buren to check on the slave Daniel he had sent there on an errand, who had fallen ill. The slave boy named Apollo was with Ridge; he's about your age, Will. The boy said they were crossing White Rock Creek when several shots rang out, Ridge slumped in his saddle, and then toppled off. When he saw that Ridge was dead, he high-tailed it to Dutchtown, said Ridge had been shot and killed, and he needed help."[120]

"Poor fellow was probably scared to death," interjected Sam.

"I suppose so," Grandfather Caleb continued. "I don't know for sure but I think this be an execution for Ridge's signing the treaty. I don't know if Ross has anything to do with it, but I'm

---

[120]Thurman Wilkins, *Cherokee Tragedy: The Ridge Family and the Decimation of a People*, Second Edition, Revised (Norman, Universityof Oklahoma, 1986),338.

thinking he does. What we have to consider is how many more treaty-signers may be in danger, and that list has you on it, James. You spoke out about the need for the treaty long before it was signed."

"That's the truth, Father. We all knew the risk we took when we signed it, so I'm not going to run away from it now."

"Son, you have to take measures to protect yourself. I just want you to be alert. I do not want you to run away. I want you to be watchful and not take risks if you can steer clear."

"I'll keep my men around me."

They talked for two hands of time about the killing of the man who had for years served as the official Speaker for the Cherokee Nation. His popularity spread far until he began to speak in favor of negotiating a treaty that would make the best terms they could expect. When Grandpa Caleb took his leave, the men had no more interest in the hay. No clouds were in the sky to threaten, so they stopped work for the day and began to return to the house and barns.

Sam, Red Wolf, and Will were walking together. Red Wolf said, "I can't believe the Major is gone. He was like an Ududu for the whole nation."

Sam said, "I always heard his name spoken with respect. It is a dishonor to all of us."

"No honor in it," Red Wolf responded. "Still I remember there was much talk when the treaty was signed. Some people expected all the signers would be killed. There was a law that no one could sign away the Cherokee lands for their own benefit. The Major had proposed the law himself. On penalty of death, it was said. My Udoda said all the signers knew that some people would bear a grudge—they wanted blood, and now they have it."

"Grudges can work both ways," said Sam. "Where will it stop? Will they kill my father too?" They were quiet after that, until they reached the barn to do their chores.

June 24, 1839, James Starr's House

On Monday two days later the morning had turned hot and steamy. After lunch the family was spread out across the front porch and under the oak trees in front of the house when David Bell rode up the trail. Dismounting he pulled off his broad-brimmed hat and ran his fingers through his black hair, scanned the scene in front of him until he saw Red Wolf coming toward him from the shade of one of the trees, and approached him with open arms. "It's sad news and a poor greeting I have for you."

Soon David was seated on a cane chair on the porch, telling his news to everyone gathered. "I know you learned quickly of Ridge's murder, but he was not the only target of the assassins. At the same time other bands of killers made their way to kill our friends John Ridge, Elias Boudinot, and Stand Watie. Stand got warning and slipped away without being found, but John and Elias had no warning. Early on Saturday morning a mob came to John's house on Honey Creek, pulled him out of the house, and stabbed him repeatedly and stomped on him. John's wife Sarah and the children carried him back into the house and he managed to breathe for a little while longer in spite of his wounds, but then he died. She has fled with the children to Fayetteville.[121]

"The attack on Elias came just as cruelly. He was working on his new house at Park Hill when a band of men approached him, asking for medicine from his supply for their sick families. When he was leading them back to get medicine, one of them stabbed him in the back, and the others bashed in his head with axes. It was as cowardly an attack as I've ever heard. His wife Delight saw what happened from a distance and came running with Reverend Worcester, but he died soon after they arrived."[122]

When David paused his hearers remained silent for a few moments, then the exclamations and questions came in a flood. "Horrible! How dare they? What cowards! What can we do?"

James was among the last to respond. "Whoever planned this will be after your brother Jack and me also."

David answered, "Yes, we think so. Jack has taken Jennie and the children and gone to Fort Gibson for protection. General Matthew Arbuckle, the commandant there, has offered safe shelter there. Stand has offered a large reward for the names of the killers, but he's also gathering a force of armed men to search for them. Your son Tom has joined him. My father-in-law, John Martin, is headed for Fort Gibson. I think we persuaded George Adair to go there also. You might want to go there until this gets sorted out."

---

[121] Wilkins, ibid., 335-336. Sarah Bird Northrup Ridge maintained her interest in the store and returned to live at their home on Osage Prairie at least through 1844, according to Edward Everett Dale and Gaston Litton, *Cherokee Cavaliers* (Norman, Oklahoma, University of Oklahoma Press, 1939, 1995), 20.

[122] Wilkins, ibid., 336.

"I know that's what my father wants me to do, but I have work to do here. No one can make a life here if we have to spend the best days of the summer hiding in a fort instead of raising food for our families. We will arm ourselves for self-defense, but I won't go hunting for trouble. If it comes for me, I'll be ready."

"I understand how you feel, James, but be ready to change your mind. You have men who will take care of the farm while you're in a safer place, just as my brother Jack does. So far it appears that only the signers of the treaty have been targeted, not their families or workers."

"And if they're not able to take out their revenge on those who signed the treaty, will they remain so selective about who gets hurt? Sarah Ridge must not think so, or she would not have fled to Fayetteville. No, I'm less concerned with protecting myself, than with protecting my family. I think I'm best able to do that here, until I have evidence otherwise."

Late that evening the boys laid their bedrolls outside under the stars about twenty paces from the house, since the sleeping loft was still hot from the day. Once they got up to chase some noisy raccoons away from the bones and food scraps that someone had left by the door of the summer kitchen. The raccoons climbed the nearest tree, so Sam placed the scrap bucket inside the door on a bench where they couldn't get to it. Before they finally stopped talking for the night, Red Wolf asked Sam, "What would we do if a gang of killers showed up tonight?"

"I've been thinking about it all day, since we heard about John Ridge's family having to watch him being killed. Dad's only got three guns in the house, and they're for hunting. I never thought about having to shoot a man with 'em, much less fend off thirty. He's always taught us to avoid a fight if we possibly could, so I don't rightly know what he means when he says he'd defend us."

"So you think he'd just try to hide us? But what if they snuck up on us like some of them did, or ambushed us from a hiding place when we were working in the field or riding down the trail? How could he defend against that?"

"I don't know, but he's thinking about it. I do know that. And he didn't have to tell me to sleep with one eye open tonight. If we hear anything, I'm running to the porch and making sure Dad's awake."

Will spoke last, "You two sure know how to ruin a night's sleep."

When the boys arose early the next morning they found that James had already packed some things and was ready to ride over to Fort Gibson to join John Adair Bell, Archilla Smith, and the others who had gone there for protection.

July 6, 1839, John Thompson Adair's House

"Eleven summers old today. Ye've lived a decade. Ye mus' think you're gettin' old," Grandpa Bell said to Red Wolf. "I'm glad ye can be here with us today. We're glad to celebrate your birthday." They sat in the open-air section of the cabin between the two large rooms on either side, one for sleeping and the other for living room and kitchen. Will was sitting on the edge of the wood platform a few paces away, and Uncle James Madison Bell, thirteen years old, was sitting beside Grandpa. Grandma Bell sat nearby on pillows, not able to get up without help, her legs and feet swollen. Sarah and Charlotte also sat nearby with the slave woman Phoebe ready to help whenever Grandma wanted assistance.

"I'm sorry you are feeling poorly, Ulisi."

"Don't you worry about me, Gigage Wahya. I'm happy you are stronger and growing well." His grandmother's voice was strong and her eyes intense, and that comforted him.

"I hear you helped put up a good crop o' hay," his grandfather said. "The corn, too, is growing well. We are fortunate to be with people who've cleared large fields and gotten used to growing crops here. Few o' the people who came when we did have even got a start growing things. Even short o' plow blades and hoes. What we've grown will be sorely needed in the year to come."

"I've been learning, Ududu. All I have to do is watch what my brothers do and try to do the same. I was awful awkward first using the scythe in the hay crop, then wielding the fork, but I got the swing of it, and plenty of blisters on my hands."

"Aye, but they toughen up and make good calluses, then it's easier next time, isn't it?"

Sarah spoke up, "I don't suppose you've added anything to your notebook, with all the farm work you've been doing?"

Red Wolf looked down at his hands, "No, you're right, Aunt Sarah. I've thought about many things, but not put any of them down on paper. Mostly we've been talking about the killings of the Ridges and Boudinot and worrying about Uduji Jack and James and the rest of the treaty signers, even you, Ududu."

Grandpa Bell sat back and put his pipe in his mouth for a moment. "One or two others join you in your worries, lad," as he nodded toward Sarah and his wife, "but I've not been in the eye of the hawk the way the others have. I mostly mind my own

Our Land! Our People!

business and try to help when needed. Still we are upset. All of us, like a carriage overturned and spilt. Now news comes from Illinois Campground, where Bushyhead and Sequoia aimed to use their good repute to bring peace to our people. The first decision may declare a pardon to all who did the killing, no questions asked, and the second, to mark as outlaws any who ask for the arrest and trial o' the killers. If they do this, I fear that peace will naw find a nest nor a hole to rest in the whole land. What comes of justice if the same James Foreman and Anderson Springston who killed John Walker, Jr., can murder and face no penalty again? And all the rest the same. But do ye want to be thinkin' on these things on your birthday, do ye?"[123]

"Yes, Ududu. These things are always on my mind, we're always talking about them at the house, and I want to know how you feel about them. Uduji Jim just returned from Fort Gibson day before yesterday, saying he thinks some of the danger's past, for the time being anyway. Since the convention is going on, the killers are busy with that. I just don't know how we can ever feel safe again."[124]

---

[123] John Ehle, pp. 271-272 on the Walker murder; pp. 393-380 on the Major Ridge murder.

[124] The "Cherokee Nation in National Convention" at the Illinois Campground from July 1, 1839 to the end of August adopted a general pardon on July 7, declared as outlaws anyone who sought revenge or redress for the killings, and adopted an Act of Union on July 12, that organized a unity government dominated by the Ross "National" Party, and established eight companies of provisional police to enforce its actions. They again declared the Treaty of New Echota invalid, laid claim to all the Eastern lands they had vacated, and called for renegotiation of all of its terms. The Old Settlers were largely absent and Treaty Party totally absent from this Convention, but they met in response on July 22 at Tahlontuskey, the Old Settler Capitol, and again on August 20 at Price's Prairie. At the latter meeting John Adair Bell and Stand Watie were delegated to go to Washington to secure support from President Van Buren and Secretary of War Joel Poinsett. William G. McLoughlin, *After the Trail of Tears* (Chapel Hill: North Caroline Press, 1993),18-21.

"Yuh certainly have lots to think about in your young years. We used to look back and say the old-timers had it tough. Now I'm an old-timer, an' I have to say, things haven't gotten easier. You've hard days ahead, no doubt about it, but you're strong and wiser than your years."

"I don't feel very wise, Ududu."

"It's the thinkin' about serious things that makes a person wise, and the doin' what you have to do before you're ready for it. In that you've got a head start, I'm a'thinkin'."

The servants had been setting up a trestle table under the trees, bringing out pitchers and plates of food, and they signaled to John Bell that all was ready. During the meal that followed Grandpa told Red Wolf about the blacksmith shop he had set up at his wife's nephew's farmstead nearby and his hope to establish his own settlement in the Cowskin Prairie area. Grandma Bell remained in her chair, out of hearing from the table, so Grandpa warned Red Wolf that the doctor didn't expect her to live many months, so he would stay close to her and be satisfied where they were. They had lived together near forty years, so he could not complain, but they must make the best of the time they had left. Uncle Jim Bell remained quiet and swallowed hard.

October 12, 1839, James Starr's Cornfield

Uncle James had returned on October 11 from a Council of Old Settlers and Treaty Party men at Tahlontuskey at the mouth of the Illinois River. They had elected John Rogers as First Chief, John Smith as Second, and Dutch as Third. Will Rogers accepted the position of treasurer, and James Starr and John Huss became members of the Executive Council. They had passed a law expelling all white men who were favorable to John Ross from the Cherokee territory, and they had authorized sheriffs and light horse patrols to enforce their laws.[125]

Uncle James and his sons and servants were shucking corn and chopping stalks when David Bell arrived on horseback, looking for Red Wolf, and attracting the attention of everyone in the field. They assembled around him to hear the latest news. David came quickly to the point, which was to let them know that his sister-in-law Jennie, Jack's wife, had died suddenly four days before, and been laid to rest yesterday at one of the Adair farms six miles west.[126] Her mother, Eleanor Martin, also had succumbed to the illness, which may have been cholera. Jennie had not been able to gain strength after the trip west, and her mother was of course older and deeply upset by the political agitation of the recent weeks. They had come to stay with relatives while John Martin continued to try to exert some influence among Ross's supporters.

Red Wolf was troubled to learn about Jennie, whom he had not seen in months. She had taken care of him like a mother during the months of the journey west. Now Andro and the other children would be orphaned like Red Wolf, without a mother or maternal grandmother or maternal uncle to care for them.

Red Wolf had not yet met his step-mother Nancy, Jennie's sister, whom David had married in March. She was still at the Martin settlement at Saline along the Grand River, and she could not travel to be with them here. David told him now that they were expecting a baby in November. If the baby was a boy he

---

[125] Foreman, p.304.

[126] The information about Jennie (Jane Martin) Bell's death, October 9, 1839, and burial at the Blakemore farm southeast of Stilwell, with mother Eleanor Nellie McDaniel Martin beside her, comes from George Morrison Bell, p. 48.

might be named after both his maternal grandfather and David's brother, so his name would be John Martin Adair Bell. If a girl, she might be a Nancy Martin Bell after her mother. Red Wolf said that there was always room for another John Bell in the family.

Jack had told David that he would take care of his own children, although he would rely on the slaves Demaris and Elijah to take care of them when he was absent. He would eventually have to find another wife to take him for her husband if he could.

David reported that Jack had just returned from his trip to Washington, D.C., with Stand Watie, when Jennie became so sick. By this time the rest of the workers were drifting back to their work in the cornfield. Uncle James asked David to stay for supper and invited him to go back to the house for rest, but David let his horse graze and stayed in the field helping with the harvest alongside Red Wolf until they were ready to quit just before dusk.

They all bathed in the creek before returning to the house for their late supper. Uncle Jim had sent a messenger to his son Tom two miles west, to let him know that David was here with news from Jack and Stand. Tom then came to join them for supper, making the doorway look small when he entered, and brightening the room with his always-smiling face.[127] When they gathered on the porch after supper, even Nellie and Sallie joined them, and David made a report about the meeting with President Van Buren and Secretary of War Joel Poinsett. Jack and Stand had made a case for federal intervention based on the guarantees of safety in the New Echota Treaty for those who signed it. They presented to the President the article they had

---

[127] This physical description comes from William McLoughlin, p. 49.

written for *The Arkansas Gazette* about the murders and the usurpation of the Cherokee government by Ross, the amnesty for the killers, and declaring Treaty signers as outlaws.[128] The President and Poinsett had agreed with their position and promised assistance in providing security, financial help for the widows and orphans, and bringing the killers to justice. Poinsett had sent orders to General Matthew Arbuckle for his troops to maintain order and make arrests as necessary. He suspended all treaty payments until order was secured, and denied the legitimacy of the new Cherokee "unity" government led by Ross, continuing to regard the Old Settler government temporarily as the legitimate Cherokee government.

Tom was first to respond. "That sounds all well and good, but who is really going to enforce it? Ross has his forces—by far the largest group, Stand has his supporters—me included, and General Arbuckle has enough soldiers to control limited areas, but not the whole territory."

Uncle Jim went on to say that the majority who supported Ross would continue to see themselves as independent of any federal government. That government was their enemy still, who forced them to move west unwillingly, brought them suffering and death on the trail and throughout the winter, and still have not paid the promised treaty payments.

"And withholding payments now," David added, "serves as a bargaining chip, but only makes most people angrier that they're not getting what was promised."

"Except they don't agree to the terms of the treaty anyway and want to renegotiate it," Tom said. "You can't have

---

[128] An excerpt from their letter is found in Vicki Rozema, *Voices from the Trail of Tears* (John F. Blair, 2003), 160-169.

the treaty payments and reject the treaty at the same time, when you're saying that you have to have a new one."

Uncle Jim agreed, "People don't understand that. They want everything they can get, as soon as possible. They've suffered too much to have patience with the government. The majority don't have any loyalty to the Old Settler chiefs. All they know is Ross."

"So what are we supposed to do?" Tom asked.

David explained that Jack was still aiming to set up his trading post on Beattie's Prairie, and General Arbuckle would probably move the post commanded by Lieutenant Colonel R. B. Mason at Fort Wayne up to Beattie's Prairie to provide security there. The Baptist Mission was now called "Breadtown." The people there with Bushyhead had taken charge of most of the food distribution that had occurred a few miles north at the old Fort Wayne site on the Illinois River. The Treaty people and Old Settlers could count on keeping certain areas secure, with the forces they had and the federal troops. Their most secure areas were right here, along the Arkansas border in the Evansville area, around Fort Gibson and south to the Arkansas River around the old capitol of Tahlontuskey, and up along Honey Creek and Cowskin Prairie over to the Presbyterian Mission led by Rev. John Huss.[129] Stand had been living at Park Hill, but he did not expect to stay there. He could continue to recruit and train a force that could maintain peace in the northeast on Cowskin Prairie and also in Beattie's Prairie.

Tom agreed that Stand Watie was the most likely person to organize a light horse militia in the north, since he already had

---

[129] Native preacher John Huss is noted in Grant Foreman, *Five Civilized Tribes* (University of Oklahoma, 1934), 365; and in John Ehle, *Trail of Tears*, p. 370.

a loyal following among the young people from both the Treaty Party and the Old Settlers. Tom volunteered that he might be one who would be capable of organizing a militia in their area, if agreeable to all of their supporters.

Uncle Jim added another matter that all of the Cherokee people had to take seriously and a reason that they would eventually have to work together. White people were already taking advantage of their disarray to move into Cherokee territory and to make a profit off of them. "They're setting up stores and selling whiskey and liquor all along the edge of the territory, charging high prices for everything they can sell. They're sneaking in and out of Cherokee land to sell and to steal whatever they can get."

"We can't allow that to happen," Tom said emphatically.

"The only way we can prevent a white invasion is to agree on laws to prevent it and have a unified police force to enforce those laws," David said.

"Otherwise it will be Georgia all over again. The whites will keep coming and eventually take over," added Tom. "If we can't get anyone else to keep them out, we will have to do it ourselves."

"I understand what you're saying, Tom," said David, "but, as you suggested a few moments ago, we'll have to reach an agreement about this. We can't take the law into our own hands. With the authority of the Old Settler Council on our side, we won't have to."

Tom stayed quiet after that, as they continued to talk, but he was obviously considering what had been said.

December 1, 1839, Evansville River Trail

Grandfather John Bell came in his carryall on the morning of December 1, 1839 to pick up Red Wolf, telling Uncle James Starr that he just needed him for the day and not explaining anything more. The grandfather wore a somber expression, and Uncle James guessed what had happened. On the way down the creekside path he told Red Wolf that his Ulisi had died the day before, and the family had buried her without ceremony on a corner of the Adair farm near the creek. To Red Wolf's stricken expression, he added that it was the way she wanted it, no fuss, no bother, no family feasting or dancing, just letting the family know one by one, but he felt that he had to show Red Wolf and some of the others where her body was laid to rest.

"She was a remarkable woman, one o' a kind," he went on to say. "Not only did she raise up ten children, and help with many others in and out o' her family, managed a large household and farm for many years, but she did a lot o' it on her own, when I was travelin' and tradin'. She sought and got help from her brother, Jim Foster, in the traditional way o' raising her children. She found her own way through many changes, among the first to break the old clan rule against marrying within the clan, accepting me as husband though we're both o' the deer clan. She encouraged her children's education in both the white people's ways and the Cherokees,' though it was not easy to find teachers for 'em."

When they reached a little rise at the corner of a cleared field and near the edge of the river, Red Wolf could see the newly turned earth where brush and vines had been cleared away. They got down from the carryall and walked up the rise a few paces to the grave.

"But she's all by herself, here, Ududu," Red Wolf said, his mouth turned down in complaint.

"Naw, she's most definitely naw here," John Bell said. "She said she was already half way to the Western horizon. She was going to hurry on and take all her souls with her, so we were not to worry about her, not about her body, as she was tired o' it and done. This is not the place for her to stay, and it looked to her that it was not for anyone else, since we already commenced to fightin' over it. So we was jus' to bury her body and let her go, and we did. Now you've seen what we did."

On the way back to Uncle Jim's place, Red Wolf asked his Grandpa if he was going to stay nearby now that Ulisi had died. He replied that he would try to do what they had planned to do earlier, but Charlotte could not. They would go up to where the Cowskin Prairie meets the Grand River and try to establish a home there in peace. If they could not accomplish that, he didn't know where they would go, because it would mean they could not live any more in the Cherokee Nation. Then Grandpa Bell began to talk about Red Wolf's uniqueness, that Charlotte had felt a bond with him because he had a destiny all his own. Because of his mother's death probably, but also because of her character, he was different from other children. He had different thoughts and different ways, not "bad" different, but all his own. He would find his own way, and not copy what he saw others doing. He would get along with people and have friends wherever he went, but he would go his own way and not follow them. "It's a good thing," his grandfather said, "to choose your own way." Red Wolf thought that he was talking as much about his own life and Charlotte's life as he was Red Wolf's future, but he stored it up in his own heart.

July 15, 1840, Natural Dam, Arkansas

In the early months of 1840 Red Wolf continued to settle into the routines of the Starr household, but gradually the world around him began to shift. His Grandpa Bell at the end of 1839 told Red Wolf that he had received a message from David at Salina that a baby boy had come into their family on December 15, 1839, and they named him John Martin Adair Bell. One had left the family, but another had entered. Samuel Bell was making his home with David near the Martins in the Saline District. Grandpa Bell bid Red Wolf farewell for the time being as he, James, Sarah, and Martha Jane were headed toward Cowskin Prairie.

Uncle James Starr did not seek help from the depot at Mrs. Webber's. Although the distribution of rations, of corn, salt, salt pork and live cattle and hogs continued, the quality of the food and livestock deteriorated further. Walter Adair, John Thompson Adair and other family members in the area tried to influence the contractors to do better in providing fair or full value, but little came of their efforts, so the misery of the crowds near the distribution sites deepened. The political arguments still prevented the per capita payments that were promised by the New Echota Treaty from being made.[130] By mid-year the rations ended anyway, and the people were on their own.

The Starr and Adair families planted their crops early, and they came up well, but rain did not sustain the growth, so by mid-summer the hayfields were brown, the cornfields and gardens were parched, except for the hand-watering with buckets from the creeks and springs that everyone took turns

---

[130] Summaries of the distribution process are found in Theda Perdue and Michael D. Green, *The Cherokee Nation and the Trail of Tears* (New York: Penguin, 2007), 143-146; and Grant Foreman, *The Five Civilized Tribes* (Norman OK: The University of Oklahoma Press, 1934), 284-288.

carrying. They would provide for their own needs, but little extra for others to share.

The boys decided to take advantage of the heat and drought and go on an adventure. Sam, Washington, Creek (who was Tom's son), Caleb, Buck, Red Wolf, and Will packed food and bedrolls, took to their horses, and headed toward Natural Dam along the trail south toward Van Buren. Stopping mid-morning at Caleb Starr's mill, and visiting with Grandpa Starr, the boys then climbed Evans Mountain and ate their jerky and bread before following the ridge road all afternoon. They arrived at Natural Dam before sunset, so they could strip and swim, above and below the falls, washing off the dust and sweat of the hot day in the cool spring-fed waters, and letting the horses graze in a clearing nearby before tethering them in a ravine for the night. With the drought and the cool-water springs there were no mosquitoes to bother them, and they didn't even light a fire, but talked late under the stars.

In the middle of the night, the noise of horses on the trail nearby roused them, with suspicion about anyone who would be roaming around in the dark. They got up and snuck through the brush until they could see the men and horses in the sliver of light from the first quarter moon. Four white men riding fully-saddled horses were leading a line of five horses, three Negro women and two Negro boys, with hands bound, from the direction of Evansville. Will was the first to recognize the captives as slaves from the household of Austin Rider, and the boys guessed that the horses were Austin's also.

The boys debated what they should do. They were unarmed, and expected that the four thieves were armed and stronger than they were. They could follow them and try to release the slaves when they stopped, but they might ride all the way to Van Buren and put the boys at the disadvantage of being even more outnumbered. Finally, and reluctantly, the boys decided they would return to Evansville as fast as they could and report to Grandpa Starr for his advice. Otherwise they would have more adventure than they wanted.

On the trail back to Evansville, Washington said, "This is just what Tom and Joe have been talking about, horse thieves and kidnappers coming into the Cherokee lands and escaping without anyone able to follow them and put an end to it."

"Sgidv!"[131] Creek agreed. "Dad says we have no one organized to patrol or protect our borders. Ross doesn't care about the Treaty people or the Old Settlers at the border. He's glad to see us raided and bothered. We can't rely on his Cherokee police, and we can't get help from the white police in Arkansas. We are an outlaw territory as far as Ross and the Arkansas officers are concerned."

"I heard Joe say that Ross's government calls us outlaws. We might have to act like outlaws in order to keep real outlaws out of our lands," Buck said. "We can't allow people to steal us blind."

Their horses a few steps behind the other boys, Red Wolf said quietly to Will, "I hope it doesn't come to that."

Will confided, "We've got to do something. This is the first time I really feel scared of what's coming. I know those people who were kidnapped. They're good people."

They returned to Grandpa Starr's house by mid-morning and reported what they had seen. Grandpa told them that they

---

[131] "Yes, that's it," in Cherokee.

were wise to come back instead of follow. "They'd as soon kill you as step on an ant. Except for Will—they could sell him and the horses. But they could not get a penny for the rest of yuh. I'll go talk to Austin, Jim, Tom and the older boys. We'll have to make a plan for what to do. Arbuckle will have to know about this, and let the officers at Fort Smith know, too."

The boys returned to Uncle Jim's place by noon with the news of their adventure.

October 25, 1840, James Starr's Farm

Sam, Red Wolf and Will had spent the day working with Aunt Susie, Aunt Nellie, and Rachel, packing hard squash, potatoes, and other root crops in the root cellar behind the summer kitchen. The pumpkins that they couldn't use soon, they stripped and hung to dry on racks along with some herbs and soft squash. He was glad to hear the voice of his father at the root cellar entrance, "Siyo, Red Wolf, Will. Can you come up for air?"

Red Wolf climbed the make-shift steps out of the root cellar, followed by Will. "Udoda, I'm glad to hear your voice. It's been months. What news brings you down from Salina?"

"Sad news and glad news, a bit of both. Gives me an excuse to come see you and the rest of the family, and learn what's really been happening around here. Rumors are flying. First, let me look at you. You look good, Uweji achuga.[132] This time with your Uduji is doing you good. You, too, Will. You must have grown half a foot over the summer."

"What's happened, Udoda? Is my baby brother well?"

---

[132] "Son" in Cherokee.

"Very well. Walking and talking, he is. We hope for another baby on the way. That's my good news. He'll be "James Foster Bell, after my own Uduji, if he's a boy.[133] But sadly, my wife's father has died. John Martin died October 17. We lost one of our best advocates with the Ross government, since he had become Chief Justice again. Nobody can twine his way into the good will of his enemies like John Martin could.

Uncle James agreed, saying that as long as John Martin was serving as Chief Justice we had some hope of things turning out better. Then he expressed his sympathy for the family's personal loss. "We are losing too many of our leaders, just when we need them most."

December 31, 1840, James Starr's Horse Barn

During the next few months, the appointment of Rev. Jesse Bushyhead in John Martin's place on the court put the Treaty Party's patience to the test when the case of Archilla Smith came before the court. Smith had been a neighbor to Major Ridge and Grandpa John Bell, having a farm on the Coosa River, and Smith had also signed the New Echota Treaty. In an altercation with John MacIntosh following a personal dispute, Smith had stabbed MacIntosh to death, claiming self-defense for his action. He was arrested and put on trial for murder at Tahlequah late in 1840. Jesse Bushyhead's son, Isaac Bushyhead, served as prosecuting attorney for the court, and Stand Watie served Archilla Smith capably as the defense attorney. All of the Treaty supporters waited anxiously for the verdict.

---

[133] James Foster Bell was actually born October 14, 1841, which would mean that David's announcement here was premature. If Nancy had been pregnant at this time, she would not have brought that pregnancy to full term.

Early on the morning of December 31, Uncle James Madison Bell came bearing the news. Grandpa Bell sent his seventeen-year-old son because he knew he would be a faster courier than anyone else in his family. Uncle Jim slowed his horse to a canter as he entered into the Starr farm lane. He headed for the horse barn, where he saw Sam, Buck, Red Wolf, and Will feeding and watering the horses. The rest of the men were soon assembled, and Jim relayed the news that the court had convicted Smith and he would be hung on the next day, January 1.[134]

Bean Starr was the first to respond, "What did we expect? No jury in the nation will miss the chance to execute a Treaty supporter. Nor will they ever convict a Ross supporter for anything like that." Soon he was angrily saddling his horse, threatening to get a group together to ride to Tahlequah and stop the hanging.

"Just how do you propose to accomplish that?" his father asked.

While they continued in agitated talk, Jim Bell drew Red Wolf and Will aside. "I've got to take this news on down the road to Caleb's place. Dad wants you to know we're living near the place he wants to develop. We have a cabin, and Rev. John Huss has some space for the girls at his mission while we're building a better house. It's all near the mouth of Honey Creek where it joins the Grand River, where he's always wanted to settle. He just wanted you to know for sure where he is."

---

[134] The elements of this story come from Foreman, p.343, McLoughlin, p.44. Shadburn, p. 141.

"He knows we can find him when we need him, doesn't he?" Red Wolf answered, thinking of Will's and his long journey by themselves to Grandpa's farm on the Coosa River.

April 15, 1841, Oak Grove

A trusted slave named Jeremiah brought news down the Evansville Creek Valley in the early morning of April 12, 1841. Nancy Harlan Starr, granddaughter and namesake of Nancy Ward, who married Caleb when he was 36 and she was 16, had died in the night of pneumonia and exhaustion. She had worked hard through the winter trying to provide for many of the poor families who had settled in the nearby valleys and ridges after the end of the government ration distribution and the drought of the preceding summer. She and Caleb were familiar neighbors to everyone, all the way from Caleb's mill to eighteen miles southwest, where the new Flint District courthouse stood at the western foot of Dahlonegah Mountain, about eight miles south of Mrs. Webber's distribution center where Walter Scott Adair now lived.

John Thompson Adair and his wife, Penelope, had already buried a little daughter in the old oak grove on his farm. Nearby stood their two story log house on the river bend three miles northwest of the mill on the west side of Twist Mountain.[135] The grove filled a shallow bowl of sixty acres about two hundred paces above the river. Centuries-old oaks grew thick enough to leave the understory open for walking around on soft shade moss and low crawling plants covering the ground. John Adair offered the ground for Nancy to be buried, and the whole neighborhood came together on the third day after the sad

---

[135] Nancy and Caleb Starr may have been buried on their own farm property, or at this Oak Grove site. Family records vary.

message went out, on a warm, quiet day promising spring. All of their children—Mary Pauline Rider, James, Ruth Bean, Ezekiel, Sallie Mayfield, George Harlan, Thomas, Ellis, and Joseph McMinn Starr—came with their many children, including Red Wolf and Will, and all of the Adair, Rider, West, Mayfield, and Bell families who lived within two days' riding distance came with baskets of food and provisions to camp in the grove as long as necessary. At age 83, Caleb looked especially frail on this day, and no one spoke what everyone thought, that he would be next and death would come soon.

Washed and dressed in finely tanned doeskin, wrapped in her favorite brightly-colored quilt with a large seven-pointed star, her six sons placed her body in the grave and slowly took turns filling it with soil, while the assembled people sang and chanted the farewell songs that they knew.

They shared the food they had prepared in baskets and hampers and sat under the oak trees to think and talk together. Red Wolf listened to his older cousin, John T. Adair, as he announced his plans to build a school in the grove as soon as he could, on the highest level area just east of the burying ground. Everyone thought that would be fitting, since Nancy and Caleb had provided schooling for several of them as children at Conasauga Creek in Tennessee. They had done more than anyone to establish all of their new homes in the Evansville vicinity. They lived to see the beginning of their dream fulfilled anyway, with all of their children and their families dwelling in adjacent valleys among the high hills that resembled their Tennessee home, complete with old growth oak, hickory and yellow pine forests. They reminisced and spoke of their determination not to give up on the hopes that had brought Caleb and Nancy west sixteen years before. For a while in that peaceful grove they seemed to put out of their minds their growing anxiety about the future of their people.

May 31, 1842, James Starr's House

In the James Starr household the end of the day provided a time to relax for a little while before bedtime. To counter the evening chill Sam, Red Wolf, and Will often set the fire in the fireplace. Uncle James took his seat in the wide rocking chair and lighted his pipe, and finally Aunt Susie, Aunt Nellie, Rachel and Janie came in after finishing the supper cleanup and sending the servants to their own cabins for the night. Sometimes James or one of the older boys announced something new they had learned during the day, or they reflected together about something that was bothering them.

Over the months they were hearing how Susanna Ridge, Major Ridge's wife, was managing to keep the store on Honey Creek that Major Ridge and John Ridge had worked hard to supply for the newcomers. While John's wife, Sarah Bird Northrup Ridge, had fled to Fayetteville and liquidated his share in the merchandise, Susanna had restocked the store and kept it going, often providing liberal credit to the newcomers.[136] Likewise Uncle Jack Bell was keeping two stores going—one in the neighborhood surrounding the Flint District Courthouse on the west side of Dahlonegah Mountain, and the other on Beattie's Prairie, near Fort Wayne. Red Wolf's Grandfather Bell had helped with the Flint store before he moved to the Grand River, and sometimes his brother David helped with the Beattie Prairie store, as he used to do at Old Coosawattee Town. Otherwise,

---

[136] Thurman Wilkins, *Cherokee Tragedy*, 341-343. Susanna Ridge continued to keep the store until her death in September, 1849.

Uncle Jack put trusted people in charge, like his slave Ezekiel, or his old partner Joseph Lynch.

Nearly every white settlement just inside the Arkansas border had a store of some kind, and entrepreneurs ready to make as much money as possible off the new settlers in Indian Territory. If nothing else was available, whiskey was.[137] As much as Uncle James and the older boys enjoyed a drink from their own home-made stock, they resented the money wasted in some of these stores instead of purchasing things more desperately needed in the Cherokee Nation. They knew that the Cherokee and missionary preachers were united in their opposition to the whiskey trade, and so were their neighbors among the Adair family. Somehow they would have to organize their opposition to this drain on the resources of the nation.

They also heard with increasing desperation of cross-border raids by thieves, while the Cherokee government response was inaction and confusion. Chief Ross was spending most of his effort trying to renegotiate the Treaty, and the per capita payments that the people needed were still being withheld. Most of the people were simply trying to establish their homes and farms, and many people were sharing what they had with people less fortunate in the traditional Cherokee way, but there were also many on both sides of the border who sought a short cut to making a living at other people's expense.

On this evening at the end of May, after a long day of raking and planting gardens and fields, the older boys were agitated about the news of recent killings. On May 9, at one of the border stores in Maysville, Arkansas, a white man named Mitchell who sympathized with the Treaty Party had stabbed

---

[137] McLoughlin, p. 388, note 4.

and killed Anderson Springston.[138] Since Springston had been implicated in the deaths of John Walker, Jr., and Major Ridge, the Starr brothers had welcomed this news, including the news that Mitchell had escaped without any consequences. "After all, how long had Springston gotten off without facing justice?" Then James Foreman, who had joined Springston in the earlier murders, had talked about Uncle Jack Bell coming to kill him at Maysville in a contest, but Bell wasn't even in the area at the time. Shortly thereafter, on May 16, James Foreman met and attacked Stand Watie in front of the same store at Maysville, David England's grocery. Watie had struggled with him and killed him. Now Watie was facing trial for murder.[139]

"What if they find him guilty and hang him like they did Archilla Smith?" Washington asked.

Their father James answered, "You have to remember—he'll face trial in Arkansas, not in the Cherokee Nation. I think he has every right to expect a verdict of innocent since he was acting in self-defense. A jury there does not have the same bias against a man who signed the Treaty. He also has a good defense attorney in David Walker, and an honest advisor in George Paschal, a white man who married his cousin, Major Ridge's daughter.[140] Not that Stand Watie didn't do an excellent job of defending Archilla, but he had two strikes against him in front of that jury. Archilla had signed the Treaty, and so had Stand."

---

[138] McLoughlin, p. 42.

[139] McLoughlin, p. 42

[140] McLoughlin, page 389, note 19; See the account of the trial in *Chronicles of Oklahoma*, vol. 59, #2, 1981, "Stand Watie and the Killing of James Foreman" by Richard Zellner.

"I'm still worried about him. We can't lose another leader, especially Stand Watie," Washington said.

"I am, too, but I think we can wait this out and hope for the best," said his father.

September 1842, George Harlan Starr's Farm

James had loaned his brother, George Harlan Starr, the use of several sons and some slaves, Red Wolf and Will among them, to finish cutting and putting up the last hay crop of the season. George had moved down from the Baptist Mission area to a farm along Evansville Creek close to most of his siblings, and a fine new house and barns now stood within sight of the hayfield.

Taking a break mid-afternoon, the boys began listing the successes of the summer. First came the acquittal of Stand Watie on the murder charges. There could be justice in an Arkansas court after all. Secondly, the Federal Government had rebuffed Arkansas Governor Yell, when he had called for more federal troops to quell what he called an "Indian uprising" in the Cherokee Nation, after several random killings had upset everyone. While the Cherokee Nation needed an adequate and impartial police force, they didn't need a hysterical invasion provoked by an alarmist governor. Thirdly, Ross's delay in settling the per-capita payment situation was finally calling his leadership into question. Some people were even beginning an inquiry into his use of tribal funds.[141]

Meanwhile, while he listened to the others, Red Wolf was adding some personal matters to his own gratitude list. His two little brothers were healthy and strong, and he had gotten to see

---

[141] Summaries of these events are found in Foreman, pp. 324-326, and McLoughlin, pp. 42-43.

his father at least twice. He received a letter, delivered by his father, from his Aunt Sarah Bell, that they had built a new house on the Grand River and were farming in the rich bottomland of that river. He still had not returned to school, and there was none in prospect yet, but he was thankful for the training he had gotten from his mother and Sarah.

Fourth on Washington's list was the large brigade that Tom, Bean, Ellis and Creek, and their cousins and friends had organized to take turns patrolling the borders of Flint and the surrounding districts. They aimed to prevent outsiders from sneaking into the Cherokee Nation and to prevent Ross's police from harassing Old Settler and Treaty families. This part of the discussion brought Red Wolf back into full attention to what was being said. The other boys were obviously excited by the new police brigade and eager to be a part of it. He was not so eager. Learning to be a farmer excited him more, but he could see that patrolling the area and claiming that police authority sounded more exciting to many of the others. They had found a solution to the issues that had dominated so many of their anxious family discussions.

October 1842, James Starr's Barn
One warm October afternoon, Red Wolf was working alone in the barn's haymow, shifting the loose hay into taller stacks and clearing a space around the ladder and the hole in the floor so he or any of the boys could pitch hay down to the animals below. Working in the mow was hot and dusty, and he had started to sweat a lot, so he had stripped to his clout. Rachel climbed up to watch. She was just a year younger than he, and they had often looked at each other, almost like looking into a mirror, the same height and weight, both thin and strong and dark-eyed and black-haired. Lately, though, changes in his voice, his shoulders,

her breasts and hips, made their glances at each other more awkward. Yet she had sought him out. At first he didn't see her, and she watched quietly.

When he did see her, he went over to where he had tossed his pants and shirt, and reached for his pants, but Rachel said, "Please don't. I like to look at you." Red Wolf blushed as he turned toward her.

"I didn't know you were there," he said. "It's easier to keep my clothes dry and clean, if I take them off."

"That's all right; it's easier on my eyes if you leave them off. I like the looks of you," she said. "I like to watch you and my brothers working in the field, when you have stripped to the skin. You look pretty to me."

"You have an advantage over me," he said. "When we were small, we would swim and play in the water naked, and think nothing about it, but when we got older, we had to stop doing that."

Then she surprised him, saying, "I think about that sometimes," and she took off her shift, revealing her small breasts, and she slowly slipped out of her skirt, and stood before him naked again and smiled. "I can let you see me again."

"Maybe you shouldn't," Red Wolf said softly, but his shaft had already begun to stiffen, as it had so often done recently as he looked at girls or thought about them.

Rachel stared down at his slim hips and smiled as she saw his clout begin to bulge. She reached for his hand and pulled him gently down beside her as she lowered herself onto the hay. "I think it's all right for us to play with each other. We're just learning what it's like to be grown up."

"What if someone finds us like this?" he quietly protested.

"Then we will put our clothes back on, and tell them we were just playing and showing each other, which is the truth. Nobody'll be surprised. Will you show me your shaft? If you will, I'll let you see my sheath."

Red Wolf's eyes were already fixed on the fine, dark hair that peeked from her groin, so Rachel reached for the belt that fastened his clout and unhooked it, pulling the cloth down and away, and uncovering his semi-erect shaft and the black hair around it. He quickly covered himself with both hands, then, looking at her face, slowly revealed himself again. "It works just like a stallion's or a bull's, but it's a lot smaller," he said.

"More like a boar's, or a dog's, or maybe a jackrabbit's, I'd say," she giggled, and he smiled. "May I touch it?" she asked.

"I guess," Red Wolf answered, and he lay back against the hay and put his hands behind his head, while she leaned over his crotch, and took a closer look, touching him lightly and briefly, jerking back with surprise at his springy hardness. He crossed his legs and involuntarily flexed his thigh muscles. "Do we have to get married now?" he teased.

"Would that be so bad?" she asked. "According to the old ways we belong to different clans. You are wolf, and I am paint clan. We could marry. Even the whites sometimes marry their second cousins, so we could do that, if we wanted to." She lay back against the hay beside him. "I'm not ready to be married yet, though. I need to know a lot more about what it means to marry. You are the nicest boy I know, much nicer than my birth brothers. If I had to choose now, I'd choose you."

Our Land! Our People!

After a few minutes lying there, side by side, Red Wolf leaned over and kissed Rachel on the cheek. Then he stood up and refastened his clout around his waist. "I like you, too, Rachel. And, wado.[142] I think you're very pretty, too." Then he went back to forking the hay, enjoying mutual glances as she put her clothes back on and descended the ladder.

Red Wolf was nervous about going to supper that evening, sitting across from Rachel, in their usual places, but when they sat down at the table, she acted the way she always did, mostly ignoring him and talking with her sisters.[143]

April 1843, Cooper's Spring

Uncle James had asked Sam, Red Wolf and Will, all near fourteen years old, and growing into full-fledged cowboys, to accompany him on a trip to sell some cattle and meet with Old Settler leaders southwest in the Illinois District. They returned by way of the Sallisaw Creek valley, south of where Walter S. Adair was now living and Mrs. Webber's depot had been, stopping for fresh water at the largest spring in the area, on the land of old Ben Cooper. Cooper was a mixed-blood, married to a Delaware (Leni Lenape) woman.

Red Wolf admired the gushing water, seeming to appear out of nowhere from a hump in the plain, forming a creek that was full of clear, cold water. Cooper had built a springhouse in the creek and his dog-trot log cabin was nearby. He encouraged

---

[142] Thank you.

[143] Missionaries among the Cherokees recorded "an astonishing degree of sexual freedom" and "tolerance of sexual experimentation" even among the students in the missionary schools, according to Theda Perdue in *Cherokee Women*, p.180. The controlling traditions of matrilineal clans and clan limitations related to marriage began to disintegrate after white contact and intermarriage with whites.

anyone to use the area around the spring, as long as they left it clean, because it was "God's gift" and no one could own it. The spring reminded Red Wolf of Rattlesnake Springs, which was larger, but no more remarkable. This spring also flowed freely even in this dry season, when everyone was short of water for their planting.

By this time everyone that they met had heard of the Border Volunteers, as they called themselves, or the Starr Gang, as many of the Ross Party and the Cherokee Advocate Newspaper from Tahlequah had begun to call them. James didn't make any effort to defend his sons. When he detected an opposing and critical opinion about them, he simply said, "They are old enough to know what they're doing," or "If we had seen any real police in our area, the Volunteers wouldn't be necessary."

When he was alone with his family, though, James had expressed some doubts. "The boys don't have enough discipline over their ranks, to keep everyone in line. I feel the resentment over the killings of my friends as much as anyone, but the young fellas have got to keep their desire for vengeance under control. It belongs in God's hands, not in ours. I worry that some of the men are going to let things go too far. Your Uncle George, Charles Reese and I wrote to Ross a few days ago. We pointed out to him that vigilante groups have organized to kill Treaty men, some of the best citizens of our nation. They are playing with war, and that is the worst calamity our nation could face. I don't suppose Ross will pay any attention to us."[144]

Apart from some brief comments and questioning looks, when people recognized James Starr, this trip had gone well. People seemed to be minding their own business, and if anyone was looking for a fight, Uncle James was not going to give them one.

At the spring Red Wolf said aloud, "The last time I was in this valley I was with Ududu Bell; both Will and I were. I miss him, but I still expect to see him again. I feel sadder to think that I won't see Grandpa Starr."

Uncle James responded, "Yes, we all do, and we will as long as we live. He was a good father, Grandpa to many, well beyond his own family. It was too bad he died in the coldest time of year. We couldn't have an appropriate gathering then. People have too much going on now to make up for it. But he was too generous a man to hold it against us. The ones I feel sorry for are those who depended on his free crib for corn. We'll have to do more to make sure we have extra crops for people who need help."

After a few minutes, Red Wolf asked a question that had been on his mind, "Uncle James, I hear people say that the Starr boys ought to act like Stand Watie, and spend more time minding their own business. Is that fair?"

---

[144] Stanley W. Hoig, *The Cherokees and Their Chiefs* (Fayetteville, University of Arkansas Press, 1998),196. The letter from James Starr, George Washington Adair, and Charles Reese, stated "Several private companies have been organized in the Nation under the title of police companies for the express purpose of killing the Treaty men, as they are called, including some of the best citizens of our nation....War would certainly be the sorest calamity with which our land can be visited."

Sam quickly interjected, "We're following Stand's example already. He recruited a group when his brother and uncle and cousin were killed."

But Uncle James quickly added, "That's right, but I sometimes wish my boys would spend more time close to home, too. We have to remember that Stand had to lay low for a while after his trial. Besides, he needed to develop his own claim close to where your Grandpa Bell is farming. As you may already know, he has an interest in that pretty little woman that you like so well."

"Aunt Sarah? Yes. I guessed a long time ago that she had a special interest in him. Her eyes lighted up too much for me to miss it, every time she talked about him. I wouldn't be surprised if they got married pretty soon."

"So, my sons are doing what they think they need to do, but they also have to spend more time tending their farms, or they'll be up at my place, asking for a hand out, and I'll have to say, 'And where were you, when we put the crop in?'" He laughed heartily for some moments. "I think Tom will get everybody to put their time into the fields before we ever get to that point. He has his head connected to his body."

July 6, 1843, James Starr's Farm

The first rays of morning sunlight shone on the top of Twist Mountain, and the birds were in full song when Red Wolf made his way down the path toward the bathing pool. This was his fourteenth birthday and he rose early, about an hour earlier than usual, as his mind wandered over many thoughts. The crackle of a footstep on a dead branch behind him alerted him to someone else. He turned around to see Rachel coming, and he was surprised to see her up so early.

"Siyo, Rachel. What gets you up at this hour?"

"Good morning, Red Wolf," she smiled back at him. "I knew this was your birthday, and I wanted to bring you a gift, so I woke up with the birds and watched for you. I knew you would get up for a morning bath today, since it's a special day. You almost always do anyway."

"It's something I got from my mother when I was a little boy. It feels like the best way to begin the day."

Rachel had moved to his side, and reached over with her right hand to stroke his bare chest and stomach, and then she moved her hand beneath his clout to touch the top of his shaft.

"Oh...well!" Red Wolf swallowed hard, and his eyes opened wider. "If that's the gift you mean...." He paused to consider what to say. "Then I guess we should find a place in the grass where we can be alone for a while, and maybe lie down?"

"I haven't forgotten our time in the haymow," Rachel said. "I'll lie down with you, and we can play."

Red Wolf took her by the hand and they picked their way through the brush not far from the stream. Just beyond a cane break, in the shelter of a cluster of willow trees, they found a gentle slope covered with soft moss. "Here...." He touched the hem of her shift and asked, "May I?"

Rachel said "Yes," as she unhooked the belt of his clout. It dropped to the ground, and he lifted her homespun linen shift over her head, and folded it over his arm, and turned and placed it on a branch behind him. He lowered himself to the ground, reaching for her hand. He saw that her breasts were fuller, her hips wider than he remembered, and the small patch of hair between her legs thicker and darker.

"You are very pretty, Rachel. I like to look at you. You are so slender, yet you are growing up and filling out as a woman."

She smiled again, and, stretching out beside him, she resumed stroking his chest and stomach, and he bent toward her to kiss her cheek and then her lips, again and again. As she was beginning to stroke his stiffening shaft, he stopped and asked her quietly, "What would your mother say, if she knew we were doing this?"

Rachel looked in his eyes fully and said, "She knows. She helped me wake up this morning. We talked about it."

"Oh.... I'm glad. That makes me feel better. I didn't want to betray your parents. They've been so good to me."

They returned to the petting and holding, and they touched and rubbed each other's genitals, and soon Rachel said with surprise and some disgust, "It's so warm and sticky." Red Wolf laughed aloud. She started to pull back, and wipe her hand onto the moss. He saw that he had offended her, and quickly said, "I'm sorry, Rachel. You're right. A man's seed is messy. The way you said it just tickled me. Before I got used to doing it myself, I had the same reaction. Sex is messy. Between a woman's monthly bleed and a man's nightly spurt of seed, it's just messy. But, Rachel, wado. I love your gift. Thank you for touching me and lying with me."

Rachel gave him a little smile. "I'm new at this."

"I am, too. Can we do it some more, or do we need to stop? I'm sorry I came so soon. I was so excited, I couldn't stop myself."

"It's all right. I'd like you to hold me some more." So they resumed the touching, but slower and easier this time. Red Wolf put his finger gently into her sheath and pretended it was his shaft inside her, until she grew more excited also, and said, "That feels so good. Please keep doing that." They kept going for several minutes, until Rachel felt Red Wolf pulse and spurt the sticky ooze again into her hand and against her thigh. She did not wipe it off so quickly this time. She slipped it between her fingers, smelled it and tasted it and rubbed it onto Red Wolf's face, and they laughed together.

"It doesn't have much flavor, but it smells like a pear tree all full of blossoms. Oh, well.... Now I know why Mama wanted me to make sure I bathed and you bathed before coming back to the house," Rachel said, as they stood up and collected their clothing. "She said she would make a special tea for you to drink, and I should wash myself well inside and out, before we left the bathing creek.[145]

Rachel and Red Wolf returned to the bathing pool and immersed themselves, and splashed water on each other and washed each other gingerly. He stood still for a moment, lifted his head, and spoke a prayer of thanks to the Creator Spirit for this day, for his life and her life, and for their time together. She listened as if his words surprised her. He climbed out, and she took special care to wash herself. He sat and watched her and then put on his clout. He extended his hand and helped her climb out onto the creek bank, and he helped her put on her shift. They headed back toward the house, and on the way, Red Wolf said, "This is the best birthday ever."

They entered the kitchen door together and found Aunt Susie and Aunt Nellie at work in the kitchen, saw them exchange

---

[145] Theda Perdue, in *Cherokee Women*, page 58, tells about traditional cleansing practices following sexual emissions.

knowing smiles, and Nellie offered Red Wolf a cup of a sweet and sour tea that he had never drunk before.

August 10, 1843, G·W·Adair's House

Many of the people from the Evansville Creek and Oak Grove neighborhoods gathered in the yard of the home of George Washington Adair on the afternoon of August 10. They had been enthusiastic about the Cherokee Nation election on August 8, especially since a popular figure represented the Old Settler and Treaty interests, Joseph Vann, running for Principal Chief. He had served as Second Principal Chief under Ross until 1840, and he chose Walter Scott Adair as his running mate.[146] Many questions had surfaced about Ross's leadership during the preparations for the vote. Election results had just begun to come in, but already they knew that not enough people had voted for Vann to remove Ross as Chief.

The more pressing problem came from arguments and confrontations between the Ross, Treaty and Old Settler factions at the polls. The most serious incident occurred in Saline District when Jacob West, George West, and John West disrupted the vote count being tallied by three men whom the Wests accused of all being Ross supporters—Isaac Bushyhead, whom they held responsible for the unfair execution of Archilla Smith; David Vann, who had renounced the Treaty and was now the National Treasurer; and Elijah Hicks, Ross Party leader and Associate Judge in the Supreme Court. In the ensuing struggle, George West stabbed and killed Bushyhead. Jacob and John West severely injured Vann and Hicks, and the three Wests set fire to

---

[146] McLoughlin, p. 44

all of the ballots before they escaped. A posse was now searching for them.[147]

Their host, George Washington Adair, a tall and dignified man, called them to order, and asked loudly, "What do we do now? We're all upset by these events. We thought we had a chance of a unity government. Instead we're looking at more division and struggle."

Walter Scott Adair responded, "I think we have no choice but to pursue a moderate course, assist in the arrest of the Wests if we have the chance, and assist in their defense. They have been loyal to our cause, and we do not have a full story by any means."

Hearing that last point, Uncle James Starr spoke, "We never get the full story. Unfortunately, we know that any trial that is held will begin with the presumption that they are guilty. I hear that some of my boys may have been involved in the argument before the fighting broke out. The rumors say they helped the Wests escape, too. I don't know for sure, but we have known the Wests for years. I'm in no hurry to help them be captured, knowing what they will face. I'm in favor of 'wait and see,' provide shelter to them if we can, and learn as much as we can about what really happened, before we make up our minds about turning them in."

Red Wolf looked around the yard at the men standing there. Few younger men were present. Perhaps they had all made up their minds already. He hadn't seen Tom, Ellis, or Bean for nearly a month, though he had heard that they were in and out of their own homes. They hadn't worked on any farm

---

[147] McLoughlin, p.44, and Foreman, pp. 326-328

projects with their younger brothers. He wondered how the border patrol was going.

G. W. Adair spoke again. "I fear that we're sitting on a powder keg. There's too much hatred on both sides. We've made too little progress in getting people settled and comfortable. Here in this valley we have a taste of what prosperity can mean, but it doesn't reach far enough throughout the country.'

"We also see that people who are trying to keep order can quickly turn on each other," Walter Adair observed. "Who's going to keep the official police and the volunteer patrols apart? I think we should seek the help of General Arbuckle before things get out of hand. People are carrying too many grudges against each other. All it takes is adding a little alcohol to the mix, and we have an explosion."

The men continued to talk through the afternoon. After a few hours most of the men had drifted away or excused themselves to go home for chores; the remaining neighbors decided to adjourn. They hadn't agreed on a course of action. They had expressed their growing apprehensions.

September 20, 1843, Evansville Creek

With their work being done for the day, the evening warm, and the sky clear, Sam, Red Wolf, and Will dug some red worms, grabbed their fishing poles, and headed to a favorite fishing hole in Evansville Creek, where the water was deep enough and the brush afforded shelter for the bass. As it turned out, only bluegill and crappie were biting, but that was enough to keep the boys interested late into the night.

Their quiet talk soon turned to news of their brothers. "Where do you suppose Tom, Bean, and Ellis are?" Red Wolf asked.

"Probably hiding out in the hills above Evansville. If General Taylor[148] sent a posse after them, they'll hide out where they know the territory real well, where they're not going to be caught," answered Sam.

Red Wolf continued, "I still don't understand what happened down at old Ben Vore's. They say Tom killed a white man by the name of Kelly, then the men killed Vore and his wife, and burned down their cabin.[149] I can't imagine how that all happened."

"My brothers wouldn't have done it unless they had to. Kelly and the Vores must have been doing something illegal. Kelly shouldn't have been in Cherokee country at all. He's a white man who's just here to make money. The Vores must have been up to no good. They probably fired the first shots. I don't see Tom or any of the Volunteers killing them in cold blood. Not the Tom I know."

Will added, "The Vores was white folks, too, I hear. They was licensed to trade in the Nation, but who knows how they got a license or what they was up to?"

"I know your Dad feels strongly that Tom and the boys must have been in the right, but I hate it, how it's come to this. Why were they so far away, down near Fort Gibson? Isn't that area supposed to be under federal control?"

---

[148] General Zachary Taylor, U.S. Army Commander stationed at Fort Smith in Arkansas in 1843.

[149] McLoughlin, pp. 44-45, and Foreman, p. 327.

"It's Old Settler country. They were probably there 'cause somebody asked them to check on what was going on."

"Maybe. But where's it going to stop? Earlier I heard that David Buffington was killed, and he's got lots of relatives that'll be looking to get even."

"Tom, Ellis, and Bean are my brothers, and I'm standing by them."

Red Wolf said quickly, "I know, Sam; they're my family, too. I just never thought it would come to this. Not even that day when the Ross Party labeled all the Treaty-signers outlaws, after they'd killed Major Ridge, and we wondered whether they'd come for our Dad. I didn't want this to keep going year after year. It's four years, and there's no end in sight. Everybody's getting pulled into the feud. There's no stopping it."

December 1, 1843, James Starr's Farm

David Bell arrived late in the morning of December 1, 1843, and asked Red Wolf to take a walk alone. Red Wolf knew immediately that his father had something to tell him that he did not want to talk about with everyone. The sky was clear, and the temperature cool. They walked east along the creek-side path southeast toward the Arkansas State line.

David was quiet at first, his hands in his pockets. "You know my sister Sarah married Stand Watie?"

"She wrote me a letter several months ago and told me they were planning to get married soon."

"I'm happy for them both. They're a good couple; they love each other. I'm sorry to say that Nancy left me. She had plenty of reasons. Upset over the death of her father. I was gone a lot, working on the cabin and the farm up the Grand River near my father's place, helping brother Jack with the store over on Beattie's Prairie near Fort Wayne. I left her alone too much. She never liked the idea of living up there."

"Why not?"

"She liked being closer to the center of things, where things are happening. I like to live where life is quieter, where I can be by myself, and work on the farm. She didn't really want that kind of life. She wanted to find someone more interesting and lively."

"I think I must be more like you, Udoda. I like the farm, and the more trouble my brothers get into, the happier I am to stay home."

"I'm with you, Son. I love my brother, Jack, and I respect all that he's tried to do for our people, but I can't see how it's accomplished very much. I haven't been much of a father to you, either, and my marriage to Nancy brought us two fine sons, but no mother for you. I'm sorry for that."

"I like being here with Uncle James, so I have nothing against Nancy for not trying to be more of a mother to me. She couldn't have replaced my mother anyway."

"No, you're right there. No one can take her place."

"What are my brothers going to do? Where will they be?"

"I don't know for sure. Right now Will's mother, Demaris, takes care of them as much as anyone, and your Ududu likes having them around. He plays with them as much or more than I do. Uncle Jack takes an interest, too. Nancy's brothers do not. Your Uncle Jack has made a good match with Elizabeth Harnage.

For a while he seemed very lost and lonely. He had three couplings that didn't last, but now I think he and Elizabeth are doing all right. They have a new baby they named Nancy, born a month ago.[150] We're not a traditional Cherokee family, if there are any of those any longer. Anyway, you have your choice now, where you want to live. You can stay here if you want, or you can come and live with me."

"Wado, Udoda. I'll think about that and talk to Uncle James. When the time is right, I will come and work with you."

They continued to walk along the path and talk about each of the family members and the events in the nation. David admitted to confusion about reports of clashes between the Light-horse Police and the Volunteer Border Patrol on the one side, and the National Party Police on the other. *The Cherokee Advocate* always took the side of the National Party and Ross's allies, and in their editorials and news articles they criticized Tom Starr and Stand Watie and their associates. David believed that people had made mistakes and overstepped boundaries on both sides.

David knew that Ross had offered a reward for the capture of Tom, Bean, and Ellis, a thousand dollars each, and that Ross always had a bodyguard with him now. The National Party government had confiscated all of the salt-works held by the Old Settlers—except for Sequoyah's—and that confiscation had further aggravated the anger between the factions. Old Cherokee allies and well-known white men, Mark and Richard Bean, had lost their salt-works. Even Old Settler Chief John Rogers lost his property at the Grand Saline. "If they don't want

---

[150] Information about the wives of John Adair Bell and his relationships and children with Tsiyahsah, Wodeyohe, and Hiahni Drowningbear is recorded in *The Cherokee Adairs*, p. 27.

to be called tyrants, they should stop acting like tyrants," David said.[151]

"Another thing, Red Wolf. Before I leave you we have something else we need to talk about. Your Uncle Jim tells me that you and his daughter Rachel are getting close to each other. I was about your age when a lovely girl and I began to dream of a life together."

"I worry about Rachel and me and what will happen to us. What happened between you and that girl, Udoda?"

"We spent more and more time together. We got to know each other very, very well. After a few years we married each other and had a baby boy together, and you know the rest of the story, because that baby boy was you. The best advice I can give you is to take your time and not move too quickly into planting your seed in her. It is a heavy responsibility to bring a child into the world. It's one I haven't done well in carrying."

"Udoda, you've always been a good example to me. I wouldn't trade my Uji or my Udoda for anyone. You let me have a family that's as large as anyone could imagine. Still, it's hard for me to think of leaving Rachel. I want to be with her whenever I can. I wonder if it's all right for me to dream that Rachel might be my udali'i, my wife."

"I don't see any wrong in it, son. She and you are from different clans. Though she's called your sister, thanks to Uncle Jim's large heart, she's not close blood kin. She's your third cousin, by Scot reckoning, and a fair match by English law anywhere. Dream as much as you want, but take your time and do not hurry your decision to marry. Try to control yourself

---

[151] McLoughlin, p. 45, and Foreman, p. 331.

when you're with her if you can. You sure chose a difficult time to fall in love."

"So did you, Udoda."

June 15, 1844, Evansville & Baron Creeks

After a day and night of heavy rain, Uncle Jim, his servants, and his boys mounted their horses and began to pick their way slowly through the trees away from the rain-swollen river to examine the damage to their fields. Flood water covered the creek path. Half of their crop stood in flowing water in the lowlands, the richest soil and the most vulnerable to flooding. "We won't have time to replant; we'll just have to make do," he said.[152] "We'll barely have enough to feed ourselves, much less help others."

They spent the day travelling downriver, seeing the Baron Fork even farther over its banks, and finding the neighbors along the way greatly distressed by the loss of their crops. Everyone knew that the heavy rains were widespread, and the Illinois and Grand Rivers were likely to be flooding as well.

"If we're ever going to get those per capita payments, now is the time we need them the most," was a frequent comment.

Uncle Jim pulled his horse alongside Red Wolf's at one point in the early afternoon. "We'll have our hands full trying to catch up after this flood. If you and Will want to join your father up on the Grand River, this may be the time to do it."

---

[152] Foreman, p. 381.

"Uncle, I don't want to leave Rachel, and she doesn't want to leave her mother's house. I don't want to leave you when you need us the most. Not unless you think we're more of a burden than a help, just more mouths to feed," Red Wolf answered.

"You always do your share, so that's not a problem. I know your father could use your help, too, in a season like this. It's up to you."

"In that case I think we'll stay here. Your older boys are busy with their patrol, and staying clear of the National Party Police. I think you'll need our help more than Udoda, unless he says otherwise."

December 30, 1844, James Starr's House

The evening fire was burning in the fireplace as Tom and Creek nervously took their places standing in front of it, facing their father and tearful mothers, Susie, Sallie, and Nellie, seated in the formal upholstered chairs. The rest of the family had gathered around, seated in chairs and on the wood floor or standing. They had just reported the death of their brother, Bean, who had ridden with them on a Volunteer Patrol foray into Choctaw and Cherokee settlements areas along the Washita River near the Texas border. After everyone had a chance to find a place where they could hear, James had frowned and set his jaw and lowered his eyebrows, and told them to explain what happened.

"What were you doing down there anyway?" came James' irritated query.

As big as he was, Tom was clearly out of practice in answering his father's anger. Nervously he adjusted his stance and looked down at the floor for a time before he raised his eyes to meet his father's. "After being chased by Taylor's dragoons, and being released by the Arkansas' sheriff who'd detained us, we decided to stay away from places where the Light-horse or the Army patrols might be looking for us. We knew there was an Old Settler area along the Washita, and we had a herd of horses and mules of uncertain ownership...."

James interrupted, "What do you mean by uncertain ownership?"

"Some we had reclaimed. We knew they'd come from Old Settler or Treaty Party families, but we didn't know exactly who they belonged to. Others were, more or less, replacements for animals that Ross's people had taken from our folks."

"So, you can't say they belonged to you."

"No, there's been some stealing on both sides of this. Anyway, we were surprised to run into a gang of Ross's people, not Light-horse; they weren't official, just a gang Daniel Coodey put together, and we had a shoot-out. Bean was hit. He had a bad wound. They outnumbered us. They got Bean and took him to Fort Washita, and turned him over to Colonel Harney. We tried to get some people in to see him, but he died in their custody there at the fort. We tried to ambush Coodey's group on the trail north, but there were too many of them and they had reinforcements from the fort."

"Tom, I am disappointed and sorrowful. Of all of you, Bean was the one who knew the least about what he was doing. He went along, and he didn't complain about anything, but I'm not sure he ever knew what this whole conflict is about. So I guess I blame myself as much as you for letting things happen the way they did. I'll find a way to bring his body back so we can give him a proper burial.

"I trust you to know what you're doing, and I'm on your side, Tom. You and Creek and Field, Jimmy, Billy, and all the boys you've rounded up to help—I'm proud of what you've tried to do, but the more scrapes like this you get into, when it's not clear you're trying to uphold the law that ought to be in place, and when our enemies can distort every story to suit themselves, well, it looks like you're just trying to keep everything and everyone upset. God knows the Ross government is illegitimate. They got the votes, but they've got no honor, to kill the very people who tried to pull their skinny asses out of the fire and give us all a chance to be a nation together. It's a damn shame. It's not right and it's never going to be right. All I can say is—you've got to do a better job of making sure you're upholding the right and not making things up to suit yourselves as you go along. We are a proud people, a peaceful people, not savages. We came here to build a nation, not tear one down. Do you understand?"

"Yes, Father," answered Tom, and the other boys nodded in solemn agreement.

March 1, 1845, James Starr's House

Conflict grew during the hungry winter months of 1844. Uncle Jim heard the news and told his family about the killing of Old Settler Lewis Rogers and Treaty Party leader John Fields.[153] When Uncle Jim saw his sons—Tom, Field, and Ellis—which occurred less and less frequently, he questioned them about what they were doing and heard their answers, and he told them that they had to keep the pressure on, keeping outsiders out, and defending their partisans against the National Party. "They have their police, and you and your volunteers are our police," he told them.

As spring approached and they were sorting and cleaning the seed for the next planting, they made what was left from the last crop available to the families in the valley who were destitute. "We can't save anything back at this point," Uncle Jim announced. "If we lose our crop this year, we'll all be in the same boat."

Will and Red Wolf were at the granary, using the gusty wind to sift, clean, and sort the last of the seed before planting. While they were talking about many things, Will made this statement, "Sometimes I'm jealous of you."

"Because I'm free, and you're a slave? I think a lot about that."

"Well, I wasn't thinking of that just now. But, yeah, that, too. Only right now I'm glad to be here. I feel free here since I'm with you and doing things I like to do, mostly when I want to do them. What I was thinking about was you and Rachel. I wish I

---

[153] McLoughlin, p. 48.

had a girl like you do. She's pretty. She's smart. She's able to take care of herself. She can do just about anything a boy can do."

"You better quit talking about her, Will, or I'll have to leave you to do the work and I'll go looking for her. I never knew a guy could feel this way about a girl. I can't get enough of her. The more we're together, the more I want to be."

"So you've got it bad, huh? Sounds like you're the slave.... No, I'm glad for you. I been lookin', but I haven't found any gal yet that I'm inter'sted in. So, that's why I said I feels jealous. I guess I shouldn't be if it makes a guy love-sick."

May 28, 1845, Fairfield Mission & School

Walter Adair had visited Uncle James after spring planting was mostly done, and he invited anyone from the family to join him at the big meeting that he had planned at the end of the month. Uncle Walter[154] was President of the National Temperance Society, and he was convinced that people could come together to oppose the illegal traffic in liquor, even if they couldn't agree on anything else. He and the society wanted to gather as many people as possible from the Flint District, where a lot of the cross-border liquor traffic occurred.

Uncle Jim gave his consent, and Washington, Sam, Red Wolf, and Will left before sunrise to make their way on horseback down the valley path about twenty miles southwest to

---

[154] Walter Scott Adair, or "Red Watt," was a nephew of Charlotte Adair Bell, Red Wolf's Grandmother. Born in 1791 Walter Scott was a son of Edward Adair, Charlotte's brother. Another brother named Walter, born in 1789, was the father of John Thompson Adair. These "uncles" are actually second cousins to Red Wolf, but regarded as uncles because of their seniority. See *Cherokee Adairs*, p. 3 in the John Adair Section II, and also p. 3 in the Edward Adair Section III. Treaty-signer George Washington Adair, born around 1805, was a half-brother to Charlotte, and a literal great-uncle to Red Wolf, and he married Martha Martin, another daughter of Judge John Martin, and settled in the Evanston and Oak Grove neighborhoods.

the Fairfield Mission. Rev. Elizur Butler, one of the revered pastors who had stayed with the people from the days of conflict in Georgia, had offered the grounds of the Mission for the gathering, and he was one of the speakers. The four boys saw the buildings at a distance at the western foot of Dahlonega Mountain—a large double log cabin, a story and a half high, with two stone chimneys; and a school house, with a stone chimney, not quite as large as the dwelling house; and several smaller out-buildings. Carriages and horses were parked and tied up to rails and fences, and dozens of people were milling around the area where benches and tables were set-up outside the school house.[155]

Beginning at 11 o'clock, the leaders led in prayers, hymns, and sermons in both Cherokee and English, until a lunch recess mid-afternoon. Uncle Walter spoke; Dr. Butler spoke; George Lowery spoke, representing the National Cherokee leadership; and George Washington Adair spoke, representing the Old Settler and Treaty leadership. Here was one place where the different points of view seemed to come together. The meeting continued until late in the afternoon, when Uncle Walter and Dr. Butler invited everyone to come forward and sign the pledge to abstain from all spirituous liquors.[156] Sam, Red Wolf, and Will went forward gladly, but Washington said he was not ready, even though he agreed that liquor had become an enemy for everyone to face in their own way.

The day was long, and Uncle Walter invited the boys to have supper with him and Nancy and stay at their place

---

[155] The mission is described by Carolyn Thomas Foreman in "The Fairfield Mission," *Chronicles of Oklahoma*, Vol. XXVII, 1949. pp. 323-324.

[156] This and subsequent meetings in Flint District are summarized in Foreman, pp. 382-384.

overnight. He had purchased the house, land, and buildings that had belonged to Mrs. Webber (the late Colonel Walter Webber's wife) five miles north of the Mission. The boys were glad to accept the invitation. They enjoyed the comforts of his pleasant home, and completed the last ten miles of their journey the next morning. Red Wolf told Uncle Walter that he had enjoyed the meeting and the trip with them, since it was his first time to see the Fairfield Mission School. He wished that it was closer so that he could finish his studies there.

Uncle Walter responded, "Your Uncles, George and John and I, have talked about that often.[157] We wanted a school at Oak Grove, but we haven't gotten the teacher yet or the money to build it. We will do it eventually, but I'm afraid it may be too late for you to benefit. The Moravians started a school on Baron Fork, but they've moved it west to Oaks. I do know that Pastor John Huss would welcome you to the school at his mission near the mouth of Honey Creek. That's close to your father's and grandfather's farms. You might plan to go there."

Red Wolf looked at Sam and Will and said, "I'll think about that, but I don't think any of us are ready to leave here yet."

September 1, 1845, Evansville, Arkansas

Early on the first day of September, 1845, Red Wolf, Sam, and Will accompanied James Starr on a quick ride to George Harnage's farm, three miles north of Evansville. When they arrived they saw a train of horses and pack mules just about ready to get underway. Forty-three members of the Treaty Party and eleven of the Old Settlers had made a plan to spend the next

---

[157] George Washington Adair, John Thompson Adair, and Walter Scott Adair are the "uncles" referred to, all living in the same vicinity.

several months exploring the lands that might serve as another location and the basis for a new government for a divided Cherokee Nation. The first assembly point for the trip was at the George Harnage farm, and other members of the group would join later. The division of the Nation had been a constant theme of conversations over several months. They had decided to visit the remnants of Chief Bowle's settlement in northeast Texas, where Devereaux Bell had inherited leadership after Bowles' murder. Then they would go to west Texas near the border with Mexico, where a settlement of about sixty Tsa'lagi lived. They called the place Mount Clover on the Brazos River. After that they planned to circle around through eastern Colorado. The expedition members present on this day included David Bell and Uncle Jack Bell; John Harnage; Joseph Lynch; Uncle Ezekiel Starr—James' brother, who lived southwest of Evansville on Honey Hill; three of James' sons—Jimmy Starr, Junior; and his brothers, Joe and Billy; Charles Reese; Jesse Mayfield; and Sequoia's son, Tessee Guess.[158] They hailed James as they saw him approach with the boys, and Uncle Ezekiel said to his brother, "Are you sure you won't change your mind and come with us?"

"I'd like to," Uncle Jim answered, "but I think I've got my hands full here. Besides, you're taking three of my workers with you, and we still have a harvest to gather."

Red Wolf said quietly to Will, "It looks to me like a group that's excited to be going on an adventure."

Will responded, "My Dad's always said Jack likes to travel. That's why he goes on so many trading trips. He can't sit still."

---

[158] Foreman, pp 336-337, and Hoig, p.202. This partial list of participants comes from the William Quesenbury Diary, 1845-1861, published by the Washington County (Arkansas) Historical Society in *Flashback*, Volume 28, #3, page 3.

"Ududu was like that when he was a younger man, too. He told me Ulisi Bell spent a lot of years raising their children on her own. I don't think he's especially proud of that."

Soon David Bell came over to the boys and introduced them to the man who was walking with him, William Quesenbury, a white man who had worked as a lawyer in Arkansas. Quesenbury told them that he was planning to keep a journal of the trip and expected that he might find a publisher afterwards. He said that people around the country would find the subject interesting, especially after all the published controversy among the Cherokees. Quesenbury noted that Chief Ross had once written to old Chief Bowles in Texas, asking whether the Old Settlers could relocate with them in Texas; maybe they would find that his idea would be the most practical outcome after all.[159]

"How long will you be gone?" Red Wolf asked his father.

"Four months or more," David answered. "I wouldn't be able to go without Ezekiel's help. He's working with your Grandfather taking care of the farm and the store. Will you keep things running smoothly here?"

"Udoda, if things were running smoothly here, you wouldn't be going on this trip."

"Right you are, Son! I only meant to ask you to stay alert. See that you stay out of trouble, which is something your older cousins seem totally incapable of doing. John Rollin Ridge may

---

[159] Hoig, p. 202.

call Tom a second Rinaldo Rinaldina,[160] but half of our people are beginning to think he's just an outlaw. We'll see if we can find an alternative to staying here and waiting for every one of our favorite people to meet his Maker before his appointed time. Stay safe, Son. Be here when we get back."

"I will do my best."

"You remember that conversation we had about you and Rachel."

"I remember."

"You are sixteen years old, old enough to take responsibility for what you do."

"Yes, Udoda. I know that."

"I'll see you, then, as soon as we get back." They embraced, and David turned abruptly and walked back to the wagons.

November, 1845, James Starr's House

Early in November Red Wolf was returning from his early morning visit to the outhouse when he saw Uncle Jim standing in the shadows, bracing himself with his arm against the trunk of an old black walnut tree, and his head was bowed. He walked up to him and asked, "What's wrong, Uncle Jim?"

Uncle Jim raised his head slowly and smiled slightly at Red Wolf, "I had a visit from Creek in the middle of the night and

---

[160] Rinaldo Rinaldina, the "border captain," was the hero of a popular romance novel, published in 1797 by Christian August Vulpius, a German novelist. John Rollin Ridge makes that comparison in a letter to Stand Watie, April 17, 1846, found in Edward Everett Dale and Gaston Litton, *Cherokee Cavaliers* (Norman, Oklahoma, University of Oklahoma Press, 1939, republished 1995), 38-39.

couldn't sleep afterwards. He said—he just wanted me to know—he and Tom and several other volunteers had gone on patrol, following a man all the way to Park Hill, to Return Meigs' house. They surrounded the house, thinking it was time to repay Meigs for his part in the killing of the Ridges and Boudinot. Meigs managed to escape, but they got carried away, killing two servants who tried to defend their master, and torching the fancy house."

"Did they all get away?" Red Wolf asked, trying to ignore the sinking feeling in his stomach.

"Yes, they did. Ross's Council hasn't renewed the authority for their Light-horse Police, but I don't think that'll keep his supporters from forming a posse when they learn about this attack. I think we're in for a storm, and I'm not talking about the weather. The last several months have been quiet. I hoped it'd stay that way. We'd actually managed to get a good crop in spite of the drought. We have our stocks ready for winter. Many of our leaders are away. I think we're going to face another siege of killings back and forth."

Uncle Jim and Red Wolf had that talk a week before November 9. During the days that followed, Red Wolf heard several neighbors complain about the Volunteer Patrol's actions, even though they had no sympathy for Meigs himself or for the people who had been killed. Uncle Jim asked Washington, Creek, Red Wolf, Will, Buck, and Sam to sleep in the barn, believing that the animals would wake them if they heard a posse approaching, and the boys would be able to alert the family asleep in the house and find cover in the woods behind the barn.

The boys awoke to the noise of horses early on Sunday morning, November 9. A large company of men, with their faces painted red and black, were riding up the trail toward James

Starr's home. As his father had instructed, Washington took a horse out the back of the barn and headed for the Rider home. Creek rode out toward Tom's place. Sam ran to the house with Buck limping behind, to alert everyone. Red Wolf and Will took up a position in the woods where they were able to see what was happening, but not be seen. Susie threw a cloak over her sleeping clothes and went to the porch where James had been sleeping. James told her to remain calm and permit the men to search the house.

Red Wolf and Will saw the posse milling around the edge of the clearing as if they were checking to see whether it was safe to approach the house. When they saw Susie and James on the porch, and James going to the washstand that sat by the front door and washing his hands and face, they proceeded into the clearing and came up to the porch, still mounted. He was still drying his face when the posse pulled their horses up. One of the men called out, "We're here to arrest your sons."

Uncle Jim started to answer, "You're welcome to search, but the ones you're looking for aren't here and I don't...," when one of the men pulled up his rifle and shot him in the chest. When Uncle Jim staggered back, the man shot him again. He collapsed to the floor.

Buck had taken a position on the porch nearby and immediately hobbled toward his father. Susie warned him to go back inside, but as Buck was moving, someone in the crowd shot him also, and Buck cried out and clutched his gut as he fell to the floor.

Nellie came out onto the porch with eight-year old Caleb, and two of the little grandsons who were staying with them while Joe, Junior, and Billy were away. She had her arms around them and her apron partly covering them, and she yelled out, "If you're here to kill innocent women and children, go ahead. We're ready."

Red Wolf thought he heard one of them say that they should kill the boys, all of them, but several loud voices were speaking to each other at the same time, and a few moments later they were all headed back down the path. Clearly at least some of them had no desire to harm the women or the children.

When the posse was out of sight Will and Red Wolf ran to the house, and Sam came out of the house where he had been hiding, but Susie, who was kneeling beside Uncle Jim, told them there was nothing anyone could do. Jim was dead. Susie said Buck was still alive, but unconscious. She had them carry Buck inside, and when they laid him on her own bed, she asked them to go for the doctor at Evansville, but avoid the posse at all costs. As if to reinforce her warning, they heard more gunshots in the distance. After they had mounted their horses and started toward Evansville, they again heard shots.

Reaching Aunt Polly Rider's home, they found her crying wildly, and learned from the servants that Sewell Rider had been shot, and one of the posse, a man named Stand Daugherty, had jumped down from his horse and stabbed him to death.[161] The boys made a brief report of what had happened to James and Buck and resumed their ride to Evansville. In about half a mile they found Washington's horse standing by the side of the trail, and Washington lying nearby, bleeding and groaning from a gunshot wound in his shoulder. Will and Red Wolf stayed with Washington to give him what help they could, and Sam rode on to fetch the doctor. In about two hands of time, Sam and a doctor returned in a carriage. The doctor checked his bleeding and

---

[161] Hill and Starr in *"Footprints in the Indian Territory."*

applied a compress and bandage. They lifted Washington into the carriage and drove on toward the Starr homestead, where the doctor proceeded to treat both Washington and Buck.

Tom Starr arrived after dark, late in the day. He found his brothers suffering from their wounds and in grave condition, and his father's body, washed and dressed in his best formal suit, lying on a table in the main living room. He swore to his mothers and made sure everyone in the household heard it, that he would find out the name of every man in that mob and make sure that he paid for what he had done with his life. "An eye for an eye," he said.

Sam and Creek assembled a plain pine coffin for their father and grandfather. Although the older sons came to the house, except for the three who were travelling with Jack and David Bell, Susie and Nellie told them not to come to the funeral. The mothers were afraid that some of their enemies would be there and turn the funeral itself into an opportunity for murder. Sam and Red Wolf were the oldest of the children who were present on November 11, when his Uncle Jim was laid to rest in the Oak Grove, near his parents' graves.[162]

In the midst of these days Red Wolf did not take time to think. He consoled Rachel and the smaller children as well as he could with the thought that their father had expected this to happen sometime and prepared for it. Their father was on his journey to the Western Horizon and would soon fly through the stars to the Creator Spirit's land beyond. Red Wolf yearned for his own father to be with him and knew he had no way to reach

---

[162] This account is based on Roberts-McGinnis.FTW; Conley, Robert J., *Cherokee Thoughts Honest and Uncensored*, Chapter: "Cherokee Outlaws", University of Oklahoma Press, October 31, 2008, and "The Light Horse in the Indian Country" by Carolyn Thomas Foreman in volume 34 of the *Chronicles of Oklahoma*, pp. 19-20. These and other accounts differ in their reports of the names of the shooting victims.

David wherever he and Uncle Jack were. He suppressed the frequent impulse to head for Ududu Bell's place. As each day passed he heard about people who had decided to seek sanctuary across the state line in Arkansas, at Evansville, Boonsboro, Maysville, and other border towns, away from the authority of the Cherokee National Party. Susie, Nellie, and Sallie stayed where they were, trying to nurse Buck and Washington back to health. As the days passed Washington gradually regained strength, but Buck got weaker as he dealt with infection. Red Wolf found visiting with him hard, as Buck cried from the nagging pain and found little relief. They both seemed to sense that Red Wolf's attempts at encouragement were hollow. Buck died a week into December.

Sam and Red Wolf both gnawed at their family's plight like it was tough gristle. Sam backed up Tom's principle of "An eye for an eye; a tooth for a tooth." Red Wolf asked him, "What happens when everybody's blind and toothless? Somehow we have to make peace with our enemies, and find a way to respect each other again, don't we? Or, we'll all be dead."

"That's not justice," Sam replied. "You can try to live like that, but a nation has to have laws they enforce fairly. They have to hold people accountable for their crimes. That's what Tom and the Volunteers are doing. That's what Stand Watie's doing when he and his brother, John Watie, are occupying Fort Wayne. Now the only way people can be secure is to abandon their homes and flee to Arkansas to seek their protection. We have to fight back."

Red Wolf replied, "I don't see how more fighting back and forth will solve anything. That's how we got into this mess. I think your Dad understood that."

With the time required to nurse Washington and Buck, and the absence of brothers Jim, Billy, and Zeke with the expedition, the rest of the family had their hands full with regular household and farm chores. Red Wolf and Rachel had no time for relaxed coupling, and their talk to each other was increasingly raw and irritable. Every day everyone in the family dealt with their mixed feelings and fears about staying in their home, even as close to the Arkansas line as they were.

The Van Buren newspaper, *The Arkansas Intelligencer*, printed an article that warned that the killing of James Starr was just the beginning of more planned reprisals by the Cherokee National Party on the Treaty Party members, including a plot to kill all of the Starr boys from two years on up. In the absence of many of the Treaty leaders, still traveling in the expedition, few people had the credibility to restore calm. General Arbuckle sent Major Bonneville to investigate. He found a hundred people had fled over the border into Arkansas. Since Chief John Ross was in Washington at that time, Arbuckle wrote to Acting Chief George Lowery that "the Light Horse must be disbanded at once, and the persons concerned in the murder of James Starr and Rider arrested." Then he ordered a company of dragoons under the command of Captain Nathan Boone to the "scene of the disorders." Chief Lowrey dispatched a delegation to Flint District to investigate the situation, including George Hicks, Rev. Stephen Foreman, John Thorn, and William Shorey Coodey. They met with some of the alarmed local citizens at the home of Walter Scott Adair, but they were unable to reassure them that they could stay safely in their homes. Refugees who had abandoned their properties, when they did return, found that livestock had been slaughtered, food stores looted, and houses plundered. Stand and John Watie gathered sixty men at the abandoned site of Fort Wayne. General Arbuckle ordered two more companies of dragoons from Fort Washita to join Captain Boone's company in the area to provide more security and order.[163]

January 8, 1846, the Border with Arkansas

The expedition returned to the Cherokee Nation in the first week of January, hearing various reports of events as soon as they entered a populated part of the Indian Territory. All of them became increasingly alarmed as they heard conflicting reports about who had been killed and other treacherous plots being formed. David, Jack and the Starrs—Ezekiel, Joe, Jimmy, and Billy—headed straight for the Starr home where they found confirmation of the murders of James, Buck, and Sewell Rider. When they had found reassurance about the safety of everyone else, Jack began to speak more strongly of the necessity of dividing the Cherokee Nation into two distinct parts, with two separate governments and territories, knowing that Indian Commissioner Medill had persuaded President Polk to present that position to Congress.[164] "Only when we have separate governments and territories will we see an end to this," Jack asserted. "We can't go on like this. We have to find a solution once and for all."

Meanwhile David had drawn Red Wolf aside. "You must come with me now, son."

"But, Udoda, they need me now more than ever."

"You're in too much danger here. The Starr boys have made too many enemies. No one will make a distinction between you and them as long as you're living here. Ask Rachel to come

---

[163] All of this paragraph's information comes from Foreman pp. 341-342

[164] Foreman, p. 335, note 33.

with you. Ask Sam, too. Besides the danger here, I need you with me. It's been too long since we've lived together as a family. I'm sure your Grandpa, my brother James, and Sarah are worried about you and eager for you to join them."

Will had listened, and added, "I'm ready to go, too. I want to see my Daddy and Mama. If things ever settle down here, I'd be willing to come back. As it is, I can't get out of here fast enough."

Sam was quick in his response that there was no way he'd leave his family at a time like this. He'd move across the border into Arkansas if his mothers were willing, but no farther. A little later Red Wolf was talking to Rachel.

"Udoda wants me to come with him to the Grand River area, in Delaware District, and farm with him. He just about insists on it, but it's still my decision. I'm sixteen. I love you. I want to be your husband. I want you to be my wife. I want to raise a family with you. I want to keep you safe."

He was taken aback by Rachel's next statement, "You're not big enough."

"I'm not big enough? What do you mean?"

"I mean you are small. I don't think you weigh as much as I do; you're not any taller either. All of your family are little people. How am I going to feel safe if I'm defended by a small man? Look at my brothers. Tom is a giant, and everyone else is bigger than you. I'm sorry, Red Wolf. I like you, I really do, but everything that's happened just makes me more sure. I want a man I can count on to defend me."

"I can provide for you. I'm a good worker. I'm strong, too. I hold my own, in whatever job we're doing. You know that. I can't believe this. After everything we've done together, everything we've dreamed about together, you hold my size against me?"

"I don't hold it against you. It's just not enough. I'm not going with you. With everything we're facing, I'm not even going to think about marrying you."

Red Wolf went to the loft to pack his things. He didn't know whether to cry or be angry, but he held it all inside and moved quickly. Will was a short distance behind. He didn't have to ask Red Wolf what had happened. Nellie gave the boys permission to take the two mares they had trained, Spring Rain and Dawn Wind, since they had brought two horses when they joined the family. Along with Susie and all of the family, they bid each other a quick and tearful farewell. [165]

Jack, David, Red Wolf and Will rode off on the trail east. A few days later Nellie, Susie, and Sallie took the rest of their family and slaves and resettled in the old Caleb and Nancy Starr house near Evansville, on the Arkansas side of the state line.

Jack and David with the two boys followed the road north from Evansville through Vineyard, where they stayed overnight at the Harnage home. On the next day they resumed their journey through Boonsboro, Salem Springs, Silvia, Simon Sager's settlement, and Maysville. Along the way they met Captain Nathan Boone and his company of dragoons. They knew one

---

[165] The romance between John Frances Bell and Rachel Starr is fiction, although they were close in age and casual sexual relationships were common among teenagers as well as adults at this time, especially from the point of view of the missionaries among the Cherokees. Rachel eventually married her first cousin, John Walker Starr, son of her uncle Ezekiel Starr, and they had no recorded children. Although they were first cousins on their fathers' sides, they were of different clans on their mothers' sides.

another from the months that Boone had served as commandant of Fort Wayne, and several years before that, Boone had met Red Wolf's grandfather during his visits in Central Missouri following their service during the War of 1812. Uncle Jack introduced Red Wolf and Will to Captain Boone, who looked strong and trim in his uniform, even though he was several years older than either Uncle Jack or David.

Boone stated that he did not expect any raiders from either side of the conflict to be out on the roads, day or night, while the three companies of dragoons were patrolling. Every traveler should still keep an eye out for small groups of troublemakers. Of course serious incidents were still occurring. Granville Rogers, the son of Captain John Rogers had been shot by Braxton Nicholson and his partner Pitner at Beattie's Prairie. On January 8, Charles Smith, the son of Archilla, had stabbed John Brown to death. Witnesses said they fought because Brown had been involved in the shooting of Bean Starr near Fort Washita.[166] Boone had heard that Charles Smith had been killed by some of the Cherokee National police when they attempted to arrest him.

Jack declared their intention to see Stand Watie at the Fort Wayne site, and Boone said that he hoped that Watie would not feel the need to continue gathering and training a force there. He believed it might incite the National police to more retaliatory actions and perhaps a major confrontation and battle. He did not know what role the United States Army might be asked to play in that event, since both sides had their defenders in the state and federal governments. He would prefer to remain neutral if he could.

---

[166] Foreman, p. 343-344

Jack and David thanked Boone for his information, and wished him well as they all remounted and parted.

January 11, 1846, Old Fort Wayne

With the sky gray and overcast, threatening snow or freezing rain, Jack, David and the boys were glad to see the cluster of log buildings and the remnant of the stockade at Fort Wayne. Even in their long riding cloaks, the cold had begun to bore through their winter garments, and the prospect of log fireplaces and hot stoves had begun to consume their thoughts. Several men were posted as guards, who hailed their approach and signaled to the men inside. With their horses unsaddled, fed and sheltered in the stables, Jack led his small party into the headquarters building to greet Stand Watie.

Red Wolf had not seen Stand for several years, and he looked broader and shorter than he remembered. He had to remind himself that he had grown almost to Stand's height during those years, and Stand had added to his already broad shoulders with the construction work he had undertaken in the last ten years. With the rough-hewn surroundings of the fort, Red Wolf was not surprised to learn that his Aunt Sarah was not there, but he was glad to hear that she was staying at a borrowed farmhouse a few miles to the northeast in Benton County, Arkansas.

With Stand's brother John joining them, they were all soon engaged in conversation about the training of troops and the advice of Captain Boone and others to disband their operation there.

"You provide a necessary check and balance to the National Light-horse Police and the random gangs, it seems to me," Uncle Jack asserted. "You don't have to patrol far from the fort or go anywhere else in order to exert a restraining influence. If you did disband though, the only thing standing between the Light-horse and us would be a small U.S. Army patrol, and I don't think that will be enough."

"Especially since the soldiers don't want to stay here very long," said Stand. "They'll be eager to get back to their own posts. They think that they can restore order and withdraw within a few months. I know our problems are much deeper and harder to resolve. We are squeezed in a vice between Ross's minions on one side and white bandits and would-be squatters and intruders on the other. What did you learn on your expedition?"

"There is not much land south and west of here that looks as productive as what we have here. Endless grazing land is available, but farmland with abundant water is not. There is already plenty of competition between Indians and new settlers for the open land that does exist. I'm not optimistic about any new location for our resettlement. A better arrangement would be to partition this area that we already inhabit into two independent Cherokee nations. That would require a standing force of well-trained militia. I think you have an advantage in that arena over the undisciplined forces under the Ross National Party control."

Stand responded, "We must plan another delegation to Washington to pursue that course. From what I hear, President Polk and Commissioner Medill remain on record in favor of partition. We have the advantage on our side right now, but Ross is in Washington trying to maintain his own control over all of the Cherokee Nation."

Uncle Jack agreed with the plan to form another delegation to return to Washington, and John Watie indicated his willingness to take command of the fort and military training so that Stand could participate in the delegation.

Before they retired to a meal and their lodging, Stand made a point of talking to Red Wolf alone. "My dear Sarah is looking forward to seeing you. She was very upset to learn that you were in the middle of the murderous outrage against Jim Starr and his boys. We have a baby boy, now six months old, and every day brings unsettling news, so I'm glad to have you here, and I hope you can bring her some comfort."

Sarah Caroline (Bell) Watie

January 31, 1846, North of Maysville

Red Wolf and his father, David, found their way north of Maysville on a cold winter day, following the directions Stand had given them, and knocked at the left door of a one-story, log, dog-trot farmhouse. Aunt Sarah opened the door. Red Wolf was surprised to find himself looking down into his favorite aunt's eyes.

"Can it be? Do my eyes deceive me? Osiyo, brother! Osiyo, nephew! It's wonderful to see you at last."

"I'm so glad to see you, too!" Red Wolf answered as he embraced Sarah and squeezed her to himself.

"Come in, get warm, tell me how you are. As for me, I' feel much better than I've felt in a long time just for seeing you."

David and Red Wolf quickly closed the door behind them, removed their riding cloaks and moved to the iron stove in the middle of the room. "We didn't know whether we'd find this place before we froze. Stand gave us good directions, though." They moved over to the basket where the baby, Saladin, whom they had nicknamed "Major," was sleeping. "He looks healthy and strong. It must be hard on you and Stand to be away from each other even for a few days."

Sarah blinked her eyes, and stopped herself from saying something. "Let me get you some hot broth. That should help you thaw out. I didn't know you were coming, or I would have something ready to eat."

"Hot broth will be good. Anything hot. I brought Red Wolf from Flint. Susie and Nellie will soon have the rest of their brood over the border at Evansville. They've been expecting their home in Flint to be fired any day." They sat down around the stove as Sarah moved to fill two cups and bring them to them.

"I am so sorry, Red Wolf. I know they've all been very good to you, giving you a family life you never had. Your Uncle James took his maternal uncle obligations seriously, just like our Uncle Jim Foster did. You've obviously grown up. I know that you've learned a lot while you were there."

"I learned that I love the farm, the animals, the soil, the work that feeds everyone. I also learned to despise everything that stands in the way of that. Unfortunately, a lot has stood in the way."

"Indeed I do know what you mean. All I want is to make a home and take care of my family. But no sooner do we have a house and I think we're settled than we have to move to some make-shift place and start over from scratch. I get so exasperated and glum, I don't know what to do."[167]

David answered, "I keep hoping, Sarah, things will simmer down. Instead they fire up, and everything gets shaken up again. I have to tell you, the only hope that we have is based on Stand leading a delegation to Washington and reaching a new agreement with the federal government. Jack, Joe Lynch, George Washington Adair, Ezekiel Starr and several other Old Settlers will go with him. I understand that Devereux wants to go, too, after his experience in Texas. He worked on a treaty with Texas

---

[167] In July of 1846 Sarah wrote to Stand from Benton County, "I am so tired of living this way. I don't believe I could live one year longer if I knew that we could not get settled, it has wore my spirits out just the thoughts of not haveing a good home. I would be very well satisfied if I was a way of[f] in some other country or in a smaller cabin of my owne, one can't feel free in other peoples places...." p. 45, *Cherokee Cavaliers*, by Edward Everett Dale and Gaston Litton (Norman OK: University of Oklahoma, 1939, 1995)

President Sam Houston, to resolve conflict there, and he will act as an aide to Jack and Stand.[168] That'll probably take several months to bear fruit. Red Wolf and I are planning to rejoin brother James and Samuel, my other two sons, and our father at the Grand River farms. If the situation is safe enough for us to stay, we will. We will be glad to have you with us, while Stand is in Washington."

"I understand, brother. I wish someone else would inherit the yoke of leadership, but it's Stand who does. I married him because of the man he is, and our people follow him because of the man he is. I have to be patient, I know. I have to pray and I have to hold onto my faith, but sometimes I have to complain. I will grieve and miss him desperately. I hope you understand."

"That I do, sister. I assure you, I understand, and I grieve, too."

Major began to whimper in his basket, and Red Wolf went over to pick him up and rock him a while. He admired his tiny fingers, missed his little sisters in the Starr household, and wondered if he would live long enough to hold his own child in his arms someday.

March 15, 1846, John Bell's House, Mockingbird Hill on the Grand River

Red Wolf stood at the riverside, remembering the other house his grandfather had built years before on the Coosa River in Alabama. The Grand River looked much like the Coosa as it flowed from north to south and then northwest again, forming a big bend enclosing the house and the Bell property on a large

---

[168] This list of members of the delegation comes from Foreman, p. 347.

peninsula of land, on which he stood near the tip. The house was a modest two-story frame house, still featuring a broad porch across the front. He was enjoying a warm, spring day, a relief after a colder than normal winter. He looked back at the house and appreciated seeing Will at the side of his parents, Demaris and Ezekiel, working on deerskins that would soon be worn in comfortably soft clothing. Will and he were both feeling much more secure after a quiet and nearly news-free month spent at his Ududu's farm. They supposed that the theft of slaves and other property was still continuing in Flint and Goingsnake Districts, and refugees were still gathered along the Arkansas border, where Stand and Sarah Watie stayed, but here on the Grand River they had found some peace and distance from the horrors of the autumn and winter.

David would soon be returning by canoe, bringing upriver from Webber's Falls the woman that he was eager to present to Red Wolf, his late mother's sister, Elizabeth Phillips-Bean-Thornton and her two-year-old daughter, Ruth Ann.[169] David told Red Wolf that he would recognize her right away, since she looked so much like his mother, Allie. Elizabeth was an Old-Settler, having come west with her first husband, Edmond Bean, about the time Red Wolf was born. Red Wolf was thinking that he was not sure that he remembered what his mother looked like, since it had been so long since he had seen her and so much had happened. Could it be that at the age of seventeen he would be a part of a family, living in peace on their own land, as an elder brother of three little children? His father was excited; Red Wolf was beginning to be excited, too.

---

[169] Information on Elizabeth Phillips comes from David Keith Hampton, *Cherokee Mixed-Bloods, Additions and Corrections to Family Genealogies of Dr. Emmett Starr* (2005), 111, 160, 181-182.

One other piece of news came to them that pleased him, though he chided himself for it—the killing of Stand Daugherty, the man who had shot Uncle James Starr, by one of the Volunteer Border Guards, Wheeler Faught. Red Wolf hoped that would be the end of the story. His experience told him that it would not be, since the Cherokee National Police were looking for Faught, to arrest him and his companions.

Last Sunday Red Wolf and several of his family had paddled east across the river and upstream from the mouth of Honey Creek to the Presbyterian Mission, where Elder John Huss, full-blood Cherokee preacher, was in charge. Huss welcomed them, and he explained that half of his congregation was sojourning in Arkansas, so he would soon go to visit them. If things remained quiet in this area, perhaps he could persuade them to return. He preached on the theme of "God in Christ... reconciling the world to himself... entrusting us with the message of reconciliation." His hope was that they would find a way to live side by side with their enemies and eventually recognize each other, not as enemies, but as the brothers that they in fact were. Even the white men, who had forced them from their own land and continued to trouble them, even though they acted like enemies, were beneficiaries of God's reconciliation, not targets of vengeance. We should do all in our power to bring about reconciliation. If he was asked to go to Washington as part of the Old Settler-Treaty Party delegation, he would do so.

Red Wolf admired the old preacher and hoped that they would all be able to see the fulfillment of his prayers.

April 30, 1846, Mockingbird Hill on Grand River
Hardly a day passed without new messages of uproar within the Cherokee Nation. The delegation, headed by Stand Watie, was in

Washington. Sarah and little Major were staying in Benton County, Arkansas, because of the renewed hostilities west of the state line. At the farm on the Grand River, David and Elizabeth, little Ruth, Red Wolf and his two half-brothers were learning about each other. David had been right about Elizabeth. Her appearance restored a full picture in his mind of his mother. Elizabeth was kind, soft-spoken, and busy, hesitant to take a full role in the new household, until she knew everyone better.

John Watie was in charge of Fort Wayne. More refugees were moving east of the Arkansas border. On March 23 the National Police had hung Wheeler Faught for his participation in the killing of Takatoka, the chief of police. One of the Starr brothers had killed Cornsilk, a member of the gang who had killed James. Turner of the Treaty Party had been killed by the police. The police had chased Ellis, Dick, and Billy Starr across the border into Arkansas on April 23, and wounded one or more of them, after one of them had killed Toonoowee. General Arbuckle put the Starr brothers under his own protection. Jim and Tom Starr killed Baldridge and Sides, members of the Ross Party gang. Then the Light-horse Police killed Billy Ryder, another member of the Volunteer Patrol.[170]

Many horses and Negro slaves had been stolen, though the thieves remained unidentified. Washington Adair, still trying to keep his property together in Flint District, had lost the horses from his corral. At Park Hill, the slaves belonging to Lewis Ross had collected arms, presumably planning to escape, but he discovered their cache of weapons and tightened his security arrangements around them.[171]

---

[170] p. 29, "H.L. Smith to Stand Watie," from *Cherokee Cavaliers*.

[171] p. 30, "H.L. Smith to Stand Watie," from *Cherokee Cavaliers*.

There were rumors about a secret council of the Ross Party on Spring Creek, attended by over five hundred partisans, that they had agreed to challenge, assault, and remove as many Old Settler and Treaty Party people as they could. Over seven hundred fifty refugees had gathered along the Arkansas border from Evansville north to Southwest City, so many that General Arbuckle was providing emergency rations for the refugees while they were waiting for things to settle down, however long that would take.[172]

David Nightkiller was one of John Bell's neighbors on a nearby farm on Honey Creek. He was also an old friend from the Coosa River country in Alabama, and head of a large family. He had been arrested by the National Police, but no one knew what charges they had against him.[173]

Important Treaty and Old Settler leaders were in Washington, and Chief John Ross and so many National Party leaders as well, that there was little restraint upon either side's police and light-horse patrols to bring recriminations to a halt. Every evening Red Wolf listened to Grandfather, David, Samuel, James, and Ezekiel consider whether their lives were in danger if they stayed where they were, whether they dared to plant the year's crops or could hope to be there for harvest, and whether Elizabeth, Demaris, and Elder Huss's families at least should be taken east of the Cherokee border to stay near Sarah for their safety. There were no obvious answers. They lived at the edge of the populated region, but they knew that the quiet of their neighborhood could quickly come to an end, since their location and their sympathies were well-known to their enemies.

---

[172] Foreman, p. 344

[173] p. 37, "Sarah C. Watie to James M. Bell" from *Cherokee Cavaliers*.

Our Land! Our People!

In the middle of April the bad news came that Ezekiel Starr had become ill and died in Washington, D.C. while participating in the delegation talks. They buried him there in the Congressional Cemetery. Elder John Huss wrote to his family from Washington about Starr's death, and the *Cherokee Advocate* circulated the news in its weekly edition.[174]

Other conversations continued around the supper table, especially related to the state of their farms. The spring had been unusually cold, with freezing temperatures, heavy rains, and heavy snow the first week in April.[175] "If we don' get this year's crop planted, we've already lost the battle," the elder John Bell said to his sons.

"And if we leave, we probably come back to ashes and dead or stolen animals," agreed David. "But if we stay and lose our lives...."

"We don't accomplish anything either," concluded his brother, James Madison.

"That's what Suzie and Nellie are facing, the worst of both choices. Their home is burned; their livestock lost. James, Bean, and Buck are killed. We don't know about Wash, Billy, Dick, or Ellis. I knew they were taking risks, serious risks, but the innocent suffer with the risk-takers." Red Wolf's eyes filled with tears as he finished, and he kept his thoughts about Rachel and the younger children to himself.

John Bell gave his decision, "I'm stayin' here. Let 'em do what they want with me. I'm too old to be a threat to them.

---

[174] p. 41, "John A. Watie to Stand Watie," *Cherokee Cavaliers*.

[175] p. 34, "R.M. McWilliams to Stand Watie," *Cherokee Cavaliers*.

James, I want you to take your sisters, and Elizabeth, and Elder Huss's wife and little ones, and find a refuge over the line in Missouri or Arkansas. David and Walter Ridge will go back and forth till it's safe to come back."

David agreed, "That makes sense to me. Demaris and Ezekiel can decide where they want to stay, here or there, and you, too, Red Wolf."

"I'm staying. We've got a crop to put in the ground."

May 28, 1846, Federal Road to Fort Gibson

David Bell rode his horse alongside Red Wolf's as they crossed the line between Goingsnake and Flint Districts on the evening of May 27. Red Wolf cast his eyes over the familiar mountains that rose to the east, picking out the bulk of Twist Mountain, and looked south to the valley where they hoped to find safe lodging at Dr. Walter Adair's house.

"I don't know why I let you talk me into taking you along on this trip, Red Wolf. If we run into any National Party partisans, who knows how it'll turn out? All they have to do is hear the name 'Bell' and we're probably done for."

"You wanted to take this trip alone? That's crazy. I'm seventeen years old. I know what can happen, and I want to be with you."

"I understand that you've already seen a lot more than you should have. By the way, you're not seventeen till July. Don't rush it."

"If Uduji Jack were here, he'd be making this trip with you for sure. Ezekiel would, too, but with all the kidnapping of slaves going on, he and Will are better off staying out of sight at the farm."

"We'll do our best to fill in for Jack, and represent the interests of the refugees along the border. Arbuckle needs to know how much relief his efforts have brought, but also how destitute the people still are. The letters we carry will plead their case. We don't know what his subordinates are telling him."[176]

"Conditions at Scott's Mill look worse than Mrs. Webbers' depot when people first arrived in this country. I remember when Ududu took us there to see it. At least people had tents then. Now they barely have blankets."

"That was the middle of winter, after a hard journey."

"That's right. This is spring, and people are healthier now, but they won't stay healthy without food and shelter."

"We'll try to get what they need. We're still waiting for the promised per capita payments. They'd really be a help now."

Red Wolf chuckled, "Does anyone still believe we'll receive those?"

"John Ross does. He's been going to Washington every year for the past eight, asking for them. Maybe if he'll agree to the new treaty, he'll get them."

---

[176] P. 44, "Robert Armstrong [from Maysville] to Stand Watie," *Cherokee Cavaliers*, reports on the "memorial" carried by David Bell, leaving May 27, to General Arbuckle, "signed by some of the most prominent men in the Nation…[concerning]upwards of 150 men women and children… under blankets near the Jas Scotts Mill in the State of Missouri."

"I'll believe that when I see it. He'd have to admit that the New Echota Treaty was legally binding. He'd never do that, would he?"

"That should be part of the bargaining positions," David said thoughtfully. "While we are on the subject of bargains, what do you think of Elizabeth?"

Red Wolf chuckled again, "She counts as a good one."

"A bargain?"

"A bargain. She's good with the boys. Her little girl is a charmer. She does have some mannerisms that remind me a lot of Uji. Mostly I like seeing you and her enjoy each other."

"I know she's different from Allie, mostly 'cause she's lived through a lot more. When she was a girl they were a lot alike. If she'd been a few years older I would've had a hard time choosing between them. But Allie chose me first, and I'm glad for the years I had with her. Now I'm glad to have Elizabeth."

The two riders, father and son, made their way to Dr. Adair's house for shelter overnight. The next day they kept their heads low and skirted other travelers as much as possible, completing their journey to Fort Gibson and delivering their message to General Arbuckle, who seemed to listen sympathetically. The General admitted that he was hearing more complaints from some Arkansas citizens about the refugees. His own superiors wanted him to reduce his relief efforts, but he still planned to do all within his power to supply help.

August 8, 1846, John Bell's House

John Bell's home on the Grand River had never been so full of eager anticipation. Charlotte and her husband, Dr. John Deupree, brought the news that the family had long awaited, that a treaty had been signed on August 6. Samuel and his wife, Rachel Martin Bell; James Madison; David and Elizabeth; Red Wolf; Demaris, Ezekiel and Will were all present with Grandpa Bell, presiding. They would hear the terms that had been agreed and accepted by the United States Senate.

There would be no partition of the Nation; the Western Cherokees would remain one people, all of whom would share one land under one constitution. That sounded at first like a defeat for the Treaty Party and President Polk's position, until they heard the rest of the terms. The legality of the 1935 New Echota Treaty was affirmed, with all of its provisions, including the per capita payments to all tribal members, including Old Settlers and the North Carolina mountain Cherokees. Treaty Party refugees would receive $100,000 for their damage claims related to losses over the past five years when they had to lose or abandon properties. The Major Ridge, John Ridge, and Elias Boudinot families would each receive $5,000 as an indemnity. Light-horse police companies, established by the Cherokee National Council, and the volunteer military organizations would be dissolved, and only civilian law officers would be authorized to maintain order. Finally, a general amnesty would cover all crimes committed by all parties over the past seven years, as long as the perpetrators returned to live inside the nation with the refugees by December 1, 1846.[177]

Samuel observed that Tom Starr would surely agree to the terms of amnesty at this point since nearly all of the men involved in the murders of the Ridges, Boudinot, and his own father had been put to death. In fact, over the past few months,

---

[177] Foreman, pp. 349-351, McLoughlin, pp. 57-58, and Hoig, pp. 203-204, 297n.

more than thirty political killings had occurred.[178] Dr. Deupree quoted words that had been attributed to Stand Watie, when he met with President Polk at the treaty signing, "I have entered into this treaty of amnesty in all sincerity; I intend to be peaceable, and have no doubt that others, who have less to forgive, will follow the example which all the leaders have set."[179] Since John Ross and the other delegates would have to travel back to the Cherokee Nation and present the treaty to the National Council, the agreement was not completely finalized, but it would be hard for Ross to renege on its terms at this stage.

"Then Jack, Stand, Elder John Huss, Jim Lynch, and George Adair will also be home soon, at last," said John Bell. "I understand that compromises had to be made, and I think it's a good agreement, if we're all wise enough to accept it. That's a big 'if,' but we've spilt enough blood to seal this treaty several times o'er."

"Does this mean Sarah can finally have her husband and her home back?" asked Red Wolf. "That'd be worth a lot."

"Yae, it does," Grandpa Bell answered. "Puttin' many families back in their own homes, takin' care o' their own business, livin' under their own vine and fig tree—that be worth a lot."[180]

---

[178] Foreman, pp. 344-347

[179] *Arkansas Intelligencer*, September 5, 1846.

[180] General D. B Brinsmade, husband of the sister of Harriet Gold Boudinot, used this biblical allusion when he wrote to Stand Waite on October 15, 1846. p. 54, *Cherokee Cavaliers*.

Red Wolf added, "Still, it makes me wonder. How many times have we all felt hopeful, then faced terrible disappointment?"

David said, "We'll still be hopeful. We could not endure as much as we have if we didn't hold onto our hopes, even when things were darkest. Today we have more than a glimmer of light."

April 15, 1847, Honey Creek

Will and Red Wolf propped their long fishing poles with rocks at the edge of Honey Creek; the poles extended over a deep pool at a bend in the river. Downstream they had taken their morning bath in the cold river waters, preparing for a lazy spring day along the river. They stretched out on a flat shelf of warm sandstone in the full sun to dry their still-wet bodies. At 18 years, Will was six inches taller as well as a few months older than Red Wolf, who stood a little over five feet, but neither had an extra ounce of flesh.

"Been a while since we took a day just to fish," said Will.

"We been too busy, clearin' land, buildin' fence and smokehouse, cribs, calvin', farrowin', gettin' set to plant. You'd think we liked to work."

"I could get used to fishin' and huntin' all day, and layin' naked in the sun."

"You think so, Will? I don' think you could stand it, more than a few days anyway. You'd be back at work, showing your muscles. I jus' wish you were workin' your own place. What's going to happen to us, Will?"

"I don' know. I can't control it, so I tries not to worry 'bout it. Maybe your Uncle Jack'll keep me; let me live near my Ma and Pa. Maybe I kin git married someday, an' have my own family. I'd like that. Your Pa likes to have you around. He likes your company, an' he likes your work."

"I wouldn't be around if it weren't for you, Will. I'd be long gone, buzzard food along Ol' Sleeping Bear."

"I don' think so. You would'a made it. Besides, you's the only brother I ever had, really. Ma couldn' have any more kids, and everbody else took me fer a slave. not a brother. You still miss that girl, Rachel, don'tyuh?"

"Like a scavenger dog gnawing at my guts. Times I get so hungry for what we had. It felt so easy, an' natural with her."

"If it hurts that bad, I guess I'll take back what I said about feeling jealous. Can't be good for yuh if it hurts like that."

"I don't hear much from the family, 'cept I heard Susie's sick, maybe dyin'. They haven't moved back to Twist Mountain. Tom's set up a place along the Canadian, as far south in the Nation as he can git, and that's likely the best place for him. But I miss her. She's a nice girl, and I wanted her for a wife. Burn it! You got me thinkin' about her again, and everything we did together." Red Wolf lay silently for a while with his hands folded beneath his head, gazing up into the cottony clouds, remembering and imagining being with her again as they used to be. Then he said, "Don't look at me, Will. I'm shaming myself. I've got to go dunk again in that cold water."

June 8, 1848, Honey Creek Trail

David, Red Wolf, and Will were riding west along the Honey Creek Trail, returning to their farm after a few days' work at

Stand Watie's farm, and visiting with Sarah in the resting hours. Earlier in May the news had disturbed them, when Mat Guerrin, Ellis, and Washington Starr had been involved in a kidnapping near Fort Gibson, and each of them had been killed, Guerrin and Wash by the posse that went after them, and Ellis after being acquitted by a jury.[181] That was all occurring miles to the south, however, and their Delaware District remained peaceful. The day was sunny and sultry. Sweat dripped from their faces, and soaked their clothes as they rode in the late morning sun, finding relief only in the occasional breeze and shady patches of the trail.

Shots rang out. David jerked and slumped in his saddle, Red Wolf's horse reared as he let go of the reins and was knocked off, and Will quickly jumped off his horse, to crouch where Red Wolf lay. Frightened, Will looked around to see if the attackers were still shooting or coming closer. Seeing none, he checked Red Wolf, who was unconscious and bleeding from his shoulder. When he looked up at David he could see that he had lost his grip and was also falling off his horse. He jumped up to catch him, but David's full weight was too much for Will to keep him from falling to the ground. Will found a large flow of blood from a hole in the center of his chest, and no response from David, no spurting of blood, no heartbeat.[182] He went back to Red Wolf, and used a bandanna to press against the shoulder wound, and felt his heart beating fast but strong. At the same time Will was looking up often to see whether anyone was pressing an attack, and threatening him as well. Suddenly he

---

[181] A summary of newspaper accounts (which are contradictory and confusing) is found in Hoig, p. 209.

[182] The death of David Bell in a shooting from one or more anonymous gunmen is recorded in George Morrison Bell, pp. 50-51, but *The Arkansas Intelligencer* mistakenly reports the death of John Adair Bell instead of David Bell in their June 10, 1848, edition.

shouted out "You bastards! You cowards! Show yourselves! Come an' get me! Where you hidin'?" All he heard in response was the crashing of horses through the underbrush, moving quickly away.

Will put his arms around Red Wolf's shoulders and held him to himself as he rocked back and forth and cried. "What've they done to us?" he repeated several times, until he heard Red Wolf moan softly. He lay Red Wolf back on the grass, and rose to get a water bag from his horse's saddle. Bringing the water back, he brought it to Red Wolf's lips for a swallow, then he wet a kerchief and washed the bloody area where Red Wolf had hit his head when he fell. He checked the gunshot wound again, finding that it was still seeping blood, and he took off his own homespun shirt. Using his knife he cut and tore strips from his shirt and tied the bandanna compress tighter.

As Red Wolf slowly regained consciousness, Will said, "I'm sorry, Red Wolf; whoe'er it was killed your Pa."

"What?"

"Your Pa, Red Wolf. I couldn't do nothin' for 'im. He died right away."

"Oh, no...no. Who shot?"

"I couldn' see who done it. They rode off. We gotta get you to your Grandpa's place, and get you fixed up. We'll have to come back for your Pa and the horses. You ride in front of me. I'll hold onto you, and I'll get you back soon as I can." Will helped Red Wolf climb into the saddle, and slipped onto the horse behind him. About a hand of time later, they reached the mission and John Huss's place, and Will asked for help there. Mrs. Huss helped Red Wolf into her house, while Will went to the mission house for the Elder. They sent for a doctor who lived nearby, and Huss sent two men back along the trail for David's body and the two horses. When the doctor had finished removing the bullet, and securing a new bandage, and they were sure that Red Wolf was stable and resting, Will and Huss went on to let Grandpa Bell know what had happened.

Huss sent for the Delaware District sheriff, and soon news was circulating throughout the area, including the rumor that John Adair Bell had been killed instead of his brother David. The second victim, reported as killed also, was actually Red Wolf, very much alive, but he was identified as any one of several Bell family members—Sam, or James, or Devereaux, instead of John Francis. "If we knew who started those rumors, we probably would know the killers," said Huss. None of the family or neighbors made an effort to straighten out the rumors; they thought it was best to let people think that there were two murdered victims, with whatever identity people assigned to them. If the shooters thought they had not killed the ones they wanted, there would be even more danger.

For David's burial the next day the family gathered with Elder Huss at the top of Mockingbird Hill. Elizabeth, Red Wolf, little John Martin Adair Bell and James Foster Bell, shed their many tears at the death of their husband and father. Huss eulogized David as the most willing to help anyone, the kindest and most compassionate, the least likely to be the target of a vendetta, of anyone associated with the Treaty Party. "In any other age he would be regarded as one of the wise citizens of the nation, but in this age he was simply another victim of injustice." He read Psalm 22 before he led the prayers at the graveside.

Red Wolf remained silent throughout the days that followed, except to say to Will that he was glad that he had not been hurt. "Again I must say 'wado' for my life. Again I say—you are my true brother." Uncle Jack was near enough to hear Red Wolf say these words, and to see the two young men lean their foreheads together, and shed silent tears.

August 31, 1848, Mockingbird Hill

Uncle Jack handed Red Wolf a collection of documents rolled together and tied with a ribbon. Red Wolf slipped the ribbon off and unrolled the documents to find a title of ownership of a slave, named William Ezekiel Bell, granted to John Francis Bell. Signed and sealed by the former owner, John Adair Bell, and the attorney of record, Stand Watie.

"What does this mean?" Red Wolf asked. "I don't want to own Will."

Uncle Jack explained patiently, "Really, Will has never been in service to me, even though legally I was his owner. I allowed him to be your companion and coworker, as long as you needed one. Now, while he lives in the Cherokee Nation, an African Negro must have an owner. Freedmen are not allowed to stay, according to our nation's laws, and as a practical matter even when they are allowed to stay, in violation of the laws that are on the books, they need to be directly under the protection of a member of the Nation. I daresay that it isn't much easier to be a freedman outside the Cherokee Nation, but that is not yet an issue for Will."[183]

"Oh, I see. Wado, Uduji. This is a great gift. It may be an answer to my prayers. Wado."

---

[183] These limitations on slaves and freedman status within the Cherokee Nation prior to 1865 are described in Rennard Strickland, *Fire and the Spirits: Cherokee Law from Clan to Court* (Norman, University of Oklahoma Press, 1975), 79-84, especially p. 79 note 42.

October 30, 1848, Mockingbird Hill

Most of the field work and harvest was completed. The members of the Bell family had remained quietly occupied with their farm work, while Jack tried to maintain a behind-the-scenes participation in his trading posts. Jim Lynch and Stand Watie remained as visible partners in the store businesses. Stung and grieved by the awareness that David's death and Red Wolf's wounding possibly came from mistaken identification—it was really aimed at Jack—he stayed out of sight for as long as possible.

Jack, James, and Sam's brother Devereaux came from Texas when he learned from his sister Sarah's letter about David's death. Three years had passed since David and Jack had visited him in Texas on the expedition they took with other Old Settler and Treaty partisans, exploring possibilities for a new location. Sam had traveled to see Devereaux on other occasions after Texas soldiers had killed Chief Bowle in the Battle of the Neches in 1838. He found Devereaux trying to rally the dispirited remnant of Bowle's settlement and becoming a community leader who was well-known as "Chicken Trotter."

"Why Chicken Trotter?" Red Wolf had asked years before.

His father David had answered, "He's small and skinny, like the rest of us Bells, kinda bird-like. When you see him walk, you'll know why."

Red Wolf watched this uncle whom he had not seen since he himself was six years old, and Devereaux, Asa, and Grandpa Bell were leaving on a trading journey west. Now he looked at Chicken Trotter and understood what his father meant. His uncle was no bigger, maybe even skinnier than he remembered, and he moved with a jerkiness and often the quickness of a chicken in a hurry.

The brothers and their father together assessed their situation. Devereaux could report that life for the Texas Cherokees in Cherokee and Rusk counties had continued to improve, especially after he and President Sam Houston and representatives of other tribes had negotiated the Treaty of Bird's Fort in 1843. Devereaux had worked with Stand Watie and the delegates in Washington, but he was discouraged about their prospects in the Cherokee Nation, especially after David had been killed and none of the culprits caught.

Only a few of the original signers of the New Echota Treaty remained alive. Stand Watie was the undisputed and obvious leader of the remnant, and, quiet and soft-spoken as he was, his reputation was unquestioned. He was a strong and purposeful leader with many people willing to follow. If anyone attacked Watie, the fragile truce of the 1846 Treaty would dissolve into full-scale recriminations. The other New Echota signers held less weight—Jack and Samuel, but also George Washington Adair and Andrew Adair—sensing that they were easier to eliminate without returning to a full-scale war among the Cherokee factions. The confusion over who really died in the June attack allowed Jack and Samuel to take a breather and think about what they should do next, although they knew that the truth was probably leaking out.

Grandfather John Bell's home was the scene of many discussions about the future. Jack returned to his position before the 1846 Treaty that he and other people closely associated with the Treaty should find a new home elsewhere, probably in Texas. At the end of October Sam announced that he had decided on doing something else entirely.

"I've been hearing a lot about the discovery of gold in California. Rollin[184] says he's planning to go, and many other Cherokees are going also. The reports agree—this the largest and easiest-to-find gold deposit in all of the Americas," Sam announced to his father and brothers.

His father responded, "You know what they say about things soundin' too good to be true."

"Yeah, I know. It may be hard work to find it, and there may not be as much as they say, but I think it's worth a try. I don't have a future here, nor do my children, as long as people hold a grudge against us."

Devereaux added to Sam's claims. "I'm ready to try it out, too. I'm convinced that we can't stay here, and I'm ready for a different kind of adventure—at least one that holds a chance of success."

"I've seen what a gold rush does, if you remember, the discovery o' gold in Georgia brought every kind of reprobate to our lands," John Bell said. "I canna' be convinced the grudge won't follow you to California an' threaten your lives there just as much as here. I'm naw goin' to stand in your way either, as if I could! I'm with Jack. Texas is as far as I wan' to go, no farther. I'll write to Asa and find out if he's still o' the mind to settle there, and ready to do it. We can gather as many as we can and start again. I don' want to do it at my age, but I think it's best. We should build a Salem there, a New Hope, or a Mount Tabor, like Elder Huss keeps a'talkin' about, a place of peace. If I could climb that mountain before I die, I'd die a happy man."

---

[184] John Rollin Ridge, son of the assassinated John Ridge.

James said that he was sticking with his father, and he'd go or stay wherever his father decided. He felt that was his duty as the youngest son.

Jack added, "If we're going to do this, going either way, Texas or far West, then we have a lot of work to get ready, selling the improvements we've made and the stock that we've gathered here, things we can't take with us. That'll take weeks, and the longer we stay here, the riskier it gets."

Red Wolf listened to these comments and pondered. Later he talked to Grandfather Bell alone.

"Slavery is the law in Texas, isn't it, Ududu? Jack and you'll take your slaves there with you?"

"Yae, that's so. With all the work to be done again, and me an old man now, near blind,[185] that's what I got to do."

"That's no place for me then. I made up my mind, long time ago, if I had to leave the Cherokee Nation, I wouldn't take slavery with me. Never again."

"You've got Will to think o'. What's he goin' to do?"

"If it's up to me, Will is going to do what Will wants to do. I hope he'll go with me, but I won't hold him as a slave, whatever he decides, anywhere I go."

"Hmmm," Grandpa murmured, but became silent. "I'll have to give that some thought."

"Ududu?"

---

[185] The 1850 Census of Rusk County, Texas, lists John Bell with his son James Madison Bell. A note by John Bell's name indicates that he was blind.

"Yes, Red Wolf."

"I can't accept what happened. Uji was alive when I saw her last, then she was gone, and I never saw her again. I knew Ulisi was dying, but I wasn't with her when she died, and I never saw her again. Udoda was riding by my side, and suddenly he was gone, but I didn't see it. I didn't know what happened until Will told me later. When I add up the number of deaths that have taken other family members from me, I lose count of how many. Now you're going to Texas, and I know I can't go with you. Is everyone going to disappear from my life?"

Grandfather Bell took his pipe out of his pocket, lighted it, and drew on it for a finger of time. Slowly he spoke. "People canna' disappear from our lives. They always leave a piece o' their souls in us, no matter when or how they leave, no matter how far away they go. Where'er ye choose to go, ye'll have your people with ye. I'll be with ye, and ye'll be with me. Y' have to remember that. E'en when ye canna' remember, it's still true, for all years to come."

A few hours later, Grandpa Bell found Red Wolf and Will in the barn, milking the cows. He watched them work for a while, and when they had finished, he asked Will to take the two pails of milk to the springhouse while he talked to Red Wolf.

"It gives an old man pleasure to see fellas work together like y'do. Y'all work like a well-matched team of oxen; maybe I should say mules."

"Wado, Ududu, I think. If it's the stubbornness of mules you're a'thinkin' of, then I know where I got it."

"Sure 'nough. I been thinkin' about where ye might go, to be free and all, in the way ye were talkin', and Will havin' a chance on his own, if he wants. Ye may naw remember the land I studied about, up in Illinois, in Pike County. An old friend lives there, who fought beside me at Horseshoe Bend. He's been farmin' there; I know he could use your help. I'll get a letter writ 'im if that's what ye want. Captain Boone's aunt and her family's up there, too, livin' a little ways east. Down the road a couple miles is Free Frank, a remarkable man, buildin' a town where freemen and mixed bloods, even some Indians, are livin' and workin' together.[186] If your Uncle Jack didn' have his heart set on a plantation in Texas, I might be thinkin' uh' livin' there myself, though it's a bunch colder'n I want when winter comes. Ye think on it. If ye want to go, and make a life fer y'self farmin', and ye'd most likely be on your own doin' it, I'll see if my old friend Richard Bean would take ye on."

Red Wolf didn't say anything right away, as he absorbed the words his grandfather had spoken. Then he swallowed and said, "I'd be mighty grateful if you'd write that letter."

"I will then. It'd be a good place fer ye. Ye'd have plenty uh' work to do to clear land an' build on it. Ye'd be with good people, decent people, who wouldna' shoot ye, that's fer sure."

"Wado. I'll think on it."

November 15, 1848, Fort Wayne

When Uncle Jack heard that Fort Wayne would soon be abandoned again, he invited Red Wolf to ride along on a trip to see Joe Lynch at the general store at Fort Wayne, and hoping to see Captain Nathan Boone before he left for his home in Greene County, Missouri. This would be their first trip in the open since David's killing, and both felt the challenge of it, since the

---

[186] The New Philadelphia community in Pike County, Illinois.

ambushers were still unidentified and on the loose. They left in the dark of a chilly early morning and made the journey with no delays, avoiding contacts with any less-than-trustworthy people along the route. By mid-afternoon the fort was in sight, more a collection of ramshackle shelters and barns than a defensible garrison. Clearly the soldiers had made no effort to locate there for the long haul.

The flags were flying. The garrison had not retired the colors yet. They soon learned that Boone was still there, helping his soldiers decide what was worth packing up and what should be left behind. He led them into his office and asked a private to fire up the iron stove in the center of the room to provide some heat. Jack congratulated him on the major chevrons that decorated his uniform.

Major Boone laughed heartily and said, "My superiors finally promoted me, just in time so they won't have to raise my pay for long before I retire. If I hadn't thought I was needed, and wanted to do what I was doing, I woulda' quit long ago."

Red Wolf took a chair and examined the broad shouldered, trim and erect, well-built Boone. He had seen him two years before, when he first took the assignment to protect the refugees along the border of the Cherokee Nation. Now he noticed the lines in his tanned leathery face that his years in the sun and weather had drawn. He thought of brother Sam Starr and Aunt Nellie and wondered whether they were well, whether he would ever see them again. Uncle Jack and Major Boone talked about their plans for the future, including Jack's interest in the land south of the Red River in East Texas. Soon, as the room began to warm up, Red Wolf also began to sag in his chair. He dreamed of sitting on a wide veranda, served by slaves dressed in formal white shirts and black suits, like Chief Ross's slaves were reported to wear. Wearing this formal attire, Will offered him a tray holding a glass of tea, filled with ice, and a cup of brown sugar beside it. As Red Wolf reached for it, he had to catch himself from falling off his chair, bringing both Boone's and Uncle Jack's amused attention.

"I guess it's already been a full day for my nephew," Jack chuckled.

"He's not on duty, not yet anyway, so I don't have to discipline him for falling asleep," Boone added, then turned to Red Wolf. "If you're interested in a military life and wouldn't mind learning some other Indian languages, there'd be a good place for you as a soldier-interpreter out west."

Later that evening, when they had eaten supper with the soldiers in the mess hall, Major Boone made a point of talking to Red Wolf alone. He reported that Jack had spoken about the possibility of Red Wolf's move to Pike County, Illinois. "It's good land, wooded, hilly and well-watered, much like my land in Missouri. My aunt and some of my friends like it there, though they say it's beginning to fill up with people, just like here, but not too many yet. I'd say it would be a good place for you, to get away from what you face here, and make a life for yourself. You won't be the first Indian to blend into that neighborhood, especially if you don't make a habit of talking about your past."

The thought that he might need to conceal his past had not occurred to Red Wolf, but he began to realize that it might be a liability around some people. Fortunately, he thought, he'd never felt the need to talk much about himself to anyone.

November 20, 1848, the Barn, Mockingbird Hill

When the feeding and milking of cows was finished, Red Wolf said to Will, "We need to talk."

"What's on your mind? I been wonderin'. You seem to be dealin' with somethin' heavy."

"I got somethin' in the post today I've been waitin' for." Red Wolf braced himself against one of the barn's main upright supports, while Will took a seat on a stool. "I had written to Aunt Sarah and asked her to persuade Uncle Stand to prepare manumission papers for you. He did, and I have 'em to give you."

Will's eyes widened, and he took a quick breath. "What? Am I hearin' you right? How'd this happen?"

"A few weeks back, Uncle Jack gave me your ownership papers. He figured he couldn't separate us anyway, you might as well belong to me. I told him I'd never own you, but he reminded me, you can't live legally as a freedman in the Cherokee Nation, due to some stupid law they passed. Anyway, it won't matter soon, since we'll all be leaving. I knew Sarah would understand, but I wasn't sure about Uncle Stand. He still thinks we need slaves to make things work. But he's the best lawyer I know, and I figured, if he drew up the papers, nobody'd get around 'em."

"I don' know what to say. I never expected this, but it's about the best thing I ever heard."

"That's not all, Will. I've got something else I want you to think on." Red Wolf paused as he considered again the best way to say this. "Uncle Jack, Grandpa, and James are planning to go to Texas and settle there. I don't know who else is going, but I know they'll take your folks with 'em. I'm not going to Texas. Ududu told me about his friends in Illinois. He's written to them to get a job and place to live for me. They live near Free Frank's town of New Philadelphia, where freedmen and mixed bloods are living together. Nathan Boone has family close by, too. It sounds like a place to get a fresh start, where people can live together the way the Great Spirit wants us to. I don't want to go without you, Will, but I don't want to keep you away from your parents either. I done that too long already." He stopped talking then, and they both looked down at their hands for a time. Soon both of them had tears in their eyes.

"I been thinkin' we'd all be goin' to Texas. I use to dream 'bout a place like that Illinois—it'd be right fine. I sees why you'd want to go there 'stead uh' Texas. Yet I sees my folks needin' me more and more as the years go by an' they gets older. If'n I was free, maybe I could get 'em free, too. So's I feel split right down the middle. You's my brother. Them's my Ma and Pa. I gotta think about it. I gotta talk to 'em."

Will stood up, and Red Wolf let go of the support beam. They reached out to each other and held an embrace for a long moment. And Will repeated, "Wado for what you're doin'."

"It's all right, Will. Whatever you think is best, it'll be all right. You're a free man now, and no one's goin' to take that away from you. You saved my life twice. I owe you everything. You don' owe me nothin'." They slowly let go, and moved toward the door.

January 30, 1849, Mockingbird Hill

The news of Samuel's death in Kansas in mid-January came as a severe blow to the members of his family. He died of a natural illness, not the result of any vendetta—that was their only comfort. His wife and children were left wondering what to do, but Grandfather Bell promised them help in staying where they were, if they wanted, or coming with the rest of the family to Texas. Jack promised his help in the move, if they chose. She decided that staying near her own parents and family was better.

Some of the stock and equipment was sold for the sake of the stake to get a fresh start in Texas, but the majority of their land and improvements along the Grand River would pass to Sarah and Stand Watie, who were determined to stay. James wanted to stay, but he realized that his father needed his help, due to his increasing blindness. Stand promised to watch over James' share of the land in case he could return someday. Grandfather Bell and Jack decided that they would need to leave by the end of February in order to get to their Texas destination in time to get set up and plant crops in spring.

Sarah and Stand were living again near Tahlequah, where Stand was pursuing his career as a lawyer. Red Wolf felt the need to write a parting letter to Sarah.

Dear Sarah,
Soon I will maek my way narth to Illinoy an noo life. I feel reddy to try to maek a life that is free from grujes an killin that stole so much frum all ov us. No slavry ether. Thank you an Stand for the papers that set Will free. He save my life an is my best frend. I owe him. Im only sad he must go hep his ma an pa an not com with me. May be sum day. I wish I cud hav a ma an pa to hep but ther long gon an I mus be on my own now. Eskuz my ritin mistax. I uz jurnal to find rite words but cant al ways find em. I fergit how to rit a lot ov em. Wen I get thar I wil rit agin an let yu no so yu can tel me abowt famli noos. Plese writ then. I miss yu. I Love yu. Love yur children an Stand. Wish yu all will b happy. For now on I will jus go by the nam John.   John Bell, yur nefew

Red Wolf sent the letter with his Uncle James just before they all were ready to leave. When the day to leave came, on February 20, Grandfather Bell reminded everyone that Cherokee words said "Hello," but did not include good-bye, and that was something he had grown to appreciate. "We will always be together in our thoughts and prayers," he said. "We hope to see one another in a better land where many of our people are already waiting. We love and we will love no matter how far apart we get and how long it takes to come together again."

For this journey the wagon train consisted of only a few wagons, although they would add to the number as they traveled south—the households of George Harlan and Nancy Starr, George Washington and Elizabeth Candy, Jesse and Ruth Mayfield, Walter Adair and Ruth Duncan.[187] Dressed in his travel cloak and heavy clothing, Red Wolf mounted his horse, Jubal, with his pack and bedroll. He watched the wagons pull out, waved to his small half-brothers and Will, and then turned his horse and headed northeast toward Missouri, with tears streaming down his face.

Red Wolf's plan was to follow the Military Road used by the majority of Cherokee travelers ten years before, until he came to the vicinity of Springfield, Missouri, where he would stop at Nathan Boone's homestead. He would travel across country northeast through Pike County, Missouri, cross the Mississippi, and enter Pike County, Illinois. The first days of travel favored his plan. The weather was unseasonably warm, and early signs of spring were in the air. Some days he made fast progress, and some days he slowed the pace, and thought about

---

[187] The records about Mt. Tabor Cemetery, in Rusk County, Texas, include the burials of many of these people and family members related to them as well as John Bell, Jr., John Adair Bell, and one of the half-brothers of John Francis Bell, that is, John Martin Adair Bell.

turning back, wondering whether he was doing what he ought to do. Maybe he should have gone with Will, and helped to secure the freedom of Will's parents, which hadn't even crossed his mind while he was with them. Still that would leave them all living in a land that was nothing like the dreams he had inherited from his parents and affirmed in his baptism. Those memories from long ago kept filling his mind and his dreams.

When he met people on the road, or found a farmhouse and asked whether they needed a farmhand for a day or more's work, or stopped and asked for a resting place in the barn overnight, he introduced himself as "John Bell." If anyone asked him anything more about himself, he told them that he was headed to Illinois and Pike County, where he would make his home and farm. His parents had tried to settle farther west, but they had died, and he was heading back to Illinois. People usually didn't ask any more, so he didn't have to stretch the truth. He didn't tell them about his Cherokee background, and they didn't recognize it in his features. Sun-tanned, black-haired, thin and wiry, he didn't look much different from any other farmhand or cowboy.

John enjoyed riding on Jubal through the hills and woods of southwestern Missouri. Sometimes he slept outside in a rock shelter or underneath the stately pines or oak forests, making a fire for some extra warmth, before wrapping himself in his cloak and blanket in a bed of gathered pine needles or fallen leaves. He found hospitality at the homestead of Nathan Boone near Springfield, and he told Olive, Boone's wife, and his children of his contact with the Captain, and of the Bell family's respect for him. Boone himself was away again. They offered him a bedroom in their fine house, but he said he preferred staying with his horse in their stables, which they readily allowed. When he left them a day later, they asked him to carry some letters to their

Aunt Margaret and cousins Tom and Uriah Elledge at the settlement of Perry, Illinois, in Pike County, a town that had at first been known as Booneville.

When he left the Springfield area and Greene County, John thought of the way the Bell detachment had moved from county seat to county seat on their route to the Western Cherokee Nation ten years before, but he did not see any advantages to that strategy on this trip. He considered adding to the journal he had kept, but the journal just reminded him of the absence of his Aunt Sarah to help with his writing, and the loss of so many people during the intervening years, so he left the journal in his saddlebag. He preferred to avoid the towns along the way, with the townspeople staring at him, a stranger. Relying on isolated settlers along the route was simpler for a single wayfarer. Still, after a month and several days' work to pay his way and provide his meals, not reducing his nest egg by even a penny, he found himself at the ferry over the Missouri River at Jefferson City, the county seat of Cole County and the state capital. Winter had reasserted its hold during February, and he saw chunks of ice on the wide river.

A much older man, craggy-faced and ruggedly built, the ferryman assured him that they would make it across the river. Then he commented that John had a strange accent, asking him where he came from. "Georgia, born there," John admitted.

"So did I," the ferryman said, "but it's not Georgia I hear. It's the soft sing-song of the Cherokee tongue."

"My Grandpa was a Scot trader, and we grew up among the Cherokees," John volunteered, as he wondered where this inquiry was leading.

"That's what I thought," the ferryman said. "I grew up east of Adairville. That's where I learned my trade, working on ferries run by half-breeds at the edge of the Cherokee Nation. It's a damn shame what that state did to your people."

John didn't know whether to admit it or not, but he went ahead, "You may have worked for some of my Adair relatives then. I never got to know many of 'em 'round Adairville. I grew up at Coosawattee."

"Small world," the ferryman said, "but I'll get you across this river and you don't owe me a toll."

After he was safely on the north side of the Missouri, John said thank-you to the ferryman. He pondered how admitting your Indian blood opened some doors and closed others. If the ferryman had family who had been killed in an Indian raid, or lost property to an Indian claim, John might have needed to find his own way across the river. As it was, the man felt a duty to help him. Then John decided that he would try to avoid the whole issue by saying he was the grandson of a Scotsman who had lived in North Carolina and Kentucky. That was true enough without opening the whole issue of Indians in Georgia. His Great-Uncle James had lived and raised a family in Kentucky without attracting any attention to himself. Not everyone would have such a good ear for a Cherokee accent. His clothes were all common shirts and trousers, since he had given the last of his hand-made and decorated shirts, leggings, and clouts to the Boone children. Until he arrived in Pike County he intended to blend into the population. After arriving he would see what he would need to do to live quietly.

An icy rain poured on him through much of the next day. The terrain seemed to level out, and the path was easy to follow, but by evening he was coughing and swallowing hard with a sore throat. Fears of a return of the serious illnesses of the earlier journeys gripped him, as he entered to the town of Fulton in Callaway County. He located an inn and boarded Jubal in the stable behind it. He would have to part with some money for the lodging, but it would be worth it to avoid getting sicker. He mixed some tea, honey and whiskey, drank it slowly, and found his way to bed. That night, he didn't have to share it with anyone else, as few travelers had ventured out on the area trails that day.

John didn't fully wake up until three days later, assisted by the elderly couple, Ezra and Maude Goodwin, who ran the inn. Old man Goodwin helped him to relieve himself in the chamber pot when he needed, and to crawl back into bed. The lady brought him broth, mustard plasters, and a bottle of terrible tasting heavy syrup, insisting that he swallow it by the tablespoon-full whenever he awoke coughing. She explained that she had lost three children to a coughing sickness when they were young like him, and she knew what to do to help him. In his misery John dreamed about her help and the deaths of young men like himself, and he couldn't separate the help from a plan to poison him, so his response was not always coherent or cooperative, but he was too weak to resist when she called her husband to hold him down. By the time he felt strong enough to get up, a week later, John was disappointed to learn that he had spent all the money he had earned on the trip so far. He would have to start drawing from the nest egg. The Goodwins made an agreement with him that he could work for his room and board until he was able to resume traveling, even as they made certain that he took on the work gradually and didn't suffer a setback. When he was finally ready to leave on the first of April, the woman told him that they had never had such a well-mannered young Indian as a guest in their house.

John puzzled about the send-off and their generosity all day. How did they know? He must have said things in his delirium. Even so, he again felt appreciation for the people who were not afraid to disregard popular misconceptions about uncivilized Indians.

In Pike County, Illinois

May and June, 1849, Northeast Missouri

Working his way across the countryside, through Bowling Green and finally arriving at Louisiana, Missouri, on the Mississippi, John helped farmers with plowing and planting their crops and gardens. He realized that, when he finally arrived in Illinois, he would be too late to clear land and put in his own crops. He might as well make his way slowly and help other farmers where he could, and plenty of work was available, even if cash was not. Gratefully receiving whatever pay he was offered, he was even more grateful for room and board for himself and Jubal, especially on the cool and rainy spring nights. He told himself that, at least, he was adding a little bit to his stake, not whittling it down.

The closer John got to Illinois the more nervous he became about the reception he would receive from people in Pike County. Richard Bean would probably be wondering what had happened to him, since John was already months overdue. Standing on the banks of the Mississippi, recognizing that he had given up so much to get here, John did not want to be disappointed. His experiences with dashed hopes kept him from taking Jubal's reins and walking down to the ferry. Instead he turned around and went back to the farmer on the outskirts of Louisiana and asked if he could work for a few more days. Two weeks later he collected his pay and tried again to approach the river. He spent the night under a rock ledge on the river bank, a mile north of the town, with Jubal grazing nearby. Strange dreams kept him in fitful sleep, imagining different nightmare possibilities, while he was awake or asleep. He thought again about enlisting in the army and becoming an interpreter to the western Indians, as Nathan Boone had suggested. He dreamed about going to see his Great Uncle James in Kentucky, and when he awoke he wondered whether he should take the dream as a sign of what he ought to do. He could learn from his uncle how to live away from the Cherokee Nation among the whites. He decided to continue to fast and pray through the next day.

When sunrise came John went down into the river and immersed himself in the water. He brewed a black drink with the roots of chicory, sassafras, and curly dock. In the afternoon when the sun was high and his head felt as hazy as the sky above, he heard field hands singing as they prepared for planting a field above and behind him. He climbed closer to hear the words of their song. "I's jest a poor wayfarin' stranger trav'lin' through dis worl' of woe," they sang in their full-throated, mellow, baritone voices, and he thought they were singing for him. "But dere's no sickness, toil or danger in dat far land whar I go." Then a little later, while he still listened, some of them started singing another melody alongside the first, "Guide my feet, Lawd, long dis lonesome way. Guide my feet, Lawd, long dis lonesome way. Guide my feet, Lawd, long dis lonesome way, cause I don' want to walk dis way in vain. I'm goin' dere to meet my mother, my father, goin' dere no more to roam. I's only goin' ober Jordan. I's only goin' ober home. I's only goin' ober home. Guides me as I go. Guides me as I go."

John returned to his spot under the rock ledge, watching the broad, brown Mississippi flow past, thinking of Will, Elijah, and other people he had left behind, his mother, his father, Uncle Jim, and other people who had died. Tears flowed down his cheeks through much of the afternoon, but by dusk he had made up his mind. He would cross the river and head for the land where Free Frank and Richard Bean had made a new start. That was going to be home for him. That's where he would see his mother's and his father's dreams come true, if he would ever see them come true.

Finally, at noon the next day, he paid his two bits toll, climbed aboard the ferry and crossed the Mississippi.

Two days later, after not eating for three days, John stood in a valley clearing five miles south of New Salem, looking toward a wooded ridge. In the village of Barry he had gotten directions to the first location he sought. Three miles north of Barry he stopped at the side by side farmhouses of John and Moses Decker, introduced himself as John Bell, a name shared with his grandfather and their step-father, and told them how his grandfather had met their step-father many years before. They welcomed him heartily and gave him more directions. Following the trail east he passed in sight of the flourishing farms and the village of New Philadelphia, resolving to come back soon and meet some of the people he saw from a distance. A few miles farther he looked north to see a two story log house standing on west end of a long low wooded ridge; that would be the home of Thomas Gray and his family, recently arrived from Ohio. A sprawling frame house stood on the ridge to the east; that would be the home of Richard Bean and his family.

July 2, 1849, Richard Bean's House

"You do look like your Grandpa, at least what I remember he looked like, when we went to war together, at Horseshoe Bend," said Richard Bean in a gravelly voice, as he examined John from head to toe. "Where you been? We expected you months ago."

John explained the time that he had spent working along the way, and then being sick at Fulton. As he spoke he took the measure of Richard Bean, as thin as a bean pole, with a long, craggy face, big ears and sharp nose, a few sparse patches of white hair on the sides of his bald head, definitely looking as old or older than his grandfather. He apologized to Mr. Bean if he was expecting his help with the spring planting or worrying about his delayed arrival.

"Naw, I'm too old for worryin'. Too many miles' travel an' too many poss'bilites to wonder what happened to yuh. But I don't have much fer yuh neither. Yer Grandpa helped me get a claim here years ago, an' I owe you a helpin' hand to git started, but I can't do much. Jest an old run-down cabin an' a forty acre patch a' brush 'n trees in a corner a' the next section west a' here, on t'other side a' Tom Gray's new place. Side'zat I could use yer help here, after yuh git set up, but I can't pay yuh much 'cept what work we kin do t'gether. Don't have much coin. But muh boy, J. B., kin do a little too. He's sev'ral years older'n yuh, married 'bout five years, got some young'ins, an' he's 'spectin' yuh too. When he gits home, afta suppa, he kin show yuh the old place where you kin stay."

John was relieved to know that a place was available for him to stay by himself, no matter how small or run-down it might be. Forty acres sounded fine. That would give him plenty to do for the rest of the year, to get a field ready for the next season. Again he gave silent thanks to his Ududu for the chance to make a fresh start.

When John Bean soon came in for supper from his day's work, putting up hay with a nearby neighbor, Isaac Conkright, he greeted John with the same friendliness as his father. Soon his wife, Ama, and their children joined them. The oldest, Robert, was five years old; James, four; and Harriet, a baby. Clearly the two little boys were eager to meet the newcomer, and they crawled all over him until Ama told them to mind their manners and leave him alone, but John enjoyed their attention, and soon they were in his lap again.

Ama set a table with an abundance of food, fresh-baked bread and cherry pie, greens from their garden, and two chickens she had killed, dressed, and fried, as soon as she knew that John Bell was joining them for supper. She was as short and plump as Richard and John were tall and thin. Black-haired and deep brown-eyed, she looked like many of the Cherokee women John had known. Ama was apologetic about the cabin, too, though they had cleaned it out in March, she said, expecting him any day then. Afterward they left it alone, wondering whether he would come. She invited him to stay in their home until they put the cabin in livable condition. John responded that he was eager to work on the cabin himself, and didn't want to impose on them any more than he had already. Likely he would need to again and again until he had a proper working farm. He wanted to go this very night, and it wouldn't be worse than staying out under the stars, as he had already done many nights. Ama frowned and pinched her eyebrows, but didn't say any more about it, except that he could change his mind when he saw the cabin.

During supper Richard, J. B., and Ama plied John with questions about their relatives living in or near the Cherokee Nation. Another John Bean, a cousin, had married Aunt Ruth Starr, also known to Ama as Lucy-Too-Yah, and they lived near Grandfather Caleb Starr, but John had to say that he hadn't heard much from them after Uncle James' murder, when he left the neighborhood with his father. He thought that Grandpa Bell had said that John and Ruth were planning to stay at their farm near Evansville, even though many of their family were leaving for Texas with Grandpa. John knew several of their twelve children, and told about them. Ama listened attentively and impressed John that he was telling her about people who meant something to her.

John mentioned that he knew that his step-mother Elizabeth had been married to Edmond Bean years before she married his father David Bell. They simply nodded as if they already knew. John didn't know what had happened to Edmond, and he didn't ask if they knew.

Richard mentioned that Grandpa Bell in his letter had called John by his "Indian name," Red Wolf. "How'd you get that name?" he asked. "It's your clan, I know, but did something happen?"

John told about his escape with Will from the stockade at Charleston, and their journey to join Grandpa Bell at his farm in Alabama. A red wolf had helped them find their way when they were lost, he explained, and Grandpa had always called him that afterward. He laughed that he liked the name better than his Uncle Devereaux's name, "Chicken-Trotter."

Did you see a red wolf on your way here?" Ama asked.

"No, I think the wolves I heard howling were probably bigger grey wolves, but I didn't hear many of them. I feel the red wolf is inside me now, so I don't feel lost even when I'm in a strange place."

They talked late into the evening about the Cherokee people and the difficult situations that Indian people faced on the frontier as the white population continued to move west, and that black people faced where the laws allowed slavery. "A generation ago those were lively conflicts in this area, but now all kinds of people live together here; everyone is more interested in making a living and learning," Richard said. The hour was late enough that John was glad to accept a bed in their home that night.

After breakfast the next morning John and J.B. rode their horses along the mile and a half to the cabin site, to make sure young John Bell was willing to stay. J.B. talked about his young children and his hopes that they could be educated in the new school he and his neighbors were planning to build.

John Bell readily affirmed what J.B. said, telling him how he had hoped to go to school himself when they reached the Western Cherokee Nation, but never had the chance, so he had to make do with the help that his family gave him, learning to read and write. Bean admitted that he never had a chance to get any schooling either, and no one in the family could help with it, but he wanted his children to have it. It was going to be more important as the years went by. More people were arriving in the area, filling up the land, and life was getting more complicated. People had to know more than they used to, and the only way to figure out what they needed was to read and be able to cipher.

When they reached the grove where the cabin sat, at the edge of a shallow ravine, John looked over the little structure, with its sides covered by a Virginia Creeper vine on one end and poison ivy on the other, its shingles cupped and cracked or missing entirely, chinking missing between many of the logs, and the plank door standing ajar, though a small well-used trail ran through the doorway. "It looks like home to me, and I've already got some company," laughed John.

"You're taking it well. I don't think you'll want the little varmint to stay," J. B. said.

"Like I told your mother, I didn't expect anything to be ready-built, and I'm used to sleeping outside, so to have this much already done gives me a head start. I'll fix it up and clean it up and be glad for it."

"Let me show you the little spring down at the head of the ravine," J. B. said. "It's a real good spring. Not enough for many cattle, but we like the water. Sometimes come up here just to fill some jugs to take home. No sulfur or iron taste to it." They took the horses down the path to a rock and moss-lined pool where a steady trickle of water flowed over the rocks into the weedy undergrowth of the ravine. Cupping their hands they drank cool water from the little pool and then let the horses drink.

"This will be just great," John said. "You can go on home and tell your good wife that I couldn't be happier." But J. B. stayed the rest of the day, joined John in his hardtack, jerky and fresh black raspberry lunch, and helped strip the cabin of its vines, clean out its raccoon nest, and replace the shingles where they could see daylight through the ceiling. They talked all day, and J. B. described all of the neighbors with vivid, often humorous stories. John was especially curious about his nearest neighbors, the Thomas Gray family, whom the man in Barry who had given John directions had described as "different." "What did he mean?" John asked.

"I spose he is different, but I like him," J. B. was quick to say. "They just came from Ohio a few years ago. His wife came from Maine to start with, and she's about fifteen years older than he is, and smart as a whip. He had an old Veteran's Tract land claim,[188] but he added to it, by trading a long rifle, a greyhound and a team of horses. In religion they're Universalists, not many of them around here, though we've got some Quakers, the Pine family, from out East, like your Grandpa Starr. The Grays are educated. They're the ones who donated a plot of ground for a

---

[188] Pike County land records contain a US Government land claim from 1836, but there is no record of Thomas Gray's arrival before 1846.

school, and got the project going. He's a crack shot, too, never misses.[189]

"They have five children. Jim's the oldest; he's just about grown up. Willie Ann's a girl yet, about 14, but she's going to be a fine lady. Then there's Tommy, Teddy, and their little girl, Alabama Carolina."

"They came from Ohio?" John asked.

"Yep."

"I wonder how they came up with that name," John said, as he silently marveled at the names that were shared with his mother and his Aunt Sarah Caroline.

"Like the man said, they're different." J. B. answered.

When J. B. left in the late afternoon, John was happy to say, "Many thanks, my friend."

"You are welcome, my friend, and glad to have you here. I leave the wolf to his den, but come on over whenever you want, and share a meal with us." And John felt that he could.

July 10, 1849, John Bell's Cabin

Catherine Gray prepared a basket full of fresh bread, garden vegetables, and dried meats, and she recruited Jim to take it a mile through the woods to their new neighbor. Willie Ann asked to go with him to meet John Bell whom J. B. Bean had told them about. When they first saw the cabin they could see the improvements. In addition to new shingles and brush and vines

---

[189] These details of the life of Thomas Gray and his wife Catherine Bennett Gray come from *The Portrait and Biographical Album of Pike and Calhoun Counties, Illinois*, 1891, page 396.

cleared from the sides, John had been filling the spaces between the logs with a mixture of clay and straw to seal the walls. They could not see where he was at first. Jim set the basket down on a newly-constructed branch and post work table in front of the cabin. Digging and scraping noises came from the ravine, so they headed toward them. At the foot of the path they found John stripped to his pants, with the pant legs rolled up, covered in clay and sweat, digging with an old shovel, filling a couple of buckets with clay from the creek bed, and lining the base of a newly dug basin with large field rocks with flat sides.

John apologized for his appearance, and Jim apologized for interrupting his work. He told John that he had brought a welcoming basket of food from his mother. Willie Ann was staring at him and his project with interest, but John quickly disappeared behind a tree to put on his shirt. When he emerged John explained that he was making a bathing basin at the same time that he was preparing the mortar with the clay and some lime he had obtained from a trip to New Philadelphia.

"I also bought the buckets and shovel there, and some other tools. Mostly I was glad to meet Free Frank McWhorter and his wife, Lucy, and son Solomon and other members of his family. He sure has worked hard to free people, even outside his own family, and it's a neat little town. They made me feel right at home."

Jim responded, "We're all glad to have you here. It's a good neighborhood; that's why my folks decided to come, too, from Ohio."

They were walking back toward the cabin when John pointed in the direction of the edge of the woods and the open prairie beyond. "I've got a lot to do to clear that land for a field. Every day I work at it a little, and I don't see much progress, but after a while I make a dent in it. I'm looking for a good pair of oxen to help clear and plow it." He explained that he had also ridden over to Perry, and then Griggsville, looking for a team of oxen, without success. He did meet the family of Thomas Elledge, son of the late Boone Elledge and grandson of Nettie, Daniel Boone's sister. He delivered letters, belatedly, from Nathan Boone's wife. "They could'a sent 'em faster by post," he admitted, "but I was glad to meet the people, anyway."

"You've been to a lot of places in a short time," Jim said.

"I feel like I've got to make up for lost time. I took too long to get here; half the summer's already gone."

"One week here and you've made a great start. You'll be fine, John. We'll see to that."

April 25, 1850, Thomas Gray's Farm

Following a hard morning's field work, plowing and burning stumps and removing rocks, John had to decide whether to return to his own cabin or head a half mile southeast to the well at Thomas Gray's farm. He decided to make a visit to his neighbors, where he expected to find fresh cool water and, if he was lucky, a dinner invitation. He left his oxen resting and grazing, tethered to a tree, and headed toward the Gray's farmstead in the distance. He found J. B. and Richard Bean there ahead of him, and Thomas Gray and Jim, also washing up and beginning a dinner break. Soon Willie Ann came down the flagstones from the house, carrying a basket of bread, jams, and sliced pork, and her mother Catherine walking behind her. John raised a bucket of water and filled a tin cup, pouring much of the bucket into the wooden trough to wash the dirt off his hands, arms, and face. As he had hoped, Catherine Gray invited him to join them for dinner.

Our Land! Our People!

Their talk began with the good weather and their plans for planting and the growing season. The "old-timer" Richard Bean talked about coming up from Kentucky with his family and settling here fifteen years ago. J. B. added that he had grown up in Kentucky, found his wife, Ama, and started his family, and come here when he was 20 with his father. This was Thomas Gray's sixth season on this land, coming with Catherine and his children from Ohio in 1846. John Bell admitted that he was putting in his first crop on his own, after years of working for his uncle or his father. The other farmers took an interest in how he was doing, noting that what he might lack in experience he made up for in diligence, and they reaffirmed their resolve to work together on the jobs that required many hands.

"This land is fertile, it's well-drained, especially along this ridge that we share. I've never seen any that's better," said Richard Bean.

Tom Gray added his two cents, "We've got good, hard-working neighbors, people we can trust, because they've earned their way. There's not a better man than our neighbor to the west, Free Frank, and his people are a good lot. They've proven themselves to be good neighbors all the while we've been here. There are a lot of newcomers to the east, south, and north, but decent folk as far as I can see. Between New Salem and New Philadelphia, I'd say we've got the best of worlds right here."

"A man needs his freedom, and he needs his peace. I think we've got a chance at both here," said J. B. "You're a quiet one, John Bell. You've been here a while now. What do you think about this place you've come to?"

John answered, "When I was growing up I learned to listen, to speak only when I had something to say. But I agree with what you've said. The land is good. The towns hereabout seem to live up to their names—brotherly love and peace—I've known a lot less, and who could want more? As to why I'm here, I been giving a lot of thought to that. I think I am here mainly for one reason—to love Willie Ann Gray, if she'd have me. Anything else that I might get or hope, wouldn't mean a hill of beans without her."

They all turned to look a Willie, who had flushed immediately to red.

"If I didn't know better, I'd say that sounded like a proposal," Willie said quietly.

"If you didn't take it as one, I'd be disappointed. If you'd have me as your husband, I'd be a happy man. If you are not ready yet, I will wait. If not ever, I'd say I've missed the whole point of coming here. I think it's a fine place to live, and I know no other place I'd prefer to be, but the real reason for my being here is this fine young woman in front of me."

Willie concentrated on the slicing of the bread, and laying out the provisions she had carried on a rough-hewn table set on saw-horses. No one spoke. They heard the cows mooing in the nearby pasture, and the wrens chirping in the tree overhead. After a lengthy wait, Willie said, "You are a fine man, Mister Bell, and I know there's a lot more to you than I know yet. I'm not going to say 'yes' right now, but if you are as serious as you say you are, I am inclined to take your proposal just as seriously, and I will hold you to it."

"That is just fine with me," John answered.

September 14, 1852, John Bell's Cabin

John pulled the wrinkled letter from his shirt pocket as he sat down on a ladder-back chair in front of the fireplace. The mailman had dropped the letter at Thomas Gray's farmhouse, asking them to deliver it to the "young fellar back in the woods." It was postmarked on August 20 at Maysville, Arkansas, and John recognized the writing as his Aunt Sarah's.

Dear John,

I received your kind letter in May, and am much pleased to hear that you are satisfactorily settled up in Illinois Pike County and have made many friends. After so many troubles here and my brothers murder you have done well to go as you did tho I was afraid for you. I am relieved to learn you are well after the past sickness. Sister Nancy is far from here in Texas and she suffers much from consumtion too. It is hard to live so far away from my dear ones. She and brother Jack let me know news that I must pass on to you tho I fear that it will burden your heart as it does mine. My father and your namesake grandpa passed from this life on July 12. They buried him there at a place they name Mt Tabor from the bible. He was blind and not able to work on his new house and his heart just stopped so he did not suffer long as some do. 70 years he got to do so many things and see so much I cant stay sad for him but I wish I was there with him at the end. He never really got to have the home in Texas he wanted and nephews Asa and Uriah bought land but have not moved their families yet. I want you to know my Saladin is growing up a fine young man and very bright and mannerly like you at his age. Things are better here than they were. We are getting more schools organized and open so someday both girls and boys will have education like we hoped. Stand and I have a new baby we named Minnehaha. We call her Ninnie a very pretty baby. I can just see you hold her as your newest cousin. Write and stay well. Do not worry over spelling and grammer. I can read it all and am always eager to hear. Your affectionate aunt.   SCB Watie[190]

John held the letter for a long time reading and rereading every line. When he put the letter down on the table beside him and gazed into the fireplace, the tears were running down his cheeks. He thought of little Lafayette, John and Ama Bean's baby, who had died in May after a life of only two weeks. Seventy years was a real accomplishment, considering everything they had lived through, but John still missed his Ududu. He gave a prayer of thanks that his grandfather was always a help when he needed him.

John looked around at his cabin, and it looked a lot like the home he remembered at Coosawattee Town. As he cut trees and cleared land, he had used many of the logs to enlarge the common room and build a sleeping wing onto the home. Window glass panes filled the casings that had been open to weather and wind. With milled lumber he had constructed tables, benches, and shelves that finished a kitchen area at one end, separate from a sitting and work area at the other. The bedroom was spacious and ready for more than one person, and he had a trunk and a nice set of large drawers that were completely empty.

October 7, 1852, near John Bell's Cabin

On September 15, Willie Ann had turned seventeen, and she had initiated several conversations with her parents, separately and

---

[190] Sarah Caroline Bell Watie wrote many letters to family members during these years, and some are printed in Edward Everett Dale and Gaston Litton, *Cherokee Cavaliers* (Norman: The University of Oklahoma Press, 1939). Although no letters between Sarah and John Francis Bell exist, I have tried to retain the tone and manner of her many letters that have been preserved.

together, since then. Catherine had married her father when she was nearly thirty, but she was not opposed to young people marrying. Thomas was concerned about John Bell's health, with the knowledge that consumption almost always caused early death, but he knew many people who were afflicted with the disease among their neighbors, and everyone had a right to be happy for as many days as they had life and breath. What did they think about John Bell's character? He was a gentleman, trustworthy, a hard worker, easy-going, friendly, a good neighbor and helper when they asked, and he never asked for more than his share of help from others, maybe even less than he had a right to expect.

"Yes," Mother said, she liked him, but that was not the most important thing. "What do you think of him?" she asked. Father echoed the same query.

"What do I think of him?' she asked herself, and her thoughts were a muddle. She couldn't keep from thinking about him, day and night. When he didn't show up as usual for two days, she became anxious, and she informed her parents that she was going to see if he was all right, she announced right after breakfast. He might have gotten sick again, or been injured. She explained that she wanted to check on him, and they allowed her to go unaccompanied by her brother.

The leaves on the trees were just beginning to turn colors for fall, no frost had yet touched the tender plants, most of the corn was still standing in the fields, and the day was warm and clear. When Willie Ann approached the house she saw no sign of John, although nothing was out of place. The door was shut and no one responded to her knock. She opened it slightly as she knocked again, but no one seemed to be there. She drew the door shut again, and thought about the unusual bathing basin, which she knew John used every day when he arose, and often in the evening after work. She followed the path down the ravine.

John heard her before he saw her, and he was embarrassed to be caught naked in the basin when the sun was already peeking over the horizon. He lowered himself in the water up to his neck. When he saw her head appear above the gooseberry bushes, he shouted out the greeting "Siyo, Willie," though he hadn't used that greeting in years. She just kept coming. When she was standing at the edge of the pool, with a full view of John, unable to hide, she just stood a minute, looking him over without saying a word. Finally she smiled.

"I think I have you at a disadvantage," she said.

"Since you are standing between me and my clothes, I think you are right," he answered.

"How cold is the water?" she asked suddenly.

"Not as cold as it's going to be in a month," he answered.

She proceeded to remove her hat, and jacket, and unbutton her dress, until she let it slip down her hips. She hesitated a moment, as if she might enter the water in her underwear, then she said, "I don't know what difference it makes," and she dropped every other item of clothes she was wearing into the pile she had made, until she stood completely revealed in front of him. "I was worried about you. I hope you haven't been sick," she said as she moved into the water, gulping a little when she felt how chilly it was.

John stood and offered his hand to help her enter, and she took it as if it was an everyday event to enter into a bath with a naked man. "I wasn't feeling very good yesterday, but I am much better today, thank you," he answered. "I think I'm going to feel much better all day."

"I sincerely hope so," she said, and slid into his arms, which embraced her very tightly, and she held him just as tightly.

"No question about it, I will feel very well, if this means what I hope it means," he said.

"That I choose you for my husband, now and forever," she said. "That's what it means, if you still want this to be, then I am yours, and you, my dear Wolf, are mine." And she returned his waiting kiss.

After several minutes of holding and stroking and no doubt that John was ready and eager to go farther right there in the bathing pool, and Willie was not resisting at all, John pulled back and held her shoulders. Looking at her eye to eye, he said, "Can we go to Pittsfield and make this legal, now, today?"

"We can. I'm ready. We can stop on the way and tell my parents they can come with us if they want, or wait here till we get back."

"You think they'll accept this?" he asked.

"Of course they will. They know I've chosen you," she answered.

In half an hour John and Willie Ann arrived at the Gray farmhouse, John riding Jubal and Willie on the mare that John had bought in May and Willie had named "Dreamer," because of "a look in her eyes," she had said. Thomas had already gone on an errand for the day, which Catherine thought would take him to Griggsville. She didn't register any surprise or dissatisfaction with their news, but she did say, "It may be best if you just go ahead and get married, and then let my good husband know afterwards. He can be headstrong at times. I think he imagined a fancy wedding at the church for you. You are seventeen. You are old enough to make your own decision. If it's my blessing you want, you have it."

In a short time they were on their way again. While they were riding, John asked Willie whether they should do this today. "Do we need your father's blessing? Among my people, the mother's advice is often sought, but it is the woman's decision whether or when she marries. I didn't even think about your father having a say."

"He does like to think he has a say, but Mother has the final word. She is nearly fifteen years older than Father. Besides, I like your people's ideas on this."

When John and Willie arrived at the white frame courthouse on the town square in Pittsfield, the County Clerk received them in a friendly manner, obtained their signatures on an application, received solemn promises that neither John nor Willie had been married before, and charged a dollar for the license to marry. "Where shall we take this license?" John asked Willie when they left the courthouse. "With the judge out of town, I don't know any of the preachers hereabouts." While they were standing outside the courthouse, trying to make a decision, John saw Willie Ann's father about a block away, with his back to them, talking to a man in front of one of the business establishments.

"What do we do now?" John asked.

"Let's see if we can leave without Father seeing us. If he wants us to wait for a church wedding, I don't want to have to argue with him about it." John took Willie's arm and they walked in the opposite direction, even though they had to circle back to get to their horses after Thomas had moved out of sight.

John and Willie still couldn't make up their minds where to take the license, so they decided to go home and think about it. While they were riding on their way home, and the sun was shining brightly and warm, John asked Willie, "We have a license. Are we married or not?"

"We're married."

"Then you and I have some unfinished business from this morning." He saw a shady spot with some brush to hide behind under a large old white oak, slid off his horse, and helped Willie down, tied the horses to a small redbud tree nearby, and unrolled his blanket onto the ground. Seating himself on the blanket, he extended his hand to help Willie join him.

They lay in each other's arms for a long time after their love-making. "When should I tell your father what we've done?"

"After we've been to a judge or a preacher," Willie answered.

"Then that won't be tonight. I hoped we could stay together and never part."

"I'll talk to Mother and see what she says about it. We'll get someone to tie the knot for us tomorrow or the next day." When they reached the Gray farmhouse, they held each other for a long time and promised they would be together as soon as possible the next day. Privately Willie told Catherine everything they had done, but Catherine did not have an answer for the question of where to take the license. When Thomas came into the house for supper, they did not tell him what John and Willie had done.

During the next two days, John and Willie spent most of their time together, but Willie went back to her house for supper and staying in her own bedroom overnight. She wanted to tell her little sister, but knew Allie could not keep a secret. If Thomas noticed anything unusual in Willie's demeanor, he didn't say anything about it. Meanwhile Catherine and Willie discussed the fact that the Methodist circuit rider who served the nearest churches would come eventually, but they did not know when, and the judges were equally unpredictable in their circuits. The nearest preacher they could count on being home was the Presbyterian one at Winchester, forty miles away. On the morning of September 10, Willie put on her finest dress, and she and John embarked for Winchester.

They had been gone more than an hour when Thomas came into his house and asked Catherine where Willie Ann was. Catherine didn't think there was any harm in telling him that they had gone to find the preacher at Winchester. Thomas didn't wait for an explanation. He rushed out of the house, saddled his horse, and started out to try to catch up with them. John and Willie had ridden steadily, but not hurriedly, so they had just reached Winchester when Thomas did finally catch up with them.

"What do you two think you're doing?" Thomas asked.

"We are asking the Presbyterian minister to sign our wedding license," John answered without hesitation.

"How's come you didn't ask me first?"

"We didn't think we needed to. Willie is old enough to decide for herself. You've known for some time what my intentions were. We did ask Catherine, and she gave us her blessing."

Thomas blanched at that, but he persisted in asking about their readiness for marriage, their elopement instead of planning a respectable church wedding, emphasizing Willie's youthful age instead of waiting like her mother, and every other delaying idea he could think of. When Thomas understood and admitted that he was having no impact on their resolve, John invited him to come with them to witness the vows, which he did.[191]

They all returned to the Gray home that evening for supper, which Catherine had ready for them, and Willie joined John at his cabin that night and every night afterward. If Catherine or Thomas said anything more about those events to each other, it was in the privacy of their own bedroom.

January 15, 1854, John & Willie Bell's Cabin

When he had shut and secured the door J. B. kicked the snow off his boots and asked if there was some coffee left in the pot by the hearth. Willie said there was, and she went to get it, while John took J. B.'s coat and hat and hung them on a peg near the door.

"You sure chose a cold day to come visitin'," John said. "You're welcome to join us for a bite to eat in a little while. Willie's got a squirrel stew going that's been whettin' my appetite all mornin'."

"Sounds too good to refuse," J. B. answered. "I hadn't seen you out since the snow came down two days back, so I thought I'd see how you were fixed for holdin' out, and I also got a letter

---

[191] The marriage license of John and Ann Bell is recorded at Pittsfield on October 7, 1852, and this is the date they celebrated as their anniversary. A note is added at the Pike County Courthouse that there was "no return" of the license. Their license is recorded at the Winchester, Illinois, Scott County Courthouse on October 10, 1852. The descendants of James Gray, Willie's brother, had an oral history of the elopement to Winchester telling that Thomas Gray rode after them and had a talk with John before he agreed to their marriage.

for you from the Post Office in town this morn. Thought you might like to have your mail."

John took the letter from J. B.'s hand and looked it over, as he knitted his brows and squinted at the writing on the envelope. "Don't get mail often enough to remember to check for it when I'm in town. It's my Aunt Sarah writing from their place on Honey Creek, where I came from." He carefully unsealed the envelope and sat down by the hearth to read while Willie handed J. B. a cup of coffee, and he seated himself at the table. John took several minutes to read the letter to himself before he looked up. "It's a mix of good and bad, as you might expect after a long time without any news, but here's what she says—

Dear John,

I had a mind to sit down and write you a letter for some time now and finly am starting it. Things change fast around here as you do know. The children grow fast. Saladin is now as old as you were when we came west and he learns to read and write from me as did you. Watica and Minnie are not far behind and eager always to do all that their big brother does. I will have another baby soon. Then my hope is to go see our family in Texas. Jack still lives with George Starr and our sister Nancy, but his house should be ready later this year. Nancy has been doing well with the consumption and I hope you do too. They write that dear Elijah has died. Your friend Will has paid for his mother Demaris. They are now free together but I do not know where they will live. [John looked up from the letter and said, "To me this is the best news of the letter. Demaris is a smart woman, the equal of anyone she ever met. She deserved to be free, for all the help she was to Uncle Jack."] There are many new schools through the nation and cousin William Penn Adair is very involvd in establishing them. Still I must also tell you some terrible news that will make you glad that you are far from here. Remember the big springs south of Mrs Webbers that Uncle Andrew Adair bought from old Benj. Cooper. On September 10th last a mob attacked Andrew and his son Geo. Wash. Adair at their home there and murdered them. We begin to feel safe and make progress toward our dreams and again we face the same demons that sent you away. Stand says we should not be afeared. There were special circomstances that led to the crime. I say the old Ross party still seeks any excuse to take revenge and we can never feel safe. Stay where you are and prosper. With my blessing and my love. Your Aunt SBWatie."

John let his hand, still holding the letter, fall into his lap. "I wonder sometimes if they'll still be fighting the old battles a hundred years from now. My dear Aunt Sarah and Stand Waite are still in the thick of it there. I don't see how they could feel safe when an old gentleman like my Great Uncle Andrew and his kin are not safe on their own place. At least Will and his mother are free and on their own. I wish they'd come here."

September 9, 1854, New Philadelphia

News of the death of Free Frank spread rapidly through the neighborhood on September 7, 1854. A stream of family, friends, and neighbors swept through their farmhouse at the north edge of the village throughout the next day and a half until the wandering preacher, Father Wolf Tine, arrived to lead prayers in the home with the family. With the gathered crowd in front of the porch, they walked down the path and followed the mule-drawn wagon with his coffin to the cemetery, south of the village, to the open grave.

Clearly Frank had a premonition that his time was short, John Bell soon learned as he talked with Frank's son, Solomon.[192]

"His biggest sorrow was he han't made 'nough money to redeem all his chillens from der owners. He made me promise I'd get duh job done, and bring muh las' three nephews 'n two nieces home, an' duh two great-gran-chillins. So I got muh work cut out fer me," Solomon said.

"How much do you need? How long do you expect it to take?" John asked.

"Don't rightly know. Probly 'nother thousan' dolluhs. Daddy set 'bout three thousan' dollars in his will, an' I got some extra saved now, but don' think it's 'nough yet. Maybe nex fall if'n we gets a good crop nex year. I'll go ta' Kentuck 'n see."

"I'll chip in some, and we'll pass the hat around. Maybe we kin help with the hopes he had. Nobody ever deserve it more'n your daddy. One of the finest men I ever had the pleasure meetin'."

"That's right kind of yuh, John. My Daddy was a good man, I know. He could be proud of all he managed to git done in his seventy-seven years."

Later, when they had another opportunity to talk, and several other neighbors had joined them, they considered the new anti-black immigration legislation that had passed the year before.[193]

---

[192] The background information for this conversation comes from "The Achievement of a Dream" by Juliet E. K. Walker, in *Free Frank: A Black Pioneer on the Antebellum Frontier* (Lexington: University Press of Kentucky, 1983, 1995).

[193] The 1853 legislation is summarized in "The Illinois Black Codes" by Roger D. Bridges in *Illinois Periodicals Online,* http://www.lib.niu.edu/1996/iht329602.html.

"So nows duh law's 'gainst us. Bars free blacks from comin', an' bars any slave comin' inta Ill'nois to git free," Solomon said. "I ain' goin' follow any sich law, but don' wanna git 'rested neither. Dese new laws made my Daddy madder'n anythin' I ever sawed."

Tom Gray said, "Your neighbors will back you up, Solomon. Nobody'll report you when you bring your family in, or we'll make 'em sorry they did."

"We cain't turn neighbor 'gainst neighbor. We cain't live like dat," Solomon said.

"It won't be like that. We'll keep it quiet. All your neighbors respect what you're doing. So nobody's going to enforce that law around here. Springfield's miles away. They don't need to know what's none of their business," responded Tom.

John entered the conversation. "I know it's not going to be right, as long as that law's on the books. None of us can bear it, so we'll jus' have to get it changed. But seein' it's unfair, and we can't abide it, we just have to keep on doin' what's right, and that's bringin' your family together and helpin' others git free. I'd like my brother Will to come here, too, but somehow I got to let him know it's not as good as I'd hoped for 'im to come. Better than Texas, I suppose, but not as good as it ought to be."

Still later, when they were by themselves, John told Solomon that he knew about the help that Free Frank and Solomon had given to runaways on their way to Canada. The cabin that he had in the woods could be used as a hiding place when they needed it. He had put a wood floor into the new part, and a trap door to a root cellar that could be covered over by a rug and the bed. "Nobody ever needs to know about it, 'cept you, me and Willie."

"Good t'know. Thanks, friend," said Solomon.

October 28, 1854, John & Willie Bell's Cabin

John had fetched the midwife, Mary Stevens, a large middle-aged black woman who had the healthy delivery of many babies to her credit, from a mile east of New Philadelphia the evening before. Much of the night he had been in and out of the bedroom, running errands for Willie or for Mary. After many months and no pregnancy, Willie had begun to worry if something was wrong with her, but her mother Catherine had reassured her that she was only eighteen, then nineteen, and she herself had not conceived until she was in her thirties. John was in no hurry. The death of his mother in childbirth was enough to make John wary of the whole process. Much as he liked the idea of being a father, having enjoyed many younger children as he was growing up, the reality of pregnancy and childbirth frightened him.

"Don't you worry. I'll be fine," Willie kept trying to reassure him, since she had the experience of her mother's and Ama Bean's deliveries to reassure her. Still John paced and needed something to keep busy. For a while he tried to whittle a toy bird out of a chunk of linden wood, but he stopped that after jabbing his finger a few times.

Willie was slow in making progress, but Mary said, "Not to worry; that's the way with first babies." Finally by mid-morning contractions became hard and more frequent, and by 11 A.M. the strong howls of a baby filled the cabin.

With great relief, John rushed into the bedroom when Mary allowed him, and found a baby boy nursing at Willie's breast. "What shall we name him?" Willie asked. John had been adamant that it was bad luck to name a baby before it was born. She persisted in sharing her desire to honor the grandparents with the name of the firstborn, and John admitted that this happened frequently in his family, too. They had dropped the subject after that, when Willie could see how uneasy it made John to confirm the choice of a name.

John looked at the red-faced wriggler and puzzled, finally asking Mary her opinion. "He looks like a 'Thomas' to me," she offered.

"A good name. Your father's name. My brother's name, too. Maybe I should say cousin's—he's a very brave man. It fits, I think. Don't you think so, Willie?" said John.

"Thomas Bell," Willie repeated. "It sounds good. What about your father, John? Name him 'David,' David Thomas, or Thomas David?"

"I don't think I'm ready for that, after everything my father went through, and how things ended. He did have another English name that he almost never used. That was 'Henry.' He used to joke about being named for two kings, but having a very small kingdom."

"Maybe we could use that name, since he never did," Willie said.

"It doesn't carry so much sadness for me, since my father didn't use it. Maybe our little boy can fill it with new meaning. I like Henry. Thomas Henry, or Henry Thomas?"

"Henry Thomas Bell sounds good to me."

"Me, too."

"You're so funny, Wolf. We could have chosen that name months ago."

"Oh, no. Nobody even suggested Thomas or Henry till we saw him, so we didn't jinx him with a name before we saw whether it fit."

Later that week John told Willie about his hope of buying a larger piece of cleared land, and building a new decent four room frame house just a mile north of New Salem, to have some room to expand with their new baby. A year later, at the end of harvest, the three of them would make that move to their new house. When they did, Willie was already pregnant with their second child. They left their cabin in the woods, but John returned to it when he farmed the land around it, enjoyed the cool spring water and the bathing pool, and kept the cellar ready for Solomon's use.

June 2, 1856, John & Willie Bell's New House

Irene Ellen Bell was born on May 18, 1856, after a shorter and easier labor for both mother and father, though John took nothing for granted and made sure that Mary Stevens was rooming with them immediately after Willie made her first suggestion of the baby's arrival. Labor didn't really start for four more days. They were fortunate that no other calls for Mary's help came in the meantime.

The naming followed a lengthy discussion, like the earlier one. 'Hannah' and 'Sarah' were considered, as family names. When they could not agree, John suggested the name 'Irene,' based as it was on an old word for peace, John said. "Being born at New Salem, which also means peace, I think the name will fit, especially since she's such a good, quiet baby." Fortunately for the name, she stayed that way. No one they knew used the name

"Ellen" either, but they both liked it, since it meant 'sunshine.' She was born on a sunny day, and that, too, seemed to match her disposition.

Although they now lived four miles north of Thomas and Catherine Gray, and John and Ama Bean, their visiting and working together did not slow down. John continued to ride to the Beans and Grays to help with farm work, and Willie and the babies would sometimes ride along in their new carriage to spend time with her mother and their friends. Thomas Gray had made repeated suggestions for the Bells to join them in worship on Sunday mornings at the new Universalist Church in New Salem. The Conkright, Preble, and Fisher families joined in making the invitation, and, finally, when Irene was two months old, and Tommy had learned to sit quietly, they went together to a Sunday service.

Rev. D. R. Biddlecome had come to serve the new church, and John was impressed with his insistence that "God is the Father of all people, and all people are God's children, and God will not let any of his children be lost for eternity. He will gather them all into his arms, although it may be harder and take longer to gather some people than others. God loves all of them, every single one, and all that is expected is their love for one another." The preacher was saying what John had thought for many years, and the message reminded him of his mother, Rev. Bushyhead, and his baptism. This was a gathering of like-minded people who didn't try to keep anyone out, and John felt at home here. An additional benefit—they got to see his wife's family on Sundays, and often they joined them for a fried chicken dinner afterward.

Late in August, when the Bells were at home, Willie in the house, and John in the barnyard, Richard Bean came riding down the road toward them. John was surprised to see him, since he had stopped coming into the field to work, and rarely left his comfortable woven cane arm chair on their porch. Old Mr. Bean greeted John, called Willie by the name 'Charlotte,' and admired baby Irene, who provided the excuse for his unusual visit. He began to talk about the battle of Horseshoe Bend as if it had just happened, and as if John were his grandfather who had fought alongside Richard there. After a few moments it was clear that Richard did not know where he was or what year it was. John asked if he wanted some company on his way home, saddled his own horse, and rode with him back to the Bean farmstead.

A few months later Richard wandered away from his house in the middle of a wintry night, and it took several hours for his family to locate him with the help of all the neighbors searching. A few days afterward, on December 10, he died at the age of 78 years. The whole neighborhood gathered on another wintry afternoon on a little hill at the southeast corner of the Gray farm, and they buried the old veteran Richard Bean near his baby grandson, Lafayette Bean, and granddaughter Marian; their neighbor, Isaac Conkright; and Lee Gray, Tom Junior and Martha Gray's firstborn son. A neighborhood cemetery had begun to collect precious souls. "Maybe we won't have to leave these loved ones behind," John observed.

"I hope not," Willie responded. "What would make you think we might?"

"Because I had to leave behind the burial place of every one I've ever loved, before I came here, and I don't want to do that ever again."

September 18, 1857, John & Willie Bell's House

When they were preparing for the birth of their third child, John again insisted that Mary Stevens come and live with them during the last couple of weeks until the baby was born. Even Mary thought that unnecessary, but John was insistent. During the summer he had even arranged for carpenters to add a third bedroom to the house that could serve as a furnished private space for Mary before it became an additional children's room. When the time came for delivery, John was in the middle of harvesting corn. They were all glad to have her there, because the baby was in the wrong position and had to be turned before delivery. Mary sent for the doctor, Edwin Gray, a cousin of Willie Ann, but the baby boy came into the world before the doctor arrived, not breathing and staying blue for what seemed like too long. He finally burst into a loud indignant series of cries, to everyone's relief.

"Since he had a hard time getting here, we'll have to call him John," Willie said.

"It would fit even better if we named him after my uncle, John Adair," suggested John. "He's always had a hard time finding his place in the world, but he's always succeeded in doing it anyway."

"I'd prefer the name 'Arthur,'" responded Willie.

"Adair's my grandmother's family name. Like Bell, it was the name of a Scotsman who came to live and trade among the Cherokee. There are a lot of fine people named Adair."

"It's a grown-up name, and we have to have a child's name. You already use 'John' and I kinda liked 'Artie,'" said Willie.

'Artie' reminded John of his half-brother Martin, whom they always called Marty, so he was willing to go along with that, and said they could sort out what adult name he would use when he was older.

Little John Arthur continued to make himself known throughout the house, crying louder and longer than his brother or sister did. He needed to be near his mother and held by her, even when he wasn't nursing. While he followed every movement with his eyes, a noise had to be loud for him to respond. Willie became convinced that he wasn't hearing soft or even normal sounds.

"There's something wrong with his hearing," Willie insisted to the doctor, but he at first dismissed her concerns.[194] After several months the child's hearing problem was evident to everyone. When he made sounds, she worked with him steadily to watch her mouth and form his sounds to make words.

"My mother told me that I didn't talk for a long time. Finally, when I did speak, it came out fully formed," John said to reassure her.

"You didn't have a problem with hearing. Artie will have to learn to speak more by looking and feeling than by hearing anything. This is something we will have to work on. It's a good thing that he can hear anything at all. With some help, he will have a normal life."

Late in the winter, in February of 1858, a quarter section of land became available just northeast of New Salem. The land connected to John and Willie's property at the southeast corner

---

[194] J. A. Bell was totally deaf in adulthood, according to his granddaughter, Doris Mae Bell. He could talk but was difficult to understand, and only those who knew him well were able to understand his pronunciations. He married and had three children, living until 1939. Doris reported that he was always friendly and good-humored.

of their eighty acres. With savings and extra cash from a good fall harvest John bought the land and more than doubled their holdings. Willie questioned him about whether he was taking on too much, but John said that he felt better than he ever had and pointed to the three children they had under their roof. "They'll have something to look forward to, if we can hold onto it," he said.

October 13, 1858, Quincy, Illinois

John, young Tom Gray, and J. B. Bean had risen early, and eaten a hearty breakfast that Willie prepared. They took a basket of food that she had packed for travel, and rode off on their horses shortly after dawn toward Quincy. Judge Stephen Douglas, who had often presided at the Pike County court, and the well-known circuit lawyer, Abraham Lincoln, would hold their sixth public debate in Quincy that afternoon as they competed for the office of United States Senator. The earlier debates had aroused great interest throughout the country and disturbed the usual comfortable ease of political conversations around New Salem. The Grays and the Beans had allied themselves with the Democrats and their frontier individualism, opposing the old Whig and Federalist elite that had steadily lost support in the Midwest and South. John had avoided declaring partisan positions, but his personal story was known to his friends.

Over the recent months John had registered his concern about the horse thieves who had been troubling people in the Barry neighborhood.[195] They reminded him of the tit for tat raiding that had produced so much heartache in his youth. A man named Lock had been shot in the midst of stealing a horse

---

[195] This report is contained in W. W. Watson, "The History Of Barry And Its People," from *The Barry Adage*, October 1, 1903.

from Squire Dutcher a mile east of Barry, and his cousin had been hung by a group of vigilantes a short time later. As they rode through the countryside north of Barry, John voiced his hatred of both horse thieves and vigilantes, and he recalled some of his encounters with both for the sake of his traveling companions.

When they arrived at the Washington Park square in Quincy, in front of the Adams County Courthoouse, a crowd of thousands had already gathered, and in their rowdy talk they appeared eager to engage in a confrontation. Many in the crowd had come across the river from Missouri as well as from surrounding Illinois counties. The sheriff had placed deputies throughout the crowd. After two o'clock the two debaters climbed the platform. The crowd responded by coming to quiet order. The debaters were both formally dressed, but they still presented an extreme contrast in appearance. Douglas was short, stocky, and neat. Lincoln was extraordinarily tall, thin, and gangly. An official read the rules of the debate—an hour presentation followed by an hour and a half response and a final half-hour rebuttal by the first speaker. Douglas and Lincoln had exchanged first position in each of the debates; Lincoln was first at Quincy.[196] Two partisans took the stage for brief introductions. Both debaters insisted that they would prefer no responses from the crowd. The crowd paid no attention to that request.

---

[196] The Wikipedia article on "The Lincoln-Douglas Debates of 1858" contained all of the references used in the speech summary that follows with the audience reactions. The full text is found in Lincoln, Abraham; Douglas, Stephen; Nicolay, John G., ed; Hay, John, ed. 'Sixth Joint Debate, At Quincy, Illinois, October 13, 1858' in 'The Complete Works of Abraham Lincoln, v. 4'. New York: Francis D. Tandy Company, 1894, 1858. Permission: Northern Illinois University. Persistent link to this document: *http://lincoln.lib.niu.edu/file.php?file=Nh458l.html*

People gave Lincoln a mixed response with much polite applause from a large contingent of women supporters. Much to his own disappointment, John heard Lincoln say, "There is a physical difference between the white and black races which will ever forbid the two races living together on terms of social and political equality." Most people laughed when Lincoln described the argument that Douglas had used against Lincoln's anti-slavery position as turning a "horse chestnut into a chestnut horse." In spite of his opposition to slavery, Lincoln said he would leave it in place where it already existed legally. John knew that would please the slave-holding members of his own family. He was glad to hear Lincoln say of a black man that "in the right to eat the bread, without the leave of anybody else, which his own hand earns, he is my equal," and again he was glad when Lincoln said that slavery was "a moral, social, and a political wrong," but on the whole he thought Lincoln was more comfortable with the continuation of slavery than he himself was.

The audience response to Douglas showed a strong and vocal Democratic Party presence. His position in favor of state sovereignty on the issue of slavery found warm support. John knew that the Beans and the Grays believed that local control of political matters was best, and he found himself nodding in agreement with much of what he heard at first. Ideally people should manage their own affairs and democracy should prevail in each jurisdiction. When Douglas began to ridicule the idea of equality, as Jefferson had written it in the Declaration of Independence, John found himself increasingly alienated.

"I ask you, are you in favor of conferring upon the negro the rights and privileges of citizenship?" Stephen Douglas asked the crowd.

While a chorus of "No, no," erupted from the crowd, John said aloud, "Yes," and both Tom and J. B. looked at him knowingly, but did not speak out.

Douglas asked again, "Do you desire to strike out of our State Constitution that clause which keeps slaves and free negroes out of the State, and allow the free negroes to flow in...?"

"Never," came the response of many in the crowd, while John thought of his good neighbors in New Philadelphia, and answered just as firmly, "Of course!"

"... and cover your prairies with black settlements? Do you desire to turn this beautiful State into a free negro colony...?"

"No, no," came the loud response from the audience, and John looked around in disbelief. Most of these people near him were agreeing with Douglas' nonsensical rhetoric, and some of these were staring angrily at him. J. B. told him that he'd better keep quiet for their safety.

"in order that when Missouri abolishes slavery she can send one hundred thousand emancipated slaves into Illinois, to become citizens and voters, on an equality with yourselves?"

"Never, no," John heard in reply while he stood in mute anger.

"If you desire negro citizenship, if you desire to allow them to come into the State and settle with the white man, if you desire them to vote on an equality with yourselves, and to make them eligible to office, to serve on juries, and to adjudge your rights, then support Mr. Lincoln and the Black Republican party, who are in favor of the citizenship of the negro."

"Never, never," the crowd seemed to say as with one voice.

"For one, I am opposed to negro citizenship in any and every form," Douglas said to cheers. "I believe this Government was made on the white basis."

One man yelled out, "Good."

"I believe it was made by white men for the benefit of white men and their posterity forever, and I am in favor of confining citizenship to white men, men of European birth and descent, instead of conferring it upon negroes, Indians, and other inferior races."

"Good for you," a man called out, and others joined in the chant "Douglas forever." John felt his stomach turn, as if he was about to lose the good lunch that he had so recently enjoyed.

By the time Lincoln took the stage for the final rejoinder, John's antagonism toward Judge Douglas was so strong, and his disaffection with the vocal Democratic crowd response was so deep, that Lincoln could have said almost anything in opposition to Douglas and found a warm response in John's heart. Lincoln spoke about human equality. Lincoln held that, by opposing Thomas Jefferson's "self-evident truth," Stephen Douglas was preparing the public mind to think of blacks as only property.

Hearing this, John mentally inserted the phrases "and half-breeds and mixed bloods and Indians" when Lincoln was speaking of blacks and negroes. Lincoln's key idea, as John understood it, was that slavery had to be treated as a wrong, and kept from growing.

Lincoln said, "That is the real issue. That is the issue that will continue in this country when these poor tongues of Judge Douglas and myself shall be silent. It is the eternal struggle between these two principles—right and wrong—throughout the world. They are the two principles that have stood face to face from the beginning of time, and will ever continue to struggle. The one is the common right of humanity, and the other the divine right of kings."

Though the audience response was not as loud, John could still hear many vocal supporters in favor of what he was saying. Laughter came when Lincoln said that Douglas' version of State Sovereignty was a do-nothing sovereignty that was "as thin as the homeopathic soup that was made by boiling the shadow of a pigeon that had starved to death."

When Lincoln referred to the quote that he had used in his "House divided" speech, that "this government cannot endure permanently half slave and half free," John thought again about his own family and his own people in their divisions. "How much our divisions have cost us," he said softly to himself.

Later, as John, Tom, and J. B. were returning home, John kept returning to the "house divided" idea. "I've lived where the house was divided, where the people were constantly opposed to each other, and it cannot work. I think Lincoln is right about this. Such inequality and hostility cannot exist side by side. It will come to blows, I'm sorry to say." Tom and J. B. both admitted that they were more impressed by Lincoln than they expected to be, and more disappointed in Judge Douglas and his disrespect for colored people than they expected. J. B. suggested they might muddle through the mess if the more belligerent voices would be quiet.

"Just like today?" John asked. "The hateful voices were the loudest; the respectful voices were the quietest. I fear for our future if it goes on like this."

J. B. answered, "For a while today, I thought we might have to get you out of there before the fisticuffs started. I'm glad you were quiet after that."

"Yes, I had to be, but I wasn't quiet inside, and I can't be when I think of the troubles that we face."

Young Tom spoke up, "It's a lot more confusing than I thought. I don't know how we're going to sort it all out."

June 17, 1859, John & Willie Bell's House

When the Illinois legislature elected Douglas over Lincoln to the Senate in a close vote, the question seemed to be settled for the time being in the area around New Salem. Still many old-time Democrats were uneasy about the positions their candidate had espoused, and Republicans had new enthusiasm. They went about their business, knowing that the issues were far from settled. With the people of New Philadelphia and New Salem living and working side by side, they hoped that the rest of the world would leave them alone.

John and Willie's children were growing. Tommy, Rene and Artie were all toddling around the house and farm buildings, trying to follow their parents in their daily duties. Willie was eight months along in carrying their fourth child, insisting that she didn't need a live-in midwife, but that her little sister, Alabama, or Allie, as she was called, now 16, could help her with the children and the chores until she was ready to deliver. Allie came to help early, and so did the baby. At eight months the baby girl was a scrawny four and a half pounds, and they didn't know whether they would get to keep her, but she fought her way during the next few months and into the new year. They named her "Mary Elizabeth" with many women on both sides of the family and in the neighborhood to count her as a namesake.

"She'll need all the help and prayers she can get," Willie said when they named her. Lizzie added the pounds that she needed, and she was a healthy eight months old when the census-taker came by at the end of January of 1860 to record their household.

The census-taker was a curious man, who added questions to the list that were not part of the census, like "how many books do you have in the house, and what are they?"

John could proudly respond, "Two," since he had just added a new book to the shelf alongside the bible they had carried back and forth to church for several years, which was a dictionary. "I read it about every other night," John offered. "I never knew how to spell anything until I got that Noah Webster Dictionary."

"I never knew a man who read the dictionary," said the census-taker.

"You have now," answered John. "I get quite a bit of entertainment from words, how strangely they're spelled, and how many different meanings each one has. Sometimes it's real comical."

"If you say so," the man replied as he made his notes and asked about the neighbors, where they lived and what their politics were.

"William Gray is next house north. He's a Democrat mostly, but wavering. He's a Union man. He doesn't like to hear about dividing up the country. Next, east down the road is Ezra Doane, definitely a Republican and a Lincoln man." John knew that the census-taker was not supposed to pry into such things, but neither neighbor made a secret of his feelings.[197]

"What party do you consider yourself?"

"One day I'm a Democrat and the next I'm a Republican," John answered. "That way I keep on the good side of everybody every other day."

August 4, 1860, New Salem Post Office

When John stopped at the New Salem Post Office on August 4, 1860, he found a letter from his Aunt Sarah waiting for him. He quickly tore it open and read it, learning that his Uncle Jack had died in Texas on May 1, 1860. "He was just wore out," she wrote. Nothing suspicious had happened to him, but she knew that John would want to know. She also let him know that she had learned that Will had taken his mother, Demaris, with him to settle in New Orleans. Sarah was still living at the Grand River plantation, returning there from several months with sister Nancy in Texas. Political sentiments were much disturbed in the Cherokee Nation, and she knew she might have to go to Texas if things became more unsettled, or if she learned that Nancy needed her.

Finishing his business in town, John returned to his home. His house sat prominently along the road north of New Salem, its

---

[197] The 1860 Census does record the households in approximate geographic order, with John Bell's neighbors listed. Ezra Doane was a major landowner north of New Salem, and his "staunch" political affiliation is noted in *The Portrait and Biographical Album of Pike and Calhoun Counties, Illinois*, 1891; pages 699-700. Ezra's brother, Dr. William Doane, practiced medicine in nearby Griggsville, and was married to Susannah Bennett Doane, sister to Catherine Bennett Gray.

cream-colored frame siding looking clean and healthy in the sunlight, and the many lathe-turned spools of the front porch added charm and an impression of prosperity. "I wouldn't trade places with my Uncle Jack for anything," he said to himself. "He always hungered for more than he had, and in the end he must have been disappointed."

After telling Willie about his news of his uncle and his old friend Will, John took pen and paper and wrote a letter, frequently consulting the dictionary to spell the words correctly.

> Dear Aunt Sarah,
> Thank you for your letter about Uncle Jack and the news about Will and Demaris. My uncle was good to me and tried to be fair and just to everyone but he faced much sadness in his life. I am sorry that he did not get to build all he wanted in Texas. I will always be proud of what he tried to do. My mind is now at ease about Will. He will surely prosper in New Orleans. I hear there are many freedmen there. Please take care of yourself and your family. It seems that the whole world is unsettled now. People hope the national election will settle things once and for all but I do not think so. I still think of you and every one in our family fondly every day.   Love, John Bell

He signed and sealed the letter, so that he could take it to town to mail the next day.

Tommy, Rene, and Artie took turns coming into the parlor to interrupt John at the writing desk. Each time John had made a bargain that, if left alone to finish his letter, he would tell a story. John went to find them, and of course Rene and Artie were "helping" their mother with laundry, as they called it, and Tommy was standing at the corner of the yard, looking down the path into the ravine where John had built another bathing pool.

"You musn't wander off by yourself, you know," John said to Tommy. "I'll tell you why." John collected his three older children and sat with them on the edge of the front porch.

A flock of crows rose suddenly from the buckwheat field. "What do you suppose scared those birds so that they flew off all at once. I'll tell you. The same thing that might get you lost if you wandered off by yourself. The little people. I learned about the little people, the Yunwi Tsunsdi, when I was your age.[198] Mama wanted to keep me safe."

"How big are they?" Tommy wanted to know.

"Oh, they are very small. The old ones wouldn't come up to your knees, but they look just like anyone, just much smaller, with hair that is thick and grows down to their ankles, so they can hide underneath it if they want to. They are the ones who can frighten the birds like that, so you can never see what it was that made them fly off all of a sudden. They live in little caves in the rocks near the bottoms of ravines or on hillsides."

"Should we be afraid of them?" Tommy asked.

"They are more afraid of us than we are afraid of them, because they are so small compared to us, but they can defend themselves. You can be sure of that. They weave spells with noises that can make people confused and get lost in the woods. If you see them, or find out where they live, they will gang up on you when you aren't looking and kill you. Just so you can't hurt them or destroy their homes. Many people have died mysteriously within a few days of seeing the little people,

---

[198] James Mooney records Cherokee stories of the Yunwi Tsunsdi in *Myths of the Cherokee* (New York, Dover, 1995), 333-335.

because they didn't promise not to tell. So, if you ever see one, you must promise out loud right away that you won't tell anyone about them."

"I'd like to play with them," Irene said enthusiastically.

"Oh, no, bad idea. You musn't try to play with them. They're not like your dolls. The older ones have a lot of work to do. And the children are so small you'd hurt them even if you didn't want to."

"You must listen at night, when you're going to sleep. Sometimes you can hear their tiny voices or their drums or their dancing a long way off. I was told many stories when I was your age, what the little people did, how they helped big people. We Bells have one advantage that other people don't have. We are small, so we probably have some of the little people as our ancestors. Some other time, when you want to know, I will tell you more, but now I have chores to do before supper." In this way John began to retell to his own children some of the stories he had learned when he was small.

James Perry Bell, was born near midnight on October 10, 1860. Willie's mother, Catherine, had been staying with them, and John had sent for Dr. Edwin Gray as soon as Willie had begun to feel contractions. "Uncle Doc," as he had come to be known, came immediately, and it was a good thing, because the water broke quickly and labor was over in a couple of hours, and Jimmy emerged strong, healthy, and loud.

Catherine stayed with Willie Ann for several days, helping with the children while John and Tommy, who at the age of six needed to be busy outside, worked in the field gathering the corn crop.

December 24, 1860, New Salem

The families of the Universalist Church and the New Salem neighbors of Thomas and Catherine Gray gathered on Christmas Eve for the wedding of Alabama Carolina to David Read. Read had come to the area from England at the invitation of his brother, William Read, who had immigrated a few years before, and Allie Gray had attracted his attention soon after his arrival. David had apprenticed as a blacksmith to Thomas Gray for two seasons, and saved enough to ask for Allie's hand from his mentor. How they had managed to carry on a courtship with his own daughter under his watchful eyes was something of a mystery to Thomas, but he found no fault in the responsible and diligent way David had conducted himself as an apprentice and helper. He had established a home of his own in a little house and furnished it before asking for her hand.

Reverend Biddlecome led the simple wedding service in the early afternoon, and David and Allie plighted their troth to each other. When the short ceremony ended, freezing rain pelted the church windows, and thoughts of any other festivities at their home evaporated. After hurried hugs and well-wishes, the congregation scurried to their carriages and horses to get to the warm dry confines of their homes and firesides. Lizzie's—Mary Elizabeth's—sore throat and fever showed up by the time John and Willie got their five children into the house. Throughout the night and into Christmas morning, Lizzie's condition worsened until she was having trouble breathing. John went to get Doctor Gray. Though he came promptly, the plasters, and cool baths, and soothing liquids did nothing to stem the infection. "Lung fever," the doctor called it. Lizzie died on Christmas evening.

Willie and the children shed tears and spoke in quiet questions. Willie was exhausted with caring for Lizzie through the night and Christmas day, so John washed and dressed Lizzie in her pretty yellow dress, went to New Salem to obtain a simple box coffin, placed her inside the coffin in the parlor, with an oil lamp burning all night. John sat by the fireplace, unnaturally still and bone weary. "We had her longer than we expected, I guess. We had our hopes for her though. She was sweet," were his first words to Willie in the morning. At John's request, young Tom Gray and his brother Jim dug the grave at the Gray Cemetery. Willie stayed home to protect the children from the cold. John carried the coffin on the back of the carriage, picked up Reverend Biddlecome, and met Thomas and Catherine Gray and their sons at the cemetery to lay Lizzie in her final resting place under a cluster of young cedar trees. John marked her grave with a walnut board that he had lettered himself with the name and dates, "Mary Elizabeth Bell, 1859-1860."

When John returned home he described for the children what they had done at the cemetery. "Where does Lizzie go now?" asked Tommy.

"I can't say that I know," John answered.

Willie quickly said, "She goes to be with God, and with all our family who have died."

"That may be the best way to say it. My people had a different idea—they used to say we had three souls—one that stayed with the body, one that stayed with people we cared about, and one that went to the Western horizon, to fly into heaven. When we go to where the body's been laid, we feel her near us; when we think about her, we feel her near, too; and we believe she is with the Great One who makes camp way beyond us with all good people who have died."

"Does she fall apart?" Tommy asked with concern.

"No. Somehow the three souls are still connected. I don't know how, but they're still tied together in one person. A person is just free to be in more than one place at the same time, when death comes." That seemed to satisfy Tommy, but John glanced at Willie apologetically, and she just shook her head slightly and smiled tearfully.

Two days later J. B. came to visit and express his family's condolences for their loss. They shared the details of Lizzie's illness and compared their experiences and ideas on how to respond to different symptoms. J. B. and Ama had lost a baby, Lafayette, to lung fever just before John and Willie had married.

Soon they were talking about other matters. Mark Bean had written to J. B. from Boonesborough, Arkansas, about growing conflict in the Cherokee Nation.[199] A pro-slavery faction was led by Stand Watie. An anti-slavery faction, organized as a secret society, was called the "Pins," or Keetoowah Society.[200] John Ross and other Cherokee leaders tried to remain neutral for the time being. Stand was working hard to organize a convention and develop an intertribal pro-slavery agreement with the other Civilized Tribes; mixed blood leaders of the Chickasaws, Choctaws, and Creeks had responded favorably.

"So it all starts again," John said. "More feuding, more blood, more losses for everyone."

---

[199] Mark Bean's involvement is noted in William G. McLoughlin, *After the Trail of Tears: The Cherokees' Struggle for Sovereignty, 1839-1880* (Chapel Hill NC, University of North Carolina Press, 1993),.171.

[200] A summary of the relationships among the Southern Cherokees, the Keetoowah Society, John Ross, and the larger forces for secession and abolition is found in William G. McLoughlin, ibid., 153-200.

"Sounds that way. Like an avalanche. Once it's started, it's not going to stop until everything winds up in a mess at the bottom," replied J. B. "I don't see how anybody can block it. We might as well let them all go. Start a new country. Go their separate ways."

"I know that Stand thinks they need slavery to build prosperity. He won't trust the North, not after William Seward said he wanted to clear out all the tribes south of Kansas.[201] Stand will think he can get promises to leave the tribes alone and independent if they take sides with the South."

"I don't know how he could trust a leader on either side to keep a promise like that. Not after Andrew Jackson's support of Georgia."

"Oh, I don't think he trusts anyone in particular. I think he's looking at the choices he has, and deciding which one to try. I just wish he and the rest of the slaveholders would choose to let their slaves be free. William Penn Adair has even talked about doing that. In the long run I don't think it will cost them as much as they'll pay to preserve slavery. I love and respect Stand a lot more than any of the so-called Pins, but I'm afraid he's going to sacrifice a lot more than his self-respect in the position he's taking."

Later that evening, after J. B. had gone, John and Willie returned to that discussion.

Willie asked, "Wolf, do you think people will let the South go its own way? I'm not even sure the Southerners would be altogether happy on their own. Even that politician, John Bell,

---

[201] McLoughlin, ibid., 166-167.

that Senator from Tennessee, said he wanted to stay in the Union."

"As far as I can see, the politicians of those states are mostly in favor of secession. I don't think it can happen without a fight. I wish it could, 'cause I don't think it will be easy any way it goes. I can't see slavery continuing there, with no slavery in the North. We'd continue to receive runaway slaves, all the more if we didn't have to arrest them and send them back. We'd still be fighting over territories in the West, which ones would belong to the North and which to the South. There'd be no end to issues we'd fight about since we share such a long border and so much trade."

"Would you join the fight?"

"No. Never. It would be the death of me. I do all right as long as I have you and my home. Without you and the comforts of this place, I'd be like that nine-year-old boy on the trail years ago. Camping out in the cold night after night, as a soldier, I'd get sick and wither away. Besides, whose side would I fight for? I love people on both sides. Who would I shoot?" After a long pause, John said, "I came here to get away from that kind of fight. Now the whole world is going to be fighting like that. There's no place to go to get away from it."

March 6, 1861, Ezra Doane's House

On Wednesday of the week of Abraham Lincoln's Inauguration as President, John Bell rode over to Ezra Doane's place to negotiate with him for the purchase of another team of oxen. The day was cold and windy. No sign of spring had yet emerged from the brown hills, patches of prairie, fields, and trees that lined the dirt road that led east and north of John and Willie's farm to Ezra

Doane's. John's properties were now too large to rely on the four teams he had in his stable. Doane had acquired a copy of the Quincy Whig newspaper with a full reprint of Lincoln's Inaugural Address from Monday. He was so excited to read it to John that the discussion of the purchase of oxen was postponed until he had finished reading and interpreting what was said in the speech.

"If that speech doesn't reach the hearts of the Southerners, nothing will. Lincoln's done everything he can do to reassure them that secession is not necessary," Ezra concluded.

"You think Lincoln's speech will change their minds?" John offered.

"Don't you? He's promised everything they wanted."

"Really, I don't think anyone's listening anymore."

"They ought to be. His plan will avoid war. They ought to listen to that. The Union has a lot more resources than the South has. If it comes to fighting, the South'll lose, mark my word! If we go to war, slavery will end when the war's won. If they relent and accept Lincoln's offer, they can keep their slaves for the time being, and let loose of them in an orderly way. Everybody will benefit, including the slaves. They'll need schooling and work that they can get paid for. That'll take some time."

"I wish you were right, Ezra. But the Confederacy has already started to organize. Even selected their leaders and generals. They're not going to stop now, no matter what Lincoln says. I've seen this before. People get headed down one road. They won't turn around even if they're going in the wrong direction to get where they want to go."

Ezra frowned and paced around without saying any more for a while. He was used to working things out successfully, and his house, barn, outbuildings, and a thousand acres surrounding them, showed the prosperity his planning and diligence had built during twenty-five years in the area. "It's not reasonable," said this staunch advocate of the new Republican Party and Free-Soiler cause. "They should listen."

"They should, but they won't," said John. They went ahead to fix a fair price for John's new team. Ezra's excitement extinguished, John left Ezra frowning and sober.

On the cold ride home, John asked himself why he went ahead and voiced such a pessimistic opinion. "I hope he's right. I didn't help our friendship any, even if I am right."

The following weeks verified John's dire predictions. After the attack and surrender of Fort Sumter in mid-April, Lincoln called up troops to defend the Union. John could count at least fifteen young men from the New Salem area who enlisted by the end of November. Two young men volunteered whom John had planned to hire for farm work—Henry Hillmann, a recent German immigrant, signed up in July; and, although he helped John during 1861 and the next spring and early summer, William Tedrow, the brother of young Tom Gray's girlfriend, Martha, signed up in August of 1862, and he did not return.

October 24, 1861, Willie Ann Bell's Kitchen

A pot of coffee sat steaming on the top of the new black and green ceramic-trimmed cookstove. The orange harvest moon shown as an oddly distorted orb through the window glass, and the sky was black with the brightest stars competing with the moonlight. Nursing a cup of coffee in his hands, John sat in a ladder back chair at the large square table in the center of the kitchen, while Willie put away the last of their supper cookware in the hutch against the opposite wall. The two leaves of a letter lay open on the table before John.

"There's an old fort in the northeast corner of the Cherokee Nation, used to be called Fort Wayne. I used to go there with my father, and Uncle Jack had a trading post there. Seems that's where Uncle Stand is organizing most of the Cherokee forces to side with the South. He holds the official rank of Colonel now; so does Bill Adair. Aunt Sarah says she's taking the children south, except Saladin, who's joined the soldiers under his father. Sarah's heading to the Red River with several families of the soldiers. She'll go on to Rusk County in Texas to join her sisters there, as long as there's danger of fighting in the Cherokee Nation. That's going to be awhile. She's not happy about it. Says she's worried about Stand and Saladin of course. Thinks Saladin's too young to be fighting and afraid what war will do to his character.[202] I'd be afraid of a lot more than that."

Willie moved to John's side and put her arm around his shoulder. "I worry about you, too, Wolf. You're working too hard, trying to do too much by yourself." She ran her hands down his chest and tickled his ribs, making him jump and nearly spill the coffee. "You're just skin and bones, no matter how much I feed you," she said, as he put his cup on the table and reached around her, pulling her onto his lap.

---

[202] In a letter to her husband, Stand Watie, on June 8, 1863, Sarah wrote, "Grady tells me that Charles and Saladin have killed a prisiner. Write and tell me who it was and how it was. Tell my boys to always show mercy as they expect to find God merciful to them. I do hate to hear such things it almost runs me crazy to hear such things. I find myself almost dead some times thinking about it. I am afraid that Saladin never will value human life as he ought." Edward Everett Dale and Gaston Litton, *Cherokee Cavaliers* (Norman, Oklahoma: University of Oklahoma Press, 1939, 1995), 128.

"You think I should just leave all that corn in the field and let the deer eat it this winter maybe?"

"You just go at it like you're fighting your own war, trying to make up for all the workers who've gone away to be soldiers. You don't have to wear yourself out."

"Billy and I are just doing what we can. It's easier when we can join hands with J. B. and your father. We'll do that tomorrow."

"But you work just as hard, whether you're here or there. You need to take more breaks, and get more rest, and eat. It's showin' on you, scarecrow."

John hugged her tightly. "You talk to me about work, when all you do is take care of the children, and the meals, and the garden, and the cows, and the pigs, and the laundry, while I'm out playing in the field. But I have enough strength left for one more thing tonight, if you have." He gave her a lop-sided grin.

Willie ran her fingers through his thick, black hair, and said, "You finish cleaning up, and I'll bank the fire. Then I'll join you in the bedroom, and we'll just see how much strength you have left."

July 17, 1862, John & Willie Ann Bell's House

David Read sent word that his wife and Willie's sister, Allie, was sick with a headache, fever, and diarrhea. He didn't know what to do and hoped her mother could help. She sent for Doctor Gray right away, and he diagnosed her illness as Typhoid Fever, which several New Salem townspeople had suffered through the spring, with some deaths. The whole family was worried over the next few days, knowing that Allie was also carrying their first child and already in a weakened state from severe morning sickness. They tried to persuade her to drink and eat, but she was unable to do either. Finally, on July 16, with her belly distended from a swollen liver, and otherwise totally exhausted and dehydrated, Allie died.

Catherine and Ama Bean washed and dressed Allie's shriveled body. Rev. A. M. Worden, pastor of the Universalist Church, led them and the family and neighbors back to the Gray Cemetery for her burial on the 17th.

John walked around the cabin that had served Allie and David as their first home, after its abandonment as a schoolhouse when Tom Gray had led the drive to build a new one. An old well sat in a depression below the cabin, and John saw that the walls of the well hadn't been cleaned for a long time, and when he tasted the water, he found it bitter. "This may be the cause, or not, but it's time to do something about it. It sits below the level of your outhouse, and it may be receiving some drainage from it," he said to David. When David said he would never use it again, John spent the next two days bringing wagonloads of gravel and clay to fill it in.

For the next several months John often found Willie with tears in her eyes, whether she was nursing Jimmy or preparing supper or hoeing in the garden, and she always said simply, "I miss my little sister," and nothing more.

The Quincy Whig and the Herald had both carried news of the Union victory at the Battle of Pea Ridge in March, and the Union's effective control of New Orleans after April, 1862. John scoured the papers to find any details about Cherokee involvement, and a few appeared, but without the names or casualties involved. The Cherokee fighters had served the Confederacy effectively at Pea Ridge, but the battle was lost when they ran out of ammunition and supplies. Clearly most of the Cherokee Nation was fighting on the side of the Confederacy, and Union support among them had diminished or collapsed by mid-summer. Chief John Ross had relocated to Philadelphia, Pennsylvania, where he could count on being safe. During his last months in Park Hill and Tahlequah he had tried to ally with the South and reassert his own leadership over the Cherokee military units, which had evidently moved into the experienced hands of Colonel Stand Waite. But John did not hear from his Aunt Sarah. He could only assume she was safe in Texas, with the younger children, south of the Red River.

By the end of the summer John could not be sure that the New Salem area would remain safe from conflict. Missouri bushwackers had begun to cross the Mississippi into Pike County and harass civilians near Barry, only a few miles away. The gangs were not large, but they were willing to steal horses, burn buildings, and assault civilians. These Confederate sympathizers used the Civil War as an excuse to do whatever they wanted, according to the scuttlebutt, and make people want to quit the war no matter who won. As the months of killing and pillage continued, and John heard of more deaths and destruction of property in Pike County, across Missouri and Kansas, and in the Cherokee Nation itself, with most of the fine houses and even many schools burned down, he wondered who would be able to say that the war was worth its cost. Yet no bushwacker was seen near New Salem, and the people of New Philadelphia, ready and alert as they were, remained free of incidents.

In Pike County, Illinois

May 15, 1863, Willie Ann Bell's Kitchen

"I am not sharing my name with a cow!" insisted Willie as she stomped around the kitchen preparing dinner.

"I am not the one who named her 'Annie.' That was Isaac Conkright. She was the prettiest and gentlest Holstein heifer he had, so it was only right he named her Annie. She'll make a good milk cow, I'll wager. The next prettiest is Clara, and I bought her for the wedding gift I promised to Tom and Martha."[203] John's eyes twinkled as he watched Willie press her lips together.

"You know near everybody calls me Ann. I am not having a cow with my name."

"So you want me to give her to Tom and Martha, and we keep Clara?"

"No, we'll have the prettiest one, but we'll name her Beulah, and that's that."

"She'll get confused, won't she, since she's used to her name bein' Annie since she was a calf, and now we start to call her Beulah. Maybe she'll get mad and won't be the milk cow she would'a been if we'd called her right."

"Better her than me, John Francis Bell. Besides, she's got time to get used to her new name. I never knew a cow that worried about what we called her."

---

[203] Willie Ann Bell's brother, Tom Benton Gray ("Young Tom"), and Martha Tedrow were married January 4, 1863, according to Pike County marriage records.

"Guess that's right. Gotta be a smart human bein' to worry about such things as sharing your name with a cow. What if we called her Francis? Would that suit you?"

"Yes, that would suit me just fine. We got a cow named Francis, named after her suitor. And you better warm up your hands when you go to milk her, too, cause they're inclined to be much too cold to touch any cow's tits."

"Oh, dear. Now we are getting feisty." John grabbed Willie as she walked past, and pulled her tight against him. His face suddenly turned serious. "I am happy to call her whatever you want, but I also enjoy seeing your dander up. It makes me a lot happier than doing what I 've got to do."

"What's that, Wolf?"

"I have to write a letter to Aunt Sarah, answerin' that letter I got a week ago. I don't know what to say, though I been thinkin' on it all week. She's mournin' the death of her boy, Meska,[204] by herself down in Texas; Stand's away fightin' a war I disagree with, and they all know that, and she's still good to let me know about the death of my little brother, Martin.[205] "

"You can tell her we understand. We do. We've all lost people we love; we can't make sense of it." Tears filled Willie's eyes. "We just have to hold 'em in our hearts, and shed our tears.

---

[204] Meska was the nickname of Cumiskey Waite, the third son of Stand and Sarah Waite, whose death is recorded in Edward Everett Dale and Gaston Litton, ibid., p.121.

[205] John Martin Bell died April 12, 1863, at about the age of 23 years, and was buried in Mount Tabor Cemetery, Rusk County, Texas. He had married Sarah Caroline Harnage and they had one son, John Martin Bell, born October 28, 1859, according to Wanda Elliott, *The Descendants of John Bell, Jr.* (Stilwell, OK, personal compilation, 10/15/2010), 9.

I knew it was eatin' on you. I know you carry those people with you. You haven't cut 'em off. They're still part of you. So you got to write and tell her. We'll love her, and the rest of 'em, whether we agree with 'em or not, no matter what happens. And we'll pray to God to watch over 'em, and take 'em to heaven, when the time comes, so we can finally be together like we should be."

"That helps me, Willie. I can git started on it now."

October 26, 1864, J. B. Bean's Cornfield

A half inch of wet snow covered the ground and the corn shocks standing in the half of the field that had been harvested. A team of oxen stood quietly, hitched to a wagon nearly full of ears of corn that were still wrapped in their light tan shucks. Fourteen-year-old Johnny Bean sat in the wagon seat, holding the reins. His father, J. B., older brothers, Bob and Jim, and John Bell pulled the ears off the stalks, threw them into the wagon, and took turns cutting the stalks and collecting them into shocks.

As they were working, J. B. asked John Bell, "Have you seen any of the wounded vets who came back from the front?"

"Yeah. I saw Henry Hillmann a few days ago. He's doin' much better. I thought he might have to lose that arm when he first came back from Vicksburg a year ago. It was so infected. But he's doin' well, and little by little he's usin' that arm again. He doesn't talk about his experiences in the battle though. I think he's glad how things turned out, even though it cost him a lotta pain."

"Bein' on a winnin' side helps. With Sherman on the way to Savannah, and Chattanooga firmly under Union control, I don't see how the rebels can hold out much longer."

Our Land! Our People!

Bell responded, "They'll fight to the bitter end, now that their backs are against the wall."

"Fraid so, but I heard from my cousin at Fayetteville that your Uncle Stand had something of a victory a few weeks back."

"Oh, you did? What happened?"

"He captured a federal supply train on its way to Fort Gibson. Five hundred wagons loaded with supplies. Near two thousand horses. Just with the few men under his command, he overcame the federals in charge of the train, and took the whole thing.[206] Quite a surprise!"

"I know he'll put those supplies to good use. There are a lot of starvin' people in the Cherokee Nation. But I'm surprised my Aunt Sarah didn't say anything about it. I just got word from her that my Aunt Nancy died September 14th. She'd been ill for years with consumption. Sarah didn't expect her to last this long. So Sarah's moved north to Lamar County along the Red River, to get closer to Stand. If it wouldn't put Stand in such an awkward position, she'd be glad for the war to be over."

"He's a brigadier general for the Confederacy and Chief of the Cherokee Nation. I wouldn't want to be in his shoes when the end comes."[207]

---

[206] Dale and Litton, ibid., p. 190

[207] The Confederacy promoted Stand Waite to the rank of brigadier general in the spring of 1864 (Dale and Litton, ibid., p. 148). With John Ross in Philadelphia, and the Southern wing of the Cherokee Nation in the stronger military position, Stand Waite had been elected chief in 1863 (Dale and Litton, ibid., p. 102).

"Being on the losin' side has made him who he is. He's strong. He'll land on his feet, whether he has shoes on 'em or not," John answered.

"If the union doesn't hang him for his trouble," J. B. said. "I'm sorry, John. I hope you're right. I respect the man."

"So do I. I disagree with him about a lot. The whole war's been a waste, and the nation's destitute because of it—the Cherokee Nation, I mean."

"You might as well say the whole nation, John. There's been no end of misery, everywhere."

"Yeah, it's been a great wrong. Yet I admire him. He's still Stand, and he's still standin'. So's Tom Starr. But one by one my family's shrinking. Now Nancy's gone. My younger brother John Martin died in April. Consumption took my Aunt Martha a few years back. My brother, James Foster, has it, too.[208] It'll get me sooner or later."

"Haven't seen a sign of it for a while. Maybe you licked it, John."

"No, this disease is like mosquitos. It's gone now, but it'll be back. First with a nibble, then with a swarm."

"You sound gloomy for a man who's got a growin' family of your own, another baby on the way, and one of the best harvests we've ever seen."

---

[208] Nancy Starr died September 14, 1864 in Rusk County TX; Martha Bell Duncan died October 9, 1857; John Martin Bell died April 12, 1863; James Foster Bell died October 14, 1867, but he was shot to death in the continuing intra-tribal hostility.

"You're right, J B. Today we get to live. Worryin' about tomorrow is a waste of precious time."

The wagon could hardly contain another ear, so they headed back to the crib, where they could unload it, stripping away the shucks and the snow moisture with them, as they tossed the ears into the crib. After two more loads they would be done with that field and on to the next.

April 17, 1865, New Salem Universalist Church

Following the Easter worship service, Rev. William Gamage greeted people at the front door beneath the bell tower that stood in the southwest corner of the white frame building. He thanked people for inviting him to come from Barry to lead their service in the absence of a regular minister, and he said repeatedly that he agreed that it was a terrible thing that President Lincoln was assassinated on Friday, and "We must pray for our nation in this time of testing." The news of the assassination had spread everywhere on Saturday, and the church was full of mourners, in addition to the regular Easter crowd.

Thomas Gray held the arm of his wife Catherine, to help her walk, since she was finding that arthritis affected her more every day. Their newest grandchild, Bennett Foster Bell, a month old, had been baptized that morning, and then his father, John Bell, had to carry the colicky baby in and out of the service, when he cried out of his discomfort. Willie Ann corralled the other children—Tommy, Irene, Art, and Jimmy—while they sat quietly. The Bells were among the last to leave the church building, following Willie Ann's parents.

"Thank you for your comforting words," Thomas said to Rev. Gamage. "We would be happy if you saw fit to come here regularly to lead us, Brother Gamage."

"I appreciate your saying that," Rev. Gamage replied. "The congregation does need someone, especially in times like these."

"Yes, we do. We were just beginning to breathe freely again, with the war finally coming to an end. Now the future is cloudy again, with more storms ahead, without our dear President to lead us. I wasn't for him at first, when he ran for the office, but he won my heart with his wisdom."

Rev. Gamage turned to John Bell, and asked, "Are those your feelings also, Brother Bell? You come from a different part of our country."

"Much the same, yes, sir. In my experience the wisest and bravest of my people are among the first to be killed, when their enemies finally have the chance to do it. We have lost many of our best leaders, in the same cowardly way that President Lincoln was taken. Somehow the God of All helps us through the troubles anyway. It takes a lot of trust to keep going, and keep believing, but God provides a way."

"Well said, Brother Bell. You could have given the message for us all today, in just those words," Rev. Gamage replied.

In that month John transferred the last of his land holdings south of New Salem to his father-in-law, and concentrated his attention on the land he held north and northwest of New Salem.[209] He owned more than enough land to support his family, and the prospect of having men home from the war and eager for work gave him and Willie hope. Maybe they could expand some of the fields and pastures, reduce the wooded areas, and hire workers to help with the farming. John might not have so much work to do on his own, and be able to keep sickness at bay.

March 20, 1866, John Bell's Bathing Pool

Wielding a short-handled digging fork with tines curved to form a shallow basket, shaped in his father-in-law's forge, John lifted the heated granite boulders from the coals of the fire pit and let them sink into the clear water of the bathing pool. The sizzling steam released the faint aroma of sulfur from the spring water. The sunrise sent its first beams into the woods of the ravine. He smiled at the thought of the season ahead, when he could enjoy the cool water in warm weather, instead of heating the rocks to make the temperature of the water bearable. The delicate white and pink blossoms of spring beauty covered the slopes of the ravines, and the first buds of the trees added a luminous yellow and green sheen to the tree branches.

Sinking into the warm water, he always listened to the memory of his mother's voice singing a chant of greeting for the new day. The leaf-covered earth of the ravine surrounded him with a comforting embrace, which he missed in the cold months

---

[209] The Pike County Clerk land records show several parcels changing hands among neighbors with John Bell releasing southern township ownership from 1857 to 1865.

that froze the pool. In those cold winter mornings he settled for a basin of hot water from the water reservoir of the kitchen range, but that had a benefit, too, when Willie Ann stood beside him and they bathed together. With the children to care for, they could not usually come to the pool together, leaving the children alone in the house.

John gave thanks for the baby that Willie was carrying, due in a month. He prayed for strength for little Foster, who did not thrive, no matter what they tried to feed him—goat milk, apple juice, various concoctions of cereal and herbs and sweeteners to encourage his appetite. Time in the bathing pool gave him moments to consider the needs of people nearby and many miles away, before the duties of the day drew his full attention.

Finally he had received a letter from Aunt Sarah Waite, now with her husband at a farm at Webbers Falls in the Cherokee Nation, although they had begun to rebuild a home at their old place on the Grand River near where Uncle James Madison Bell had returned to live. Uncle Stand had been the last general to surrender, during the past summer, and the federal authorities had imposed no punishments. They had a chance to begin again. That gave John a cause for gratitude every time he thought of it, but even more gratitude that his aunt could report that several of their freed slaves continued to work for them, receiving a wage for their efforts. "Why couldn't they do that before?" he asked aloud, when he read it in the letter.

South of the boundary of John's farm, surveyors were marking a route for the Hannibal and Naples Railroad that might be constructed on the south side of New Salem and east to west through central Pike County. John's friends at New Philadelphia were disappointed that the planners were bypassing their village. The railroad would be an economic boon to the communities along it, or so the community leaders said, including Ezra Doane and Thomas Gray.

John's cultivated acreage expanded by twenty acres during the previous year, as they cleared forest and plowed fresh earth. Eddie Coss now lived with them. He was a seventeen-year-old orphan who was eager to learn to farm, ready to try anything, and a good worker. The veterans, John Gray and Henry Hillmann, came to work the fields whenever John needed them. For crew work the old neighbors—the Beans, Grays, Conkrights, and Fishers—could always depend on John, and John on them.

John felt a fullness of contentment that exceeded anything he had felt before.

September 27, 1866, Gray Cemetery

Willie Ann stood at the highest point of the low ridge that rose above the surrounding farm fields and woodlots, cradling in her arms the bundled baby girl, born three months earlier, whom they had named Nancy Alabama Bell. The rest of the Bell children gathered around the legs of their grandparents, Thomas and Catherine Gray, who stood beside her. From the carriage John carried a small wooden coffin, about two feet long and a foot wide and deep, to the side of the open grave where young Tom Gray stood with ropes in his hand for the lowering of the coffin.

Reverend Gambage was dressed in a formal black frock coat, his Sunday best, facing the family and friends, his back to the south where, a few feet behind him, a grave was marked, "Lizzie, Dau of T. B. and M. A. Gray, Died Aug 10, 1865, Aged 11 Days." Each of those present on that ridge top glanced over to that grave at some point during that afternoon, and remembered the death of the young couple's firstborn daughter, so soon after birth.

"Now your Lizzie and our Liz will have another companion nearby," said John Bell to Tom quietly.

"Eventually we'll all rest here, won't we?" answered Tom.

"So true," John responded.

Reverend Gambage quoted the passage that read "Suffer the little children to come unto me, and forbid them not, for to such belongs the kingdom of heaven." He paused, looked around at their faces one by one, then continued, "It doesn't say, 'Let the little children suffer.' It's just a word that means 'allow.' God allows great suffering, and suffering even for those who never did a thing wrong to deserve suffering. God allows it. That's a hard thing to accept. We do not want to accept it. Are we to think that God wants to allow the suffering of innocents little ones? No, but still we do not know why in any case.

"The scripture promises us that the kingdom of heaven belongs to them, even before anyone else, before anyone who is older and has had more chances to do right or do wrong, to enjoy life or not to have much enjoyment in life. The kingdom of heaven belongs to the little ones first, with all of its glories and wonders, beauties and comforts, delicacies and delights. I think we should use our imaginations to peek around the corner of our sad thoughts and see the little ones with God and with Jesus, with their blessed grandparents, aunts and uncles and cousins, a whole host of relatives and neighbors glad to hold them and comfort them.

"We love our children. We must know that God does, too, and has a multitude of arms and laps to hold them. Perhaps they will even grow up there, become the people we had hoped to see grown up. Perhaps they will enter into another life on earth and have a chance to live it. I do not know. But I believe that God does not waste the effort you have poured into this baby's life in his first hard, suffering year and a half, when he could barely keep down the little nursing milk that you got him to swallow. And when he suddenly became even sicker, and the scarlet fever took him, I think he had healers waiting for him, and arms to reach out to him, so he would be lifted up to heaven to live an eternity of joy. A year of suffering, an eternity of joy."

Gambage paused again and looked around at them. "I think the toughest bargainer among us would accept that deal," he said quietly. Then Reverend Gambage led them in prayers for the baby and for themselves, John and Tom lowered the little casket into the hole that they had dug, and each of them took a handful of soil and let it pour onto the casket lid. Even the children did.

A few weeks later John and Willie Ann would bring a stone marker and place it on the grave. It read, "Foster, Infant son of J. and A., died Sept 25, 1866, 1 ½ years."

February 3, 1867, John Bell's Stables

John had spent a cold night in the stables as one of his mares, the one he had named Wadulisi[210] because of her color, was foaling, and she seemed to be having a hard time of it. Tommy, nearly twelve years old, had stayed with him and slept most of the night in the hay, covered with blankets, next to her pen. When the

---

[210] Wadulisi is the Cherokee word for honey.

In Pike County, Illinois

birthing finally came, Tommy was awake and watchful, but he remained as quiet as he could be outside the pen, as his father had warned him. His eyes were wide. The colt's hair was a dark reddish-brown with the dampness of birth. When the little colt struggled to stand so quickly, he asked his father if he couldn't help, but John told him it was best that the colt and the mare took care of it themselves.

As they watched the colt finding his legs, Tommy asked, "Is this how people are born? Do we come out of our mamas like that, with all the blood and water?"

"Yes, that's how birth happens for people, too. It's harder for women than for mares. At least women have words to tell about the pain of birth. When our baby comes this summer, you can stay with your Mama and me, and you'll learn why people call birth "labor." It is very hard work. It was harder when you were born, because you were the first baby your Mama had. You had to open the way for your brothers and sisters."

Tommy frowned. "I don't remember that."

"No, nobody remembers bein' born. That's probably a good thing. It's probably hard for the baby as well as the mama. We remember the good things that come to us later."

At daybreak Tommy ran into the house to wake Irene, Art, and Jimmy, so that they could come out, one at a time, to see the new colt.

John coughed as usual to clear his lungs, but for the first time in years, he saw flecks of blood in the phlegm that he coughed into his handkerchief. He looked at those specks for several moments before he folded his handkerchief and put it in his pocket.

Our Land! Our People!

When John and Tommy were alone again in the stables, John asked his son what he wanted to name his colt.

"My colt? Daddy? You mean he'll be mine?" Tommy asked.

"Yes, it's time you had a horse of your own to care for and to train. You should get to name him. No hurry. You want a good name that'll last a long time. He'll be a riding horse, not a work horse, so you'll teach him to take the saddle."

"Oh! Yeah! That'll be fine! I can do that. You will help me, won't you, Daddy?"

"Of course. I will help, but you will be the master of this horse."

"That's wonderful! This is the best day of my life!"

"So what will you name him?"

"I don't know. I'll have to think about that."

"You think about it. Come up with a good name."

After a few minutes of quiet, Tommy spoke up, "You remember, Daddy, when you were teaching me to use a blowgun, and when you were teaching me to make the bow and arrows, and to use 'em, you told me stories of the lucky hunter, Kanati?"[211]

"Of course, I remember."

---

[211] A collection of Kanati stories is found in James Mooney, *Myths of the Cherokee* (New York: Dover Publications, 1995), 242-248.

"Could I name the colt Kanati? He will take me hunting and I will be lucky."

"Kanati is a good name. It will remind you of our people, and you will have your own stories to tell of your great hunts."

July 9, 1867, John & Willie Bell's Bedroom

Willie Ann's mother, Catherine, was not able to help with the preparations for the delivery. John and Willie Ann decided that they could proceed without any outside help, if the doctor could come when called. "Doc" Gray expressed reservations about having a boy in the birthing room, but when John made it clear that Willie Ann and he wanted Tommy and Irene to be there, he agreed. "I've had young girls helping; I guess boys should know what it's about, too."

Willie Ann's water broke as she was preparing breakfast. John sent their farmhand, Eddie Coss, to get Uncle Doc. Since this would be their eighth child, and the labors had been shorter almost every time, John began to prepare the hot water and cloths immediately. Willie couldn't sit still or lie in bed, so she had Tommy help her walk around until the labor pain became intense. Then he helped to fan her, since the morning quickly became sultry hot. He ran to the ice house to get ice for the cloths that Irene used to wipe her Mama's forehead and arms. With his father, Tommy took turns going back and forth to Art and Jimmy, who were also supposed to be watching Allie.

An hour and a half passed without any sign of Eddie and Uncle Doc, and Willie declared, "Doc or not, this baby's comin'." With a few minutes of pushing, the baby's head crowned fully and pushed through. John received the little girl into clean white cloths, gently pressed on her chest, and she began to breathe and cry a soft clear sound. He cut the umbilical cord and tied off the belly, and Irene and Tommy gently wiped the baby, while John assisted with the afterbirth.

"I'd like to name her "Sarah," since she's come into the world ready and willing, no matter how hard it will be," John said.

"I've always liked the name "Melissa," since I first heard it. It sounds so sweet. That will be her middle name. Sarah Melissa," Willie Ann said.

When Uncle Doc arrived he found "Lissa" loosely wrapped and nursing at her mother's breast. He checked mother and baby and pronounced them both fit and healthy. "This is how I like to deliver babies," he said. "Nothing to it. No problems at all." He did stay for a while to make sure things stayed that way.

Tommy disappeared from the bedroom while the doctor was there, and John went in search. He found him in the barn with the colt and tears in his eyes. "It was scary, Daddy," he said.

John had tears of his own when he looked straight into Tommy's eyes. "Yes, it's scary. Your fear for your Mama or your wife doesn't go away. We should face it with them, though, since we have a part in makin' the babies. And the babies are the future of our people. I've never told you, Tommy, but my Mama died when she was givin' birth to my little sister. They both died. So I was full of fear when you were born, afraid I'd lose your Mama and you, too. The Great Spirit has been good to us, to have you and your little brothers and sisters, so we will be happy, and grateful, and brave, just as you saw your Mama be brave." They held each other for a moment, then wiped away their tears and returned to the house.

April 25, 1868, New Salem

John and Willie Ann Bell arrived in their carriage at New Salem mid-morning on April 25, a bright spring day with trees budding out in redbud pinks and locust whites and the chartreuse luster of new oak and hickory leaves. They crossed the new railroad tracks, and wondered how the big engines would change the quiet and fresh air of the town when the workers finally finished laying the tracks and a regular railroad schedule began. They made their first stop at the post office. John came out waving a letter and proceeded to stand beside Willie, still seated in the carriage, opened the letter and read it aloud.

> Dear John and Ann,
> I have a chance to send a letter to Fort Smith so that it can be mailed there, you know there is no office here at Webbers Falls. I think often of you and wish you was not so far from us but know it has been a great benefit to you. You have had your share of sadness in the loss of two little ones. You also watch your children grow and prosper in peace which is far from what we have seen and a great blessing. I write with new sadness, after Saladin gave us a new house here which he built for himself but insisted we use it through this last winter, his dear friend cousin Charles Webber died. Saladin was alredy feeling poorly but went downhill fast and died also. We miss him terribly and think how noble and generous he was and what we had counted on for his future. Now we pray for God to grant him the life he misses here in the joys of heaven. Now we have just our Watica, Jackie and Ninny. They have had me as their teacher just as you did. They are good students but have a poor teacher. Soon all three will go away to bording school and I am already lonely for

them but they cannot succeed here with what I have to give. Stand is tired and sorrowful but still works to make a life for our little family. He is a good and wise husband and father, and I know you to be one also, so I pray for you and ask your prayers for us and send my affection. Your aunt Sarah Watie.

John finished with his head bowed and folded the letter slowly.

"It saddens me—all the troubles they've had, so many losses. I would not trade our lives here with anyone. We'll see what we can learn from your Uncle Doc Gray." John took the reins and urged the horses away from the hitching posts, as they pulled the carriage down the street toward the doctor's house. Doctor Gray's house stood two blocks away, a two-story house with light brown-painted wooden clapboards, fronted by a full porch and neat hand-turned spindles for bannisters, and decorations at the top corners of the upright posts painted in hues of red, yellow and green. A sign at the door read, "Come In—the Doctor is In."

A bell attached to the inside top of the front door jingled as they opened the door and entered the house. From the front hall, a parlor to the right served as a waiting room with comfortable armchairs; a stairway led to private rooms upstairs; and an open doorway led straight ahead into a wide hall lined with cabinets filled with bottles, boxes and apothecary equipment. No one was waiting in the parlor. Doctor Edwin Gray came out of the wide door to a room beyond the parlor, where an examining table sat in the middle of the room. His first words were, "I'm glad to see you, John, Ann. I've been expecting you since we spoke on the street a few days ago."

Uncle Doc was going to take John into the examining room by himself, but John said, "There's nothin' you want to look

In Pike County, Illinois

at that Willie Ann hasn't seen, and nothin' I want to keep from her, so I'd just as soon she came in, too."

Doc said, "Sure, she can come in." He had John remove his shirt and undershirt, and his boots and pants. He told John to step on the scales, and extended the rod to measure his height, announcing that John weighed 111 pounds and stood 54 inches tall. "You've lost twenty-five pounds since I had you here three years ago. You don't have a bit of fat on you anywhere."

"I feed him, but he still loses," Willie Ann said.

Doc just nodded, "That's part of the sickness. He'll keep losing as long as it eats away at him."

John sat on the examining table in his undershorts, while Doc listened to his chest and his back with his stethoscope for several minutes, sometimes thumping and pounding lightly with his hand. He looked carefully over John's skin and felt his neck, underarms, and groin with his hands, and along his extremities and joints, noting places where he found swellings and asking how sore they felt.

John answered consistently, "Not very. They don't bother me much."

"One thing I can say for you, John. You're about the cleanest man I know. The arthritis is not going to kill you, but the consumption is. Not a damned thing I can do for it, either, except the few things you already know that bring a little comfort."

"I know, Doc. This is one disease that the plants haven't yet revealed their cure for."

Doc answered, "I don't know what you mean."

"It's an old story from my people," John answered. "According to the story, the animals brought all the diseases into the world to keep people from spreadin' so fast that there wasn't any safe place for animals any more. But the plants were kinder to people, and provided a medicine for every disease, so people could survive. We just don't know what their cure is for consumption, do we?"[212]

"Right. That's a pretty good story. It's true about plants providing most of our arsenal for combatting disease. We use other chemicals and minerals, too, but plants give us our most helpful medicines. Those old Cherokee doctors must have learned about a good many beneficial plants. I wish they had something to cure consumption. We'll learn eventually, but we don't know now."

"What can you tell me about how long I have?"

"Not much. You've been fortunate to have many years without a lot of trouble, but once you get to this stage you can't expect many more. Any other sickness that affects your breathing can come along and bring a crisis, so stay away from colds or grippe if you can, and stay away from dusts and mold, too. I'd advise you both to get ready because the end can come at any time. Ann, since you've been free of any symptoms so far, I hope you can stay free of it, but be careful with the phlegm or mucous that he coughs up. Keep it away from the children, too. It probably carries the disease, so you want to burn it or clean anything with alcohol or bleach that it touches. Sometimes people are lucky enough not to catch it, even when they are

---

[212] James Mooney, *The Myths of the Cherokee*, pp.250-252.

exposed as much as you have been. When the disease is in its active stage, as it is now, it seems to be much harder to avoid."

"What about our marital relations?" Willie Ann asked.

"I can't tell you to avoid them, can I? It's probably the mouth kissing and saliva that will bring the most risk, not anything else that you do. You've had eight children without becoming sick, so you've done pretty well. When his symptoms are more obvious, as they are now, the danger of catching it is probably greater, too."

When they left Doctor Gray a little later, John said to Willie Ann that he thought he would take the offer from Bill Laird to sell him the 84 acres northeast of New Salem. "He's offered a good price, since people expect the railroad to bring more business and new people to New Salem.[213] I can't continue to farm as much land as I have. You like Isaac Cooper's place up at the edge of Fairmount Township. It's smaller. We can be comfortable there, away from the noise and smoke of the steam engines. Tommy can help me farm it, and take it over eventually, whether I'm here or not. It's cheap, and we'll have quite a bit of money to save for the family after I'm gone."

"I don't want to think about it," Willie said.

"Then I'll think about it and plan for it. We both will enjoy what we've got as long as we can."

---

[213] Pike County land records show the sale of most of John and Willie Ann Bell's holdings near New Salem in April and August of 1868, and their purchase of land from Isaac Cooper at the boundary of New Salem and Fairmount Townships in September.

August 25, 1869, Perry Springs

Summer heat had been near to unbearable from a week before John's birthday in July throughout the month of August. John himself had done more watching than working during the hot weather, with his wracking cough, hard breathing, and sleepless nights, the causes of persistent weariness. Tommy and Eddie Coss did most of the chores and brought in the wheat, oat and hay crop with the help of some of their neighbors. John kept working, but he had to take frequent long breaks to recover.

John found relief in the spring house that he and Tommy had constructed in the previous fall, shortly after moving to the Fairmount Township farm. The main farm house itself was spacious and similar in layout to the James Starr house that he had remembered from his childhood and youth. The two big rooms upstairs served as boys' bedroom and girls' bedroom. The kitchen at the back of the house was connected to the summer kitchen separated from the main house by a roofed walkway. Down the hill from the summer kitchen was an all-weather spring. There they set in place a rock foundation with the spring flowing from a sink, available for dipping containers to carry water to the house, down an open chute into a bathing pool, and out the opposite end into a brook that led into Bay Creek as it meandered south. They built a fireplace on one side to warm the room through the winter cold, and to heat rocks for the pool, to provide a steamy and comfortable bath. They built the spring house with clay-chinked logs and a low roof, like John had often seen in Coosawattee Town. In the summer the coolness of the water provided respite from the heat of the day.

Willie Ann's mother, Catherine Bennett Gray, had died on May 9, and they had buried her in the family cemetery. Her mother's months of weakness and frustration before her death had prepared Willie for the inevitable. Her children's needs, John's illness, and her pregnancy had left her little time to mourn. Two weeks before her due date she moved into Uncle Doc's home, still nursing Lissa, but leaving the rest of the youngsters in Irene's care.

John encouraged Willie to spend the last days of pregnancy at Uncle Doc's. He didn't want her to take any chances with this delivery, so soon after her mother's death, when their own home was now farther away from their family doctor at New Salem. To add to John's anxiety, at the end of May he received a short sorrowful letter from his Aunt Sarah, telling of the death of her and Stand's son, Watica. Watica had died suddenly of pneumonia in April, while he was attending boarding school at the Cane Hill Academy in Arkansas.[214] Only their daughters, Ninnie and Jackie, were left to them.

The deaths of Catherine Gray and Watica and John's own frailty brought memories of his own mother vividly to his mind. He wanted Willie to have everything she needed for this baby's delivery, and Uncle Doc Gray was readily agreeable to having her stay with him. John waited a few days after getting Willie situated at Uncle Doc's, then he moved into a room at the new hotel, next to the Unitarian Church on Main Street, just two days before the baby came. They named the baby Catherine Star Bell, 'Kate' for nickname.

While they were staying in New Salem they heard people talking about their experiences at the health resort that B. A. Watson had built at Perry Springs.[215] People were coming from

---

[214] Reports of Watica's death are included in *Cherokee Cavaliers*, pp. 265 and 284.

[215] B. A Watson built the Perry Springs Hotel in 1865. He planned it to provide the finest accommodations in the region and advertised it widely.

all over the region to enjoy the healing effects of the springs—iron, sulfur, and magnesia springs—and the commodious facilities of the hotel.

"Wolf, let's take the babies and Irene to help, and spend a few days. It could do us all some good," Willie Ann suggested.

"It's probably no healthier than our own spring. It comes out of the same earth, and carries the same minerals."

"Don't you think it's worth a try?"

"We already enjoy the Siloam Springs that Rev. Reuben McCoy found. The advantage at Siloam is—they're closer and we have them to ourselves most of the time."

"The advantage at Perry Springs is—fine lodging and good food, according to the reports, and lots of help, so that people can rest and heal. We can treat ourselves to some luxury. What do you think?"

"I think, if you want to go that much, we should go."

So they made plans to go the fifteen miles to Perry Springs toward the end of August. Hitching their matched pair of bay horses to their carriage, John and Willie loaded their baggage with Irene, baby Kate, Lissa, and Allie, and headed for B. A. Watson's Health Resort.

The four-story hotel towered above the trees and they saw it three miles before they reached it. An American flag flew above a central square tower where a few people were standing on an observation platform from which they could see and be seen for miles. As they came nearer, John and Willie saw that the hotel was one of several buildings, a stable and carriage house, kitchen and laundry, and several scattered, small, open pavilions located above springs, that sat in a well-trimmed glen along a brook and several smooth lanes and pathways. Fronting the hotel a two-decker porch ran the entire width, with seven large windows spaced evenly along the width on each of the four floors, including the mansard roof dormer windows on top. With equal spacing fifteen windows stretched back the length of the building, so it was more massive than any building they had ever seen, including the new court houses and hotel buildings they had visited in Quincy and Pittsfield. Trees and shrubbery gave the whole landscaped area the look and feel of a pleasant public park.[216]

A doorman met them at the carriage when they pulled up in front of the main entrance, and soon he had the assistance of a valet, taking charge of the unloading of their baggage, and a stableman, who led the horses and carriage toward the carriage house. They entered the lobby and registered at a main desk at the center of the room, and a bellboy and the valet led the way up the central staircase, carrying their luggage, toward their second floor rooms. They walked down a hallway and the valet opened the door to a small sitting room with two transom-windowed doors leading to two bedrooms—one a spacious large-windowed nursery with a junior bed, a cradle, and a cot for Irene, and the second bedroom of equal size with a large bed and two overstuffed chairs sitting next to its large open window. The valet showed them the white linen garments used for the bathing springs and described the rules and schedules for immersions, open and private, and he also invited them to the meals served family-style at 8, 12 and 6 each day in the dining

---

[216] Photographs and descriptions of the facilities of the Perry Springs Health Resort are found at the Quincy, Illinois, Public Library.

room. They were invited to consult with the staff physician about the benefits and uses of the waters available, particularly suited to their personal needs.

"If nothing else, we'll learn what it means to be coddled, and you do deserve that," John said, when the valet finally left them alone.

"Maybe a miracle cure for you, Wolf?" Willie offered.

"I have had my share of miracles through the years. Of all of them, you yourself are the greatest."

They spent the next three days eating the ample, well-prepared meals, drinking water from and soaking in the several springs, enjoying the shade and the occasional breezes in the park while they talked and read to each other. Then they decided that they were missing their home, their own bed, their children, and their own work.

"If I kept living like this, I think I'd just get weaker and weaker. If I get home and back to work, doing as much as I can, I'll be stronger, and live longer," John said.

"You're right. We may never do this again, but I'll never forget this time we've had together. Thank you for it," Willie answered.

They paid their bill, summoned their carriage, had two bellboys' help loading their luggage, and made their way home.

May 15, 1870, John Bell's Spring House

In the cool mists of first light, Willie Ann led John down to the spring house, trampling on the spring beauty, mayapples, and trillium that lined the path. The banked fire sprang to life as John placed tinder upon the coals, and added light and heat with ever larger pieces of wood. While the rocks were heating, they took off their clothes, and reclined on the fur-lined ledge, and added their own heat to the room with tender and eager embraces, stroking one another, slipping into each other, and breathing heavily. Afterward John dropped the heated rocks into the pool, filling the air with clouds of steam, and they stepped down into the pool for their morning bath.

"We welcome the day with love, bathing, and prayer, like my parents did years ago," John said. "I count myself blessed since we have had years of peace together, my love, but they have gone much too quickly. I have lived as long as my father lived, and we have children as a comfort for the years to come."

"I am blessed as well as you, my Wolf. I dream of growing old with you, as my parents got to do."

"You know my end will come at any time."

Willie Ann quietly shushed him and put one forefinger to his lips.

"You must be ready, Willie. I don't need my mother's turtle bones to tell the future. I'm just glad you've shown no sign of getting sick with the same sickness. God must'a given you the "resistance" Uncle Doc said you might have."

"I'm glad for that, 'cause I never could resist you, and we'll have another baby on the way if we keep doin' this."

"Maybe a George or a Georgia, or a Carl or a Caroline? We have our Alabama. Maybe we could keep adding the names of the states our people came from. You have some people from

Virginia. That's a girl's name for sure. A boy would never forgive us if we named him for the state of Virginia. Maybe we could name a child for the love chapter in Corinthians."

"I thought you didn't believe in naming children before they'd come."

"Oh, I'm just thinking out loud. We couldn't really name 'em ahead of time. We always thought about their names, though, even if we didn't choose 'em, didn't we?"

"You jus' never admitted it before."

October 1, 1870, John & Willie Bell's House

When Willie entered their parlor, John was seated on a ladder-back chair in front of the open door of the pot-bellied stove, feeding torn-out sheets of paper into the fire.

"What're you doin', Wolf?"

"Cleaning up is all," John answered.

"But that's your old journal. Why're you burnin' it?"

"Willie, when I'm gone, there's nobody can read it anyway. I can't read a lot of it myself any more. I don't remember all of the signs I wrote with or what they mean. It's just as well most of this is forgotten."

"I'm not so sure about that. Those are your memories, even if we can't read 'em. You know you've got people down south who could make sense of those hen scratchins."

"They're moving on. That's a good thing. They don't need to remember the old days. They have a fresh start."

"Wolf, I don't know. From what you've told me, you went through some hard times, but you learned a lot from 'em. Our memories make us who we are. I don't want our children and grandchildren to forget who you are."

"They'll remember what they need to. And it's our hopes that make us, more than our memories. They don't need all this old stuff."

"If you say so."

"You just let 'em know that John Bell was raised among the Cherokees, and they were good people, people like anybody else, people who belonged to this land...who deserved...more than they got...respect. Tell them I love them, and I always will love them. That'll be enough. If they know that, they'll remember enough."

Willie looked down at John and the leather-bound journal in his lap with already half of its pages torn out and burned. She put her hand on his shoulder, then leaned over and put her arms around him. "I can tell them that. I can tell 'em, nobody earned their respect more than John Bell, and the people who made him who he is, whoever they were."

John returned Willie's hug, then turned again to the tearing of pages from the bindings, feeding them into the fire. "Besides, if I don't do this, somebody else will have to, soon enough."

October 10, 1870, John & Willie Bell's Farm

On October 9 John had stopped work and walked over to lean on the corn wagon in the middle of the cornfield, while Tom, J. A. and Jimmy continued to pull the ripe ears out of the husks and off the cornstalks and toss them into the wagon. John went into a spasm of coughing and soon fell to his hands and knees, choking and coughing up large clots of blood. He was too weak to stand, and gasping for breath. With Tom grabbing his father by the armpits, and J. A. taking his legs, they carried him to the house, and Willie put him to bed. She tried to get him to take some of the syrup that soothed his throat, but he refused it. She sent Tom to fetch Doc.

Doc Gray listened to his lungs and said he didn't know how John had managed as long as he had; he had so little lung capacity left. "Only will power has let him last this long. Just let him rest. I can't do anything for him."

Willie was in her fifth month of pregnancy. When her uncle said he felt sorry for her in her condition, she responded forcefully, "You don't need to feel sorry for me. I've had everything I wanted and more. I don't ask for anything more than a healthy baby. We knew what we had in store. We've known for a long time."

Through the night John kept his eyes closed unless Willie or one of the children made noise as they came and went. Then he opened his eyes and gave a half-smile as he worked to breathe. Toward morning he whispered to Willie, "Part of me stays here...always...watch over you."

"I know, Wolf," she answered. "I remember."

Soon after sunrise on the morning of the tenth, he stopped breathing. Willie and Tom gave him his last morning bath. J. A. went to get the undertaker in New Salem, who brought a coffin, and helped to dress John's body and lift it into the coffin. Family members and neighbors came in a steady procession throughout the day, offering the family their condolences, bringing food, and some stayed to watch over the body during the night.

No pastor was serving the Universalist Church at the time. When the undertaker brought the casket to the Gray Cemetery, he invited whoever wanted to speak to say a few words. Isaac Conkright, whose father had helped to start the church, was himself 63 years old at that time. He said that John was a good worker and steady neighbor, whose quiet and peace-loving ways would be missed. David Preble, another church founder, said that John had some unusual ideas, but perhaps in spite of them, maybe because of them, he had learned a great deal from him about what it meant to believe that God would eventually bring everyone to their heavenly home. Daniel Fisher, also one of the church founders, echoed Preble's words, "No one had a more open mind, or open heart, or knew more about loving their enemies, than John Bell." J. B. Bean said, "I don't usually talk in public...but I owe this to John. He was my friend, from the first day he came. I knew I could count on him. He opened my eyes...that the world is bigger than I thought, and all the people in it are brothers and sisters."

Willie Ann's father, Thomas Gray, said, "John was all a father could want in a son-in-law, a man who loved wholeheartedly and provided well for his family." Her brother Thomas added, "He is a brother I will miss as much as the brothers born to me. I learned from him that we belong to the land, more than the land belongs to us, and we must take care of it, as well as it takes care of us."

Solomon McWhorter thanked John for his encouragement to fulfill his father's dreams of reuniting his family at New Philadelphia, and his help in other ways that he could mention.
Henry Hillmann thanked John for giving him a job before

the war, when he was just a newcomer to the area, and especially after the war, when he was still struggling with his injuries and no one else thought he would be able to work again. Standing with Henry was his new wife, Margaret, her grandfather, and her father, both named William Pine. Ninety-one-year old William, Senior, had brought his family to Pike County as Quakers in 1838, making a War of 1812 veteran's claim, and his son had recently plotted a town named Pineville, a short distance southwest of John Bell's home in Fairmount Township. They had gotten to know John through Henry, but also through their tree nursery and the sale of fruit trees to John for his properties. William, Senior, spoke in a shaky, but insistent voice, "John knew the ways of the Indian, and they were in his heart, the ways of peace. I was a Quaker, yet I felt I had to go to war for my country, and I served with an Indian guide, back in the War of 1812...." William, Junior, cautiously interrupted his father, reminding him that he had told his story many times before, and the people there did know it, but they also knew that he was right about John. They went around the circle of friends and neighbors, and no one had a bad word to say, nor were there any words left unsaid.

1871-1901, Fairmount & New Salem Townships

Willie Ann gave birth to George Corinth Bell on December 18, 1870. At the end of the next September, she received a letter from Sarah Caroline Watie that Stand had died on September 9, at what she called the Old Place on the Grand River. Willie asked Irene to write back for her and let her know of John's death. "Thank her for her letters. They meant a lot to John all of his life. Tell her I will pray for her and need her prayers for us as well."

Willie Ann continued to care for her family and face trials through the next years. Thomas married Berthada Jane Allen on

September 11, 1873. They had six children—three boys and three girls. On September 23, 1875, Irene married Oscar Manker; they had one daughter. The Lewis Manker family had lived southeast of the Bell properties near New Salem, Lewis and John had worked together, and the children had gone to school together. John A. Bell married Mary Johnston, and they had two sons and a daughter. While Allie was preparing to be married, she became ill with typhoid fever; she died and was buried at the Gray Cemetery on her planned wedding day, February 13, 1882, next to her father. James Bell married Amelia Manker, Oscar's sister, on September 12, 1883, and they had six children—four sons and two daughters. Sarah Melissa married Alfred Elliott Hillmann, the son of Henry, the Civil War veteran and farmer, on January 13, 1889, and they had two sons and two daughters. On April 2, 1893, Kate Bell married Joseph Manker, brother to Oscar and Amelia, but they had no children. George Bell married Alice Riley on November 24, 1895, and they had three daughters and one son.

Willie Ann lived with her children for a few years at the Fairmount Township farm. She sold it to her cousin, George Bennett, in November of 1876, and moved back to the old neighborhood, south of New Salem and near the Gray Cemetery, after the death of her father on September 1, 1876, and after the division of the farm property between her brother, Thomas Benton Gray, and herself. When her children were all grown and married, she moved into the home with J. A. and Mary to help with their children. Lissa died after a strange accident on July 7, 1899. She swallowed pins that she was holding in her mouth while sewing. She left Alfred Hillmann with four young children, and Willie Ann moved into their home in New Salem, while Alfred continued his work as a postman.

Our Land! Our People!

When Willie Ann and her family visited the cemetery, and when the children shared a memory of their father, Willie Ann would sometimes remind them that their father had grown up among the Cherokees, in a family with twenty-one other children, and he wanted them to remember him, as he loved them and said he always would love them.

In Pike County, Illinois

Willie Ann Bell with grandchildren Bede and Glen Hillmann, 1901

May 11-26, 1901, Alfred Hillmann's House, New Salem

On Wednesday afternoon, Alfred Hillmann got a copy of the Pittsfield paper and read the news story to the family from *The Pike County Democrat*, which had been published that morning, May 15, carrying the item under the heading "Come to Life Again:"

> A dispatch from New Salem under date of May 14 tells the following story of the supposed death and coming to life of a prominent lady of that village: This community has been startled by the apparent death of a well known woman and the return to life of the supposed corpse. Mrs. Anna Bell, daughter of the late Thomas Gray, a former treasurer of Pike County, and one of the most prominent women in this community has been very ill for some time and all hopes had been given up for her recovery. Mrs. Bell, a pious Christian woman, had herself given up all hope, and was calmly awaiting the end. She bade her family and friends good-bye while she still had strength to talk. Sunday she passed into a trance, which was pronounced death. The doctors were summoned, and after a close examination they said she was dead. There was no pulse and no perceptible beat of the heart. Neither did she breathe. The usual tests were made, the tests that are generally regarded as infallible, and all indicated death. A lighted candle held before her mouth and nostrils did not flicker in the least. The lighted candle was held back of her hand, and there was no dim light between the fingers. There was no doubt that she was dead, and while the family mourned, preparations were made for the funeral. The undertaker was summoned to prepare the body for burial, and it was decided that the funeral should be held Tuesday. The body grew cold while the preparations for the funeral went on, but after

In Pike County, Illinois

several hours it became warm again, and then the supposed corpse gave signs of returning life. The undertaker was sent home and the physicians were again called, and after several hours more Mrs. Bell returned to consciousness. She is still alive but is very low and weak. The family is rejoicing.[217]

Alfred carefully folded the paper and put it on the drawing room table. "They got the story right, didn't they? It's a miracle, isn't it, if there ever was one," he said, as he proceeded to light his pipe and draw from it.

Anna still lay in the main bedroom off of the drawing room, and the members of the family took turns waiting on her and going in and out of the bedroom to check on her and try to talk with her. When she was awake, she often tried to speak, but her words were soft and garbled. "He th...th...th...thaw me. h...Uh...I...th...thaw...uh...Wuh...Jaw...John...yuh...Pah." No one had been able to make any sense of what she said, and Anna was plainly frustrated that she could not make herself understood, although her eyes shown brightly, and her mouth, twisted oddly on her left side, smiled on the right. "Ah won... uh won...oh, shoo!" she said suddenly, and Irene asked if she wanted them to leave. Immediately Anna said clearly, "No. No! Shay!" She still could not form any other words to be understood.

J. A. came the next day, Thursday, afternoon. No one expected him to be able to hear or understand anything, since he was already so limited in his hearing and speech. He asked them to leave him alone with his mother for a while, and they respected his request. About a half hour later, he came out of the room with his face beaming.

---

[217] *The Pike County Democrat*, Pittsfield, Illinois, Volume XLIV, Wednesday, May 15, 1901, page 2. *The Barry Adage* also carried the story.

"See woll ress now," he said. "We have a guh talk. I unnerstan er. See have a guh visi wi her Jown an mee wif many pee-pul fum ta pass, many pee-pull see neva mee befo, aw wiff ow Papa, aw wash ovuh uss, aw love uss, see say."

Alfred's children were present in the house. The oldest, Burl Elliott Hillmann, was 12; Lila Furn was 9; Glen Otto was 6; and Leta Bede was 4. They had no more of an idea what their uncle was saying than they had of their grandmother, but Irene, and Thomas and James and George knew their brother's speech patterns, and knew what he was saying, and were amazed.

"I think she must have been dreaming while she was gone from us," Thomas said.

But George took J. A.'s words to heart and said, "She wasn't just dreaming. She saw our father and people who've gone before us. She's always told us they were watching over us, and they always would be, and they've let her come back to tell us. She wants us to know this and to know that we remember this before she goes."

In the days that followed, while they were with Anna, they all acted as if they heard and believed what their mother and grandmother had said, even if they marveled about it when they were away from her. The children of the family repeated the refrain that their aunt and uncles taught them, "John Bell grew up among the Indians. He had twenty-one brothers and sisters. They belong to this land, and we belong to them, and to their land. They watch over us now, and they always will.... We will not forget."

Two weeks later, on May 26th, Willie Ann died, and was buried alongside her husband, John Bell, in the Gray Cemetery.

Afterword

The footnotes scattered throughout this narrative are available for further research and as a help to sort out fact from fiction. Obviously the dialogue is fictional since no one recorded these conversations, although they at times contain information that is as accurate as the author could make it. The letters, if there ever were any, are long gone, even though many extant letters of Sarah Caroline Bell attest to her prolific letter-writing. The journal is only a literary device to provide a reconstruction of daily events during the time of the Cherokee migration. That John Francis Bell, born in Coosawattee Town in 1829, is the same John Francis Bell who came to Pike County, Illinois, in the early 1850's, has not been proven, given the paucity and inaccuracy of the written evidence, and the dozens of "John Bells" who lived in the Midwest at the time, but during the research it was often surprising to find many connections that made the claim plausible, and to exclude connections to other John Bells who came to light.

That Asa Bell of Madison County, Alabama, and Cherokee County, Texas, was the nephew of John Bell, Junior, who settled finally a few miles away in Rusk County, Texas, is also unproven. The 1860 census showed a "John Bell" living with Asa and Barbary Bell, who also had a young daughter named Francis, and this John Bell was also 31 years old, as was John Francis Bell in Pike County, Illinois, in 1860, giving us another tantalizing coincidence, or possibly an alternative and interesting story.

A few suggestive traces of the Ezekiel, Demaris, and William Bell family have been woven into a much larger part of the whole narrative. They provide a motivation for the resettling of John Francis Bell close to the Free Frank McWhorter- New Philadelphia community, the residual interest of some family members in that community, and the anti-racist standards of the Bell descendants.

Even if the reconstructions of family connections prove to be mistaken at some future point, and this researcher is ready to admit that possibility and to rewrite significant parts of the narrative as more information comes to light, perhaps the basic truths of the story and of John Ridge's insight remain intact and inspiring for the readers. There are many who can claim the heritage of the people who walked the trail on which they wept, and all of the people of America benefit by remembering and respecting that heritage.

Appendix A: Cherokee Wordlist

Cherokee words used in this narrative come from the *Cherokee-English Dictionary*, by Durbin Feeling, edited by William Pulte, in collaboration with Agnes Cowen and The Dictionary Committee, published by the Cherokee Nation of Oklahoma, 1975. Common words from other sources are noted with an *.

Cherokee word forms have been simplified for the English reader. Prefixes are added to the root forms of personal words, indicating direct address, singular and plural, first, second, and third person uses of relationship words. The specific prefix may also change the pronunciation of the root word slightly. A complete table of such changes is found in Lesson 20 on "Relationship terms in Cherokee," and specifically on page 160-161, of *Beginning Cherokee*, by Ruth Bradley Holmes and Betty Sharp Smith, published by the University of Oklahoma Press (in Norman), Second Edition, 1977, fifth printing; 1989. The reader should be aware that inexact usage is presented in this narrative, and different forms would have been present in the original period conversation that is simulated here. I apologize to speakers of the Cherokee language for the liberties that I have taken with their words.

Ani'Yun'wiya   the people, the principal people, an early self-designation of the Cherokee people*

Doyu   really, very

Galieliga   I am happy, glad, grateful

Ganugogv'I   spring, the season

Gayugi   communal show of support*

Gigage wahya   red wolf

Our Land! Our People!

Gusdi — cousin*

Equoni — river*

Osiyo, siyo — hello

Sgidv — yes, that's it

Tsa'lagi — Cherokee

Udali'i — wife

Udo — brother or sister

Udoda — father

Ududu — grandfather

Uduji — uncle

Uhlogi — aunt

Uji — mother

Ulisi — grandmother

Usdi wahya — little wolf

Uweji achuga — son

Wado — thank you

Wadulisi — honey

Appendix B: Ududu John Bell and Ulisi Charlotte Bell's Children

John Bell, Jr.　　　　　　m. 1805　　**Charlotte Adair**
　　　　　　　　　　　　　　　　　　　　[daughter, **John Adair**
　　　　　　　　　　　　　　　　　　　　and **Gahoga**]
b. 5/1/1782　d. 7/12/1852　　　　　　b. 1785　d. 9/1838

1. **John Adair [Jack] Bell**　　m. 1832　　**Jane Jennie Martin**
   b. 1/1/1806　d. 5/1/1860　　　　　　　b. 3/16/1816　d. 10/9/1839
   　　　　　　　　　　　　　　m. 1841　　**Elizabeth Harnage**
   　　　　　　　　　　　　　　　　　　　　b. 8/20/1820　d. 5/27/1847
   　　　　　　　　　　　　　　m. 1849　　**Sabra Lynch**
   　　　　　　　　　　　　　　　　　　　　b. 1808　d. 2/23/1863

   a. **Andromache Bell**
     　b. 1832　d. 11/28/1906
   b. **Maria Josephine Bell**
     　b. 3/26/1834　d. 10/27/1876
   c. **Charlotte Bell**
     　b. 1836　d. 1865
   d. **Lucien Burr [Hooley] Bell**
     　b. 2/13/1838　d. 1/27/1915
   e. **Nannie Ellen Bell**
     　b. 6/17/1841　d. 1920
   f. **Nancy Abigale Bell**
     　b. 1844
   g. **Nancy Ann Bell**
     　b. 1850　m. 4/1/1861
   h. **John R. Bell**
   i. **Elizabeth Bell**

Our Land! Our People!

2. **Elizabeth Hughes Bell** m. 1826 **George Washington Candy**
   b. 1807 d. 7/28/1848   b. 1805 d. 5/9/1856

   a. **John R. Candy**
      b. 1826 d. 1866
   b. **Maria Candy**
      b. 1830 d. 1851
   c. **Samuel Worcester Candy**
      b. 1832 d. 1854
   d. **Charlotte E. Candy**
      b. 1/20/1834
   e. **Martha Jane Candy**
      b. 1836 d. 1860
   f. **Juliette Melvina Candy**
      b. 8/7/1841 12/7/1930

3. **David Henry Bell** m. 1828 **"Allie Phillips"**
   b. 1809 d. 1848 m. 1839 **Nancy "Nannie" Martin**
                              b. 5/22/1821 d. 12/6/1871
                    m. 1844 **Elizabeth Phillips**
                              [-Bean-Thornton-Bell- Post]
                              b. 1818

   a. **John Francis Bell**
      b. 7/6/1829 m. 10/7/1852 d. 10/10/1870
   b. **John Martin Adair Bell**
      b. 12/15/1839 m. 1/20/1859 d. 4/12/1860
   c. **James Foster Bell**
      b. 11/2/1841 d. 10/14/1867

4. **Samuel W. Bell** m. 1844 **Rachel Martin**
   b. 1812 d.1849   b. 1823

   a. **George Bell**
   b. **John Bell**
   c. **Eliza Jane Bell**
      b. 1/30/1848

5. **Nancy "Nannie" Bell**   m. 1834   **George Harlan Starr**
   b. 7/14/1814   d. 9/14/1864   b. 5/4/1806   d. 9/28/1879

   a. **Jane Starr** [mother= Nellie Carr]
      b. 10/30/1830   d. 1854
   b. **William K. Starr**
      b. 3/9/1835   d. 9/9/1858
   c. **Charlotte Starr**
      b. 12/28/1840   d. 9/28/1848
   d. **John Walker Starr II**
      b. 7/8/1842   d. 6/19/1862
   e. **Mary Frances Starr**
      b. 3/24/1844   m. 2/10/1876   d. 10/28/1928
   f. **George Colbert Starr**
      b. 3/21/1847   d. 6/29/1876
   g. **Ezekiel Eugene Starr**
      b. 8/11/1849   d. 10/5/1905
   h. **Joseph Jarrett Starr**
      b. 12/21/1851   d. 8/16/1872
   i. **Caleb Ellis Bose Starr**
      b. 5/26/1854   d. 9/21/1925
   j. **Samuel Jesse Starr**
      b. 10/13/1857   d. 4/1/1942

6. **Devereaux Jarrett Bell**   m.   **Juliette Lewis Vann**
   b. 1817   d. 1867   b. 5/18/1826   d. 2/13/1905

7. **Sarah Caroline Bell**   m. 1843   **Stand Watie**
   b. 1820   d. 1883   b. 12/12/1806   d. 9/9/1871

   a. **Saladin Ridge Watie**
      b. 1846   d. 2/13/1868
   b. **Sloan Watica Watie**
      b. 1850   d. 4/9/1869
   c. **Cumiskey Watie**
      b. 1851   d. 1863
   d. **Nannie Josephine Watie**
      b. 1853   d. 1875

  e. **Charlotte Jacqueline Watie**
    b. 10/9/1854 d. 3/17/1875

8. **Charlotte Bell**   m. 1851   **William J. Dupree**
 b. 1822 d. 1902   b. 12/25/1824

  a. **Emma Dupree**
  b. **William E. Dupree**
    b. 11/9/1857
  c. **Annie Eugenia Dupree**
  d. **Maude Ethel Dupree**

9. **James Madison Bell**   m. 1852   **Caroline Lynch**
 b. 10/15/1928 d. 3/23/1915   b. 1830 d. 1866

  a. **Minnie Caroline Bell**
    b. 1853
  b. **Mattie Charlotte Bell**
    b. 1854
  c. **Delia Palmer Bell**
    b. 5/31/1856
  d. **Joseph Bell**
    b. 1858
  e. **William Watie Bell**
    b. 10/21/1864 d. 12/25/1894

10. **Martha Jane Bell**   m.   **Walter Adair Duncan**
  b. 1827 d. 10/9/1857   b. 1820 d. 1906

  a. **Marianne Celeste Duncan**
  b. **Anacreon Bell Duncan**
    b. d. infant
  c. **Jarrett Merini Duncan**
    b. 1856 d. 1884

Ruth Bell died in 1835, and would be the eleventh child of John and Charlotte Bell, but I have found no indication of where she should be placed in the order of birth.

Stand-alone years are often estimates. Most of this data came from Wanda Elliott in her manuscript *Descendants of John Bell, Jr,* printed at Stilwell, Oklahoma, on January 1, 2011.

Some data came from the *Mount Tabor Indian Cemetery*, Rusk County, Texas, as researched by J. C. Thompson, and submitted by Gloria B. Mayfield, online, June 22, 2009.

Other information is the responsibility of the author. The chart is provided for the sake of recognizing the extent of the second and third generations of John and Charlotte Bell's family. A significant portion of this family lived to contribute to the fourth generation and to hundreds of descendants living at the time of this writing.

Appendix C:
James Starr, Son of Caleb and Nancy Starr, His Wives and Children

James Starr was born in 1796, and was killed on November 9, 1845. At least twenty-one children were born to James Starr and his three wives. The following list is compiled from several sources with arbitrary assignments of dates of birth and mother where records vary. The children are listed under their own birth mother. Roman numerals indicate the birth order of all twenty-one children of James Starr.

Nellie Maugh
   b. 1800   m. 1818
   d. 1847

i. Joseph
   b. 1818 m.

iii. Field
   b. 1820   d. 1845

iv. Washington
   b. 1822   m.
   d. 1848

vii. Samuel
   b. 1827   m.
   d. 1858

ix. Mary
   b. 5/1829   m.
   d. 1909

xii. Leroy Buck
   b. 1831
   d. 12/15/1845

xiii. Rachel
    b. 1832 m. 1848
    d. 1853

xv. Jane Z.
    b. 3/18/1833
    m. 7/15/1857
    d. 6/12/1916

xvii. Caleb Suake
    b. 1836
    d. 1856

xix. Lucinda Malzerine
    b. 10/19/1838
    m. 1859
    d. 8/24/1925

xx. Sarah "Sallie"
    b. 1841 m. 1858
    d. 8/20/1867

Susie "Sukie" Maugh
    b. 1800   m. 1819
    d. 1845

ii. Thomas II
    b. 1819 m. 1839
    d. 10/7/1890

v. Bean
    b. 1822 d. 1845

vi. James, Jr.
    b. 1824 m. 1845
    d. 5/13/1867

viii. **William**
    b. 1827   m.

x. **Ellis Creek**
    b. 1829   m.
    d. 4/1846

xi. **Jennie**
    b.1830   d.1834

xiv. **John**
    b. 1832

xvi. **Ezekiel**
    b. 1835 m.

xviii. **Pauline "Polly"**
    b. 12/14/1837
    m. <1853   d. 1872

Sallie Bacon Acorn
    b. 1826 m. 1843
    d. 1900

xxi. **Nancy**
    b.1844   d.1890

Appendix D: John Francis Bell and Willa (Willie) Ann Bell Family

John Francis Bell was born July 6, 1829. Willie Ann Gray was born August 15, 1835. They were married October 7, 1852. John died October 10, 1870. Willie Ann died (the 2nd time) May 26, 1901.[218]

1. Henry Thomas Bell
Born October, 1854
Married Berthada Jane Allen,
September 11, 1873
Died October 26, 1937

2. Irene Ellen Bell
Born May 18, 1856
Married Benjamin Oscar Manker,
September 23, 1875
Died May 9, 1939

3. John Arthur Bell
Born September 18, 1857
Married Mary Jane Johnston
Died January 5, 1939

4. Mary Elizabeth Bell
Born 1859

---

[218] The author was aware that DNA analysis could disprove the oral history of John Francis Bell, if no traces of Native American DNA were present in his descendants, ruling out other family sources of Native American descent as much as possible. Using the resources of 23andMe.com and gedmatch.com, a male and female descendant of Henry Thomas Bell, and a female descendant of Sarah Melissa Bell did undergo genetic testing and did show genotypes consistent with Cherokee and Scot ancestry. A female descendant of Thomas Gray, Jr., the brother of Willa Ann Bell did not show any evidence of Cherokee ancestry.

5. James Perry Bell
>Born October, 1860
>Married Amelia Pernice Manker,
>>September 12, 1883
>
>Died 1910

6. Nancy Alabama ("Allie") Bell
>Born 1866
>Died February 13, 1882

7. Bennett Foster Bell
>Born March, 1865
>Died September 25, 1866

8. Sarah Melissa Bell
>Born July 9, 1867
>Married Alfred Elliott Hillmann,
>>January 13, 1889
>
>Died July 7, 1899

9. Catherine Star ("Kate") Bell
>Born January 18, 1869
>Married Joseph Manker
>Died after 1880

10. George Corinth Bell
>Born December 18, 1870
>Married Alice Luellan Riley,
>>November 24, 1895
>
>Died December 9, 1943

Bibliography

Adair Family Reunion Book Committee. *The Cherokee Adairs*, (Cherokee Nation, 2003).

Arkansas Historic Preservation Program, online, research paper. *"Memphis to Little Rock Road—Village Creek State Park, Newcastle Vicinity, Cross Country,"* undated; also citing Clarence E. Carter, comp. and ed., *Territorial Papers of the United States, XIX, Arkansas Territory, 1825-1829* (Washington, D.C., 1954).

Arkansas Intelligencer, September 5, 1846.

Army and Navy Chronicle 8 (April 25, 1839): 266.

Bell, George Morrison, Sr. *The Genealogy of Old and New Cherokee Indian Families* (Cherokee Heritage Center, 1979).

Dale, Edward Everett, and Gaston Litton. *Cherokee Cavaliers* (Norman, Oklahoma, University of Oklahoma Press, 1939, 1995).

Lt. Edward Deas to General W. Scott, October 22, 1838, National Archives Record Group 75, Records of the Bureau of Indian Affairs, Letters Received, Cherokee Emigration, Roll 115, S1555 No. 2.

Ehle, John. *Trail of Tears: The Rise and Fall of the Cherokee Nation* (New York, Doubleday, 1988).

Elliott, Wanda. *The Descendants of John Bell, Jr.* (Stilwell, OK, personal compilation, 10/15/2010).

The Encyclopedia of Arkansas History and Culture, www.encyclopediaofarkansas.net

Feeling, Durbin; Edited by William Pulte. *Cherokee-English Dictionary* (Tahlequah, Cherokee Nation of Oklahoma, 1975)

Foreman, Carolyn Thomas. "The Bean Family," *The Chronicles of Oklahoma*, vol. 32, pp. 308ff.

Foreman, Carolyn Thomas. "The Fairfield Mission," *The Chronicles of Oklahoma*, Vol. 27, 1949. pp. 323-324.

Foreman, Carolyn Thomas. "The Light Horse in the Indian Country," Vol. 34, *The Chronicles of Oklahoma*, Vol. 34, pp. 19-20).

Foreman, Grant. *The Five Civilized Tribes* (Norman, OK: The University of Oklahoma Press, 1934).

Foreman, Grant. *Indian Removal: The Emigration of the Five Civilized Tribes of Indians* (Norman, OK. University of Oklahoma Press, 1932, 1972).

Garrett, J.T., and Michael Garrett. *Medicine of the Cherokee; The Way of Right Relationship*

Georgia Chapter, Trail of Tears Association, www.gatrailoftears.com

Gibson, Wayne Dell. "Cherokee Treaty Party Moves West: The Bell-Deas Overland Journey, 1838-1839," *Chronicles of Oklahoma* 79 (Fall 2001).

Hampton, David Keith. *Cherokee Mixed-Bloods, Additions and Corrections to Family Genealogies of Dr. Emmett Starr* (2005).

Hampton, David Keith. *The Descendants of Nancy Ward* (Cane Hill AR: ARC Press, 1997).

Harvillle, Logan D. *Treaty Party—Disbursements for Subsistence; Disbursements for Transportation*, Edward Deas Papers, Sequoyah Research Center.

Hill, Sarah H. *Cherokee Removal: Forts Along the Georgia Trail of Tears*. (Draft Report by under a joint partnership between The National Park Service and the Georgia Department of Natural Resources/Historic Preservation Division)

Hill, O. E., and Helen Starr. *Footprints in the Indian Nation* (1974)

The History of Adair County, (Cane Hill AR: ARC Press, 1991)

Hoig, Stanley W. *The Cherokees and Their Chiefs* (Fayetteville, University of Arkansas, 1998).

Holmes, Ruth Bradley and Betty Sharp Smith. *Beginning Cherokee*, 2nd Edition (Norman, University of Oklahoma, 1977).

King, Duane, and David G. Fitzgerald. *The Cherokee Trail of Tears* (Portland, Oregon, Graphic Arts Books, 2007).

King, Duane. "The Emigration Route of the John A. Bell Detachment of Treaty Party Cherokees within the State of Arkansas, November 25, 1838 - January 7, 1839," Research Paper, 2001.

King, Duane. *"Report on Recent Research Regarding the Cherokee Removal,"* 17 April 1996; National Park Service, Trail of Tears National Historic Trail -- Map Supplement, Maps 222-247.

King, Duane. "Terminating Points of the Cherokee Trail of Tears," for Cherokee Heritage Center, *The Columns*, June 2006.

Lincoln, Abraham; Douglas, Stephen; Nicolay, John G., ed; Hay, John, ed. *'Sixth Joint Debate, At Quincy, Illinois, October 13, 1858' in 'The Complete Works of Abraham Lincoln, v. 4'*. (New York: Francis D. Tandy Company, 1894, 1858). Permission: Northern Illinois University. Persistent link: *http://lincoln.lib.niu.edu/file.php?file=Nh458l.html*

Lipscomb, Carol A. "Cherokee Indians," HANDBOOK OF TEXAS ONLINE (*http://www.tshaonline.org/handbook/online/articles/bmc51*), accessed April 07, 2015. Uploaded on June 12, 2010. Published by the Texas State Historical Association.

Logan, Charles Russell. *The Promised Land: The Cherokees, Arkansas, and Removal, 1794-1839* (Little Rock, AR. Arkansas Historic Preservation Program, 1997).

Lutens, Allen. "Prehistoric Fishweirs in Eastern North America" (Binghamton, State University of New York, 1992, updated by the author in 2004).

Mayfield, Gloria B.; researched by J. C. Thompson. *Mount Tabor Indian Cemetery*. Txcherind@aol.com

McLoughlin, William G. *After the Trail of Tears: The Cherokees' Struggle for Sovereignty, 1839-1880* (Chapel Hill: North Caroline Press, 1993).

Miles, Tiya. *African American History at the Chief Vann House* (University of Michigan, 2006).

Missionary Journal of the Moravian Missionaries at Springplace, (manuscript photocopy, manuscript photocopy at New Echota State Park library).

Mooney, James. *Myths of the Cherokees* (New York, Dover, 1995).

Mooney, James. *Sacred Formulas of the Cherokees*, 1891.

Murray County [Georgia] Museum. *Murray County Heritage Book,* http://www.murraycountymuseum.com/book_01.html

The New Georgia Encyclopedia, "Cherokee Missions," www.georgiaencyclopedia.org

Perdue, Theda, and Michael D. Green, *The Cherokee Nation and the Trail of Tears* (New York: Penguin, 2007).

Perdue, Theda. *Cherokee Women, Gender and Culture Change, 1700-1835.* (Lincoln, University of Nebraska, 1998).

Phillips, Joyce B., and Paul Gary Phillips, ed., *The Brainerd Journal* (Lincoln, Nebraska; University of Nebraska Press, 1998).

The Pike County Democrat, Pittsfield, Illinois, Vol. 44, Wednesday, May 15, 1901.

Pike County History (Pittsfield, Illinois, Pike County Press, 1964).

The Portrait and Biographical Album of Pike and Calhoun Counties, Illinois, 1891.

Pulaski, Tennessee
http://www.nativehistoryassociation.org/giles_tot_memorial.php

Quincy, Illinois, Public Library. Files of photographs and memorabilia of the facilities of the Perry Springs Health Resort.

Reed, Marcelina. *Seven Clans of the Cherokee Society* (Cherokee, North Carolina, 1993).

Roberts-McGinnis. FTW; Conley, Robert J., *Cherokee Thoughts Honest and Uncensored* (University of Oklahoma Press, October 31, 2008).

Rozema, Vicki. *Voices from the Trail of Tears* (John F. Blair, 2003).

Shadburn, Don L. *Cherokee Planters of Georgia, 1842-1838* (Cumming, Georgia: Don Shadburn, 1989).

Snell, William R. *Candy's Creek Mission Station 1824-1837* (Cleveland, Tennessee, Two Penny Press, 1999);

Southeast Tennessee Tourism Association, "Cherokee Native American Guide" 2009. "Research provided by Dr. Duane King."

Strickland, Rennard. *Fire and the Spirits: Cherokee Law from Clan to Court* (Norman, University of Oklahoma Press, 1975).

Walker, Juliet E. K. *Free Frank: A Black Pioneer on the Antebellum Frontier* (Lexington: University Press of Kentucky, 1983, 1995).

Watson, W. W. "The History Of Barry And Its People," from *The Barry Adage*, October 1, 1903.

Wikipedia contributors. "Lincoln–Douglas debates." *Wikipedia, The Free Encyclopedia.* October 29, 2014, 14:47 UTC. Available at: *http://en.wikipedia.org/w/index.php?title=Lincoln%E2%80%93Douglas_debates &oldid=631617634*. Accessed November 15, 2014.

Wilkins, Thurman. *Cherokee Tragedy: the Ridge Family and the Decimation of a People*, Second Edition, Revised (Norman, University of Oklahoma, 1986).

William Quesenbury Diary, 1845-1861 (Washington County [Arkansas] Historical Society in *Flashback*, Volume 28, #3, page 3).

Zellner, Richard. *Chronicles of Oklahoma*, vol. 59, #2, 1981, "Stand Watie and the Killing of James Foreman."

Acknowledgements

All of the people listed in the Bibliography who have devoted much of their lives to the study and preservation of information on the people who are involved in this story.

Duane King for his meticulous efforts to document the Bell Route of the Trail of Tears, making possible the four trips I have taken to retrace the steps of that detachment of Cherokee Nation citizens.

Tom Mooney and other staff at The Cherokee Heritage Center at Park Hill, Tahlequah, Oklahoma, for many hours of assistance, searching through the library and records of the center for more clues about the Bell and Starr families and the communities of which they were a part.

Wanda Elliott, the late Betty Barker, and other volunteers at the Adair County Historical and Genealogical Center for their assistance in locating and providing resources on the families, settlements, and geography of Stilwell, Oklahoma, and Evansville, Arkansas, areas.

David Gomez of the New Echota Cherokee Capital State Historic Site in Georgia and its library for resources to find my way around the Coosawatee River Valley and surrounding areas and their history.

Debby Brown of the Chieftain's House and Museum, who received me on one icy and another stormy afternoon to have extended conversations about the kind of book that might emerge from my research.

First readers, including my wife Janet Chapman, son Nathan Chapman, cousin Larry Waite, friend Dr. Timothy C. Downs, sister-and-brother-in-law Bonnie and Steve Sorrells, for their encouragement and specific suggestions for the improvement of this novel. In addition to Janet and Nathan, Polly Rein and Connie Krieger proof-read the novel.

For many people throughout the years who have said to me, "If you write a story about that, I would certainly want to read it."

About the Author

Gary Chapman received a Methodist license to preach when he was sixteen years old, going on to graduate from Illinois Wesleyan University and earning a doctorate of ministry from Chicago Theological Seminary.

After being ordained in the United Church of Christ, Chapman spent the next thirty-five years serving three Midwestern congregations. For twenty-one years, he also taught numerous courses on philosophy, religion, and contemporary issues at Southeastern Community College in Iowa.

Chapman is married with two children and three grandchildren.

He is the author of two other books in a series on *A Family's Heritage— Out of My Hands: The Stories of Harold Hunsaker Chapman*, and *The River Flows Both Ways: Following the Mekong Out of Vietnam and Cambodia*.

Made in the USA
Middletown, DE
04 May 2016